BLUE

LN Bey

BLUE is a work of fiction. All names, characters, places, and actions are the result of the author's filthy imagination. The author in NO way condones any kind of activity, sexual or otherwise, without the full consent of everyone involved.

WARNING: This novel contains explicit sexual situations and mature content.

BLUE

Published by Visconti Press
PO Box 1094
Lawrence, KS 66044

www.lnbey.com
www.viscontipress.com
www.strictmachineartist.com

ISBN: 978-1-944814-00-7

I would like to dedicate this novel, my first, to the four women who have cost me countless hours of sleep but showed me how fun it could be to put entire worlds, and all the filthy things that go on within them, down on paper:

Molly Weatherfield, Laura Antoniou, A. N. Roquelaure and Pauline Réage.

Part 1: Driveways

Chapter One

Janet could not get the piece of gum scraped off the bottom of the coffee table. She was on her hands and knees in front of the sofa, butter knife in hand, chipping away at the hard, stubborn little lump of blue. She looked up at the clock. It was already seven o'clock.

Damn it. They would be here any minute. Everything needed to be *perfect.*

Over the past year, Janet had transformed her home into the coolest house in the neighborhood, no doubt about it. It was the one thing that she had won in the divorce, and it was all that she had wanted. She had rid the house of the traditional furniture and beige color scheme that her equally beige ex-husband had favored, and replaced it with a bright white and blue modernism.

She had painted the walls blue over the dull earth tones herself. She had ripped out the tan Berber carpet, and had the oak floor beneath it bleached to near white. She'd sold off the costly but somewhat pedestrian occasionals he didn't take and used the money to purchase sleek modernist furniture, all white: one featureless sofa and three cubic chairs, which she arranged in a U shape around the long plastic coffee table cast in cerulean blue. It rested upon a ridiculously thick rug of long white fake fur, in joyful Retro contrast to the minimalist seating.

Gone were the knick-knacks and clutter that her husband had preferred and she had grown to hate. She now decorated the room with a very few, carefully selected artifacts of personal significance on smaller tables and on the walls—a subtle cyanotype nude she'd purchased at a gallery in New Mexico; a large, smooth gray river stone she'd found on a mountain hike and lugged back to the car like Sisyphus with his boulder (not one of her smarter moves; the Sun had fried her fair skin). Now, when she walked into the room in the mornings, everything was clean, bright, and new. Pure.

Except for this unyielding nubbin of gum. She had bought the table at a yard sale, deep blue and perfect. She hadn't noticed the underside, though, until she'd just now felt it as she'd moved the table a few inches to the left. She felt her stomach tighten.

She chipped away, sawed at it. It was the only detail left undone—every inch of the house cleaned, every morsel of food prepared perfectly. Just appetizers, she was told; finger food.

This cannot be a good idea, she thought. *What the hell was I thinking?*

The gum flew off into the jungle of thick acrylic fibers. She felt around, crawling, until she felt its disgusting hardness in the fluff of carpet.

She rose to her knees and rechecked the spread of food atop the table: slices of pears and gorgonzola wrapped in prosciutto; tomato slices with mozzarella and basil, drizzled with extra-virgin olive oil and balsamic vinegar and held together with toothpicks. Brie, aged gouda and some unpronounceable cheese recommended by the vendor with several shapes of exotic crackers; vegetables with dips and hummus; strawberries dipped in dark chocolate; and her masterpiece, rum balls drizzled in white chocolate. Five settings, each a small plate, napkin and wine glass; two bottles of reds decanting, a Malbec and a Cabernet. She adjusted the position of a wine glass a fraction of an inch.

She trusted Jon. That was the thing to remember, the thing she kept repeating to herself. He'd been something of a friend before the divorce, a better one since. He would never let her come to harm. Why did she even need to keep reassuring herself?

Because she'd talked a big game, that's why.

She nearly tipped the glass over when the doorbell rang. *They're here.* Would they time how long it took her to answer the door? She'd been told they did not like to be kept waiting. Still holding the gum, she licked it moist and stuck it back under the table, then cringed as she stood, tasting chemical blueberry.

She straightened the collar of her smart blue 3/4-sleeved top—chosen to accentuate the blue in her eyes—and nearly ran toward the door. She stopped at the little mirror beside the doorway and brushed a curly strand of her jet-black hair out of her face. Her hands were shaking. She opened the door.

"Jon! How nice to see you again!" Was she really saying this? Like it was just another day? "Please come in!" So the neighbors wouldn't see? Why would they think anything about it?

Jon, a head taller than Janet, gave her a peck on the cheek and stepped through the doorway. He was wearing jeans and a nice white shirt, black sport jacket. A woman walked in behind him, which she had been told to expect. She was dressed in a gray skirt and white blouse with matching gray jacket over it, casual but elegant.

"My God, Janet! What you've done to the place," Jon said as he looked around the room. His intense brown eyes took in everything. "You've made so much progress. This is amazing."

"Thank you. I've put a lot of time into it. And quite a bit of money, but I've found ways to stay within a budget. This won't affect my rates, will it?" Stupid nervous joke.

"It shouldn't. You actually have *less* stuff. I'm not sure how it would affect your real estate values, though." He looked around, appraising. "This is a pretty traditional neighborhood, very conservative."

"Yea…" Again the tightness in her stomach.

"The outside still fits in. But this interior décor is a little… radical, for what most people want around here."

Story of my life. "Well, I'm not going anywhere." Were they still talking real estate?

"Good girl."

Jon was Janet's insurance agent, and a realtor as well. He'd found them this house, when she was married. When Thomas left, Jon stayed on with the house—and her. There had always been a little something between them, but neither had ever acted upon it—until Janet left that book out on the blue coffee table one day, when she knew he'd be stopping by. Or was that the old coffee table?

Janet extended her hand toward the woman.

"Janet, this is my wife, Amanda. Amanda, Janet."

Janet froze, her hand still extended. His *wife*? Jon had prepared her to expect many things, tonight—but he had never said he was married. *Never.* She felt even more apprehensive and confused.

Amanda shook her head and then shook Janet's hand.

"Don't believe everything he tells you, dear." She wore no ring.

She looked a little older than Janet, maybe mid-thirties as was Jon, but very well put together. Her sandy blonde hair was cut just above her shoulders, and her compact frame and… well, ample figure made her look somehow complete, self-contained. Decisive—she had remarkable posture. Yet somehow her grayish blue eyes were comforting.

"Relax, darling. We're your friends, and we've all been dying to meet you. You'll be fine."

Darling. Janet didn't know what to believe.

"Look at this place, Amanda," Jon said. "What do you think?"

Amanda walked slowly around the furniture, first taking in the arrangement and then the space itself.

"It's very nice," she said. "Simplifying?"

"Trying to, anyway." Which was a bit ironic, considering tonight's plans.

"Very orderly. Very…strict," Amanda said. She looked right at Janet.

Janet felt her face warm and redden.

"That's Amanda, doll," Jon said to Janet. "Very orderly, and very strict."

"Um…yes, well. Would you like something to drink? I have wines, drinks, soda…" She tried to stop wringing her hands.

"Not until everyone is here," Amanda said.

Something about Amanda was both intimidating and reassuring. Janet wanted to make her more comfortable, to please her—or to be comforted by her; hugged, maybe?

Janet jumped, to Jon and Amanda's amusement, when the doorbell rang again.

"Excuse me," she said, as she walked to the door. Again she straightened her shirt.

"Hello," she told the very striking man standing in the doorway. He was a foot taller than Janet, with hair as black as hers and eyes to match. "You must be Jack?"

"Hello, little honey," said the man. His accent was southern, from exactly where, Janet had no idea. "I am indeed Jack." He strode through the door without being asked.

"Hello, Jon. Hello, Amanda." He looked Janet up and

down as she stood holding the door open, then pointed toward her with his thumb. "This her? Not bad."

Janet had no idea what to say.

Jack definitely hit the gym, Janet could tell. His shoulders were broad and powerful beneath his black sports jacket, his skin tanned. *Wow.* He calmed his thick black hair, and put his hands on his hips as he took in his surroundings.

"That you?" he said, his eyes going straight to the cyanotype across the room, the female nude in a haze of blue tint.

Janet shook her head, even though his back was to her.

"Ha! No. I don't know who the model is. I bought that in Santa F—"

"Too bad. I thought maybe you modeled." He gave Jon a sly look.

Janet started to close the door. "Oooh, no. I couldn't. Um, whatever we do tonight, there can't be any photographs, okay? I—"

"Oh, Little Miss Sunshine is right behind me," Jack said.

As Janet pushed the door shut, she felt an obstruction, heard the sound of wood scraping against what turned out to be shoe. She jerked the door back open.

"I'm so sorry!" she said. "I didn't hear you coming."

A woman, one foot in the door, was staring down at her very polished high-heeled shoe, which was now severely scuffed.

"Oh no," Janet said. "I am so sorry. Can I—" She froze as the woman straightened and fixed Janet with a severe glare. Janet opened her mouth to speak again, but stopped.

The woman had amber eyes, set above the most perfect cheekbones Janet had ever seen. She also had the most perfect eyebrows Janet had ever seen, which were now furrowed in anger.

"I'm sorry. I'm—" Janet extended her hand, but the woman walked into her house without saying a word.

Janet looked out the door at her street, the guests' cars in her driveway. There was a light breeze blowing in the trees, helmeted kids clickety-clacking down the sidewalk on skateboards. All so…normal. Just another day in Oakdale. Part of her wanted to step onto her porch and close the door behind her, leave these people alone in her house and tip-toe away.

She shut the door from the inside, turned the deadbolt. Tight.

"Carolyn!" Jon said. "How have you been? It's been a while, hasn't it."

The woman named Carolyn replied, "Jon, Amanda."

She exchanged little kisses on the cheek with both of them, and Jon touched her face when it was his turn. Janet watched Amanda—she did not seem to mind. Which maybe wasn't so surprising, considering…

"Jack," Carolyn said, as though forced to. "How goes the oil business?"

"Quite well, Sunshine," Jack said, and Janet stood by the door, wishing she could stay at the side of the room and watch. "People still crashin' cars?"

"Reliably." Neither person looked particularly enthralled with the encounter.

Carolyn's light brown hair was pulled back into a tight bun, and her clothes were very similar to Amanda's, white blouse with gray pencil skirt and jacket. But while Amanda's outfit hung on her body like an afterthought, proper yet sexy, Carolyn's clothes were like a military uniform—starched, rigid, a shell. Like Amanda, her posture was flawless in her high heels. Which Janet had just ruined.

"How goes the alphabet, Jon?" Carolyn asked.

"Making progress, thanks. Seven down, so far." Janet had no idea what this meant.

"Carolyn, this is Janet," Jon said. "Our hostess for the evening. Janet, meet Carolyn." He made a little gesture for her to approach—which she did, and felt a little strange about, in her own home. "She and I work for the same insurance company," he said. "We didn't even know it for years, completely different divisions. We go way back."

"Oh how nice." They never talked about work for years? She tried to smile at Carolyn, but Carolyn wasn't watching. She was looking around the room, ignoring Janet.

"So nice to meet you," Janet said. "I'm sorry about your shoe."

Carolyn grunted, then turned to look her over as Jack had done. Janet looked away.

"Could I get anyone anything to—"

"Not yet," Amanda said, a little firmly, and Janet remembered why they were all here.

"Carolyn, what do you think of Janet's house?" Jon said. "She did this all herself. It started out your basic boring. Sort of like your ex, eh, Janet?" He laughed.

Jon had an interest in aesthetics, Janet knew, in design and art. He was too polite and business-savvy to say much about the old version of the house, but always sounded approving when she would tell him her plans. He always told her she should be an artist, she had such a good eye. She thought the idea was ridiculous—what would she do? She hadn't gone to art school, though she'd always kind of wished she had. She didn't know how to paint or sculpt or take real photographs. But Jon wasn't flattering her, she didn't think. He genuinely seemed to admire her house and how hard she worked on it. Her house was her art, she guessed.

"I thought you might appreciate the design choices," Jon said to Carolyn.

Carolyn said nothing; her heels slowly clicked with authority against the hardwood floor as she inspected the living room. She even ran a finger along one of the tables displaying three sizes of blue Art Deco vases: checking for dust. Janet eased when Carolyn said, "It's very nice."

Then she said, "Very…disciplined," and Janet felt herself tense again.

"Well, listen, y'all," Jack said as he checked his glimmering Rolex, "I'd love to stay and chat until the cows come home"— Janet noticed Carolyn roll her eyes at the cliché—"but I've got an appointment later on tonight."

"Yes," Carolyn said. "As do I. Let's get this going."

Janet was incredulous, and a little insulted, considering.

"Oh, like you have something better to do?" she asked, trying to add a little levity. *She* certainly needed some levity.

Carolyn turned to face her, took a step closer.

"Actually, yes," she said. "I do have other things to do this evening. Things I really didn't want to be taken away from."

Everyone was looking at Janet. She wiped her sweaty hands on her pants.

"Oh, um…okay. I'm sorry. Please," she gestured to the furniture. "Make yourselves comfortable?"

Her guests moved to seat themselves, Jon and Amanda on the sofa, Jack and Carolyn in the two chairs across from them, studiously ignoring each other.

It was starting.

Janet stepped toward the center chair at the head of the table, but stopped.

"I…don't know what to do, I'm sorry. Do we sit, first? Talk …a while? I know what I'm supposed to say, but this is new and—"

"How thoroughly did Jon instruct you?" Amanda asked.

"I…I don't know. I mean, pretty well, I guess?" They'd talked for hours about this, over the course of the last few weeks, and she suddenly regretted acting like she knew what she was doing the whole time. Now she felt like she'd forgotten everything he'd told her. Her mind was racing all of the sudden, as was her heartbeat.

He'd actually been very thorough—even arranging for her

to be tested at a doctor's office, and sending her the most recent results of everyone else's tests. *That* was quite a surprise, picking up her mail that day. Drug and disease free, indeed.

"Janet, relax," Jon said. "I know you're nervous, but you definitely get this. We're all friends here and we want you to do well. You've been looking forward to this—just do what I told you. How many times have you told me you couldn't wait?"

Too much was going through Janet's mind to focus. Was it really she who'd initiated this, when he was coming over to help move some furniture and she'd so "casually" left that book on her coffee table? That very kinky book. Which coffee table *was* that?

"But I do agree that it's time we got things started. Don't you?"

Janet could only nod. She looked around the room, stalling. The open end of the table, of the "U" in the furniture—she'd decided days ago, when it still seemed like a fantasy: that would be the spot.

She walked behind Carolyn and Jack to take her place. She turned to face them, all arranged in a little arena. She stood as straight as possible, hands at her sides. *It's not too late, Janet,* some part of her mind urged her. *Tell them you can't do this.*

She cleared her throat. She tried to slow her heart rate down, tried to will it to slow. Jack folded his arms across his chest and crossed his legs.

"Okay," Janet muttered, almost a whisper. She wasn't supposed to talk during this part of it. "So…we're starting?"

"Yes!" Carolyn nearly shouted. "Jesus, where did you find this one, Jon?"

Jon shushed her with his hand. "You're doing fine, Janet."

Okay then, Janet's inner voice relented. *Do it or don't.*

She reached for the top button of her shirt and unbuttoned it as her fingers trembled. She fumbled for the next one. At the third one she stopped, but when multiple eyebrows were raised she unbuttoned it as well. She continued through the last two in a daze, trying to think of anything else, unable to think of anything. She reached up to the lapels, and hesitated again.

"Do we—" But she said no more and pulled her shirt off of her shoulders, tossed it to the floor behind her. She kicked off her shoes without thinking, her little comfortable shoes.

She reached for the fly of her tan Capri pants, stopped before unfastening it. On seeing the disapproving looks of her guests, she unzipped it. She slowly—out of nervousness, not dramatic effect—bent over and slid the pants over her hips and down her legs. She stood straight, her head a little dizzy, and tossed them behind her onto her top.

Standing before them in black bra and panties, she started to speak.

"Keep going, darling," Amanda said.

Janet looked to Jon, the only person here she'd met before a few minutes ago. He nodded in agreement.

Janet reached behind her back, and unfastened her bra. She closed her eyes as she crossed her arms to pull the thin straps off her shoulders. She kept her breasts covered as long as she could, but knew she would have to expose them to toss it onto the growing pile of clothes behind her—or to continue the evening at all. She lowered her hands to her sides and looked up. All eyes were on her chest. Jon shifted in his seat.

Janet moved her hands to her hips and lowered her matching underwear that she'd selected after her shower to look skimpy but not trashy. She thought she'd be wearing them a little longer. She lifted each knee to step out of them and tried to ignore her now-exposed pubic hair, a small patch of jet-black fur. Her breasts swayed with the movement, and she reached behind her again, dropped her panties without looking.

She was completely naked. She wanted, more than anything, to cover herself. She started to do so, then she straightened her arms, tightened her hands into fists and held them at her sides. Letting everyone look. These were the rules Jon had given her; this was her fantasy. She could barely glance at each guest as they looked her over, assessed her. She looked down to the floor.

Janet's skin was smooth and pale, "alabaster" as Jon had once called it. Now Jon wasn't just taking in her body, with his eyes, but the room around them as well, the whole scene.

"See what I mean?" he said, to whom Janet wasn't sure. "I'd never guess she'd match the *house*. What a perfect picture."

"No pictures!" she blurted out. Eyebrows were again raised, and she looked back to the floor.

Janet had always hated her fair skin, so easily burned rather than tanned, but she had always taken care of it. It had never been quite so on *display*, before. She blushed, and realized that her face was probably the only red in the room. Well, except for her exposed nipples, two dots of pink against a sea of white. Her face turned even redder.

Jon motioned for her to turn around. She did so, relieved for the chance to look away. She could feel their eyes on her backside.

"All right," Jon said, and she turned again. He was leaning back, approving.

There was an awkward silence as everyone kept *looking*.

"Put your hands behind your back," Amanda said, and Janet obeyed, feeling even more exposed. More silence, unbearable. She bent one knee slightly in front of the other, a modest, girlish pose.

Carolyn saw the move.

"Spread your legs," she said.

No—this was too much. And yet this was nothing. She closed her eyes and spread her feet.

"Wider."

Janet spread her feet further as she fought the urge to bring her hands around and cover her exposed sex. Even her husband hadn't spent so much time looking.

"Why isn't she shaved?" Carolyn said.

Janet's mouth dropped open as she stared at the floor.

"She doesn't need to be," Jon said. "Look at how nice and tight that little patch is. It's adorable."

"Yea, I'm with Jon on this one," Jack drawled.

"She should shave the lips, at least," Carolyn said.

"Fair enough," Jon agreed. "You want to do it tonight?"

Janet covered her face until someone cleared their throat. She lowered her arms.

"C cup?" Jack said.

Janet looked at him, surprised.

"What?"

Someone *tsked* disapproval. He pointed to her breasts.

"Oh. Y—Yes."

"Yes, what, darlin'?"

"Yes…thank you?"

Carolyn cleared her throat and looked at Jon.

"She was told," Jon said, a little defensively.

"Do you know the line, Janet?" Amanda asked, "Or were you not told that, either?"

"She was told!" Jon said.

Janet took a deep breath. She had been informed of what to expect. This was the kind of thing she had always fantasized about, all her life. She knew the line.

"Welcome to my home," she recited. "How may I serve you?"

There. *Done.*

Carolyn raised her empty wine glass and struck it with her fingernail; it rang like a bell. Despite her embarrassment, Janet snapped into motion.

She nearly ran to Carolyn's chair, bending over between her and Jack's chair to reach for the wine on the table. She stood and poured from the bottle into Carolyn's offered glass.

"My God, Jon, you really didn't teach her anything, did you?" Carolyn said.

Jon shrugged and shook his head.

"You will kneel when serving your guests," Carolyn said. "Always. Were you not told this?"

Janet fell to her knees, the glass already filled.

"Y—Yes, I was." Then it occurred to her: "Ma'am. Oh! Sir!" She turned to face Jack, who was holding his glass toward her. "Yes, Sir. I am a C cup, Sir." She lifted the bottle to fill his glass.

"Then why didn't you kneel?" Carolyn said.

Janet felt a pang of inadequacy, plus stupidity for feeling it. She focused on pouring the wine, not wanting to make things worse.

"I'm sorry," she said, as she felt a warm hand caress the underside of her right breast. She hesitated as she fought the urge to lean away from Jack's reach. It had been a long time since anyone had touched her there—*any*where, for that matter.

"I forgot. I'm terrified," she confided, but Carolyn didn't seem to care. "I will try to do better. Ma'am."

"Hmm," Carolyn said, tasting the wine. "Not bad. Cabernet?"

"Malbec. Thank you, Ma'am." She stayed kneeling as Jack's hand lifted her breast, then he very gently squeezed it before letting her go.

She felt another rush of blood to her face. This was all too strange. What would her family think, if they knew she was doing this? They were all so straight-laced. Her ex?

Why was she thinking about any of them? She tried to concentrate. She saw that Amanda and Jon were both holding their empty glasses.

"Do I walk around to you, or do I have to walk on my knees—Ma'am?" she asked Amanda.

"You may walk to serve us or to run to the kitchen. But you will always kneel when serving or picking up after us. Do you understand?" Amanda was speaking as if Janet was a first grader.

"Yes, Ma'am," she said as she got up, walked behind Jack's chair. The sofa presented a new problem: she was not able to get between the guests as she could between the chairs. *Always serve the wife first,* she remembered reading somewhere. *She's his wife?* Too many thoughts. She kneeled near Amanda at the end of the table, poured her wine first and then Jon's, who mercifully held his glass out to her rather than making her walk around the entire couch.

"I am hungry," Amanda said, leaning back and watching her. Janet set the empty bottle down on the table, picked up the nearest serving plate and held it in front of her.

"May I offer you these, Ma'am?"

"Never hide your breasts, dear. They are on display for us. Never hide anything. Understood?"

This should have come so easily to her, after reading so many kinky, filthy books with naked slave girls always serving someone or other. But here, in real life, it did not feel natural at all—just awkward.

"Yes, Ma'am," she said. She bowed her head and lifted the plate higher, offering it.

"Thank you, Janet." Amanda took a prosciutto appetizer and bit onto it. Janet waited patiently, unsure of what to do. "Mm, pear. What cheese?"

"Gorgonzola, Ma'am."

"These are wonderful. Pass them around."

"Thank you, Ma'am." Janet offered the hors d'oeuvres across to Jon, then to her left to Jack. She got up to walk to Carolyn, nervous that she was serving her last. She kneeled.

"Appetizer, Ma'am?"

Carolyn took one without comment and set it on her small plate.

"Get me the cheeses," Carolyn said.

Janet reached all the way across the length of the table, her breasts almost falling into the bowl of hummus, but she didn't think she should rise from her kneeling position. She bowed her head as Carolyn, then Jack, each took small handfuls.

"We would like some too, dear?" Amanda said, and Janet stood, walked quickly behind Jack's chair again. She kneeled again before Amanda and served her first, then reached across to Jon.

Carolyn cleared her throat—her plate was already empty. She pointed to the serving plate of tomatoes and mozzarella near Jon, farthest from Janet at the other end of the coffee table. Janet stood and walked behind the sofa, kneeled at what was supposed to be her own place at the head of the table but was still only a very empty chair. She offered the food to Carolyn as properly as she could, then Jon, who was nearest, then got up to walk to the other end. She hoped the little toothpicks would keep the slippery assemblages together as they loaded their plates.

As soon as she kneeled again to serve, Jon held up his wine glass, which was now empty.

"Sweetie…" he said.

Janet stood and nearly ran around the sofa, kneeled, and poured—just as Jack held his glass up from the opposite corner of the table. She stood again. She glanced at her own place at the table again; empty.

"Ignoring the women, are we?" Carolyn asked her as she lifted her empty wine glass.

"No, Ma'am! I'm sorry." Janet ran to serve her.

Janet was beginning to understand—this was all kind of a big joke, and it was on her, to see how she would react. Yet she still wanted only to please everyone. They were all taking this ridiculous scenario very seriously, so she would, too.

"There are empty plates, Janet," Amanda said, gesturing to her own and Jon's.

Janet was losing control of the situation, not that she had ever been in control. They kept her constantly running, kneeling, pouring, serving. She was getting frantic. It was becoming too much to keep straight, and she regretted every decision she made because each one meant neglecting one person to serve another. Her plan to always serve the women first fell to shambles in the rush. Her breath became heavy, her legs aching. She was starting to sweat. And all the while her body was on full display, only hers, and looking none too graceful in her chaos.

Amanda held out her glass for more wine, and Janet was mortified to discover that the bottle was almost empty. She had only brought two bottles to the table. She poured what little there was, and looked up at Amanda.

"Ma'am, should I—may I—go and get you more wine?" She could hear little *tsk-tsking* sounds from Carolyn.

"I think you'd better, dear."

Janet stood and ran into the kitchen, feeling the air rush across her perspiring body. No time to reflect. She grabbed a bottle of red and a corkscrew and scurried back to the group, breasts bouncing and jiggling. She kneeled, and—looking very awkward, she knew—placed the bottle between her thighs, inserted the corkscrew, pulled out the cork with a pop.

"Good girl," Amanda said, while Janet kneeled up straight and poured. Amanda sniffed the wine, tasted it. "You have excellent taste in reds, Janet."

"Thank you, Ma'am." She checked the others' glasses.

"But you put no water out for us. Why don't you go get us some glasses?"

Water. *Damn it.*

"I'm so sorry, Ma'am." She *was* sorry, aware of her little failings. How could she forget water? She set the bottle down and ran to the kitchen again. Was this the next phase, to watch her run naked back and forth to the kitchen, demanding something new each time?

She grabbed four glasses—no point in five—and walked to the refrigerator. She felt the blast of cold air across her chest as she opened the freezer door and her nipples tightened. It felt wonderful. She filled the glasses with ice, then took a bottle of water from the fridge and filled them. She returned to the table at a slower pace but still hurrying, carrying the four glasses in a bunch.

The serving plates were all empty but for the desserts. Janet had worked up quite an appetite. She sighed.

"Would anyone care for dessert?"

All agreed, and Janet served them, both the strawberries and the rum balls. She set the plates on the table, the last fat strawberry looking very tempting. She wanted to ask Amanda if she could eat—funny how she was looking to her for authority—but instead she stayed kneeling at the head of the table, waiting for instructions.

"Have you seen Dmitri lately?" Jack asked Jon. "Is he working on anything new?"

"He's still in Latvia, I think," Jon answered. "Or is it Lithuania. He should be back in a few weeks. And yes, he will be looking to start his next project, so he tells me."

"Aw, I can't wait! But shoot, if he's just startin', it'll be a while won't it."

Jon nodded. "Yep. A couple of months, probably. He's a perfectionist."

"Jon idolizes Dmitri," Amanda said.

"We all do," Jack said.

"I idolize his ethic," Jon said. "His devotion to craft. He's a big influence, I have to admit."

"So, is he, uh…" Jack shoved the last of his strawberries into his mouth. "Is he looking for a new subject?"

Janet noticed a silence that perhaps only she found awkward.

"Yes. I believe he might be." Jack and Jon both turned to

look at Janet; both examined her torso carefully. Who the hell was Dmitri?

"We have been served," Amanda said. "You may eat."

"Oh. Thank you, Ma'am."

Janet reached for the last big strawberry, the only thing left on the table, and stuffed nearly all of it into her mouth, starved and not caring if she looked like a foolish savage. She already felt like one. The chocolate melted in her mouth, its sweetness intermingled with the tartness of the berry. She wiped a trail of juice off her chin with her wrist.

She heard the sharp ring of fingernail on empty glass. Carolyn was staring at her. Janet put down the rest of the berry and resigned herself. She chewed her mouthful as she kneeled to serve Carolyn and poured the last of the bottle into her waiting glass.

"Clean this mess up," Carolyn told her as she nodded toward the tableful of plates and glasses. "And prepare to present yourself. Where is your bathroom?"

Present myself? What had she been doing, until now? But she knew this whole thing was just getting started. Her heart rate sped up again, a complex mix of thrill and dread.

"Down the hall. First door past the kitchen. Ma'am."

As Carolyn stood and walked across the room, straightening her jacket, Janet picked up the scattered plates and trays and started into the kitchen.

"I like that lily white little backside," she heard Jack say to Jon. "Pity it won't stay that way."

❖

She put the whole pile into the kitchen sink. She would worry about dishes tomorrow.

Dishes?

She stood at the sink and tried to calm her thoughts. She

couldn't imagine what she would be thinking when doing these dishes tomorrow.

The one outdated design feature of Janet's house that she disliked but couldn't fix was that the kitchen, painted in a more serene sea-green/blue than the living room and open to the formal dining room farther into the house, was so separated from the living room—only the narrow doorway connected them. Cutting a wide hole for a bar-type countertop for better entertaining would leave her almost no cabinets, and the refrigerator was already against that wall, with nowhere else to put it.

Tonight, though, she was glad for this isolation, this moment of not being watched, to gather her thoughts.

"Wonderful party," a deep voice said behind her and Janet jumped, startled. She turned, crossed her arms across her chest.

Jack.

So much for her moment alone. She regained her composure and lowered her arms.

"You're doin' a great job. Very nice choices in wines, I have to say."

"Thank you." She wanted to call him Jack, make this the normal conversation it could have been while standing in her kitchen and talking with a handsome guest. But this wasn't normal at all. "Sir."

He stepped closer to her, and fighting the urge to back away—she was already backed against the sink—she stood straight, placed her feet together.

Jack noticed this. "I like your instinct," he said.

He stepped closer, uncomfortably so. His breath smelled of chocolate and wine. He placed his hand on Janet's stomach, and she sucked in her breath. He *was* an attractive man, but…

He raised his hand to Janet's chin, lifted it.

"Jon was right about you," he said. "You do have amazing eyes."

Janet looked away, toward the refrigerator, toward anything

else.

"Thank you."

"Don't speak."

Jack placed his thumb under Janet's lower lip, and gently pinched her chin. He leaned in and kissed her lips, holding her steady, and all she could do was blush. Examining was one thing, kissing was so...*intimate*. It had been a long time.

Did she try to kiss him back? She couldn't remember. He released his thumb and lifted her chin higher, forcing her to stretch her neck. He raised his hand higher yet, and she yielded to him—she could not help but rise as he lifted, stretching her to stand up on her toes. He backed up a step, and held her there at arm's length.

She glanced at his face as he looked her over, evaluating her body like some racehorse or something. She held her position as he gazed at her breasts, her stomach, her hips, her thighs. Her sex, or her public hair, at least. She felt his eyes on every inch of her, and she expected him to tell her to turn around. Would she have to stay on her toes? She lowered her eyes again as he evaluated her face. She tried to look anywhere but at him as she was immobilized, her feet and calf muscles beginning to quake.

He started to speak.

"Trying to claim her for yourself?" Carolyn said, from the kitchen door. "Not yet. She's community property, tonight." She was holding Janet's own razor and a bar of soap from her shower. Carolyn headed to the living room, businesslike.

Jack released Janet; he had never actually *held* her.

She collapsed from the overwhelming release of tension, not just back to standing but falling to the floor, her own kitchen floor, stopping herself on her hands and knees. She wanted to grip his legs, wrap herself around them and beg for...what?

She strained to look up at him.

"Come on," he said. "It's time."

Chapter Two

Janet again resisted covering herself as she followed Jack and Carolyn through her kitchen doorway and back into the living room. She had never been quite so aware of the feeling of oak floor beneath bare feet.

Her guests sat down in the same chairs and Jack indicated the spot where she should stand, the same place where she had stripped off her clothes for them. Someone had moved the coffee table out from the center of the furniture to the space now behind her, so that that the little U-shaped arena was empty, only the thick fur carpet still between the sofa and chairs.

"You remember what's going to happen, Janet?" Jon said. "First, we're going to thoroughly inspect you, to make certain that we are indeed interested in this property." It took her a moment to realize he meant her, not her house.

"Then, we will tally up your errors and breaches of etiquette from dinner."

She nodded; this had sounded so erotic, so intense, during their talks. But now all her little inadequacies were coming back to her.

"Then you will plead your case."

She looked at him, confused. He'd never mentioned this.

Jack spoke up. "You will tell us why we're here," he said. "You will convince us that we should stay. You will tell us, in detail, all the things that you will do for us, as individuals and as a group."

Janet was mortified. She'd have to *say* it? Not just do it?

"Why should *we*," Amanda said, waving toward the others, "*let* you into our little club? You have to prove your worth to us. You'll have to plead your case."

Janet blanched at this. Following orders, obeying commands, that was one thing. She'd known that was what she was getting into. But explaining and even requesting what they could do to her? That was a far more embarrassing thing altogether. She swallowed hard, a lump forming in her throat.

"Understand," Jack said, "that pleading your case is consent. It is commitment. Do you agree to that?"

Janet wondered how far they intended to go. Was this some sort of last chance to back out? Did this mean they wouldn't stop even if she wanted them to? That would be illegal, regardless of this initial consent, wouldn't it?

"Is there some kind of…safeword, Sir?"

She heard Carolyn snort derisively.

"If you want," Jack said.

"I do."

"Name it."

Janet thought. She'd never *ever* needed one with her husband; the entire concept was foreign to him. She looked around the room.

"We're waiting, dear," Amanda said.

The walls. She wouldn't be able to forget the color of the walls.

"Blue," she said.

"I want you to acknowledge this, Janet," Jon said, "When

you plead your case, you will be asking *us* to do things to *you*. The things we've talked about. Right?" So—she could still call it all off, and go back to her normal life.

But maybe she didn't want to go back to her normal life. At least not now.

"Yes, Sir," she said. "I understand."

Jon leaned back, a satisfied smile on his face.

"See?" he said. "What did I tell you guys?"

Carolyn was resting her chin on her knuckles, elbow propped on the arm of her chair.

"Stand where you are," she said, "And spread your legs again. As wide as you can, this time."

So. Now it was really starting. Janet complied, moved her feet apart as far she could manage. She rested her hands on her thighs, not sure where else to put them.

She felt the cool air between her legs. Except for her earlier stance like this, she'd been trying to maintain as much modesty as possible through the evening.

"Newbie or not, I want no nonsense from you," Carolyn said. "No reluctance, or you're just wasting my time. Raise your arms high, and clamp your hands behind your head. Keep your elbows as far back as you can. Do *not* bring your elbows forward. Never try to hide your face in your arms. Do not hide anything—ever. These are the most basic rules; we shouldn't have to tell you."

Janet knew from her books these were the basics. She lifted her arms as ordered. Her breasts were elevated higher and thrust forward by the move, her armpits exposed. This was familiar, she'd read it a thousand times—an inspection stance, a presentation. But it was so unnatural, actually *doing* it. She glanced around at her guests, but they weren't returning her gaze. They were staring at her breasts, her stomach, her...

She blushed, again.

"Ladies and gentlemen, meet the new kid," Jon said.

"She's your find, Jon," Amanda said. "Why don't you be-gin?"

Odd that she would make this decision—maybe they *were* married.

"If no one else minds?" Jon asked.

Jack gestured towards Janet as Carolyn leaned back.

Jon stood and slowly approached Janet. He stopped right in front of her. He stared into her eyes as she alternated between looking back at his and looking away. She knew how he felt about her blue eyes, and she tried not to look away, look down. But in the books, slaves were *told* to look down—which now seemed like the easy way out, quite frankly.

He looked her over not as though she was a racehorse or livestock, as Jack had, but as a sleek new car that he had been waiting to see—admiration. He looked down at her body— she'd never been so close to him—and placed his hands on the sides of her torso, feeling her ribs and her deltoid muscles. He brought his hands to her breasts and she inhaled sharply. He held them, fondled them, pinched her nipples between his thumbs and middle fingers. She could feel them harden. She closed her eyes, her breath coming faster.

She reopened them as Jon kneeled down on one knee. He placed his hands over her hip bones, squeezed, then ran his hands up and down her stomach. He felt the flesh between her belly button and pubic hair; he felt the soft muscles of her thighs.

"She's so *supple*," he told the others.

Janet was fairly fit from daily walks and the work on her house, but not incredibly muscular. She wondered if he would prefer more of a hardbody. Jon placed his palms on either side of her small black bush, and with his thumbs he began stroking her outer labia, examining them. He slipped his thumbs just inside and spread them, and Janet squeaked at the intrusion.

Jon stood. He walked around behind her and again placed

his hands on her hips. He held them firmly, and shook her. Was he getting the feel of her, from behind, what she would be like? He grabbed a buttock, and squeezed, a little too hard. He ran his hands up and down the backs of her thighs. Only her paralyzing shyness in front of the others prevented her from bending over for him. She was tingling everywhere he touched her.

Carolyn stood up next, and gave Jack a disdainful glance as she passed him.

"I wasn't joking when I said I had other things I'd rather be doing," she said to Janet. "*Do* you understand this? That you are a distraction, an interruption?"

Janet didn't know how to answer. She didn't know what more she could do than stand here naked and take orders.

"Yes, Ma'am."

Carolyn sighed as she stopped inches in front of Janet. Her breath smelled of wine.

"I guess I might as well make the best of this."

From too close, Carolyn looked Janet directly in the eye.

"Yes, Ma'am. Thank you, Ma'am."

"Quiet."

Damn, this woman was scary, and Janet wished that Jon hadn't invited her. She didn't know where to look as Carolyn stared her down from only inches away—no one had told her what to do with her eyes, yet. Carolyn's eyes weren't just amber, Janet noticed, but a complex mix of amber and green.

"Chin up," Carolyn said, and Janet adjusted. "Better."

Carolyn crouched down on her haunches in front of Janet, her back perfectly straight. She tapped Janet's inner thigh.

"Wider," she said, and Janet struggled to spread her feet a little farther, uncomfortably so.

Carolyn outlined the edge of Janet's pubic hair with a fingernail, drawing a line along its borders. She spread apart Janet's labia, less gently than Jon had, and went straight for her clitoris, seeing if it was hard.

It was. Janet was too shocked to breathe.

"My," Carolyn said as she ran her fingers farther back, everything wet and slick and incredibly sensitive. "Little Miss Shy and Proper seems to be quite enjoying this."

Carolyn's fingers returned to Janet's clit, and she gave it a vigorous little workout as Janet stood red-faced and open-mouthed. This was a *woman*. Yes, it always sounded hot in the novels, but she'd never actually been with one—well, except for kinda that one time. Okay…two.

Carolyn pulled away.

Jack, who had been watching with fascination, stood and stepped up as Carolyn walked behind Janet, keeping one hand with its wet finger on Janet's hip. Jon stepped aside to allow Carolyn to move in behind Janet as well.

Jack brought his face very close to Janet's. He touched her lips with his fingers, felt their softness. Janet kept them parted for him, opened her mouth a little wider. As she enjoyed this gentleness, someone—Carolyn, judging by the fingernails—began playing with her ass, squeezing her buttocks. Janet felt Carolyn, and possibly Jon as well, spread her buttocks apart, stroke the crack of her ass, touch her anus. *Oh God.*

Jack leaned forward and kissed her hard, his tongue probing her and sampling every surface inside her mouth. Someone behind her started fingering her more forcefully, as though about to enter. It was probably Jon, as she felt no fingernails—she realized that Carolyn was spreading her cheeks wide apart with both hands, digging her nails into her ass to help him out.

Her heart was racing. She managed to meet Jack's tongue with hers; she licked and tickled it back as he felt around in her mouth. No one was touching her where she most wanted it, and neither could she, with her hands still locked behind her head.

Everyone pulled away at once, like they had practiced this,

and Janet felt tingly and abandoned, and very, very wet.

She hadn't even noticed Amanda approaching. Amanda examined Janet's rising and falling breasts as she tried to catch her breath. She put her hands under them and lifted, felt their weight. She gingerly touched both nipples, sending another shiver through Janet's body. She gave Janet one of her almost maternal, comforting smiles, took Janet's right nipple between her thumb and finger, and pinched it—*very* hard, twisted it outward.

Janet cried out in surprise and pain. She had grown to trust Amanda, to feel comforted by her presence. Amanda had *advised* her during dinner, more than demanded. Now she was the one giving her serious discomfort, not pleasure. Amanda held the nipple and pulled it, stretching Janet's breast.

Janet groaned, fighting the urge to release her hands from behind her head. But she managed to stand motionless, not wanting to offend Amanda. She clenched her teeth, imploring Amanda with her eyes to ease up. Amanda stared back as though she were evaluating, calculating.

After what seemed like an eternity, Amanda released the nipple, and Janet's breast bounced back to its natural shape, the nipple bright red. The uneven ache of only one side throbbing made it worse yet.

"Get onto the table, darling, on all fours," Amanda said, and gestured to Janet's new coffee table behind her.

Janet brought her legs together, her hips stiff, and nervously walked to the table. She glanced back at them, and climbed onto her prized new possession. She remembered when she had fallen in love with it at a neighbor's lawn sale. She kneeled on her hands and knees, wrapped her fingers around its edges.

Janet held on as eight hands fell upon her body, sampling very inch.

"Her back is so smooth," Jon marveled as he ran his hands up and down the full length of her spine. Hands were feeling her ribs, fondling breasts and ass, stroking her thighs.

"Too smooth," Carolyn said. "She could use a little time in the gym."

Janet knew that she was not the prettiest or fittest woman in the room—Carolyn was, sleek and severe and in incredible shape. Maybe Amanda, too—Janet didn't know how to judge. She lowered her head.

"You're too critical," Jon said to Carolyn.

"If she were mine, she'd have a workout routine. Or else."

"How many do you have out there, Carolyn?" Jack asked.

"You'll never know, Jack."

Someone was massaging her sore nipple, easing the twinge of pain.

"Spread your legs, honey, as wide as the table," Jack commanded, interrupting her moment of comfort. "And arch your back, raise your little ass as high as you can."

She complied, embarrassed, spread her knees almost to the edges of the table. She lifted her behind, exposing herself to full view. She shook her head in disbelief at her own behavior, and tried to hide in the curls of her hair. But Carolyn removed the hair tie holding her bun in place and pulled Janet's hair back into a ponytail. Carolyn's hair fell straight and shimmery over her shoulders.

"Chin *up*. You will maintain this posture, understand? No slouching."

"Yes, Ma'am."

Hands separated her buttocks. She quivered as she felt a tongue flicker across her anus. She felt a mix of shyness and need as the lips of her sex were separated, examined. Someone—a man—placed his hand over her pubic area, fingers brushing through her fur, and inserted his thumb into her, penetrating deep.

She moaned out loud—this was the first real penetration of the night. *First—out of how many?* The thumb was feeling around inside her, stealing her secrets. She wanted to collapse her arms and rest her head on the table, ass up, let him do this. But she stayed in place, elbows locked straight, head held high. She stared at the pretty row of Art Deco vases, arranged by height on a nice maple table she had found at the mall.

The thumb withdrew, leaving a lonesome void. She felt the wet thumb swirl around her anus, moisten it, press against it. Her shoulder muscles tightened. Finally the man inserted the digit, and pushed through her tight little hole. She cried out in surprise, more than anything.

"Oh God," she whispered.

No one had ever done this to her before, not even her.

"*Tight,*" Jon marveled. It was Jon.

"Too tight? We can do something about that," Carolyn said, in a clinical way that frightened Janet.

"There's no such thing," Jon said. Carolyn snickered.

"Roll over onto your back," Jack said.

The thumb was withdrawn. She lowered herself onto her stomach, and then slid and rolled awkwardly on the narrow table. She looked up at them standing above her, around her. Carolyn leaned down, inspecting her face.

"Her eyes *do* match the table," she observed, though without Jon's enthusiasm.

Carolyn straightened, and watched Jon as he ran his hands along the backs of Janet's thighs from her ass to behind her knees, then lifted and pressed her legs up to her chest. He pushed her knees outward to her sides, which spread her wide.

"Hold these here," he said, his face just above hers. She gripped her knees. Jon looked her over, and pushed her feet outward, away from her exposed genitals.

"Keep these spread, too."

She found this position humiliating yet deeply arousing, and her face turned red once more. Jack joined Jon between her feet, and suddenly it was like a clinical exam with two doctors, slippery fingers everywhere.

One of them—Jack, she saw as she glanced down—thrust two fingers into her, as deep as he could until his hand blocked his penetration. She arched her back, wide-eyed, and moaned at full volume. She looked up at him with her mouth open, speechless.

"Tight is right," Jack said, then he began to stimulate her clitoris with his thumb, while also reaching down and teasing her anus with his pinky finger. The sensation was overpowering, one withering mass of pleasure. She was unable to tell where one stroking began and another started. She panted, rocked her hips and pulled her knees back farther, begging him wordlessly for more. The smell of her own arousal filled the room. He inserted the tip of his wet pinky into her anus.

Carolyn was watching Janet's unoccupied mouth. She bent down over her face. She grabbed a fistful of hair and kissed her hard, wide-mouthed, her tongue penetrating deep into Janet. Janet's head was immobilized as Carolyn explored her, her tongue aggressive, shoving Janet's tongue out of the way—dominating her even within her own mouth.

Janet was spread open and pinned, every orifice filled. She felt like a butterfly pinned into a glass case by a collector—four collectors. She moaned into Carolyn's mouth and felt herself nearing climax, when as if on signal everyone pulled away at once, watching the intense mix of desire and disappointment on her face.

Carolyn still held her by her hair, but looked up at the others.

"Where's the razor?" she said.

❖

"I counted nine errors," Amanda said.

"Nine, yes, that's what I got, too," Jon agreed. He was stroking the newly smooth lips of Janet's sex, driving her insane.

"No, no—ten," Carolyn said.

Janet waited; she still held her spread knees to her ribs as they sorted this out. Her nervousness increased along with her desire as Jon left her labia to run his fingers through what was left of her pubic hair. She tried to rock her hips up to meet his hand, but he wasn't having any of it—he placed his hands on his own hips as Carolyn argued her point.

"Standing while serving wine," Carolyn said. "Talking out of turn. Ignoring Amanda and me while serving you two men, big one. Leaving me there holding out a glass because she didn't know enough to start a new one before pouring, and then *mixing two wines in one glass to fill it up*. Forgetting *water?*"

She continued enumerating grievances until Janet couldn't bear to listen as the others tried to convince her that some perceived slight or another was not actually a breach of any specific rules.

Finally Carolyn relented. "Okay…fine. Nine it is. On your hands and knees again," she told Janet. "Ass up. High."

Janet rolled over, lifted herself.

There was a pause. Jon said, "Well then, who wants to do the honors? Amanda, you brought it, didn't you?"

"Of course I did. Who's the thorough one in our house?" *Our house?* So they did live together?

"But I'll defer to Jack," she said. "He hits harder."

Hits harder? There was a hesitation, then she thought she heard the sound of a—

She cried out at full volume as the white hot blaze of pain shot across her upraised behind, matched with a terrifying *crack!* as some sort of whip slashed across it. It was a movie sound, a whipping-scene sound effect.

She wondered for an instant if her neighbors might have heard her scream. The sting was unbearable. *Eight more?* No— she turned to look over her shoulder at everyone as her eyes watered up. This was much more painful than she'd expected. This was not the spanking she'd always thought she wanted. *This* was what it felt like?

"P…Please," she said.

"No speaking!" Carolyn shouted, more at the others than her. "*That's* ten—now she'll get nine more. And she should get ten more!"

To Janet's dismay, the others agreed. Janet made a moaning sound and fidgeted, trying to figure out a way to talk them out of it. She was reluctant to use her safeword so soon, but…

She hadn't actually told Jon that she'd *been* whipped, no. She'd told him, in their talks, that she "liked whipping." She was certain she would; the thought of it was what got her hotter than anything else ever had.

What the hell had she been thinking?

Amanda crouched down in front of Janet and gently slipped her hands under Janet's jaws, lifting her face.

"Janet, dear. Listen. Calm down."

She waited until Janet focused on her. "You're going to be whipped, child."

Amanda was only a few years older than Janet, but Janet certainly felt like a little child at the moment—in trouble, back when they used to let teachers beat the kids. Why had she always thought this would be sexy?

"You knew this was coming," Amanda continued. "This is what's in all those books of yours, yes. Jon told me you have quite the collection. It's not quite what you thought it would be, I can tell.

"But I know that you want, more than anything, to please us. Well, this is the bare minimum. If you're going to learn to serve, to make it real, not just stories, then owning up to your mistakes is not going above and beyond the call of duty, pardon the cliché—it is the basic starting point. Anything less is cheating us, making us look like fools for believing in you.

And I know you'd never forgive yourself for doing that."

But wasn't this the initiation *into* the club? Was she also supposed to serve them once tonight was over? She'd never really thought that far ahead, beyond what she thought this evening would be.

"So. Are you ready?" Amanda asked.

Janet would have to think this over later. She did know what was expected *tonight*, it was true. And she'd wanted it. She nodded, and resumed her correct posture.

"Yes, Ma'am."

The whip slashed across both sides of her ass again; she shuddered as she cried out. She couldn't *help* it. This just wasn't what she thought it was going to be like. She knew it would sting, sure, but...

Jack must have found her cries very exciting; he hit her even harder on his third stroke. She reeled. Her elbows began to give out, but she caught herself from collapsing forward just as she was about to fall off the table. She straightened, braced herself again.

"Oh God," she moaned.

She quivered again at the fourth, regretting her decision to ever join this awful club. Why did she think she wanted this? *Thomas.*

Her husband. *Ex*-husband—this was why they would never be compatible. These fantasies she'd always had, about being bound and whipped—he wasn't one of those people who thought kink was abusive or wrong, it was...

On the fifth stroke she buckled again, tried to hide her face on the table yet still offer them what they wanted.

"Straighten up," Carolyn said. Janet pushed herself up, locked her elbows and then arched her back.

...he thought it was *ridiculous*. "Worthy of ridicule," he'd once said. Every single thing she'd found erotic, he'd found worthy of derision. "All these goofy fuckers with their whips and chains," he'd said, sneering—*laughing*—as he thumbed through one of her paperbacks. "You can't be serious, reading this stuff."

On the next stroke, the whip struck lower, where her ass met the back of her thighs. This was even more sensitive than her cheeks, and caused her to cry out at her loudest volume yet.

She bit her lip. *God, please don't let the neighbors hear.* Mrs. Janski? It would be all over the neighborhood, all over town.

Another lash, and Janet thought she could take no more.

She'd left him, because of that. A weekly fucking wasn't enough. *Fucking* wasn't enough. She needed *more*. Was that fair, to him? To kick a decent man out of his own house, just because she wanted to be—

She screamed, despite her efforts to stay quiet. The sting was beginning to accrue as the strokes were laid on top of each other, crossed over each other. Her ass was a searing mass of hot agony, each blow worse than the last.

—because she'd *thought* she wanted to be whipped—and used. Like this. But not like this!

Another, and she could hear the others breathing harder, enjoying her torment.

Or maybe this was what she…deserved? This beating? Good God, she'd left him, made him leave her, whatever—over sexual *fantasies*.

Why the hell did I wait until we were married to tell him? She'd fucked it all up—their families, security, friends choosing sides, so many people…

She cried out in agony at the next stroke. God, this hurt—*hurt*. But yes, maybe she had this coming. This was her punishment, this surprise that a whipping was actually painful.

Fine, then.

"That's nine," Jack said. "Are you okay, little darlin'? Are you ready? This last one's gonna smart."

Janet saw that she had two little puddles of tears on her

lovely new coffee table. She almost had to laugh. *This* one's gonna smart.

"Yes, Sir," she said, and straightened her posture.

And then she realized that while yes, maybe this pain was indeed justified, there was *something else*—here, on her hands and knees, waiting for the whip…

"Sir?" she said.

"Yes, darlin'?"

"Carolyn was right, Sir. I committed ten errors. At least. I deserve another stroke, Sir. At least one more." *Many more.*

Janet heard braided leather twist in Jack's hands.

"Well, color…me…impressed," Amanda said.

Jack hit her again, without mercy. She heard a squeak, a whimper, realized it was her own. A sob.

"Thank you, Sir."

Yes, she deserved some punishment, for more than this evening's little mistakes. But she now understood what this "something else" was, that she had been missing: leaving Thomas wasn't just for some frivolous fantasy, some lark. She couldn't live a lie, with him, anymore. One way or another, she had to be herself—and this was what she was.

She raised her face to the ceiling when she felt the final blow, gasped. She was crying, the tears running off of her cheeks onto her favorite new piece of furniture.

"Wow—her ass is the only red in this room," Jon said.

"Her quivering hindquarters were the only red within the serene, blue space," Amanda said, either quoting a book, or probably making it up. Janet didn't recognize it, but she wasn't exactly thinking clearly.

The others laughed, the tension in the room released.

For them, at least.

Carolyn lifted Janet's wet, blushing face.

"Are you ready to plead your case?"

The plea. Janet had forgotten all about that. Her mind

teemed with regret and confusion and pain. How did sex slaves ever concentrate on *any*thing?

"Y—yes, Ma'am," Janet said. She started to raise her hand, to wipe off the sweat and the tears, but Carolyn grabbed her wrist.

She stayed on all fours as the others made their way back to their comfortable furniture. *Her* comfortable furniture.

"Now, honey?" Jack said from across the room.

Reluctantly, she got up from her hands and knees, climbing off the table onto her feet.

"Crawl," Carolyn said. "You will have to earn walking privileges."

Janet dropped to her hands and knees, and crawled toward the others across her gorgeous but very hard bleached oak floor. She kneeled up, her face a mess.

"You may begin."

"May… May I fix my makeup?" she asked, wanting to at least clear her mascara from her cheeks.

"No."

Janet inhaled, exhaled; tried to gather her thoughts. She tried to think of something eloquent to say, or at least coherent. She had no idea what they wanted. Well, yes she did.

She couldn't look them in the eye.

"First of all," she said, "please forgive me for my mistakes I made while serving you your dinner. They were all my fault." She paused, unsure, feeling silly and her ass still burning.

"Please know I that I am so…honored, by you coming here, and asking me to join you. I am so sorry that I couldn't make it perfect for you. If you choose to accept me, I would gladly serve you again, and I would work even harder to get it right." But she would be one of them, then, wouldn't she?

Stop thinking. Just do this.

"I was told, when I was approached by Jon, or maybe I approached him, that I would be your slave, pet, and toy, tonight." She cleared her throat. "I was shocked that this could be real, but I was excited. It sounded so…"

What—wrong? This was her lifelong fantasy. Weird? Well, yes, but—

"I not only accepted this, I embraced it. I am here to please all of you." She cleared her throat again. That *was* what gave her the most pleasure, alone in bed at night, reading, her fingers between her legs—the idea of being *made* to *give* pleasure.

"I will do whatever it takes to make all of you happy. I understand that if I fail I will be punished. If you feel I should be restrained for whatever reason, I will not protest. I will not protest at anything you do."

If that wasn't the ultimate submissive speech, she did not know what was. What was the safeword, again?

Jack shifted in his seat, an erection nearly bursting through his pants.

"But what's in it for me, darlin'?" he said. "What do you consider your skills, that you can offer *me*? What are you offering to *do*, to please me?" He waved his hand like he was negotiating a business deal.

"I…I've been told that I give…that I have a very talented mouth," she said. "I would be very happy to prove it to you."

"Details," Jack said.

Jesus. She had never had to spell all this out before.

"I will suck your cock for you," she said, eyes closed. "Gladly. I will do it any way you like. If you permit me, I will use my tongue in very creative ways to please you."

She had never said that. What a sheltered life, she'd led. "I would swallow you."

Now everyone shifted.

"Janet," Amanda said, "that's all well and good for the gentlemen. But what about Carolyn and myself? What good are your astounding fellatiatory abilities to us?"

Amanda sounded both serious and teasing. And Janet

wanted Amanda's approval, still.

"Ma'am. I…have never been 'with' a woman. …Well, there was this roommate in college that I—"

"Get on with it," Carolyn said.

"Actually, I kind of wanted to hear that," Jack said.

"Yea, me too," Jon agreed.

"Focus, everyone," Amanda said. "Continue, dear."

"I have a very talented tongue, and I know what a woman likes. My lack of experience will be made up for by my effort."

Janet wanted to raise her hands and cover her face even more than her body.

"I will happily lick… I know how to please you. I will give full attention to any part of your body you want me to. I will do whatever you tell me to do."

She looked at Carolyn, then Amanda again, then down at the floor, red-faced.

"Lick my what, Janet?" Carolyn said, with a sideways smile.

"Your…"

"What do you call it?"

The truth was, Janet had never known what to call it, out loud at least.

"Whatever you would like me to," she said.

"I call it my cunt."

Price of admission, Janet thought.

"I will gladly lick your cunt. Ma'am."

"Fix your makeup," Carolyn said.

Chapter Three

Ken was stopped on the 147th Street overpass, stuck in traffic. He was already late, and there was no telling how late he would be when he finally got to his Mistress's house. This was not going to go over well at all.

To make matters worse, far worse, he had left his phone in his cubicle at work. He wasn't able to call or text Her to let Her know where he was—not that She would have accepted a texted apology. She thought them cowardly. He took off his sunglasses and rubbed his forehead, trying to massage the stress away. This was a clusterfuck of unprecedented proportions.

He had been staring at the back of the Toyota minivan for nearly a half-hour, trapped between it and a large orange work truck of some sort behind him. He looked in the rear view mirror, first at the enormous grill of the truck, then at his own worried eyes. He ran his fingers through his dark red hair and put his sunglasses back on.

His inability to see over or around the two taller vehicles made the situation even more frustrating; he was helpless against circumstances. Whatever disaster was ahead—car wreck? the radio said nothing—it was making him *late*, damn it, and his stomach was in knots.

Because, of course, the traffic itself wasn't the problem. The problem was that more than anything, his Mistress hated waiting. He looked at the clock in the dashboard. 6:02. *Shit.*

Ken tried to calm himself, to take temporary comfort in numbers. When stressed, he liked to make lists, numbered lists. Bulleted lists. Lists of options, lists of components to a philosophy. Lists of lists. Lists of permutations and combinations of other lists. It helped. It brought order to the chaos.

He began thinking up a list.

Oh, here was a good one, the big one: He counted the Seven Basic Rules that his Mistress had given him when they'd started together, when She'd claimed him. The rules that structured his Life.

Not his "life"—his job, the gym, hanging around his apartment—but his Life: from Friday evening until Sunday night or Monday morning, and the rarer and highly cherished weekday evening.

His day job was nothing *but* structure, which he liked. Programming code that worked or didn't—finding the problem, fixing it, moving on, all within the restrictions of very specific standards and protocols that must be followed and accounted for with endless forms that required their own proper procedures.

The coding process itself, while comforting in its clear-cut goals and yes/no clarity, still required some degree of problem solving and risk-taking, jumping out ahead of the rules to see what worked and what didn't as the test runs judged his efforts. But while he should have enjoyed that bit of initiative, the guesswork, it actually made him feel nervous and out of control. He always waited anxiously for the test runs, so that his next steps could be laid out for him. Black and white, please. No shades of grey, thank you very much.

Then there was the gym, except for weekends, which had exercise programs of a different sort. But even in the gym the workouts were carefully pre-planned and followed, no exceptions, with only minute changes over time to work on specific new problems—a bit more cardio after too many doughnuts, a bit less if muscle tone was flagging.

Overall, things were nicely ordered: work, gym, Life.

Then there was this mess. He tried to see around the minivan, but couldn't. It looked like an ambulance helicopter was flying in for a landing, far, far ahead on the freeway.

A calming ritual was most definitely needed.

So. Those Rules, and how he was trained to understand and obey them:

Rule One: *You will obey all commands given to you—immediately, without hesitation, without protest, without comment.* Simple enough. This was the basis of all: the one rule to obey, is that you will obey all Rules. Structure at its purest. And strictly enforced. *Very* strictly enforced.

Ken's heart sank at the thought of what awaited him when he showed up late for his Friday night appointment. He clenched his teeth and thought about slamming his fist into the steering wheel to hurry things up. But he knew that it wouldn't help, and it would hurt. Plenty of that later. He would not punish himself, but would let ("let?") his Mistress do the punishing for him. Okay maybe this exercise wasn't so calming. Next thought, please.

Rule Two: *You will do nothing that you have NOT been commanded or given permission to do.* This was an even more complete form of control than the first Rule. Far more complete—it put his entire life, at least while She was watching, under Her control. Not being able to scratch an itch (see also Rules Five and Six), or even ask permission to scratch an itch (see Rule Four), without first being given an explicit command, or a verbal allowance, was a far deeper surrender than just following commands. And it took far more mental discipline on his part.

He remembered back to Training Week, Day Three, when he was taught Rule Two: She ordered him to stand at full attention, naked, while She methodically applied a series of clothespins to his body. One by one, the little wooden clamps were attached to his nipples, his scrotum, what loose skin She could pinch from his fully erect cock; the tip of his cock, his earlobes. Then, as an afterthought, his lips. She smiled with gleeful anticipation as She administered the clamps.

At first he enjoyed it. Just being touched, gently at first, then more intensely as the clamps squeezed his most tender parts. The nipples hurt a bit, but he stood at attention, keeping his eyes straight ahead and not daring to watch Her. The feeling of Her kneeling before his swollen cock and balls, and stroking them before applying the clamps was the greatest experience he had ever had in his sheltered life.

Then She left, without saying a word. He could hear Her in another room, making phone calls, starting the dishwasher. When She came back She ignored him completely, and turned on the TV. She first watched the news, the traffic reports, then flipped between horrible reality shows and finally watched an hour of financial news, which was what She had been waiting for.

She left him standing for almost two hours. The pleasurable intensity of sensation had evolved into discomfort, and when he realized that She wasn't going to remove the clamps for quite some time, titillation turned to confusion, then dread, then uncertainty again. The discomfort increased and boredom, of all things, set in. He was sure that his blood was no longer circulating to certain areas. Should he pluck the clothespins off? Say something to Her, sitting there on Her sofa, watching garbage on TV? (The reality shows, all mindless contests of endurance and personal politics, were worse torment than the clamps.) At the very least, he should have adjusted his stance, scratched at his nipples, moved one or two of the more uncomfortable clothespins on his genitals to slightly preferable spots.

Yet he held still, perfectly still, thinking She would surely come back to play any minute—and also because he did not want to displease Her.

This was quite a realization. His cock had long before gone soft, and yet there he stood, hands at his sides, working to maintain his posture.

Because it was what She had told him to do.

The clothespin that clamped the end of his once-hard cock was pinching severely, and he wanted—needed—to move his hands, only a few inches, and pull it off. His nipples ached. The clamps on his balls were also becoming incredibly irritating, and he was overwhelmed with a kind of claustrophobia as the ceaseless pinching all over his body became too much. If he could just bend his knee, lift one foot up behind him and stretch a little, that would relive things so much.

He began to breathe harder. Why didn't he move? Tell this Woman he'd had enough, put on his clothes, and leave? What kind of idiot was he? She couldn't stop him from doing so. She'd said so.

His breathing became more unstable, his thinking cloudy. In his rising panic, he let out the slightest of moans.

His Mistress, as he had recently agreed to call Her, snapped Her fingers, just once, without moving Her eyes from the television.

The finger snap cut above the noise of the TV and rang in his ears louder than the crack of a whip, with which he had become acquainted over the previous few weeks. Still terrified but calmed, the panic stopped. She had refocused him, completely: *Do Not Move*, even though She had never said it out loud.

The single finger snap, Her only communication with him for nearly two hours. He knew then that he would defer to Her authority, without question. He had not been given permission to move, so he would not. Until She said so. He settled into a long evening of staring at the wall and listening to television as the financial news droned on. He did try flexing his pectoral muscles to ease the aching in his nipples, to little effect. Only one part of him had been given latent permission to move, as it had sunk in earlier disinterest—but it was starting to move again.

When She finally returned to him, both he and his cock stood at full attention. She removed the clothespins with an excruciating slowness, then made him stand fifteen more minutes without the clamps. The return of his circulation and nerve endings was worse, far worse, than the numbness.

When She gave him permission to move, he was aching to scratch or rub at the clamps' absence, but he did not do so. Instead he fell at Her feet, kissing Her leather shoes and apologizing profusely, for what he did not know.

Three: *You will accept whatever is done to you, without protest, complaint, or comment.* Amusements, She called them. He called them torments.

Whippings. Dildos. Clamps, bindings, and the dreaded Deep Storage. They had no safeword; acceptance was total or not at all. "You are free to go at any time," She'd told him at the very beginning. But of course, he would not be allowed back.

Enforcement of silence, he learned, was arbitrary: She often enjoyed a short, sharp cry of surprise when he didn't hear the swish of the whip before it struck him; or a proper, helpless whimper. As long as there was no speech, no long loud moans. If he was making a serious effort to remain silent through his grief, She usually forgave him.

Unless She was in a temper.

Four: *You will never, ever speak, unless asked a question or are specifically told you may do so.* He had found this one a bit surprising. Not even a "Yes, Ma'am" or "Yes, Mistress" when given an order. Simply obey, in silence. He had expected a more conventional "No speaking unless spoken to," the stuff of his fantasies, but that was not thorough enough. That would have still given him permission to speak his mind, occasionally, and speaking his mind was not part of the plan.

She deprived him of speech, an important facet in maintaining Her control. Any exercise of free will was seen as a rebellion, and rebellion would not be tolerated in Her house. He often wondered if he would be thanked or punished should the house catch fire and he were to barge in on Her relaxing to warn Her. Probably both. But why ponder on hypotheticals, when the Rules were so clear?

Five: *You will remain exposed. You will never cover any part of your body with your hands or any other object.* Nakedness at all times was expected for all Her slaves, and he had gathered early on that there were more. And what was expected was delivered, without question. Exposure did many things: it was a thrill, for both Mistress and slave. It maintained the proper power ratio. Mistress was rarely fully naked before Her slaves, or at least this one. The slave remained always so, for the viewing pleasure of the Mistress, and because it made apparent the slave's proper, humble place. The Mistress had the choice of what to wear; the slave had no choice whatsoever. It was much harder to *feel* equal, to argue or rebel in any way, when so self-consciously naked. Or perhaps She chose only people who felt that way.

His Mistress enjoyed grooming his body Herself. She had exacting standards, and did not trust him to meet them. She would order him to stand in the bathroom, legs spread, arms raised while She would shave his balls. It drove him insane with desire. Crouching down before him, She would trim his dark red pubic hair just so, moving his agonizingly erect cock with Her hand while trimming with the scissors.

"I have always preferred redheads," She'd said. "But only very specific shades. You should feel privileged." He did.

Modesty was not an option: the Rule against covering one's body with one's hands was of central importance, as he learned on Day Four of Training Week, when he was also taught the closely related Rule—

—Six: *You will never, ever use your hands or anything else to pleasure your own body, or to relieve it in any way without explicit permission.* No masturbation, no scratching an itch, no bathroom without permission. Certainly no rubbing out the sting of a whipping.

He was ordered to stand at attention, hands not at his sides but against the fronts of his thighs, inches on either side of his stiff cock. Her fingers snapped, but he did not know what he was supposed to do. He held perfectly still.

From behind him, he heard voices entering the room—several, male and female. His Mistress smiled and greeted them, and said that She would like them all to meet Ken.

Ken's face became flushed with heat and blood, but he was frozen in place. This was easily the most embarrassing moment of his life. His instinct was to cover himself and walk away, look at no one. He could simply walk forward, exit the living room into the hallway, and figure out what to do then. But his clothes were in the other direction. He could wrap up in a blanket or sheet from Her bedroom. Except that he didn't know exactly where Her bedroom was, having never been allowed into it. This was Day 7 of Training Week. He had barely known Her a month, back then.

While he was trying to find a solution, panic setting in and heart racing, Her guests had walked up to him and were looking him over, smiling, laughing, talking to his Mistress but never him. What to do in such a bizarre situation? Try to make small talk? By covering himself, at least some of his anxiety would be relieved, wrapping his hands around his exposed balls and trying to hide his erection with his forearms.

But he didn't move. She'd had him place his hands there, so close to his genitals, for this very reason—She'd planned to bring him to maximum embarrassment solely to force him to obey this Rule.

This was also, he realized, an important moment between them: was he Her slave, or not? Some people are *shy*, damn it. He could walk out and never come back, hope that he would never run into any of these people again. How devoted was he willing to be?

"Everyone, have a seat," She told Her guests. They sat down, two men, three women, on the expensive Modernist furniture in the living room. All eyes were on him, face red, his cock still hard and uncovered.

"Ken, I want you to make everyone feel at home. Take off their shoes for them. Find out what they would like to drink, and remember it, because you cannot ask them again. Then get their drinks. You know my favorite wine. You will address them as 'Sir' and 'Ma'am'."

Ken's instinct was to say "Yes, Mistress," but he remembered Rule Four. He went to the nearest guest, a beautiful blonde, and, kneeling, began to remove her shoe, a shiny black high heel.

"Ken," his Mistress interrupted, "I also want you to show my guests the proper respect."

Ken hesitated, then lowered his face to kiss the woman's shoe. He removed it, then the other, and when he kneeled back up she said, "Gin and tonic."

He walked on his knees to the next guest, one of the men, and hesitated again before bending down to kiss his shoes as well; he untied them and pulled them off of his feet.

This was not what Ken had signed up for. No. He thought again of leaving. But he held still, looking at the man, who looked back at him, waiting. Ken had seen this exact expression only once before in his life, in his one art class back in college. Most of the nude models, male and female, always had bored, distracted looks on their faces as they maintained their poses, but there was one guy who would look from one male art student to another, sort of smirking at them—"Yea," he seemed to be saying, "How do you like drawing my cock?"

"What would you like to drink, Sir?" Ken asked, trying to retain any dignity he could while kneeling before the man.

"Bourbon. Neat," the man answered, sounding bored but looking Ken in the eye, smirking exactly as the art model had done.

Ken kissed and removed all shoes, took all orders, then retreated to the bar to make drinks. His bartending skills had always been questionable, and as he worked he began to lose his erection while concentrating on the drinks. His hands were trembling, his fingers already cold as he handled the ice cubes.

He finally had all the wine poured and drinks mixed, and returned to the living room. He served the drinks from a tray while on his knees—something he had not yet been taught, but felt right doing. His Mistress then told him to remove the coffee table (heavy, She loved watching his muscles flex) from between the two long sofas. She told him to kneel where the table had been, right in the center of everyone, and to replace his hands onto the fronts of his legs, where they had been when the guests first arrived. At some point his erection had returned.

His Mistress then directed, or perhaps more accurately orchestrated, an evening-long, unbalanced five-on-one orgy, in which he had to provide full satisfaction to all but Her, who watched, and they provided him with what could be called very intense teasing. He wasn't certain of the status of these people—She had definite authority, they did whatever She said. But She never actually commanded them, instead always making them feel like honored guests.

After licking the blonde's clitoris for what seemed like hours while the others stroked his body, he was horrified to be confronted with the Smirking Man's erect cock, jutting out from black trousers as the man leaned back. He tried not to look at it. He was disgusted to know that he was going to have to suck it, to finish him—or else leave and probably never come back. He had never done such a thing, and had never wanted to.

But he was undoubtedly in a highly aroused state, being the naked center of attention for the first time in his life. And the job was made much easier by the blonde stroking his balls from behind. He wet his lips and took the cock into his mouth.

It tasted of man, ugh. He had always thought that women were disgusted by the sight of men having sex together, but these women certainly seemed to enjoy watching his naked, kneeling self suck another man's hard dick. It was the first time he had ever tasted semen, and he decided that he did not much care for it.

While he orally serviced every guest, they stroked his balls, his cock, but never enough to finish him off. And all the while he had to keep his hands planted on the fronts of his thighs, but never, ever pleasure himself. It was an exquisite torture, designed to test his will and obedience. It was nearly overwhelming.

It was also so unfair, everyone experiencing such pleasure and here was his own cock, exposed, throbbing, useless.

His Mistress insisted that the second man, who sported a cock so huge that Ken had to struggle to accommodate it, come in his mouth and not on his face. Apparently he had a habit of doing this? Ken learned that he was prepared to make considerable sacrifices for his Mistress.

He was on his knees licking the reclining third woman's shaved pussy when his Mistress took the second gentleman by the hand, willing him up from the couch. She pulled him by the arm, and headed toward Her bedroom.

"Ken," She said, "Keep them satisfied. You will do whatever they want. If I hear you have disappointed my friends in any way…"

She left the room with Her companion, not even bothering to finish Her sentence. He watched Her leave from between woman number 3's spread legs.

Ken was filled with a new and profound sense of humiliation. He brought the shaved woman to a quiet but high-pitched orgasm, then was ordered, to his chagrin, to suck the Smirking Man off—again.

He obeyed, hands on thighs, his head bobbing up and down on the stiff cock while the man watched with his obnoxious grin. All the while Ken thought of Her in the next room, getting thoroughly fucked by that huge cock. Which he would never get to do. Instead, he was out here, by Her command, naked and sucking another man's dick, and getting no release himself. No one was even bothering to stroke his balls anymore, yet his own cock was swollen and hard, his balls aching.

In this deep new shame, the Smirking Man came into his mouth.

❖

Traffic was beginning to move. He watched anxiously as the minivan pulled away from him, and another car from the next lane cut in front of his. *Jerk.* This time, though, no one stopped, and all the lines kept moving, however slowly. The clog had been removed. He glanced again at the dashboard clock, 6:11. *Damn it.* Whatever had caused this jam might now be gone, but it would still take time for things to get moving along—people would be filing in from on-ramps, fighting for priority and position, the more polite drivers letting others in.

He was going to be very, very late.

Blue

❖

Rule Seven: *Eyes down, unless otherwise instructed. When at attention, eyes forward. You will never look Me in the eye until explicitly told. You will not stare at your own body unless given permission. It is Mine.* These sub-rules were listed and given in order of importance; this one always seemed anticlimactic. But it maintained control even further: She already controlled the body, the hands, the will, speech—all that remained were the eyes, where he was allowed to look. Even what can be passively taken in, rather than actively done. Her face, Her body were off-limits not only for touching, but even for looking. And so was his own—what he once thought of as his own body was now Her property. Looking was not a passive activity, but an active expression of will. And there would be no usurping Her will.

This Rule was the least enforced, especially as time had passed between them. Pleading looks were often enjoyed, even forced. Eyes were often raised, eye contact briefly made. As long as it didn't become a habit, as long as he didn't stare. He cheated frequently, on this Rule. She was too beautiful, with those green and amber eyes, that incredibly fit body. As long as She was not in a temper—which She surely would be tonight.

❖

He was off the freeway now, past the off-ramp, through the gauntlet of convenience stores and strip malls and the older neighborhoods that preceded Hers, speeding into the maze of winding streets and cul-de-sacs that held the larger homes in this particular suburb, Cedarvale.

Then straight streets again that were once country roads before the suburbs enveloped this area, back when the City was growing east instead of west. He turned one last corner, went past two more streets, and turned into the driveway of the sleek Modernist home that was Carolyn's house.

Chapter Four

Everyone was just staring.

"Well?" Jack said, "What are you waiting for?"

But she didn't know what to do. Jack beckoned her with his finger. Janet crawled toward him, a lump in her throat.

"Have you been trained to show respect?" he asked when she reached him.

"No, Sir."

"She was told!" Jon protested.

"Can you figure it out for yourself?"

Janet hesitated, but she knew. She lowered her face to kiss his shoes. She heard a zipper.

When she raised herself up, his cock looked like a missile emerging from its silo—perfectly straight, incredibly smooth. *Oooooh God.* It had been well over a year since she'd last had one of these, and not very often for quite a while before then.

She looked up at his face.

"What *are* you waitin' for, darlin'?" he said. "An embossed invitation?"

Janet licked her lips, leaned forward on her hands and

knees, and took the cock into her mouth. She moaned at the sensation of it filling her mouth and she held it there, savoring it, tasting it. *Man*, she thought. *Male*. A man freshly showered but driving here in warm weather. She felt a surge of pure, primal lust. She slid her tongue up and down it inside her mouth, feeling every feature of its smooth, warm surface. Jack inhaled sharply. She backed off, and swirled her tongue around the cock's head—feeling its firm ridge and licking the very tip, slick with pre-come.

For the first time all evening, she was no longer embarrassed; she did not *care*. She thrust her head downward and took in as much in as she could, moaned again as its hardness nearly filled her throat. She considered how she must look to the others, down on her hands and knees, head bobbing up and down, red ass up in the air, and it now thrilled her. *This* was what she was wanting, when she'd listened to Jon's idea weeks ago. Slave-girl-in-castle, slave-girl-in-mansion, slave-girl-on-pirate ship, she'd read them all—and never mind all the submissive-to-a-billionaire stories. If this was what it was to be put in her place, to be a sub, she was all for it. She could feel her own wetness and she spread her knees apart, wishing Jon or whoever would move behind her.

"You know," Carolyn said, "If she's going to be trained properly, she's going to have to learn to take a whipping while servicing her betters."

Okay, maybe never mind about that slave girl thing. Janet stopped, and looked up at Jack's face with his dick still in her mouth—*You're not going to let her, are you?* her eyes pleaded. But his expression was quite different.

"Couldn't agree more," he said, grinning and watching her intently. Janet lowered her lips down the cock again, and could swear it had firmed up even harder.

The crack of the whip was a complete surprise; she hadn't heard Carolyn move. Janet screamed, her cry muffled by Jack's cock, and it took everything she had not to pull away from it—but she had the feeling doing so would make things worse. She looked up at Jack, who watched her with fascination. Begging him with her eyes wasn't going to work, apparently.

Carolyn struck her again, causing her to moan, her mouth still filled. She hesitated once more from the pure, painful surprise of it, but only for an instant. What had she been expecting, these last few weeks? Let's face it, this was what she'd been picturing in her mind for tonight, what had got her all slippery sitting at work or trying to watch TV—being on her hands and knees, sucking a man, being whipped.

The next blow came quickly and Janet whimpered again, but she did not stop or even slow her sucking. If anything, she sped up, worked harder. The fourth came after a long pause, Carolyn apparently making her wait for it. Did she know that the anticipation could be as agonizing as the whip itself? Janet flinched when it came, but she did not ease up on the cock.

Carolyn swung three times in rapid succession across Janet's ass, which already hurt from the previous whipping, and once more against the tender backs of her thighs. Janet squealed, prodded to suck even faster at each blow. Carolyn whipped across her shoulders, which she did not expect. That seemed almost rude, somehow, though she didn't know why.

But she remembered what Carolyn had said: she was being trained. To suck a cock while being whipped.

Okay then. She sucked furiously as the whip struck twice more across her back.

"You wanna trade places with her?" Jack said to Carolyn, and Carolyn struck her harder.

"In your dreams, Jack."

Jack moaned and leaned back in his seat. Carolyn whipped her again and again as Jack began moving his hips in perfect timing with her bobbing head, as he fucked her mouth. He grabbed her head on both sides, held it in place, and with a loud and ecstatic groan he erupted into her. Janet continued sucking, kept her head still as his hips slowed, and he began thrusting in time with his ejaculations. Carolyn timed her blows with his orgasm, each thrust into Janet's mouth met with a stinging crack across her ass. She could only moan at each convulsion, partly out of what was becoming actual pain from Carolyn's whip and partly from the shear subservience she felt each time Jack's cock penetrated her deeper, releasing its hot come into her throat. She let its salty taste dominate her.

Carolyn's whipping stopped. Janet relaxed, as did Jack's cock; it softened until she could take it all in and bury her lips in his pubic hair. Carolyn returned to her chair and reclined back into it. Jack still held Janet in his hands, and he lifted her head as his dick flopped against his stomach. He smiled beatifically.

She expected him to say something grateful, but instead he turned her head toward Carolyn sitting in the chair next to his.

"Now her, darlin'. Maybe you can bring a smile to that sour puss."

Carolyn's eyes narrowed into an angry glare at Jack, then she either realized he meant her face, or that she was fulfilling his insult. Her lips curled into a smile, but those eyes—achingly beautiful, Janet couldn't help but notice—weren't smiling.

Janet backed out from between Jack's knees and crawled to Carolyn, eyes down. She lowered herself down to Carolyn's shiny black shoes and kissed them both, felt the brand new scuff mark against her lips.

There was a snap of fingers, and Janet snapped her arms straight.

"Listen, you little—" Carolyn started, then took a deep breath.

"All right, newbie. I've given up something tonight to be here. Something special—for you. You've already ruined one pair of shoes. So I expect you to make this worth my while.

Can you handle that?"

"Yes, Ma'am. I'm sorry about—"

"Push up my skirt, and pull off my underwear. Gently."

"Yes, Ma'am."

"Don't say 'yes, Ma'am,' just do it."

Janet kneeled up and slid her hands along the outsides of Carolyn's thighs, trying not to touch her too much as she slid the tight skirt higher. Carolyn raised herself off of the cushion to let her. Janet pushed the skirt up to her hips, and noticed that Carolyn's thighs were hard and sculpted, like marble. She reached for the band of her underwear, black and skimpier than her own, and pulled down. She pulled them over Carolyn's knees and brought them down to her feet. Carolyn lifted one foot, then the other as Janet pulled them off.

Unsure of what to do with them, Janet carefully folded the panties and placed them on the arm of the chair.

Carolyn slowly lifted one leg and brought her foot over Janet's shoulder and placed it behind her back. She pulled Janet toward her spread legs with her foot, and Janet yielded until her chest was against the cushion of the chair.

Janet had never been so close to another woman's...parts, just inches away. Announcing, earlier, that she would gladly service one was not the same as doing it. Carolyn's sex was as sleek and perfect as the rest of her—shaved, or waxed, the lips swollen and plump. With her legs spread, her labia were slightly parted, showing the pink inner lips and clitoral hood inside.

Janet's face felt very hot.

She had drunkenly made out with her roommate in college once—okay, twice. They unhooked bras, felt each other up, squeezed breasts and butts as they tongued each other, but they never got inside each other's jeans. They just couldn't do it. She'd never done *anything* with a woman since; in fact she and her roommate always pretended like nothing had ever happened...either time.

Carolyn's eyes gleamed as she stared at Janet. She slid down into the chair and brought her hips forward in anticipation. Janet started to back away, but Carolyn pulled her forward with her foot.

"Going somewhere?"

This was all happening too fast. Yes, she'd always found certain women attractive, found the girl-on-girl scenes in books kinda hot—but this was *real*. There were smells and…tastes, to deal with. Janet took a long, nervous breath, wishing that there was some way to stall. Make small talk, maybe.

"You promised to be very enthusiastic," Carolyn said.

"I, um…"

"Let's hear you say it."

"Say what? Ma'am." She could barely whisper.

"Ask me."

"Ask you what, Ma'am?"

"Don't be stupid. To let you. Beg me."

Janet shook her head no, wanted to turn back to Jon and Amanda for help. They would understand.

"Beg me, you little whore. Tell me—exactly and precisely—why I should let you do it."

Janet didn't like being called a whore. She tried to shrink back, but couldn't move away. She also couldn't say it—it was too much. Now she did look back at Jon and Amanda, seated on the couch behind her. Neither had said a word since she'd started with Jack, and Amanda looked less than sympathetic.

"Did you really invite us here for nothing, sweetheart?" Amanda said. "We can leave, if you prefer."

Janet looked at Carolyn, still staring her down. No way would *she* respond to a pleading look.

"I'm waiting."

"Please let me…please you," Janet said.

"I'm giving you one more chance," Carolyn said.

"Please let me…lick you," she said. "Let me lick your clit.

Please, Ma'am." She closed her eyes as she again felt the rush of blood to her face.

Carolyn leaned forward, grabbed Janet by her makeshift ponytail, and pulled Janet's head back until her eyes—and mouth—opened wide.

"You made some big promises, earlier, newbie. Was that all just talk? Just a fantasy? Do you know what I gave up for you tonight?"

Janet tried to shake her head in Carolyn's grip.

"No. No, Ma'am," she said. "Okay."

Carolyn released her hair, but not her dominating gaze. She leaned back, again shifted her hips toward Janet. Janet remembered the word Carolyn liked, which Janet did not.

She felt very, very naked.

"Please, Ma'am, may I please lick your...cunt for you?"

Carolyn looked at her with a deep satisfaction.

"Permission granted."

Janet swallowed hard and lowered her face. Her pulse pounded in her ears; she could feel Carolyn's heat as she neared. She ran the tip of her tongue along the inside of Carolyn's outer labia, and Carolyn tensed. The musky scent of Carolyn's sex—why was it so hard to call it what Carolyn did, she'd read it a thousand times—was potent. It was so familiar, yet so strange, to be down here. She ran her tongue up and down the smooth outer lips, and tasted her. Carolyn was clearly aroused. She ran the very tip of her tongue along the smooth, shaven outsides of both labia. She was reluctant to go deeper.

But Carolyn grabbed Janet's ponytail and drew her in.

Janet found the clitoris, and began licking with urgency. She could do this. Hell, she'd tasted herself—on cocks after sex, on her fingers. Carolyn gasped at the friction and stopped breathing, her hips rocking.

Janet realized that even though she was in the obvious subservient position—on her knees, face buried in another

woman's crotch—she actually had some control in this situation. She could give Carolyn exactly as much pleasure as she
wanted. She left the clitoris long enough to find the inner lips,
and probed into them, once, twice, a third time, the taste even
more pungent; then she returned to the clit, tickling it with
the tip of her tongue. She glanced up at Carolyn's face, red and
open-mouthed, but when Carolyn looked back down at her,
she averted her eyes immediately.

Carolyn was breathing hard, but regained her composure.
She looked over at Jack sitting in the next chair.

"You do know, Jack," she said, "An important part of any
slave's skill set is to be able to lick cunt while being whipped, as
well as sucking cock."

Janet tensed; her ass was still on fire. She sensed Jack rising
up from his seat and moving behind her. She braced, and
pondered what to do. Should she let up on Carolyn, be less
aggressive? She could—

"*Aaagh!*"—open-mouthed, tongue wrapped around Carolyn's clit, Janet groaned at the sting Jack had inflicted. He had
spanked her flank with his hand, not the whip. She moaned
again with her next breath, before Jack could swing again.

She kept her extended tongue pressed against the hardened
clitoris. So much for being in control—she was no longer
doling out pleasure as she saw fit, but intensely, desperately,
wanted to make Carolyn happy, or at least not angry.

She began licking the clit again, focused entirely on it.
She quaked at the next slap of Jack's powerful hand, warm and
firm, and the next as it smacked the other side.

Humbled by the pain and the taste of another woman,
she buried her face into Carolyn's sex—okay, her cunt—and
licked, licked, licked, begging her with her tongue for mercy.

Carolyn's back arched; her breathing sped up. She again
grabbed Janet's hair and pulled her head in tighter as she came,
grunted and moaned from deep in her chest. She kept her shoe

pressed tight against Janet's shoulder blade.

Jack was able to get in a few more spanks, and gave one last, loud, hard one as Carolyn began to relax. Janet shuddered, but did not stop licking, not having been told to.

Carolyn brought the point of her stiletto heel against Janet's chest and shoved, pushing her backwards onto the rug.

"Next."

❖

Janet lifted her stinging behind off of her white rug. Even the soft, fake fur of the rug against her burning skin was too much to take. She felt the need to wipe her chin.

"Carolyn, sunshine," Jack said as he sat back down, "I could watch you come all day."

Janet didn't dare look up at Carolyn's reaction.

"In fact, I think you and me could have ourselves quite a—"

"Not. Gonna. Happen, Jack," Carolyn said as she pulled down her skirt and resettled into her chair. "Not even in your pathetic dreams."

Jack laughed. "Think you're in charge of those too? You *are* quite the control freak, ain't ya."

"Listen—" Carolyn started, but was interrupted by Amanda:

"Jon," Amanda said, "You look like you're about to burst. Why don't you go next? This poor girl needs something to do, look at her, lying there."

Janet looked up. Her head was near Jon's feet, and his cock, hard and erect, was already extending above her from his open fly. She wanted to thank Amanda for curtailing the hostilities, but stayed silent. She kneeled up.

Jon tilted his head toward his cock and Janet lowered her mouth onto it. She moaned at the pleasure of it. *Male*, again;

good to be back. She was determined to give Jon, who had been gentler with her than the others this evening, pure ecstasy. She tightened her lips around the head of his cock and wrapped her hand around its base, began stroking his balls with her other fingertips. Jon grunted in approval.

"Would you like her whipped?" Carolyn asked in a very perky voice, almost a joke. Almost.

"No," Jon said, "No. I want her to associate my cock with relief, with pleasure. I want her *grateful* to suck my cock."

She was. Gratitude was exactly what she intended to show him, eagerness as well. She made her mouth into a pure wet pleasure zone and sucked him with long, forceful strokes, trying to imitate what she thought he might feel if he were thrusting it into her sex. Her pussy. Her cunt. She pulled her mouth off of the cock and licked up and down the sides and bottom of the shaft, full-tongue, mouth wide open.

She lowered herself to lick at his balls, took them into her mouth one at a time, all the while jacking his wet cock with her hand. She licked up his shaft again, opened her mouth, and began truly sucking. *Make. Him. Come,* she thought, and did not care how humiliating this might look to the others watching her.

But Jon had other ideas. He gently grabbed her head, his hands on both sides, but rather than holding her there as Jack had done he lifted her face up toward his. She looked at him, mouth still open, afraid she'd displeased him.

"Lie back on the rug," he said.

Janet reclined back and brought her legs out from under her. As Jon pulled off his jacket and unbuttoned his shirt, she couldn't help but spread her thighs.

Jon slid his jeans off and dropped to his knees, now naked. He was fit but not overly muscular; hairless chest. He kneeled and she let him spread her legs wider, short of breath as she realized what was about to happen. It had been a *long* time. Jon took her by the waist with both hands, gripped her hips, and pulled her onto his kneeling thighs, raised her still-sore ass up off the floor.

He thrust himself deep into her. She moaned loudly in surprise and pleasure, and the pure exposure of it. She did not care if the entire neighborhood walked right in and watched, let alone heard her cry. She was being *fucked*, in a most exhibited manner, on the floor with everyone around her watching. And she was fine with that. God, was she fine with that.

Jon thrust again, pulling her deeper against him, manipulating her like a toy doll. Was that why he called her that, "doll?" He didn't call Amanda that name. She spread her thighs as wide as she could, calves hanging limply. Her back arched as he began working her. She caught herself moaning again— would he prefer she stayed silent, like a proper slave/toy/doll? She wasn't sure if she could control *anything* at this point.

Jon gripped her hips tighter, pumped her faster, pulled her harder and harder onto his cock. She could feel the weight of her breasts bouncing each time he yanked her body toward him.

She was going to come. Was this allowed? Or was she supposed to maintain some kind of discipline, to be used only for *their* pleasure?

Not that there was much she could do about it. Janet tried to control herself, to stay silent, but the orgasm swept over her and hit her hard—an immense release from the tension of the entire evening. Hell, the last few weeks. The last few *years*.

Janet's fists grasped the white fur of her rug. She let herself cry out, mouth open wide as she felt Jon's cock slamming into her, felt the heat and soreness from the whip and Jack's hand— which she suddenly found very, very exciting, pain and pleasure too mixed up to define or separate. How had that happened?

Jon didn't let up. He continued pulling her onto his cock by her hips, sometimes holding her tight against him, grinding deep. She was getting close again. She tilted her head back, eyes shut tight. She thought of Jack's cock in her mouth. God, if only he would join them here on the floor, let her take two at once.

"I definitely know what I'm doing for my second round," Jack said.

Second round?

"Sure you can function twice in one night?" Carolyn asked him.

"You kiddin' me, darlin'? What do *you* think?"

"Jack, *put* that away, you creep."

"Come on, darlin'. They're busy. You and me, we could make our own fun. Bend ya over the chair, there. Let's have—"

"I'm warning you, Jack. Do *not* mess with me. You do not want to see me angry."

"I've never seen you anything *but* angry, darlin'," Jack said.

"People. Play nice," Jon said, annoyed. No one seemed to care if Janet had anything to say.

"Care to join in, my love?" Jon said to Amanda as he regained his rhythm. "You look a little bored."

"I thought you'd never ask," Amanda said.

"Idle hands are the devil's…whatever," Jon said. He looked back down at Janet's spread and writhing body, ran his hand up her stomach.

Amanda stood, one foot on each side of Janet's head. Janet looked straight up and watched as Amanda unzipped and stepped out of her skirt, revealing no undergarments at all—which was kind of thrilling, that she had come over like that. Amanda then slipped her blouse over her head and reached back to unfasten her bra.

Janet gazed up at Amanda from the floor, looking up along the front of Amanda's naked body to see trimmed sandy-blonde pubes, barely-rounded stomach, the bottom sides of her large breasts—and a gold chain around her neck, with…a gold band hanging on it.

What?

"Are you ready, dear?" Amanda said down to her. "Carolyn was correct, you did promise satisfaction."

"Yes…Ma'am," Janet managed between Jon's thrusts.

Amanda lowered herself over Janet, straddling her, facing Jon. Her shaved labia were just above Janet's mouth. Janet sensed that Jon and Amanda were kissing, and she knew what she was supposed to do.

Concentrating on the wonderful cock inside her, she raised her head and extended her tongue to meet Amanda. She licked between the labia, tasting her tangy wetness. She probed deeper. Why was this easier than with Carolyn? Was it because the woman she was basically sixty-nining was kissing the man she was being fucked by? Or because she actually liked Amanda, wanted to please her for the *right* reasons?

Things could be worse, she decided; God what a night.

Janet brought her arms up and wrapped them around Amanda's hips. She worked her tongue, but Amanda was positioned too far forward for Janet to be able to reach her clit, which was what would surely please her most. Amanda was making her work for it—she had to arch her back, thus forcing herself tighter against Jon, but she reached it, and now Jon was even deeper inside her, grinding against her cervix.

Janet teased the clitoris, worked at it. Amanda wrapped her arms around Janet's body as she came, and Janet was pushed again over the edge by Jon's thrusting, a third orgasm rocking her as she licked Amanda's clit. She had to stop for breath.

Amanda straightened her torso upright and slid forward, and Janet was now confronted with the tight button of Amanda's anus. Lost in lust—how long could Jon *go*?—she accepted her place, this role she'd agreed to, and extended her tongue up to it. Amanda, appropriately, tasted of soap.

To hell with it. Janet abandoned all reservations. She licked, swirled, danced her tongue around it. Another first for the evening to think over later. Amanda squirmed and moaned as she rocked appreciatively.

Jon must have fed off of Amanda's excitement. He pounded even harder, faster, then hesitated, ground against her until he could go no deeper—and he came, filling her with his warm—no, hot—come. She gasped, tongue still extended, as Amanda came as well, her fingers reaching down and stroking her own clit above Janet's chin. Someone grabbed her breasts and squeezed them, pinched the nipples.

❖

They both rolled off of her, panting, and leaned against her furniture on the floor. Janet let go of the fourth orgasm that had been building within her; three was a pretty good night.

"Nicely done, girl," Amanda said.

Janet was alone on the rug, spread wide and well fucked, cooling down. Her face was wet from sweat, saliva and two other women, and she tried to catch her breath.

She wanted to kneel up and suck her own juices from Jon's glistening cock. She wanted to invite everyone down onto the rug with her, feel them all at once and let them feel her again, a warm, horizontal inspection different from the earlier one, which from her newly satisfied perspective seemed incredibly naughty and enticing.

"Round two?" Jack said.

"Jesus, Jack, give it a break," Carolyn said. "I've donated enough of my time to the cause. I'm going home. You may all continue without me."

Amanda pulled herself up onto the sofa and started putting on clothes.

"Oh, come on, Carolyn," Jack said. "This girl needs a break. I would give you one hundred thousand dollars for a blowjob."

"Sure, come on over. I've got a boy at home right now who'd love for you to give him one. He's in quite a state, at the moment." She almost smiled. "I need to get back."

"Aw, sweetheart, if I came by your house, wouldn't be no boy involved. I'd have ya bent over my knee, beggin' me to *let* you make me a sandwich. Then I'd start in on ya."

"Fuck off."

"Exactly. 'No coming yet, Carolyn,' I'd tell you, then I'd—"

"Fuck *off*, Jack. Use her. That's what she's here for."

Please, don't piss her off. Just let her go home. We'll have fun.

Carolyn stood, and Janet felt a palpable sense of relief. But Carolyn didn't head toward the door. She was heading toward the bathroom.

"Need any help in there?" Jack asked after her.

Carolyn said nothing, that sharp, authoritative click of her heels on the bleached oak the only sound in the room other than Janet's heavy breathing.

Click, click, click...thump.

Click, then *thump.*

Oh no.

"What...in the hell...is this?" Carolyn said.

Please, no.

"*Gum?*" Carolyn nearly shouted, incredulous.

Janet flipped over onto her stomach, jaw hanging open. Carolyn was standing on one foot, her other lifted so she could examine the bottom of her shoe. She turned slowly—painfully slowly—toward Janet.

"You left *gum* on your floor, where I, where any of us could step in it?" Carolyn was glaring down at her. "You already trashed my other shoe."

Janet was too petrified to move. She shook her head no, not knowing how to explain. She had worked *so* hard.

"I—I thought I'd..." She had stuck it back under the table when the doorbell rang. It must have fallen off when they'd moved the table. And now it was stuck on the bottom of Carolyn's shoe, her gorgeous, gorgeous, perfectly polished shoe—LaBoutins, were they?

"I'm so sorry," she said.

Carolyn removed both shoes and headed back to Janet.

"You little trollop," she said. "You're going to lick this off."

Janet shook her head again. "No," she whispered.

The hard nubbin of gum dropped onto the floor with an audible click.

"What did you say?"

Janet was too scared to repeat it, but she shook her head again. She pointed down at the little blue wad. It shouldn't be a problem, now.

"I'll pick it up."

Carolyn headed for her like she was going to hit her. Before Janet could move, Carolyn had grabbed her by the hair, by her sloppy ponytail, and Janet yelped as Carolyn lifted, pulling her upward.

"Stand up, you little whore," Carolyn said.

Janet strained to get upright, her hair still in Carolyn's grip. She felt incredibly naked again, but not in such a fun way.

"Stand *perfectly* straight," Carolyn told her. "At attention. Stretch your arms up as high as you can. Higher! *Struggle* to reach higher, and keep struggling."

Janet raised her arms high, tried to reach for the ceiling. She could feel the cool air against her exposed armpits, perspiring from sex and now fear. No one was stepping in to help her.

"Where's the whip?"

To Janet's horror, Amanda handed it to Carolyn. Janet got a good look at it for the first time: one braided leather strand, about three feet long, gradually thinning from its handle to its tip.

"I gave up a very special evening to be here," Carolyn said.

"Yes, Ma'am," Janet felt compelled to say. "Thank you,

Ma'am." She was *thanking* her? "I'm so sorry."

"Up on your toes," and Janet obeyed.

"Stay there, and do not move," Carolyn ordered.

Janet stood as straight as a rail, feet together.

Janet cried out as the whip slashed across her stomach. A whipping on the ass was one thing, but her front was something else. So…*personal.* She wanted to reason with Carolyn, to apologize again, to be friends. Well, not *friends.*

But instead she held her position, arms up, against all her instincts yet too scared to move.

The whip struck across the fronts of Janet's thighs, much harder, as though Carolyn knew the muscles there could take it. Janet gasped. Carolyn whipped across her pelvis, and then her breasts, causing red streaks across them darker than her light pink nipples. Her breasts!

Carolyn cycled through these four zones—belly, thighs, hips, breasts—again and then again as Janet's cries became both louder and higher in pitch. How could she get out of this? Only Jon was in her field of view, and she looked down at him, hoping for help. But he only watched from his chair, looking slightly concerned, as if to see how she would react.

Just run away, she told herself, but she stood still. Paralyzed.

"Turn around," Carolyn ordered, and Janet obeyed again, ashamed of herself for doing so. This just *hurt,* no pleasure intertwined as there had been a few minutes ago, and she was starting to panic. She was facing the kitchen, and the back of the house—she could start walking, running, and lock herself in the bathroom until they all left. So why couldn't she seem to move?

She was still holding her arms up, but no longer precisely straight. Her shoulders were hunched forward, hands spread wide, barely above her head.

"Posture!" Carolyn said, and Janet snapped her feet together and stretched, arms straight up toward the ceiling.

She flinched as the whip struck across her already aching behind. She gritted her teeth as it smacked across the backs of her thighs, then her shoulders.

She glanced down at Amanda, who like Jon seemed to be evaluating her, and then to Jack, who to her disappointment was quite visibly aroused. She could feel tears welling in her eyes. Carolyn was beating her with a steady rhythm, with no indication she would stop.

This was, finally, too much. Janet whimpered, then cried out as the whip hit her unbearably sore ass yet again.

"Please," she said, almost whispering. "Please stop."

Carolyn didn't stop. "What did you say?"

"Please stop. I can't do this anymore. I—I just can't." Janet felt tears roll down her cheeks, fall upon her sore breasts.

"Turn around."

And Janet did, absorbing Carolyn's anger and more blows and wondering why no one would step in.

"Please!" she shouted, sobbing. "Please!" she said directly to Jon, who only shrugged and nodded, maybe even smiled a little.

Oh, fuck. They were waiting for her safeword.

The whip struck onto her breasts again, leaving instant welts, and Carolyn whipped her tender stomach even more.

What the fuck is my safeword? Her mind raced, her body cowered.

"Arms *up*, I said."

But Janet wasn't even listening, just trying to remember what the hell she could say to get out of this pain—real pain, now—without offending Carolyn, God damn it.

She couldn't think. She couldn't remember at all.

"Fuckin' safeword, already!" she screamed.

"*What?*" But at least Carolyn stopped her whipping.

"Safeword. Whatever it was. I'm sorry. My fucking safeword. Please stop. Please."

Janet broke into loud sobs, no longer caring about maintaining any semblance of dignity. Her entire body was on fire—not the localized sting of that first whipping, for breaking the little rules, but real agony, real, burning pain. She stood with her arms still up, her chest heaving, her face covered in tears.

"Carolyn…" Jon said.

Carolyn stood staring at Janet. She wiped away a bead of sweat from her own forehead, and let the whip drop to the floor.

"Fucking amateur."

She walked away toward the hall bathroom without saying another word.

Janet stood still, sobbing, arms still in the air, until Amanda signaled her to come down in front of her.

She gratefully kneeled before Amanda, not sure of what to do now that the game was so obviously over—everything, everyone looked different, all of the sudden.

Amanda took out a tissue from her purse and wiped away Janet's tears. She cleaned her streaking mascara from her cheeks.

Janet fell forward onto Amanda's lap, gripped her around her hips. She was finally getting her hug.

"I don't understand," she said. "Why does Carolyn hate me so much?"

"She hates all women," Amanda answered.

"She hates all men, too," Jack added.

Janet wanted to say, *Then why the fuck did you invite her?* but she held her tongue. Amanda started rubbing her back, which both hurt and soothed the hurt.

"Now, stop it, you two," Jon said. "She's not… She's not usually so… Something's up, with her."

Gee, ya think?

Janet tensed as she heard the sharp click-clack of Carolyn's approach from the bathroom. She hugged Amanda's legs tighter; didn't look up. She just wanted to hide.

"For what it's worth, I do like your house, Janet," Carolyn said. "It's very elegant, and very restrained. Congratulations." She walked out the door, leaving it wide open to the neighbors and the outside world.

The outside world. Was there one? Janet wished someone would please shut the door, but she didn't want to get up to do it. Or know if she was still supposed to ask permission, or what.

"Does this mean there won't be a second round?" Jack said.

Janet stifled more sobs, accepted Amanda's embrace.

"Can I just speak now, as a person, not a…toy, or whatever?" Janet said, no Sir or Ma'am, her head still in Amanda's lap.

"Of course," Amanda said. She smoothed Janet's hair.

"You guys are a bunch of cruel motherfuckers."

Amanda looked over at Jon.

"You really *didn't* tell her everything she needed to know, did you…"

Chapter Five

Ken sprinted from his car to the entryway of Carolyn's house. Tucked between two garish McMansions, Her house—or lair, as he thought of it—was a low, older Ranch style built before the city had expanded this far out, but it was so thoroughly altered that it had lost all of its Ranch-ness. Long and horizontal, it recalled the glory days of Modernist functionalism, combined through Carolyn's own designs with a sort of Asian asceticism—She liked things simple, and disciplined. To say the least. It was also surrounded by the last remaining cedars in Cedarvale. The neighbors hated it.

To enter the house, one had to first pass through a small walled courtyard tucked into a front recessed corner. A gateless entryway led into it from the side facing the driveway, and one turned to the left to find the heavy wooden front door. The rectangular courtyard had a stone floor, plaster walls that hid the door from the street, and a built-in bench along the entire length of one wall. Tall bamboo shoots provided shade. Despite the lack of a gate, it was all very private, very restful; it provided a peaceful transition from outdoor to indoor as visitors waited at the door.

It was also where other transitions took place. Ken entered the little courtyard, raised the hinged seat of the long bench, and undressed as fast as he could. He threw his shoes, khakis and polo shirt into the box, then his underwear, and picked up the leather collar he recognized as his own. Still breathing heavily from effort (and panic), he locked the lid of the wooden seat closed. His clothes were now Hers. He then locked the tiny padlock on his collar. He was now Hers as well.

He kneeled, as always, and pushed the button for the doorbell. He waited. He had once been caught by a UPS guy there, very awkward, but it was too late in the day, today. He was very, very late.

The door opened.

"Do you have any idea how fucking *late* you are?" She was still dressed from work.

"Yes Mistress! I'm sorry! I—"

Carolyn snatched one of the steel loops in his collar and yanked him forward onto his hands and knees. She pulled viciously, almost dragging him in as he struggled to crawl forward. The heavy door closed behind him.

She pulled him hard down the long Earth-tone hallway, bent over him, Her arm extended behind Her. He crawled as fast as he could, knees thudding and skidding as Her sharp heels hammered across the bamboo floor.

Where the entry hallway opened into the spacious, spare living room, there was a tall arched alcove recessed into the wall to the left, usually filled with some kind of Asian art that was supposed to have some kind of calming effect that it never managed to achieve.

Today, even as he was being violently pulled along, Ken couldn't help but notice that the alcove contained a beautiful young Asian woman, standing naked and perfectly still with her hands behind her back and with one leg slightly bent at the knee, the swell of her hips accentuated. She wore only a wide polished metal collar around her neck, and a very thick rope ran down her back to a precisely coiled cone of more rope beside her. Artfully lit from above, she did not look at him, but kept her eyes lowered.

"Ignore her," Carolyn said, not bothering to look back at Ken. "I said *ignore* her," and Ken looked away. Who *was* this?

His Mistress dragged him by the neck into the living room, so serene: the far wall of glass looking out toward her Zen garden of a back yard, surrounded by cedars. The ring of minimalist furniture in front of the equally minimal fireplace, its original bulky stones replaced by polished concrete. Contrasting with all of this simplicity, the 18th Century Anatolian carpet upon which the front legs of the furniture sat, so complex in its dark abstractions that it boggled the mind when he wasn't busy orally servicing some guest or another while being beaten with a flogger. "It looks like traffic patterns," She'd said of it, back when he was still permitted to speak freely in conversation. "Those weavers *must* have studied advanced stochastic processes."

Ken's knees yearned for that complicated but soft carpet as he struggled to keep from tumbling onto his face, but She was pulling him the other way—through the dining room which was open to the wider living room and on into the kitchen, also part of the same huge space, separated by a peninsular counter surfaced in concrete.

She released him at the doorway that led downstairs, next to the hallway that led into the mysterious back of the house—Her bedroom, Her office, guest rooms. She pointed down the carpeted steps; unlike the upstairs, most of the basement was carpeted.

"Down. Crawl."

Ken started down the stairs on his hands and knees. He nervously navigated the gravity and physics of a situation he was surprised he had never before encountered, but he was at least thankful for the softer surface. The going was slow as he struggled to keep from falling and sliding downward.

Carolyn stepped down behind him. He reached the basement floor, much relieved and out of breath, and waited at the bottom of the stairs on his hands and knees.

He was in the media room, a big TV and a sofa along the wall with a stocked bar in the corner.

"Stand."

He stood. She paced back and forth in front of him and around him, restless. Like a shark.

"Don't worry, you won't get the whip," She said. He kept his eyes most definitely lowered. "I don't trust myself with it. I am furious at you."

Ken felt an odd sense of relief. No matter how he craved the whip during the rest of his boring life—its *intensity*—he was glad to avoid it right now, with Her mood.

"Are you not happy to see me?" She asked as She looked down at his limp cock, curving downward. Before he could answer, She said, "Usually you're about to burst when you get here. Today you can't even get it up for me."

When he remained silent, She repeated, "Are you not happy to see me?"

"I am always thrilled to see you, Mistress. I live for it."

"You don't look happy to see me."

"I am terrified, Mistress."

"Terrified? Why?"

"Because I know I'm so late."

"So you know you deserve to be punished," She said. "I do not trust myself with the whip tonight," She said again. "How do you think you should be punished?"

"However you see fit, Mistress."

"The reason I am furious at you, besides your *incredible* rudeness at not even calling me to let me know that you would be late, is that I had a very special evening planned, and you have ruined it. What do think about that?"

"I am so sorry, Mistress. I was caught in traffic. I gave myself plenty of time to—"

"I don't want to hear your excuses! Why didn't you call me?"

Ken grimaced. "I left my phone at the office, Mistress."

Carolyn stepped back, Her weight on one high heel, and crossed Her arms. Ken found this semblance of a normal conversation, however chastising it was, to be somehow arousing. He imagined himself married to Her, a rolling pin in Her hand like in the old cartoons—except that he was naked. His cock began to thicken, all the more embarrassing as She could watch it happen—which quickened its rise. He expected a severe criticizing for forgetting his phone, but there was a long silence as She stood observing. When She finally spoke, his cock erect, She was much more calm.

"I have to leave early tonight for an appointment. We had a short night as it was, and you have ruined it. I have to leave in just a few minutes." Another pause. "And I was planning a little cock play for you tonight. Wouldn't you have liked that?"

Ken let his shoulders slump.

"Yes, Mistress."

Unlike many nights, when Ken's stiff cock was merely an ornament, barely touched by his Mistress, certain times were reserved for cock and ball torments. They were heaven for Ken; they meant that Carolyn's hands would be on him nearly the entire time, administering torments, stroking it hard, teasing, tickling, binding. Clothespins, clamps, ropes, maybe just fingernails digging in—sometimes it was too intense, sometimes not enough, but at least his cock was the center of attention.

He was also almost guaranteed an orgasm. Most nights he was allowed to masturbate at the end of the evening, long after he had satisfied Her desires. On those nights, it was a sort of performance, with Her seated and watching as he was ordered to stand still or kneel as he got himself off. If She were not yet satisfied, She might participate. She would whip him while he jerked off, or torment him in some other way. Or give him a limited time period to come.

On the best nights, the rare ones, one of two things would happen: either She would masturbate him Herself, usually while he was bound or ordered to maintain some uncomfortable posture; or, absolute heaven, he would be allowed to jerk off while orally pleasing Her. So long as She finished first, of course.

There were also the disappointing nights, when he would be sent home rock hard, or kept restrained all night and not allowed to come. Something told him this was going to be one of those nights.

"So? What punishment do you think you deserve? I am calmer now, and I promised there would be no whips." Her arms were still crossed, but Her posture had relaxed.

"Whatever you wish, Mistress," Ken said to the floor. "I deserve to be severely punished for ruining your special plans."

"Well, then. Let's go to the playroom."

❖

Ken stood next to Carolyn as they stared down into the wide drawer in the long counter that ran along one wall of the playroom. The room was bright and evenly lit, clinical in its white walls, light maple cabinets and stainless steel—this was no medieval dungeon. It even contained a medical examination-type table, and many, many hooks and metal loops fastened into the walls, floor and ceiling. There was also the one incongruous piece of furniture set in the corner, a chartreuse faux-Romantic chaise that She thought was ironically hilarious.

"What will it be, Kenny? Black Mamba, White Python, or Blue Anaconda?" She asked as they regarded three massive dildos arranged in a neat row, each increasing in size. The first two were molded from a couple of porn stars who specialized in S&M videos; the third and largest was a blue, abstracted zeppelin with a penis head, which he had never encountered nor had any desire to.

He was relieved when She softly muttered, "No…"

She was speaking to him very differently now, calm and almost distracted, like a girlfriend browsing a jewelry counter on a relaxed shopping weekend. She even—lovingly—placed Her hand on the small of his back, before lowering it to run Her fingers down the crack of his ass. She placed Her middle finger over his anus, as if poised to strike. His cock throbbed in response.

Keeping Her hand there, She guided him down the counter to the next drawer and pulled it open with Her free hand. *My God, we* are *shopping*, he thought.

He recoiled from the drawer. In it were laid out, in precise rows, dozens of metal instruments with handles and various sharp points; spurs for riding horses. Carolyn shut the drawer.

"No…"

She looked wistfully at the rows of whips, crops, and canes hanging from the wall above the counter. He could tell She was regretting Her promise to not use them.

This was when She could be the most dangerous—when She seemed to be the most loving and affectionate. He thought of the one time She had drawn blood from his welted flanks. It was a Sunday; She had been in just such a friendly mood the entire weekend, demanding obedience, of course, but never dishing out harsh punishments for the slightest of perceived errors. And he had eaten more pussy that weekend than he had in his entire life. She was relaxed and reclining while he did his chores, calling him over again and again for more personal duties. At some point, he had crossed some little line that he shouldn't have—talking out of turn, he guessed, as they had almost begun engaging in normal conversations.

Without warning, She became furious. She tied his hands behind his back, looping the rope over his neck to keep him from lowering his hands, and ordered him to bend over the leather ottoman in front of Her chair. She tied his knees and ankles together so he could not move. She then proceeded to whip him mercilessly, the worst he had ever received, before or since. It was a ruthless thrashing, reducing him to whimpers and full sobs, before he finally cried out, for the first time, for Her to please stop. She continued, harder, insulted at the breach of rules, flailing at his immobilized body until a few of the welts began to bleed red.

"Safeword, safeword, safeword!" he shouted, since they'd never had one. She stopped, leaving him there bent over until his wailing and blubbering had ceased, blood trickling down the backs of his thighs.

He had flinched in fear when She returned with a wet cloth, but She untied him, and led him into the guest room, where She ordered him onto his stomach on the bed. She came back with antibiotic creams and bandages and nursed his wounds with a great tenderness, though She never apologized. The next day She permitted him to call in sick to work, and did so Herself, for two full days. She nursed him with care, but as the two days progressed, She began to restore order, made sure that after the first night he continued fulfilling his chores and duties. She allowed him to masturbate, any way he liked, while She watched. Actually, She ordered him to—he wasn't in the mood, for once.

On that Wednesday morning he was awakened by Her early and told that he needed to go to work. She admitted, though still without apology, that She had gone too far. She had never gone so far since.

It was a painful week sitting at work. The next Friday, they continued as usual, Her thorough strictness resumed. Neither of them mentioned it again.

Now he watched as Her face lit up with excitement, eyebrows (those beautiful, perfect, sculpted eyebrows) raised, Her mouth open.

"I know!" She exclaimed, an idea forming in Her mind like a bored teenager just thinking of something fun to do after a lazy day with her boyfriend.

She placed Her free hand on his hip (Her other hand still nearly penetrating him), pushed him to the very end of the long counter, and opened its final drawer. She reached in and pulled out a small metal box, with a coil of red and black wires coming out if it, each with a tiny metal clips on the end. It also had another, thicker cord coiled from it. The burnished metal box had a black dial and a black button on the top surface.

Oh, shit. Electricity. He truly, truly regretted leaving his phone in his cubicle.

The drawer was laid out with other gadgets, all meant to dispense electric punishments. She slapped the box against his chest and he grabbed it up in his hands.

"Let's go," She said. "Up to my office."

He followed Her back upstairs, all the way down the hall and opposite Her own bedroom, a room into which he had never been allowed.

Like the rest of Her house, the office was clean and minimal, with few distractions. He wanted to examine the one piece of art in the room, some kind of drawing of a twisted nude male torso, but he kept his head obediently cowed.

Carolyn walked around and sat behind the uncluttered desk while he stood before it, as though he were preparing for a reprimand from a boss or teacher. She reached into a low drawer and pulled out another metal box with a cord, this one a flat platform with a clamp of some sort extending up from the surface. Ken's dread was now tempered with curiosity.

"This," She began, showing Ken the little machine, "is

something I had the boys downstairs at work fabricate for me a while back. I'd almost forgotten about it."

She was speaking almost in business mode, as though She were explaining something in a meeting. Her office at work was in one of the top floors, Ken knew, though She rarely talked much about Her job—he knew it involved complex numbers, statistical analyses. This was one reason why She liked Her house, and Her rules, so simple.

"I told them I needed a device to mount a digital camera onto, to automatically capture still images of traffic as it passed by on the freeway. And I needed the images to be taken at random intervals. A few seconds between shots, or a few minutes, there should be no way of knowing how long the next interval will be, but within limits that I could control."

Mathematics and random processes had been one topic of conversation during their brief "dating" period, since his work involved some statistics as well. But the levels at which She thought were orders of magnitude above his—at work, and at play.

She stood as She continued, holding up the device for him. "The boys suggested that I just hard-wire a camera and write up the software, and I told them to shut the fuck up and asked them how much they really knew about the relationship between collision insurance and traffic-related complexity studies."

Ken stayed quiet.

"I said no, I want it to simply *push the button*. A little more expensive project, but I knew what I wanted."

Ken watched as She placed the cruel little device from the basement onto the metal platform and clamped it into place, the little metal armature fitting over its black contact button. She plugged its power cord into one of the jacks along the side.

"And they wanted to know why I wanted electrical outlets on the thing. I told them again to shut the fuck up, it was for external flashes. I also mentioned that there were an awful lot of young engineers out there looking for jobs just like theirs.

"Of course, it was all bullshit, Ken. I wanted *this*."

She smiled and held the little platform up for him to see: the small box with dial controls, atop the platform that it was plugged into—the platform's timer would activate the other box, timed randomly, by pushing its little button instead of the camera buttons as She had requested from the boys downstairs.

But what did the smaller box *do*? He had the feeling he wasn't going to like it.

He promised himself that he would never, ever, ever forget his phone again.

❖

"Put it on the corner of the table." She gestured down at the low glass and burnished steel coffee table in front of the sofa. "And plug that cord into the wall by the fireplace."

Ken bent down to carefully align the platform with the corner of the table nearest the outlet, and unwound its cord. He dropped to his knees near the wall beside the polished concrete fireplace.

From where he was kneeling, he could see the alcove set into the wall across the room and hallway. He glanced at the Asian girl still standing there, and took in as much as he could in one quick scan down her body: her black hair pulled back into a tight bun, as was Carolyn's; her smallish breasts with dark, erect nipples; a supple and flat stomach leading down to her trimmed pubic hair. He could not tell if her hands were tied behind her back or merely held there, and he thought she might have shifted her weight to her other leg since he last saw her. The weight of her wide and thick shiny metal collar, and the very thick rope falling down her back before resting on the giant coil of more rope, must have been quite a burden. She did not return his glance.

"I told you to ignore her!" Carolyn said. "That'll cost you a few extra volts, my friend."

Volts? *My friend?* Ken could not recall ever being called that. His Mistress was in a very strange mood, tonight. He stood quickly.

Carolyn snapped Her fingers, pointed to the thick glass surface of the table. Ken stepped up onto it; he had been there before. No doubt She had thoroughly researched weight capacities and structural strengths of all the coffee tables She'd seen, or perhaps had designed it Herself and had the boys downstairs fabricate it. Yet it always made him nervous, climbing onto glass. He stood straight, facing the middle of the room and away from the alcove with its mysterious new art.

He stared straight ahead, but he could see Carolyn in his peripheral vision as She bent to unwind the pair of wires from the box.

He stood still as She stroked his scrotum and attached a clip to one side; She was careful not to pinch an actual testicle with it. He gasped—it smarted already. She clipped the other clamp onto the other side of his sack, then gave his balls, and his cock, one long gentle stroke upward. She ran Her hand across his stomach.

"Hm. I don't want your abs to get *too* defined," She said. "Only gay boys have those ridiculous six-packs."

She brushed Her fingers through his reddish-brown pubic hair. "You're also due for a trimming."

After regarding him, She stepped to the side and bent down, and pressed the button on the electrical timer.

Nothing happened. She backed away to Her chair, its old and worn leather cushions still maintaining their strict geometric integrity, and She sat, legs tucked under Her in an unusually feminine pose. She did not take Her eyes off of him.

They waited.

Ken jerked forward and shouted a short, sharp cry at the shock—literal as well as emotional—to his balls. He caught himself, nearly falling forward but catching his balance. He straightened and braced himself.

Oh Jesus.

He whimpered closed-mouthed as his body convulsed at the next shock. Then there was a longer wait, even more excruciating. He clenched his fists, still at his sides, and gasped when it next hit.

He glanced for the quickest of moments at Carolyn, who sat absolutely transfixed. He had never seen Her look quite so...entranced.

He tried to regain some self-control. Now that he knew what to expect, he could brace himself for the next shock. The next one came, with more intensity than he had ever felt when She'd used Her hand-held zapper on him. He cried out.

"The voltage randomly changes as well," She said.

He was not going to be able to get used to this. He could only flex his muscles to keep his posture as straight as he could, and wait for the next shock. He was determined not to shout or whimper again.

But it was the waiting that drove him crazy. Not knowing the timing or the severity of the next shock, he could never fully prepare for it. This was an all new torture, mental agony as well as physical. As this ordeal continued, his convulsions and cries, which he was never able to stop after all, were the worst when his sense of timing and anticipation was the most off.

The next was a low-level, almost pleasant buzz, something he would have liked had it not been for the previous shocks conditioning him to fear it. It did not help to relax him.

He heard the television turn on. Carolyn was watching the local news, ignoring his suffering, his confusion. Didn't She realize how intense this was?

Of course She did. He began to step from foot to foot,

walking in place, trying to mentally escape.

"Stand still."

The news program was an annoying white noise of squawking and barking, adding to his mental torment as he tried to concentrate on enduring the jolts.

"Did you hear that, Kenny?" Carolyn asked, Her unusually warm voice piercing the chaos in his head. "There *was* an accident on the eastbound interstate. Three people were killed. That must have been what held you up."

Ken waited and hoped that She might see in this new information reason to forgive him and stop this torture.

But the broadcast wore on as his balls tingled with agony, even between shocks.

Carolyn sighed as She checked Her phone. She swiped and touched its screen, probably checking Her traffic app.

"I should make good time, at least," She said. "Do you think I can make it to Oakdale in twenty minutes?"

She turned off the set with Her remote. Ken couldn't focus as he awaited the next shock.

"I—I don't know, Mistress? I'm sure you—" He braced as he was sure another jolt was coming.

She stood and pushed the button that turned the machine off before it did. She unclipped the nasty little clamps on his balls.

"Down," She said.

He stepped off the table onto the floor. He was still clenching his fists. He glanced at Her face, but he saw that Her expression had changed again.

"Downstairs. Now," She said.

He turned and walked ahead of Her to the basement. He needed to massage his balls, rub out the clip-marks and painful electric numbness. He made absolutely sure to not look at the Asian beauty in the alcove.

Blue

❖

"The reason I am so angry with you...*was* so angry with you, besides the fact that you didn't *call*"—anger building up again, then dissipating—"is that I have to be somewhere. I don't want to go, but I have to. I promised a friend."

Ken stood, feet together, with his back against one of the three supporting steel columns in the basement storeroom, next to the playroom. He had been here before. Unlike the rest of the basement, this room was bare concrete, both walls and floor. There were cardboard boxes and plastic organizers on shelves against one wall, but the center of the room, where three columns of steel tubing stood to support a wall above, was empty. He was in the very center of the room, against the middle column. He placed his ankles together, against the bottom of the steel pole. He raised his arms out at 45-degree angles above his shoulders.

"That is why I've decided that instead of sending you home, I am putting you into Deep Storage until I can get back. I will come back as soon as I can get away."

Carolyn crouched down in front of him, always a thrill. She wrapped a leather strap tight around his ankles and buckled it. She then buckled a second strap around his knees. The straps were bolted onto the column, to keep them from slipping down. She fastened a third across his thighs as his cock throbbed right in front of Her face, and a fourth around his waist. He could feel Her breath upon his hardness.

She stood and met him face to face, leaned against him as She reached around him to grab both ends of the longer chest strap. Her breasts pressed against him.

"I will probably be gone two or three hours. It's clear on the other side of town, in Oakdale. You're *sure* you don't need a bathroom break?"

"I am fine, Mistress."

She buckled the strap around his chest, loose enough for him to breathe but not move. Much more gently, She brought a shorter strap around under his chin, and carefully fastened it over his collar. She stepped to his side and wrapped his outstretched wrist in a leather cuff hanging by a chain from the joint where the next pole met the ceiling, which pulled him to that side.

He watched Her while he still could, and She took his other wrist, pulled him toward the other waiting cuff. He was now stretched tightly into a Y shape, legs and torso firmly fastened to the cold pole behind him, arms reaching toward the ceiling. She placed a ring around his middle finger that was connected to a thin hanging chain. If he were to pull that chain downward, the heavier chains stretching his arms would be released, and he could free himself if there was a fire or some other emergency. But he had better have a good reason for doing so.

Ken opened his jaw wide as She inserted a thick penis gag into his mouth, pressing until its flat base fit against his lips like a binky. She fastened its strap behind his head.

Deep Storage.

"I'm going to see some friends, not that that's any of your business, darling."

Darling?

"We're meeting tonight to fuck and whip a new volunteer slave that my friend Jon has found. He told her that we're a dinner club with an initiation." She laughed. "Isn't that the best? Some little raven-haired whore over on the west side, I guess, divorced and desperate and eager to please, so I'm told."

She stopped laughing and sighed.

"Gorgeous blue eyes, willing to do just about anything. So I'm told."

Carolyn pulled a fitted leather hood over Ken's head. It covered his entire head except for a square notch below his nose, where the gag was.

"How does that make you feel, hmm? Some horny little bitch licking my cunt while you stand here in the dark all alone?"

Ken was glad that he was unable to answer that particular question, struggling with the head of the rubber cock deep in his mouth. Besides, it was a trick question, having been made to *watch* various women and men do exactly that.

"I can tell you how it makes *me* feel," She said as She reached for a set of bright yellow workshop earphones, big and padded.

But She didn't tell him. She sounded less than happy.

"I wonder what she looks like?" She teased instead.

"I wonder if she can take the whip as well as you. I wonder how pleasing and eager her wet little tongue will be for me. *Very* pleasing and eager, I would bet."

Finally, She placed the set of earphones over Ken's hood. Its tight, form-fitting and foam-lined shells were designed to drown out almost all exterior sound, to leave him totally alone with his helpless and jealous thoughts.

He shivered as Carolyn massaged the skin of his scrotum. She pinched the indentations where the clips had dug in, then squeezed and fondled his entire balls, rubbing the electric numbness out. She stroked his stiff cock with the barest touch of Her fingertips, and left him starving for more as She turned to leave.

She stopped and placed Her hand on his chest.

"But I would rather stay here with you," She whispered. She must have thought he couldn't hear.

He sensed the vibrations of Her footsteps through the house he was strapped to as She walked up the stairs and across the floor above him. A door shutting, a car door shutting. A garage door opening and closing, as She drove toward whoever the hell was taking Her away from this otherwise delightful evening.

Part 2: Culs-de-Sac

Chapter Six

The latte was too hot to sip, so Janet pulled the lid from the cup to let it cool. She looked around the bookstore's coffee shop, nearly empty, and thought about how sad it would be when they eventually went out of business. She was in the last big brick-and-mortar bookseller in the whole metropolitan area, clear out on 135th Street, and by the looks of today's business—or lack of it—they didn't have much longer.

All the hip bookstores were downtown now, independents, and who had time to head all the way there?

She blew on her latte. She looked at her stack of books on the table, and rested her chin in her hand.

Stupid. *Stupid, stupid, stupid.*

She hadn't really known what she'd come in here for, just the comforting feeling of a bookstore. She'd wandered around the so-called "chick-lit," as they still called it, and found nothing. She'd wandered into the Romance section—wasn't *that* a funny one—and wondered where those kinds of men were.

Two weeks. Almost three.

She'd ambled into the Erotica with very mixed feelings, and

left when she noticed two pasty-faced teenaged boys watching her from the Science Fiction section. They weren't so much snickering as in awe of her, their eyes wide and mouths hanging open, but she left anyway.

So what had she picked out, for perusal in the coffee shop? *Throw the Perfect Dinner Party!*, *Ultimate Entertainment: Make Your Guests Love You!* and *Appetizers as a Meal*. What the hell was she doing? So much for the comfort of the bookstore.

She pushed them away without opening them.

Two fucking weeks. Seventeen days, to be exact.

❖

After everyone left, that night—Amanda had *still* insisted that she kiss everyone's shoes as a farewell ("It's the rule," she'd said, as if it were obvious)—Janet watched their backs disappear into the darkness through the door's peephole, clicked the lock and the deadbolt, and then slid down against the door and cried. And cried.

She fell asleep there, naked and hurting and curled up against the door. She woke up around three in the morning and dragged herself into the bathroom, leaving the glasses and plates for later.

She couldn't look at herself in the big mirror, but then couldn't not look. She was covered in red stripes, some of them turning purple already, all of them still welted up and painful to the touch. She didn't know what the whip that Carolyn and Jack had used was called—she knew that the long, braided whips were called single-tails; this had been some kind of shorter version of those. A fucking whip. It was no flogger, anyway. This one left sharp, crisp lines that crisscrossed her entire torso, and still hurt like hell. She pulled Carolyn's stupid hair tie from her hair and let her black curls fall around her shoulders, then threw it into the toilet and flushed.

She turned around, and saw that her ass and upper thighs were a mass of redness from so many strokes as well as Jack's spanking. Splotches of purple bruising were beginning to show. Her back was welted and striped, as well.

She took a shower. A thorough shower. She still had the taste of, well, everyone, in her mouth, and she brushed her teeth, then went to find a bottle of wine. She nearly drank the whole thing, lying on her stomach in bed until she fell asleep again.

She awoke around noon on Saturday with a severe hangover but famished—she hadn't eaten anything but that half a strawberry in twenty-four hours. She wolfed down a piece of leftover pizza from the fridge and went back to bed.

God, she had been such a fool.

That night, more cold pizza, more wine; another bottle. She avoided the living room assiduously.

Sunday she knew she had to do some cleaning up. She found her ex-husband's cotton wife-beater tank top—how's that for irony?—and wore nothing else, her backside still hurting when *anything* touched it, becoming blacker and bluer all day, as were most of the stripes across her front and back. She replaced the coffee table, feeling like a total idiot. She loaded the dishwasher. She remembered being evaluated by Jack right there in the kitchen. She tried to think of other things.

Sunday afternoon was spent watching comforting Lifetime movies in which no one hit each other with whips and the man and woman lived happily ever after with the new stepchildren. She drank wine until she ran out.

She called in sick that Monday, and again on Tuesday, and she found the gin. She couldn't *sit*. Wednesday morning, missing the world and out of booze, she decided she would go back to work. She put on her softest cotton underwear and sat at her desk in the Medical Records department and thanked everyone for their concern, and wondered why the hell no one from that horrible night had bothered to call her even once. Not Jack, not Amanda, not even Jon, who she thought would, and, thank God, not Carolyn either.

That psycho fucking bitch from hell. It still hurt Janet to sit at her desk for very long, and since all the desks were in one big open room, she volunteered for the more annoying jobs like going down to the basement and looking through actual paper files to find lost or outdated information. Her boss Ron was happy she was back, happy with her willingness to take on the little odd jobs that everyone always stalled on, but was concerned that she was a little…distracted.

He asked her into his small office, cluttered with fishing souvenirs and art. Ron was a nice guy, very sweet, a tad bit overweight.

Please, she thought. *Don't let him start talking about his fishing lures.*

"Janet, how are you feeling?" he asked. "You wanna sit?" He gestured to the chair in front of his desk, covered with folders.

"Oh, no, I'm fine. I caught a little flu or something last Friday, but I'm good."

"Well, you've certainly been ambitious these last few days. Thanks for taking care of all the little bullshit no one wants to do."

"Glad to help. I felt bad for missing a few days."

"Oh, you shouldn't if you were sick."

"Yea. I know." *Does he not think that I was sick?*

"You're a great worker, Janet."

All those hours, cooking and cleaning the house. Cleaning and cleaning and cleaning the house. But not clean enough.

That fucking gum.

"We are lucky."

"Thank you, Ron. That means a lot." It did.

He ran his hand through his dishwater blond crew cut, the bristles snapping back into place. He stroked his matching moustache, as though stalling.

"But you seem a little distracted, even though you're working more. Not that you don't always work hard!" Ron raised his hands as if in apology. "But you seem worried. In some ways, it's none of my business, so don't feel like you have to tell me anything—but I want to make sure you're okay, that there's nothing you feel like you need to talk about?"

Did he know? How could he? What was he getting at?

"No, really, I'm fine. I've been a little tired, that's all."

Ron nodded. "Well, okay, take it easy, then. You don't have to keep going downstairs, just stay at your desk, if it'll help. No one'll think less of you."

"Oh. Well, no. I'd rather be up and around, I think." *If they only knew, everyone here would think less of me.*

"Everyone here has the *highest* opinion of you."

What does that mean?

"You know what might do you some good, Janet?"

She knew what was coming.

"No, what?"

"Have you ever done any fishing?"

"No. Not really."

"It is *so* relaxing, Janet. Just you, the fish, the sky, the water. Nothing is better to get away from it all."

Not that she'd mind getting away from it all.

"Listen, um," he said.

She waited.

"Listen, I'm not asking you out on a date, or anything, okay? I don't mean it that way."

Oh, no.

"But if you'd like, I'd be glad to take you fishing, sometime? You'll feel so rejuvenated, so…relaxed. It's the best thing for you, I'm sure it is."

Janet slowly backed out of his office, and almost knocked over the little carved wooden fisherman on the low bookshelf by the door.

❖

Two weeks ago. Since then, the bruises had faded, one by one, the dark ones on her ass taking an incredibly long time. Her fair complexion had always meant that she bruised easily, and they were slow to fade. And she'd never had bruises like that.

Her general feelings of foolishness had taken even longer to fade. In fact, they still hadn't. She'd been played, like a college freshman on her walk of shame from the frat house. Except it had been in her own house, serving them her own food, with nothing on, until…

And worse yet, over the last week or so, when she finally did let herself think about that night, there were parts that she had enjoyed—intensely. She *did* like some of it. Pinned on her back, with everyone inside her? Even if she was holding her own legs back and spread wide because they'd told her to? Yes, *because* they'd told her to. Getting fucked while another woman sat on her face? Everyone she knew would be so shocked. God, if her sister Marj ever found out. But she'd been so… thoroughly…fucked. Even that first, searing whipping, her punishment (and just that *word*—"punishment"). Yes, it had brought tears to her eyes, but—

"Well, aren't we a snazzy pair."

Jon's voice.

Janet looked up from her stack of recipe books. Lost in thought (drifting towards filthy thoughts), she'd forgotten she was still in a bookstore.

She didn't know what to say. He was holding the lapel of his light denim jacket, the same thing she was wearing.

"Matches your eyes," he said.

She could only stare. He had never once called her. She had

wondered what she'd say to him the next time she saw him, probably to renew her insurance or some such thing. She had thought of a few choice words.

But "Yours, too," was all she could muster. Yes, she knew his eyes were brown.

"Mind if I sit?"

She shrugged, gestured at the seat across from her.

He slid into the chair, tilted his head to see what she was reading.

"Interesting," he said, and looked up at her face.

"Why the hell haven't you called me?"

Jon leaned back, looked away. "I'm sorry," he said.

"Why? I want to know why. I've felt like a total idiot for two weeks now."

She wanted to hit him, but that felt like a cliché from some romantic comedy, the jilted beating in the bookstore.

"I thought maybe you needed time."

"For what?"

"To sort out your feelings. Away from us. Away from me."

Janet started to argue, but clenched her jaw shut. He was kind of right. "What did you think I'd be feeling?"

"Anger. Fear. Joy. Lust." God damn him.

"Add abandonment to that list."

"I am sorry Janet. It got harder to call you the longer I waited."

"What are you, sixteen?"

"You got me, there. I apologize. Sincerely."

She saw him looking at her stack of books again. She looked at his.

"What do you have, there?" she said. "Why are you even in this store?"

He held the big square book up for her to see.

"I couldn't find this anywhere on the Internet. It's out of print. I started calling around town, and what do you know!

They had one here, of all places. The store that Time forgot."

The cover was a black and white photograph of three female models, dressed in tall Marie Antoinette wigs and not much else. They were standing in some sort of formal garden and looked very worried, and Janet noticed that their hands were all bound behind their backs, all six wrists tied together in one fancy bundle.

"What is that?" she asked.

"Sergei Daniels. Ever heard of him?"

"No."

"Photographer. This is a series he did about the French Revolution, except that the Royal Family and aristocracy were sold off as sex slaves to the masses instead of being executed."

Janet smiled and shook her head.

"You doing okay, doll?"

"What's your 'alphabet'?" she asked.

"I'd like to show it to you, sometime."

"Who's Dmitri?"

"I hope for you to meet him, someday."

So he still had intentions for her? Plans?

"You've got some things to answer for." She wasn't sure whether she was talking to her friend Jon, or the Jon who had sat in her living room and watched as she'd taken one hell of a beating and never called her back. Or if they might be the same person, which was what she was suspecting.

"Oh?" Jon said.

"Yes. I'm not so sure I trust you, anymore."

"I'll do whatever it takes to regain your trust."

Janet took a deep breath. "I have questions."

"Ask away."

Janet thought a moment. She'd been formulating these for two weeks now, imagining herself pinning him against the wall and shouting each question as she jabbed her finger into his chest.

"Are you married?"

He paused, surprised. "No."

"You share a house with Amanda."

Again he paused, tilting his head one way then the other. "Sort of. Yes."

"What the hell does that mean?"

"It's—"

"Don't say, 'It's complicated'."

"Okay."

"Why does she wear a wedding band around her neck?"

"You can ask her."

"Are you two married, or not?"

"…No."

Another deep breath. "Why would you invite a psychotic bitch like Carolyn into my home?"

Jon laughed, then stopped. "I am sorry about that, doll."

"Why are you laughing? And if you're so sorry, why didn't you call to apologize? To see if I was okay? She beat the *shit* out of me, Jon."

She looked around the coffee shop to see if anyone had heard. So did Jon.

"And you could have stopped it at any time. When you asked for a safeword, that meant you gave consent to whatever happened until you said it. That's the *point* of safewords—no matter how you say 'No, please stop', I—or Carolyn—have permission to keep going. You're a big girl, Janet. I thought you were taking responsibility. I was impressed, quite frankly."

"Impressed."

"That you could take that. Yes."

"I was sobbing like a baby."

"And not moving. I was impressed!"

"I was too scared to fucking move, Jon."

"How was I supposed to know? You didn't say your safeword."

"I was crying and…"

"You cried when you were punished for your infractions, too," Jon said, a bit of a smile on his face.

Janet felt herself blush.

"That was…different."

"You didn't seem to mind when Carolyn whipped you while you were going down on Jack, either."

Janet glanced around the café again, her face a deep red.

"Shut up."

Jon raised his eyebrows.

"That was…"

"Different?"

Janet closed her eyes. "Why did you invite her over? She's unstable. She's…"

"A fucking bitch, yes. We go back. Way back. She wasn't always so…unstable. I'm a little confused, actually. I'm kind of worried about her."

"What? Why? She's insane."

"No."

"Evil."

"Yes." He smiled as though remembering something.

"She and Jack don't seem to be friends."

"They hate each other."

"What about her and Amanda?"

"They tolerate each other. Professional differences."

"What does that mean?"

"Amanda's been trained, you know. She was a pro, before she quit and went to cooking school and started her own catering business."

"A pro what?"

"Dominatrix."

"What?!"

"Look, I didn't know Carolyn would be so…volatile. She's always been very *controlled*. Very strict, but very controlled."

"Is Carolyn a dominatrix?"

"No. That's the problem."

"Why did you think I would like her?"

"I thought she would like *you*."

Janet froze at this.

"Shouldn't you have been looking out for me?"

"Yes. But I'll say it again. You—"

"Okay, okay, okay. Fine." They sat in silence a moment. "I just don't see why anyone would want anything to do with her."

"Are you kidding? People *line up* to serve her. Men and women. She is exactly what some people have been searching for their entire lives."

"Psychotic beatings?"

Jon fiddled with the corner of his book.

"Most people who are into this kind of thing like to play, Janet. You do, if you'll ever play with me again."

Janet made an angry face, but she knew her blushing skin was giving her away.

"And from the looks of it—" he gestured to her stack of books, "—you very well might." He looked up. "I like to play, too. We set aside a few hours, and we take or give up control, within limits that we've agreed to."

"But I didn't agree to—"

"To what? To be whipped? Yes you did. Before—for weeks!—and during. Until you didn't. And then she stopped."

Janet fell back against the back of her chair.

"But some people don't just want to play," he said. "Some people want it all day, every day. The real thing. Real life, not fantasy. And let me tell you, it's not easy to top twenty-four seven. You have to think of something for your sub to do, or it slides back into playing games and letting them do what they want the rest of the time. Which can kill off the fantasy. Carolyn has *no* problem topping 24/7. She demands it. She has schedules in her head, of when everybody will show up and when they'll leave. She's got them coming and going. And she is strict, oh my God."

"What do you mean? You sound like you…*know*."

"Some people would kill for that, doll. She's everything they've ever wanted."

Janet exhaled, her anger diffused but not her embarrassment.

Jon shrugged. "You've got nothing to be ashamed of. My God, you were…"

"What."

"Magnificent."

Janet looked up at the ceiling; she saw that someone had somehow launched butter pads for the café's muffins and stuck them up there.

"Everything that people like us look for in someone who's new to it," he said.

"Carolyn called me a fucking amateur."

"You were. It was your first time." He looked her straight in the eye. "Nothing a little training can't fix."

She looked around to see if anyone had seated themselves nearby. No one had. She could feel her arousal even now. Damn it.

"I don't know, Jon."

"I would never ask you to do anything you don't want to do."

She knew he was right.

"What did Jack say, later?"

"Haven't talked to him since. At least not about that. But guess what?"

"What."

"I'm on my way over to his place right now. What are you doing this afternoon?"

"Oh, no. I don't think I'm up—I'm not sure I—"

"No, no, no. I'm going over to have him sign some papers. He's a client, that's how I know him. Then we're going to watch a ball game, drink a couple of beers. I know he'd love to have you along."

"Mm-hm. 'Have' me."

"It won't be like that. I promise. You're in the club, now, remember? Nothing you don't want to do, Janet. Ever. It's just a ball game."

Janet wasn't sure. But she knew he was right: she could have stopped the evening at any moment. Maybe that was why she'd felt so stupid.

She had certainly found Jack attractive. She thought of his big, smooth cock in her mouth, as Carolyn whipped her naked ass right in front of everybody. And she had enjoyed it, that time, even if she wished she could deny it.

She looked up at Jon, who was watching her expectantly.

It was a ball game. What could it hurt?

"Okay," she said. "But I'm taking my own car."

Chapter Seven

She wished she had ridden with Jon. He was in an incredibly cool ancient blue Buick convertible, bigger than most delivery vans, while she followed in her tired old Honda. He wore Ray-Bans; his brown hair waved in the early summer breeze.

She followed Jon north down six-lane streets, then four-lane streets until they turned off at a Hills Heights sign, and she was glad for her navigation app as she'd never find her way out of the knot of curved Streets, Courts, and Terraces, all with the same half-dozen names: Pinnacle, Apex, Summit…

Finally they circled around in a cul-de-sac and pulled up in front of a beige McMansion almost identical to the two on either side of it. She joined him on the sidewalk and Jon rang the doorbell.

She was surprised to be greeted by a young blonde woman wearing nothing but a black leather collar. The woman was shorter than Janet, with large breasts that were remarkably pointed, like you only see in the old nudie magazines—the *really* old nudie magazines. They just don't make tits like that, anymore.

"Hello, Jon," she said, like this was nothing unusual. Maybe it wasn't.

"Hi, doll," Jon said—did he call all women "doll"? "Jack in?"

"Yes, of course. He's expecting you. He's in the living room."

"Hannah, this is Janet," Jon said. "Janet, Hannah."

Janet instinctively held out her hand.

"Nice to meet you," she said, afterward noting how odd it was to be shaking hands with a collared naked woman, door to the cul-de-sac wide open.

"Nice to meet you," Hannah said, not overly excited. "Follow me, please."

❖

"Jon! How ya doin', ol' boy?" Jack said. He saw Janet enter the room. "Janet!" He stood up from his overstuffed sofa to meet her—a gentleman, Janet thought.

She almost called him "Sir." "Hello, Jack."

He took her hand in both of his, met her gaze and kept it.

"How have you been, blue eyes?" he said.

"Okay. Good. It took a while to—"

"Why are you two dressed alike? Somethin' goin' on?"

She looked down at her denim jacket and shrugged. "We just—"

"Hannah, get both of these wonderful people a beer. You do want a beer, don't you Janet?"

"Sure, that sounds great."

So, was she one of them, now? She watched the naked Hannah walk into the kitchen. She was slender and curvy, and had a remarkably pert little behind that swayed as she walked.

"You watching the game with us, darlin'?" Jack asked.

"Yea, I guess so," Janet said.

"Sports fan?"

"Sure. What are we watching?"

"Hoops. The pros. I don't care about either team, but it's all that's on."

"Okay."

"Have a seat, darlin'. Jon and I need the sofa. You wanna sit right there?" He pointed to the matching overstuffed leather chair behind her.

"Mind if I take off my shoes?"

"You can take off anything you want."

Janet kicked off her shoes, then sat and tucked her feet underneath her.

Hannah brought a tray with three bottles of beer on it, cheaper beer than Janet had expected given the size of this house. She kneeled down in front of Jon to offer it, then kneeled in front of her.

Janet felt a dark, awkward thrill. She took the beer and Hannah stood. Janet looked around as Jon handed a folder to Jack, and Jack opened it and signed several papers within it.

The room was enormous. The ceiling must have been thirty feet high, tall windows on either side of the wide-screen TV hanging above the fireplace. But aside from the fat leather sofa and chairs and the tiny tables between them, there was nothing else in the room.

"That it?" Jack asked Jon.

"Yep, that's it. Easy peasy."

"Excellent. Hannah, get us some snacks."

"Yes, boss," Hannah said, and left again.

"How goes the alphabet, Jon?" Jack said. "Any more progress?"

"I'm stuck on the B," he said. "It's kind of a bitch."

Jack chuckled at the joke.

Janet wanted to ask what this was all about, but Hannah returned and kneeled before her again, and Janet was so entranced she forgot what she was going to say. She took the little bowl of pretzels, and Hannah placed a bigger bowl between the men, kneeling again. Janet recalled with a twinge of embarrassment how tiring all that constant kneeling was.

"Heard from Dmitri?"

"You ask that every time," Jon said. "He is back in the city. Looking for inspiration."

Both men looked at Janet, and she nervously took a sip of her beer.

"Game's startin'," Jack said. "Go get them, Hannah."

Janet watched as Hannah walked out of the room, and came back with yet another tray.

This one had no food upon it: it had one black leather flogger and a riding crop too long for the tray. She kneeled, looking a little pale, this time.

"Choose your weapon, sir," Jack said, and Jon took the crop and Jack the flogger.

"Assume the position, Hannah," Jack said. "They still have to introduce the players."

Hannah turned and stood between Jon and Jack in front of the sofa, facing the TV up on the wall. She spread her feet and raised her arms, locked her hands behind her head just as they'd told Janet to do for her inspection that night.

Janet's throat was so dry she almost coughed, then she remembered she was holding a cold beer. She took a sip.

"Janet, to explain—Hannah here is being punished," Jack said. "I spoil her, I admit it. I find her adorable—I mean, look at her—and I let her get away with far too much. But she pushed me a little too far, the other day, and so now she has to pay a little forfeit to me. Isn't that right, sweet thing?"

"Yes, boss," Hannah said, still facing the TV.

"Jon and I have played this before. We each pick a team. Every point gets her a stroke. Not each basket, each point."

"Don't they get some pretty high scores in these games?" Janet asked.

"Yes, little darlin', they do."

Janet could feel the familiar heat rushing to her face.

Jon looked over at her. "Whoever's ahead at halftime gets her mouth. Whoever's team wins gets whatever orifice they want, at the end of the game."

Jack looked thoughtful. "I sure wish there was some way to let you play, Janet," he said. "One way or another."

"We'll have to think about that," Jon said. He pointed up to the screen. "Ah! Tip-off."

Everyone was watching the TV except Janet, who was watching them.

All eyes were raised, but within seconds the men's lighted up while Hannah shut hers tight. Jack struck her twice across the ass and she gasped, despite the advanced notice.

Janet looked up to the screen in time to see the replay: a player had jumped and tipped the ball to another, who promptly ran to the basket and dunked it. She looked back to Hannah.

Hannah was watching the screen with dread. Again she grimaced, and Jon struck her ass twice with his crop, making a harsh sound against her skin.

"Damn, they really don't play much defense in the pro's, do they?" Jon said.

"They say they do, but they don't. Different game than college altogether."

"Doesn't bode well for Hannah, does it?"

Jack smiled his evil smile that Janet hadn't seen since the dinner party.

"No. It doesn't." He raised his arm to swing again.

"Three pointer!" he shouted.

❖

They switched whips during the break between first and second quarters. Jack used the restroom, and Hannah was told to fetch more beers. Janet hadn't even noticed that she'd barely touched hers. But when Hannah kneeled in front of her with a new cold one, she gave her the old warm beer and made sure to say "Thank you."

Hannah replaced the bottle on her tray and stood.

"You okay?" Janet asked.

"What do you think?" Hannah said, and left Janet alone. Janet watched her go, her ass a mass of red, a few defined streaks from the crop on her upper thighs.

"Doin' okay, darlin'?" Jack asked Janet, ignoring Hannah, as he seated himself on the couch. "You need anything?"

He stared at her intently, focused.

"I'm fine, thanks."

"'Cause I can have Hannah get you anything you need." Jack put down the flogger, cracked his knuckles, picked it back up.

Janet looked up at the TV; the second quarter was about to start. The score was 27-23. Hannah had taken fifty strokes in the last thirty or forty minutes, fifteen minutes of playing time. Janet tried to remember how many blows she'd received that night. There were the ten—no, eleven—harsh ones from Jack in that first painful session, her punishment. Then she'd lost count.

She looked over at Jack, swinging the whip through the air, taking practice swings. She felt a tiny bead of sweat on the back of her neck.

"Hannah!" he shouted. "Get your perky little ass back in here. Now."

❖

"I've got to go use the bathroom," Jon said.

Janet was so involved watching Hannah's pained expression that she didn't realize he was talking to her. She sipped on her empty beer bottle.

"Would you take over for a minute?" he said.

"What?"

He was holding the handle of the flogger toward her. "I need to run to the bathroom, but I don't want to miss a point. Take over for me."

"You want me to...?"

"Yea. Just for a minute—oh, damn it!"

He turned and gave Hannah two hard swats, and she moaned and leaned forward as if to get away from them. She sniffled. The blows were adding up on her. Janet knew how that felt.

"Okay?" Jon said, and stood, and pressed the handle into her hand. "Don't miss one. Look! They stole the ball! Come on, Janet, come over here—give her two—he just dunked the ball, didn't you see it?"

Janet stood and almost ran the few steps to the sofa. She knew what she was supposed to do, but somehow it wasn't that easy.

"Hit her! Come on, I've got to go."

Janet swung the whip at Hannah with a flick of the wrist, but it didn't seem to do anything, no loud smack like the men had coaxed out of it.

"No, watch," he said, and wrapped his larger hand around hers. "Don't stop when you make contact. That works with a crop, but not a flogger." He swung her hand in his, slowly across Hannah's red ass. It couldn't have hurt her.

"You have to *follow through*," he said. "See?"

She jumped when Hannah cried out twice at Jack's crop hitting her.

Another basket for Jon, and he was looking impatient.

"Now, Janet."

Janet swung the flogger like she'd been shown, and it did make a sort of smack; she could feel it making solid contact.

She looked up at Jon, standing above her.

"Better. But the basket was two points, and you need to hit her harder."

Janet turned to Hannah.

"Sorry," she said, and swung the whip with more force than before. This time she felt it through the handle—the leather tendrils of the flogger made solid contact and a loud *snap*, dozens of tiny snaps all at once.

"Sorry," she repeated.

"You apologize one more time, I'm gonna whip *your* little fanny," Jack said without taking his eyes off the TV. "Damn it!"

Janet looked up. One of the players on Jon's team—now her team—had stolen the ball again, maybe the same player. He ran down the court, about to dunk the ball yet again, but was leveled by a player running up from behind him and the ball went sailing out into the audience.

"What does that mean?" Janet asked.

"It means I've got to go," Jon said, and headed out of the room.

"Free throws," Jack said. "But this guy ain't very good at 'em."

Janet watched the players line up. The man who'd been hit missed his shot, and the men stayed put. She waited.

He made his second, and the men broke up and one player took the ball off the court and threw it to another, who started dribbling the ball toward the other basket.

"One point," Jack said.

"Oh." Janet lined up her swing. "Sor—"

She stopped herself from apologizing. She hit Hannah across the ass again, once, and Hannah didn't react much at all.

"No, darlin'," Jack said, and after his player made a basket from a very long way out, he turned to face her.

"You're going to have do better. Consider this your do-better talk. The point of this game is to teach Hannah a lesson, and tickling her with that thing ain't gonna do it."

He struck her three times with his crop, so hard that Hannah shuddered, saying "Oh, God," before clamping her mouth shut. Janet heard her stifle a whimper.

"Why don't you tell her why your being punished, sweetie?" Jack said.

Hannah's voice quivered as she gathered herself together. "I...I threw a little fit at the jewelry store," she said. "I'm so sorry, boss."

"I know you are, sweetie," Jack said, and put his hand on her thigh. She flinched. He looked up.

"Now! Janet—now. Two points, damn it, there's no defense at all in this game."

Hannah moaned in dread even before Janet swung the whip. She hit Hannah twice, good full swings—not as hard as the men hit, but harder than she had before. She still wanted to apologize when Hannah made a small squeaking sound.

Janet looked down at Hannah's red behind, once so white, and saw that she was shaking. Janet felt an odd mix of pity, empathy, and thrill at the "perky little ass," as Jack called it, so reddened and so close to her. She placed her palm against it and felt its heat.

"God damn it!" Jack yelled, and this time, Janet decided to whip Hannah a little lower, on her thighs, which had only been hit a few times.

"Three," Jack said, shaking his head. Janet swung the flogger once, twice, three times, each time understanding the physics and kinetics of it a little more—the way the tendrils caught the body, the resistance she felt, the way that it *was* necessary to follow through like it was a tennis racket.

Hannah cried out with each stroke.

"What did I miss?" Jon said, standing behind her.

"Your girl's getting better at this," Jack said. "She'll be a top in no time."

"Well, I am in the club," Janet said.

Jack looked at her. "The what?"

"You know," Jon said, still standing behind Janet. "The club."

Jack looked up at him.

"The *club*," Jon said, and Janet saw Jack raise his eyebrows, having caught some gesture or expression from Jon.

"Oh, yea. Yea! The club! Welcome to the club, Janet. Now hit her again." Another basket.

Janet felt something very familiar—that feeling of being chumped that had haunted her for the last two weeks.

There was no "club." She knew it for sure, now.

Damn these bastards. She wanted to start yelling at Jon, like she'd imagined doing before he found her in the bookstore.

She clenched her jaws. She hit Hannah harder than ever, once on her pretty little ass and once just above it, on those adorable little dimples on the small of her back. Hannah cried out, and wrapped her elbows tight around her head, keeping her hands locked behind it.

"Posture, sweetie," Jack said. "Jon, you've almost caught up. No tellin' who's gonna get her at halftime." He was completely unaware of Janet's anger, that she'd figured it all out.

Did he even care? But then Janet looked up at the TV, at the clock in the corner. She—Jon?—was only one point down, with twenty seconds to go. What would she do if she were ahead? Jon had said whoever was ahead at the half got Hannah's mouth. What if it was her? She'd never gone down on a woman before the dinner party, and she'd still never had one go down on *her*. She looked up at Hannah, naked and humbled, and decided this might be fun, club or no club.

"Ha!" Jack shouted.

"Oh, damn it," Jon said.

Janet saw that one of Jack's players had stolen the ball from one of hers, ran the entire length of the court and dunked the ball with only two seconds left. Her team threw it in bounds and one of them threw it as far as he could across the court; it missed by a mile. The buzzer buzzed, and the half was over.

Jack was ahead.

"Turn around," Jack told Hannah, and she did, her cheeks covered in tears which had run down her face and onto those large, heavy, pointed breasts. Janet hadn't noticed her crying. Little rivers of tears glistened toward those pointed nipples, and Janet was fascinated as the breasts jiggled with her every move.

"Finish telling her why you're being punished," Jack told Hannah.

She sniffled, her arms still up.

"I threw a fit at the jewelry store," Hannah said, trying to stop her crying. "And made a fool of both myself and Jack. I wanted a diamond necklace that he said he couldn't buy right then, and I made everyone in the store think he couldn't afford it."

"Could I afford it?" Jack asked.

She nodded, sniffling.

"Yes, boss. Of course you could. In fact, you'd just bought me a better one, a bigger one, as a surprise. I am so sorry."

"I know you are. But you're going to have to finish your punishment, right?"

She nodded again, more tears dripping off her face onto those incredible tits. Janet watched as they spread into tiny deltas, some little rivers flowing down between the cones of flesh and some rolling toward her nipples, her hard, pointed nipples.

"I will not do it again, I promise."

They all watched her. She saw them looking, and bowed her head again.

"We'll all need another beer," Jack said. "But you have something to do for me first."

She started to kneel, but Janet leaned forward and placed a hand on Hannah's flat stomach. She had been staring at those breasts since she'd arrived—now so wet, from *tears*, and so unique. Janet reached up and felt one, the one closest to her, lifted it to feel its weight. It was a handful. She leaned forward and took the hard nipple into her mouth. It was warm and wet, and the tears were salty.

Even at her dinner party, the party where she'd been played, she now knew, she hadn't been told to take a breast into her mouth. Just cocks and…cunts, as that bitch Carolyn called them.

She suckled Hannah's breast, squeezing it with her hand, until she heard Jon take a deep, deep breath. Then Jack. She released the nipple from her teeth and tongue, watched the breast quiver back to its original shape. Both men exhaled at once.

"I'll get those beers, boys," she said. "You—" pointing at Hannah, "—suck your boss's cock."

She mic-dropped the whip onto the sofa and sashayed toward the kitchen. For some reason she couldn't explain, she felt better fetching and serving anyway. Was that wrong?

❖

Fourth quarter, and Hannah was definitely looking worse for wear. Her posture had slacked, she seemed to have run out of tears—Janet had insisted they give her water—and she was pretty much whimpering at every stroke, no more protesting cries.

The boys had traded toys again, after Hannah had sucked Jack's cock as Janet and Jon watched. She'd served another round of beers before resuming her position after halftime, and yet another round after the third quarter. Janet was getting a little drunk.

She was in awe of Hannah, in a way. She felt deeply sympathetic—this was quite an ordeal—and she wondered if she should say something. But Hannah could stop this too, right? Just as she could have? She looked down Hannah's entire backside—blotches of purple and crimson, and all those welts. She wanted to touch them, to feel them on someone else's body. Hannah's front was covered, too—red breasts and stomach, marks across her thighs. Did she have a safeword? She wasn't using it, if she did.

Janet was worried but impressed, and a little thrilled.

The score was 103 to 99: 202 strokes since they'd started, what, three hours ago? Janet looked around for a clock, but there weren't any. There wasn't anything hanging on the walls, nothing but the bare minimum of furniture and TV, even if they were huge and expensive.

She pulled her phone out of her pocket to see what time it was. How long had it taken Hannah to receive so many blows? There were only a couple of minutes left in the game. She held her phone out in front of her, trying to remember what time they'd arrived here.

"Please, no pictures," Hannah said, her voice hoarse. She was a wreck—she didn't wear much makeup, but what she wore had streaked down her face and dried, her tears long evaporated.

"Oh. No, I wasn't going to take any pictures," Janet said. She understood. That would have been the *one* thing that would have sent her guests—"guests"—packing, that night. She smiled reassuringly.

Hannah was facing the TV again, after having been turned away from it for a while. The men had grown tired, sometime in the early fourth quarter, of having to be careful of where they hit her with the crop down her front. The flogger had been no problem, whipping anywhere on her they'd wanted, but whichever man held the crop had to avoid her tender stomach, take it easy on her breasts after a few decent blows. They'd been pretty much restricted to her thighs so they told her to turn around.

"Can you take good pictures, Janet?" Jack asked. He was looking at her phone.

"What?"

"Jon here is quite an artist with a camera. Can you take a decent picture? I think we need to document the occasion."

Janet looked at Hannah, standing there with her legs still spread.

"But she just... I guess so, yea," Janet said.

"Jon can't take the picture, he needs to be in it," Jack said. He looked at Jon. "Yea! We'll both sit nice and straight, displaying our tools of the trade, on either side of her. Nice and... and symmetrical, right, Jon?"

"Absolutely."

"And Hannah here will straighten up. You shoot us from directly in front, we'll be all balanced, like in Jon's photos. And then hey! We'll make it all sepia-toned, like an old-fashioned 'Wanted' poster or something."

"Awesome," Jon said.

"Oh! Hold on."

Jack stood, and rushed out of the room.

He came back with something dangling from his hand, something gold and shiny. He fastened the necklace behind Hannah's neck, then turned to face Janet. The necklace had a sizeable diamond on it, dazzling as it caught the reflections of the big screen TV and its cruel game. It hung right between her breasts.

The game ended, and Jon's team had won, coming from behind with a last-second shot that he took out on Hannah with glee.

Jack looked gleeful as well, happy for his friend.

"Your lucky day, Jon," he said, and turned to Janet. "Take the picture, while the moment is still fresh."

Janet hesitated, looking Hannah in the eye. Hannah nodded very subtly.

"Now," Jack said. "Posture, Hannah," and Hannah straightened her arms and back.

Janet moved directly in front of the trio and framed her shot, Hannah standing in the exact center, legs spread and her body striped and beaten, her face defeated. Her streaked make-up was haunting. The two men sat up straight like Old West outlaws, whips across their laps like six-shooters.

"I'm sorry," she told Hannah, and she took the picture.

Janet looked at the image. The diamond in the center of Hannah's chest twinkled from the flash. The woman had taken a pretty severe whipping and had stood perfectly still for almost three hours to let them do it. She looked completely worn out and defeated. Why was Janet so turned on?

"Let's see it," Jack said. Janet handed him her phone. He smiled wickedly, victory in his eyes matching the defeat in Hannah's. He tapped numbers into her phone, texting it to himself. Janet heard his phone beep. He looked up at her, as intensely as he had at Hannah.

"What did I tell you about apologizing to her?"

Janet's mouth dropped open.

"You told me…not to," she said.

"What did I tell you would happen?"

"…You told me you'd paddle my little behind."

"Mm-hm." He stared up at her, with his dark eyes—almost black—dilated and focused on her like a cat on a tiny mouse.

She stammered to speak. She hadn't been this close to him since, well, since she'd sucked his cock on her hands and knees.

Most every erotic novel she'd read had the perfect Dom for the surrendering maiden, the one who'd sweep her off her feet whether she liked it or not—but of course she always did, even if it took her a while. Was Jack hers? Beneath his goofy laid-back drawl and good ol' boy rural charm, there was someone extremely centered and in charge. She looked down at his searing eyes, his full lips, his thick black hair and the muscled shoulders underneath his shirt.

He slid her phone into the pocket of her jeans, and patted his thigh.

Janet swallowed hard, and unzipped her jeans. Without being told, she slid them down to her knees. She bent over his knee, grasped his other thigh.

"Hannah, do what Jon says," Jack told Hannah, and Hannah turned to face Jon.

"On your knees," Jon said.

"You can use her any way you want, ol' buddy," Jack said as he pulled Janet's panties down over her hips. He gave her a little squeeze. "Take her little ass, if you want. You won fair and square." So generous, this man.

"I've always been more of a mouth man," Jon said, and Hannah kneeled down in front of him as he unzipped.

Janet cried out as Jack's hand slapped against her left flank. She inhaled sharply as he matched it on her right.

Hannah was only a few feet in front of her, kneeling between Jon's spread legs.

"*Ah!*" Janet cried, as Jack's hand came down on her ass again.

She knew from experience that Jack could spank hard. She tried to put the memory of their last such encounter out of her mind—bent forward as Hannah was now, tongue against that awful bitch Carolyn's clitoris.

He hit her again.

Hannah was sucking Jon, licking up and down his shaft. Janet could smell the musk of Hannah's arousal—or was it her own? Somehow, it felt more natural to be over Jack's knee, not behind Hannah swinging the whip.

As Jack hit her again, and again, bringing a stinging heat to her backside, she felt the confusion of the last two weeks. She'd sworn she wouldn't be chumped by these people again, yet here she was—literally bending over for him.

"Janet," Jack said, as she watched Hannah move her mouth faster and faster over Jon's swollen and stiff cock.

"Yes, Sir?" *Sir?* She was falling right back into it.

"I have to go to Texas next week, to look over some oil fields of mine."

He was an oil magnate? She remembered Carolyn asking about his oil business.

"Okay…"

"How would you like to come along with me?"

Janet looked at Hannah, who didn't stop her sucking or even break her stride. What would she think?

Jack stopped his slapping, ran his hand lower, and slid his fingers between her wet labia.

"Good God," he said, feeling her slippery folds. Her incredibly slippery folds.

Janet whimpered at his touch. So harsh a moment ago, so tender now.

"Okay," she said.

"Good girl. I'll have my secretary set it all up. We fly out Thursday."

"Okay." She would have to take a day off. She pressed herself against his exploring fingers.

How fun, a trip to someplace else, her first trip out of town in forever, flying in his private jet. Would he make her fly naked, serving him all the while? But what about Hannah?

"Hannah, did you hear? Make the arrangements, will you?"

Janet watched as Hannah released Jon's cock with a smack of her lips and straightened, her diamond necklace bouncing against her chest.

"Yes, boss," she said, and returned to her work.

"She's—she's your secretary?" Janet asked, as Jack found her clit.

"Of course. Didn't you hear her call me boss all day? What did you think she was—my girlfriend?"

Jack laughed, and with his hand, wet with her juices, he slapped her ass hard, one-two-three.

Four. She cried out in surprise, both at the sting and Hannah's situation. Hannah's head was bobbing even faster over Jon's hard shaft. He placed his hand behind her head and pushed down, making her take it in deeper.

Janet had no idea what was about to transpire, here or next week, nor how she felt about any of it. But she felt like everything was somehow back in its proper order.

Chapter Eight

The jet wasn't private. It wasn't even corporate; it was commercial—and the seat wasn't even First Class. There was no First Class on this short of a domestic flight.

And, either by design or because her seat was booked last, Janet sat ten rows behind Jack—and Hannah.

To top it all off, she was in the middle seat. On her left was a rather large man who smelled of beer and wanted to talk about, of all things, professional basketball. On her right was a very thin older woman who wanted to know if Janet had heard the Good News, and handed her several anti-pornography pamphlets. She recognized one from her sister's house: "So You Think You Know What's In-Store," bad grammar and all, which oddly enough showed an image that had to be pirated from a porn shoot—a man in a red devil suit, about to whip the naked backsides of a bound man and woman with a cat-o-nine-tails.

Janet spent most of the flight learning about which teams still used the Triangle Offense and how best to defend against it.

Why had she assumed Jack owned his own jet? Because

they always do in the books, that's why. She watched out the little window as the plane descended into an endless grid of green circles within yellow squares: fields, watered by sprinklers that go around in circles to irrigate the crops. They went on forever.

❖

Janet sat in the front of the rental car, under, she felt, the watchful eye of Hannah in the back seat. They headed south from the airport, then turned west onto another freeway and headed into vast, open prairie.

"So," she asked Jack, and gave Hannah a friendly look, "How did you two meet?" She still wasn't quite sure what their status was, or, considering what had gone on last week at Jack's house, if it mattered.

That day might as well have been a porn movie that her fellow airline passenger would have condemned: Janet and Hannah on their knees sucking the seated men, Janet's pants around her knees, red ass on display; Hannah naked and severely whipped. The men chatted and slowed the women down or urged them to speed up, so they could come at the same time. Such good friends, they must be.

Janet was then dismissed after being told to give Hannah her phone number. Standing on Jack's front porch with the taste of his semen still in her mouth, she wondered if she'd perhaps overestimated his gallantry as Hannah closed the door behind her.

"I saw her in *Eye of the Storm (Yellow)*," Jack said, big smile on his face. "I had to have her."

Janet waited for more, looked back at Hannah, who was smiling for the first time on the trip. Beaming, in fact.

"Not the girl in the center, of course. Hannah was one of the extras. But I couldn't keep my eyes off her, up there in the corner, and I hunted her 'til I found her." He flashed a smile at Janet.

Janet looked back at Hannah again, then at Jack.

"Is this a movie or something?"

"She doesn't know," Hannah said, looking disappointed and a little irritated.

But Jack was still smiling. "You still haven't met Dmitri?" he asked. "I thought Jon would be a little more on the ball with this."

Janet looked at them both again. "Who *is* this, this Dmitri?" she said. "What's the big deal about him? Why does everyone look at me when they say his name?"

Hannah giggled.

"I'll just let you find out when you find out," Jack said, and turned on the blinker. He slowed to take the off-ramp. They were in the middle of nowhere, but the edges of the empty pastures had reconfigured into housing blocks, identical beige and gray apartments. She saw the lighted sign of the hotel.

"Oh," Janet said. "I kind of thought you'd have a ranch out in the grasslands. A bunkhouse. Cattle hands."

Jack laughed.

"No money in *that*," he said. He turned into the parking lot.

❖

The room was nice, a suite. Dark green carpet and earth tones; a little living room with a bar/kitchenette in front, bedroom in the back. Janet wondered what kinds of adventures she would be having, here—two beds, she noticed. Stocked bar. Generic floral art, not even "western" flora.

Jack set his suitcase down.

"Okay. You two set for now? You saw the restaurant downstairs, they're pretty good, or you can order in, there's a menu somewhere 'round here."

"Where are you going?" Janet asked.

"I've got to meet my people," he said. "Meeting's in… twenty minutes. You two entertain yourselves."

Janet glanced at Hannah, and Jack laughed.

"Don't get *too* entertained," he said. "I don't want to miss anything." And he left.

Hannah flopped down on the couch, kicked off her shoes, and started massaging her feet. She picked up the TV remote.

"Welcome to my life," she said. "Might as well get a nap in, if you want."

❖

Hannah wasn't hostile, but she didn't really want to talk, either. Janet checked her phone for messages; none. She thought of taking out the smutty novel she'd brought, one in which a woman on a wagon train making its way across west Texas is kidnapped by Native Americans, who the author had insisted on calling "savages," brutish and sexually demanding. But she is rescued—"rescued"—by even more brutal and demanding outlaws, fond of rope, before being rescued—"rescued"—by a sheriff's posse that puts her through her paces themselves, before returning her to her husband in the caravan. But by then, of course, the woman had lost all interest in him, and, flipping ahead, Janet learned that she ended up riding alone into the sunset in search of the handsome but strict deputy who'd understood how she wanted to be treated: sternly, yes, but not callously.

It had seemed like an appropriate read. Janet still had most of the good parts to go, but she left the book in her suitcase. She watched a little TV with Hannah, but Hannah liked incredibly stupid and depressing reality shows, and Janet for some reason deferred to her—odd, considering how she'd whipped Hannah pretty good with that flogger last week.

Did that carry any authority now? Would Jack want her to

whip Hannah again? Would he want Hannah to whip her? She looked at Hannah, who was fascinated by the hillbillies and their intra-family hijinks, and wondered. Hannah ignored her. She got up to look out the window in the bedroom. There was nothing out there—just grass, until a new housing development started at the far end of the big pasture. It was getting dark. She wondered what the view was from the other side of the building. There had to be a town, here. She knew there was a university. Maybe they had a nice little museum they could go see, if they weren't going out to some ranch like she'd thought they would.

"Should we go ahead and order room service?" she asked Hannah.

"Sure," Hannah said. "Tell 'em I'll take the usual."

Janet picked up the menu. Hannah raised her index finger as though remembering something.

"Oh. He'll want us showered."

❖

She was awakened by a forceful kiss from Jack. She was on the couch, wearing her terrycloth bathrobe provided by the hotel. He tasted of alcohol. Red wine, odd for such a manly man of the frontier out with his posse. He slid his hand under her head on the sofa and gripped her hair, not hard enough to hurt but forceful enough to keep her in place.

He explored her mouth with his tongue, lips pressed hard against hers, and she felt helpless and pinned and her heart rate surged. He unfastened the belt of her robe and opened it.

She was naked and clean underneath, and she felt his hand explore her skin as his tongue continued to investigate her mouth. She moaned. His hands felt her breasts, squeezing each, pinching the nipples to hardness but not too hard, nothing like Amanda had done to her at her house.

Why did her mind keep going back to that night? Comparing every kiss, every touch, every stroke of the whip. Her nerves sizzled as he ran his hand down her stomach, bypassing her sex to feel the muscles in her thighs, then back up—running his fingers through her trimmed pubic hair, but going no lower. She wanted to raise her arms around him, but she kept them at her sides, as he'd found her. He pushed her robe apart and over her shoulders, then stood and motioned for her to follow. She let the robe slip off of her and he led her into the darkened bedroom.

Hannah was asleep on one of the beds, wearing nothing. Odd that he'd chosen a double room—oh wait, Hannah had probably made the reservations.

"Wake her up like I did you," he whispered, his breath heavy with wine.

Janet wished that she'd had some. She climbed onto the bed as Jack settled into the wingback chair in the corner of the room. He reached up and turned on the small reading lamp above his head.

Janet looked back at him; he nodded. Hannah was on her side, curled up for warmth. In the dim light, Janet could see the web of bruises on Hannah's back and thighs, dozens of dark lines and a mass of blue and purple covering her ass. She had helped do this.

Janet tilted Hannah's face up toward her. She glanced at Jack one more time—why was she so nervous? She kissed Hannah full on the mouth.

Her main thought was *please don't let anyone find out.* Her parents, her sister, her co-workers, her neighbors. Her second thought was how sweet Hannah's mouth tasted—toothpaste from hours ago, sleep, woman's tongue. Hannah moaned and Janet kissed her deeper, as she'd been told to do.

Still on her elbows and knees, she reached behind Hannah's head and grasped her blonde hair, pinning her. Hannah moaned again, and rolled onto her back. She let Janet feel her body, as Janet had passively done for Jack.

Janet felt those amazing tits of Hannah's, marveled at how firm and vertical they remained while she lay on her back. She felt her stomach, ran her fingers through her pubic hair, slid them down over Hannah's warm labia without penetrating.

Janet slid one leg straight, then the other, lying on her stomach against Hannah's chest. Hannah was wearing no scent; her skin smelled fresh and young and her hair smelled of shampoo.

Hannah kissed back. The two of them were making out, kissing each other with equal enthusiasm. *What the hell am I doing?* Janet looked back to Jack, who watched intently. He was dressed entirely in black, and the lamp gave him a glow from above, his face cast in shadow. She could barely make out his features, his look of amusement. The bad guy in a cowboy movie. With a deep breath she kissed Hannah even harder than he'd kissed her.

Hannah reached behind Janet's head and grabbed a mass of her hair, just as Janet was doing to her.

With a sudden pull, Hannah lifted Janet's head up and away. Janet cried out as Hannah pulled back hard and flipped her onto her back, so fast there was nothing she could do about it.

Hannah maintained her grip and rolled over, rose to her knees and straddled Janet across her stomach. Janet tried to raise her arms but Hannah squeezed her thighs together and pinned them against Janet's ribs. She was trapped.

Janet was panting. "Jack?" she said.

"Yes, lil' darlin'?"

"Is this okay with you?"

"Perrfkly okay," he said. He was slurring. "Keep a-goin'."

Hannah kept Janet pinned by the hair with one hand, but with the other she reached and pinched one of her nipples, this time as hard as Amanda had so cruelly done.

Janet groaned, and Hannah said, "*Shhh. Sh.* Neighbors."

Janet bit her lip because Hannah didn't let up as she said this. She kept squeezing, leaving it to Janet not to awaken the people in the next rooms.

"Please!" she finally said, louder than she should have.

Hannah let her go, but then pinched the other, just as hard if not harder. Janet wriggled under Hannah's spread legs. She gave her an imploring look that never seemed to work with these people.

"What do you want?" Janet said.

"Why?"

"Why what?" Janet was in pain.

"Why do you ask?" Hannah said.

"So I can do it."

Hannah smiled and released her nipple but not her hair.

"What do you say, boss?" Hannah said over her shoulder.

"I say, there's—there's a deff'nit…high-archy. Hierarchy— that needs played out," Jack slurred. "You're doin' good, sweet-ie. Keep a-goin'."

Janet was starting to panic. What had she gotten herself into? Were these two some kind of hotel rapists/killers? Was Jack sober enough to stop Hannah if things got out of hand? Would Hannah stop Jack? Who the hell *was* he, anyway? She thought of yelling for help. But Hannah saw her look of panic, and raised her finger to her lips: "*Shhh.* You're fine."

Janet tried to calm her breath.

"What do you want me to do, boss?" Hannah said over her shoulder.

The black flogger from their previous meeting landed on the bed beside Janet with a tangled thud. Hannah picked it up with an evil grin on her face.

"How many, boss?"

"Aw…ten…twenny…" Jack was sounding a little distant.

Hannah dismounted Janet.

"You heard the man. Turn over, on your hands and knees."
This was the most Hannah had talked to her since they'd met at the airport. Since they'd *met*.

Janet obeyed. Why was she obeying Hannah? She didn't know what *anybody's* relationships were.

"And keep those legs spread," Hannah said.

Before she could think about it, Janet felt the sting of the flogger across her ass and heard the loud *thwack* it made. Janet tried to keep her whimper as quiet as possible; they *were* in a hotel with thin walls—how thin were they? She listened for their neighbor's TV through the walls, but her concentration was broken when Hannah struck her again, with a *swish* and a *thwack* and Janet's own gasp.

"Can we keep it quiet?" Janet asked as politely as possible. "Someone might turn us in or something."

Another strike and Hannah giggled.

"More like they've got their ear to the wall, jerking off," she said, and hit her again. "How many is that?"

The flogger felt very different than the whip they'd used on her at her dinner. That one had a very sharp, stinging pain to it, almost like a knife that drew no blood. This one hurt, most definitely—but it was a wider, almost "softer" kind of pain.

That was adding up. Janet pictured herself from Jack's viewpoint, her legs spread, her sex wet, her ass reddening with each cruel stroke. Hannah was on her knees on the bed behind her, but she dismounted and stood to the side of it, and suddenly the blows got harsher.

"I asked you a question," Hannah said, and swung at her full force.

Janet's face was inches from the wall; she was desperately trying to keep quiet.

"Um…six?" she whispered.

"Count them for me," and she kept up the whipping as Janet spoke to the wall, trying to keep her composure—and hoped she wasn't speaking to someone on the other side, mere inches away.

At twenty, Hannah stopped. Being flogged by Hannah still wasn't nearly as bad as being whipped by Jack and then Carolyn, but it definitely smarted.

"What now boss?" Hannah said, but Jack only mumbled something unintelligible. Janet stayed still, held her pose.

"You want her to eat my pussy?"

"…Yea, yea…"

"Get on your knees on the floor," Hannah said, and Janet crawled off the bed and glanced over at Jack, who was leering at them with heavy eyelids. Hannah sat on the edge of the bed in front of Janet and leaned back, her legs spread.

"You heard him."

Janet leaned forward. Hannah's thighs were still heavily bruised, a mix of straight lines and dark blotches. Rather than the teasing she had done with Amanda and Carolyn, she went straight for Hannah's clit. No point in trying to impress her.

Hannah was already wet, her scent formidable. Janet wrapped her arms around Hannah's hips and dove in. Her clit was hard and swollen—she'd had fun, swinging that whip. Janet lapped at the little knob, flicked it with her tongue. She felt Hannah arch and shudder.

This was, despite her embarrassment, what she had more or less pictured for the weekend: on her knees, ass whipped red, servicing one of her travelling companions while the other— what? Whipped her? Fucked her from behind? Oh yes—either. She'd still only known Jack's cock in her mouth, nowhere else.

She looked up at Hannah, who was watching her with a look of satisfaction and domination. Okay, yes. She could get used to this, if Hannah didn't get too rude about it. She looked from Hannah's face to the undersides of those magnificent breasts, huge and looming over her. She reached up for one, took it in her hand and squeezed, pinched the nipple between her thumb and finger. Felt it harden.

When would Jack join in? Janet arched her back, offering her ass. Her bright red, whipped ass. She dove in deeper into Hannah's sex, tonguing the clit with the broad surface of her tongue. She heard...

She heard...

...the sound of snoring.

She pulled away from Hannah, labia shiny from her saliva, and looked over her shoulder. Jack was hunched over, chin against his chest—sound asleep. She watched him until Hannah turned her chin back toward her.

"Like I said, welcome to my life," Hannah said.

"Should we...should we wake him up? Put him to bed?"

"No. He doesn't like that. He'll have to pee, he'll take care of himself."

Janet looked back at Jack, slumped uncomfortably in his chair, then back up at Hannah's jaded expression. Hannah placed her hand behind Janet's head and pulled it toward her again.

"He never said you could stop," Hannah said.

❖

Janet dropped her suitcase and went through her mail: bill, bill, junk, bill, junk; something from the West Oakdale Neighborhood Association.

A chill went down her back. *Oh shit. They know.*

But how could they know? Had Carlotta Janski, her neighbor across the street and two houses down, heard her screams that night? Peeked through the curtains? Tracked down all the cars at her dinner party and researched their owners' histories? If anyone would, it would be Carlotta, head of the Neighborhood Association and spymaster extraordinaire. It was probably some sort of public censure, some Notice of Banishment. Best not to open it yet.

She tossed the mail onto the coffee table.

❖

The whole weekend went on much like the first night.

The next morning, Janet awoke in her bed alone. Jack was in the other bed with Hannah, woke up wanting his cock sucked, and so it was—by both of them, alternating sucking and licking balls, until he wanted to come into Janet's mouth.

Then he was off for business, and Janet spent the day alone with Hannah, not talking much, not fooling around at all, just *there*. They both stayed showered and dressed in bathrobes, ready and available at any moment in case he came back.

"You don't curl your hair?" Hannah asked as Janet came out of the shower, curls dripping.

"Nope. Natural."

"Bitch."

Janet stared out the window as Hannah watched insipid TV; it didn't occur to her to take control of it. Janet suggested a card game. She suggested finding out if the university's museum was worth visiting; maybe they could call a cab? She read the last of her filthy book—goodness, that deputy had a lot of rules—then downloaded a murder mystery onto her phone, anything to take her out of this room, not bothering with anything erotic. There was already entirely too much time to meditate on the discrepancies between fantasy and reality.

Janet suggested room service and Hannah thought that was a very good idea.

That night, Jack feel asleep again while watching her and Hannah perform for him. They were sixty-nining—*sixty-nining. For him.* Hannah said that he liked to alternate fucking one pussy and one mouth, then switch ends—and who knew where he'd come? But he dozed off, drunk and exhausted.

"What does he *do* all day?" Janet asked his secretary. Shouldn't she know?

"It's all money stuff, all day," Hannah said. "Oil stuff. Then he goes drinking with his associates."

"And leaves his secretary here?"

"He has another office secretary. I'm his personal secretary."

Ah. Well, that explained a lot.

"Why are we even here?"

"I'm here in case he needs me. The question is, why are you here?"

Next day: repeat. Last day: repeat again. Fizzled sex at night, blowjob in the morning—with Janet doing the swallowing. And no orgasm for her, other than the one she gave herself in the shower. But as the weekend progressed, she cared less and less.

She had burned two vacation days for this.

◈

Before unpacking, Janet went into the kitchen and opened a bottle of Cabernet and poured herself a glass. She opened the cabinet door under the sink and pulled out a white plastic trash bag. No—she stuffed it back in the box, pulled out one of the dark green ones, the opaque ones.

She took the glass and the trash bag—and the bottle—into her bedroom.

She opened the bottom two drawers of her wide dresser, both completely full of books. Her porn collection. The two drawers were like horizontal bookshelves, books arranged by author then date of publication. Their spines all faced up, hundreds of them. This was the paper collection, never mind the downloads.

She took a swig of wine and methodically began going through the titles A to Z. She had to pull a few volumes up enough to see the cover art or the description on the back, but most of them she remembered well.

Any book that had anything to do with a dark, mysterious Dom with a regional American accent, especially a southern or Texas drawl, she pulled from the drawer and threw into the trash bag. She considered tossing any book with a dominant male with *any* accent, but that would eliminate almost half her collection.

She took another drink. *Accents.* Just who was this Dmitri, anyway? Some Russian, or something? Why was he always in Latvia or wherever, and why did everyone smile and look at her when they brought him up?

Another sip.

When she had collected a good fifteen or twenty books, she pulled the drawstring on the trash bag, stood, and took it to the door to the garage in the kitchen. Recycling day was Wednesday; maybe someone would find them and have fun with them. She'd had enough of cowboys and good ol' boys.

Oh, she almost forgot. And her wine glass was empty. She went back into her living room, opened her suitcase, and took out the book she'd taken to Lubbock: *Rustled.*

Into the bedroom to get her bottle, and into the kitchen to pour another glass and toss the book onto the plastic trash bag.

There was something she was going to do, something that needed looked at. What was it? Some phone call or email. Or letter.

Later, maybe.

Right now, she needed a nap.

Chapter Nine

"And how are we doing this evening, darling?" his Mistress said.

Again with the "darling."

"Fine, Mistress," Ken answered.

In truth, he was sweating from the strain. He had been waiting in the playroom for hours, two at least; it felt like three. His collar was fastened to a chain from the ceiling, high enough that to breathe comfortably he'd had to stand on his toes until he couldn't take the strain any longer. Then he would stand flat-footed, nearly hanging by the neck, until he felt lightheaded or had the strength to try again. It had been exhausting. His hands were free, at least. He could reach up and use his arms to pull himself up. His Mistress had unlocked his collar, in case of emergency, but he knew better than to unfasten it no matter how miserable he was.

"Ken, this is my friend Jennifer."

Carolyn was leaning against a woman Ken did not know, a brunette like his Mistress, her hair several shades darker. They stood close, supporting each other's weight, their arms around each other's shoulders. He could smell the alcohol on their breath.

"Jennifer, this is my lil' Kenny."

"Oh my God, you weren't kidding."

Jennifer was dressed in stylish work clothes, a gray skirt and jacket like his Mistress usually wore. His Mistress had apparently changed into a more casual skirt and top after She'd fastened him into place before going back out.

"I rarely kid. Do you not know me?"

"So is he—will he—"

"Kenneth, tell my friend Jennifer what you'll do for her."

Ken lifted his head to speak, but kept his eyes lowered.

"I will do whatever my Mistress's friend wants." He had said all this before. "I will serve you in any way that you like. I will pleasure you in any way that you like. If my Mistress wishes, I will be your entertainment. You may do whatever you wish to me."

"Holy shit," Jennifer said. "How can I get one of these?"

"You can borrow this one, if you like."

"Take him home?"

"No."

"Can I touch him?"

"Touch him? You can…" She gestured toward the selection of whips and crops hanging from the walls, the long counter with all its evil drawers.

Jennifer reached out and caressed Ken's chest. She rubbed across his clavicles, felt his pectoral muscles.

"Jesus."

"Yea." Carolyn looked pleased.

"He's kinda sweaty."

The two women smelled interesting, of drinks in an outdoor terrace on a hot summer's night, an evening breeze cooling them off. Not a bad smell at all.

"Is that good, or bad?" Carolyn asked. "We can watch him

shower."

Jennifer ran her hand down Ken's stomach. Still holding onto Carolyn for support, she bypassed his rising cock and reached for his balls. She squeezed and looked to Carolyn. Carolyn shrugged, deferred the decision.

"I don't know," Jennifer said. "I kinda like it."

"Men," Carolyn said. "Workout sweat good, ditch-digging sweat bad."

"Yea. You're right. I, uh—"

"Ken, Jennifer here is having a few problems at work. Seems the men—the *males*—in her department aren't taking her seriously." *Oh, no.* "I thought about things as we were having drinks, and I thought I'd offer her a chance to work out some of her frustrations. About men."

This was going to be a long night.

"Jennifer, are you interested in taking me up on my offer?"

"Ooooh, yea," Jennifer said, her hand feeling up and down Ken's torso. "Yea."

Carolyn reached behind Ken's neck and unhooked his collar from the chain. He exhaled in relief. He could finally just *stand*. His legs were shaky.

Jennifer was staring at his erection, now at full size and elevation.

"That bothering you? You want it down?" Carolyn stroked the length of Ken's cock, fondled his balls. "He's eager for punishment, you know. Just look how eager he is. But if you want—"

"No, no… It's okay." Jennifer looked him over. "So we can—"

"Yes."

"What if I want to—"

"Then do it. He'll let you."

"But what if he—"

"He won't. He does as I say. And tonight, he'll do as you

say. I'm giving you a rare gift, you know."

Jennifer looked like she was evaluating a coat hanging in a store.

"I want to whip him."

Carolyn raised Her hand toward the whips, crops, and floggers hanging on the wall.

"Be my guest."

Jennifer went straight for a short leather whip, some four feet long, as though she'd already thought this out.

"Can I whip him anywhere?"

"Yes. Try to stay away from his balls. Sometimes men will just up and lose their lunch if you hit those too hard."

"'kay."

"And see this?" She dragged three fingers across his lower back. "His kidneys are here. Don't whip this. Got it?"

Jennifer nodded. "Okay."

"Arms up," Ken's Mistress told him.

"Good lookin' guy," Jennifer said, and Ken flinched at the sting of the whip across his ass. She hit surprisingly hard.

"Yes, he is."

Another stroke. He'd expected a few tentative, easy strokes at first, before she felt her way into it. But this Jennifer woman whipped hard from the start. She'd been thinking about this. How had their conversation begun and progressed, on that terrace?

"Do you like redheads?" Carolyn asked Jennifer.

Jennifer stopped her whipping. She looked thoughtful, regarded him again.

"I like this one. Certain shades of red look kind of ridiculous on guys but okay on girls."

"Hmm. Good answer."

The third stroke came across his shoulder blades, then another across his ass.

"I'm thinking of getting another one," Carolyn said.

What?

"How do you get these? Where do you find them?" Jennifer said, amazed. "Is there a sex slave store, somewhere?"

Carolyn giggled—giggled?—and looked Ken over.

"I found this one at the gym. Total nerd, but look at him. I think he's gorgeous. I'm thinking maybe I want more of them. Him. Another one, at least."

Another me? What's wrong with the one You've got?

Carolyn looked down, a little sad. She furrowed Her eyebrows in thought, like She was troubled by something. Ken looked away before he was caught staring at Her.

"You want another drink?" She asked, but Jennifer hit him with the whip again. "Fun, isn't it?"

"Oh, God, yes. I—" another stroke, then another. She was into it. "I've got to get me one of these. No wonder you're so empowered at work."

"We'll get you there. You just need a few lessons."

Two more strokes across his back.

"What if I go too far?"

"I only have once," Carolyn said, and again the troubled look. "He'll let you know. Just don't draw any blood."

"You can go *that* far?"

"No. I just said, that's too far."

"Okay. Got it." The next stroke was slightly softer, then she returned to the harsher whipping. Jennifer moved forward a step.

"Anywhere?"

"Anywhere but his balls. We don't want him sick."

Ken braced, and flinched as the whip landed across his chest, his stomach, his thighs. One stroke crossed his vertical cock, and sent a shock wave through his entire body. Jennifer paused; waited to see if she was in trouble. But Carolyn said nothing, and Ken was harder than ever. She whipped him several times on his thighs.

He received three hard strokes against the backs of his
calves, then she worked her way up again.

"Look, his legs are shaking," she said.

"He's been working them hard, all evening," Carolyn said.
"It's time you had a man show you some respect, anyway."

Ken waited to be told to lower his arms.

"You heard me," Carolyn told him. "Show your Mistress's
friend some respect."

Ken fell to his knees, bent forward and kissed Jennifer's
shoes.

"Oh. Wow. God, yes. *That's* how I want to see a man," Jennifer said. "Stay there," she said, and stepped to his side. Ken
felt the whip cross his upraised ass; up the length of his back.
He was glad to be able to hide his face. She started down his
back again. "I can't believe this is okay with him."

"He does what I say. He is very obedient."

Jennifer pulled up on Ken's collar.

"Up on your hands and knees. Like a dog." She lifted his
chin with the handle of the whip.

"Good. Stay." She whipped his ass again.

This was becoming painful. He hoped that his Mistress
would intervene.

But Carolyn said, "I'm gonna hit the bathroom," and
walked out of the room.

Jennifer continued the whipping. All Ken could do was
flex his behind and grit his teeth. His collar tightened as it was
pulled up again.

"Up on your knees," Jennifer said. She lifted his chin with
the whip, leaned close and looked him straight in the eye.

"Men are such pigs," she said. "Admit that you're a pig."

"I'm a pig, Ma'am."

This woman was very different than his Mistress. Carolyn,
for all Her cruelty, talked to him sweetly, or matter-of-factly,
even when She was doing horrible things to him. He'd never

felt such…hostility.

"I should make you squeal like a pig," she said. "Squeal like a pig, boy!" And she laughed, quoting the hillbillies in the movie.

Ken prepared to make a squealing sound, but Jennifer grabbed his chin and forced him to look at her. She stood straight, feet apart, and letting go, she stretched the whip between her hands.

"Call me Mistress."

Ken's eyes widened in indecision. He had never been told to call anyone Mistress but his Mistress. But he had been told to do whatever this woman said. He sensed a trick; his Mistress was fond of setting up traps for which he would pay a price.

He looked up at the woman towering above him. She was almost as beautiful as Carolyn, though not quite, of course. Dark hair, dark complexion, deep brown eyes. Angry brown eyes. A body to die for, all the men at work seeing her as an object when she wanted to be taken seriously.

He had only one Mistress. But if he were to disobey this woman, things would be far worse, given Carolyn's orders. What was it about angry, beautiful women that he couldn't resist?

"Yes, Mistress."

Jennifer stood taller, breathing in the power.

"Good. Grovel at my feet."

Ken obeyed. He kissed both of her black leather pumps. The whip came down across his ass, which was becoming quite tender. He watched as the shoes stepped back toward the chaise lounge, the only piece of comfortable "furniture" in the playroom—a gaudy chartreuse with gilded wood; he had never understood why his Mistress had chosen it. Something to do with an ironic play on Romance novels.

"Crawl to me. If you are fast enough, I won't whip you so hard."

Ken crawled as fast as he could—which was pretty fast, he'd had practice. He bent down to her feet.

"Sorry, not fast enough."

The whip slashed across his back.

"Now crawl across the room and back. You should try harder. Maybe if you put in a little more effort, things would go a little easier for you, hmm?"

Ken turned to crawl. Something told him that last sentence had a certain meaning behind it—something she'd been told at work, perhaps more than once?

"Stop."

Ken froze in place, not halfway across the room. The whip struck his ass as she approached, and she again lifted him up by the collar.

"Why didn't you say, 'Yes, Mistress' when I gave you that order?"

Ken knew there'd be no right answer, so he told the truth: "I've been trained to obey in silence, Mistress. Only to acknowledge my Mistress when asked a question."

"Well that's going to change tonight, understand?"

"Yes, Mistress."

"You will 'acknowledge' every command and show me respect, understand?"

"Yes, Mistress."

"What did you call her, Ken?"

Carolyn was standing in the doorway, back from the restroom.

He knew whom to obey without hesitation: "My Mistress's friend has ordered me to address her as 'Mistress', Mistress."

Carolyn walked into the room. She stood directly in front of Ken, but wasn't looking at him. He bowed his head.

"You are free to use him as you want, tonight, but he has only one Mistress," Carolyn told Jennifer.

"I wanted to keep him in his place. I thought that calling me that would—" Jennifer stopped speaking. Ken risked a glance up. Carolyn was staring right at Jennifer, not saying a word. "Okay. Sorry. I understand. I wouldn't let him call anyone else that, either, I guess. Or maybe I'd—"

"So we understand each other?"

"Yes. Yes, M—"

Jennifer was about to call Her Ma'am! This was getting interesting.

"Good, sweetie. I brought you here to have a good time, to work some things out. I should have made a few things more clear." She sighed. "And here I am trying to build up your confidence. I'm so sorry. We'll have fun, okay?"

"Oh it's okay! I'm sorry I got…"

"You want another drink?"

"Sure."

Damn. Things weren't going to get as interesting as Ken had hoped.

"White wine. Two," Carolyn said, and Ken got up, in silence, and ran to the bar in the media room.

❖

Jennifer was seated on the chaise and Carolyn was leaning against the counter when Ken returned. Both looked amused. Whatever they were talking about, they stopped when he entered the room. He kneeled and bowed when he served their glasses of wine.

"What would you like to do to him?" Carolyn asked.

"He's a man. Let's kick him in the balls."

"You *are* angry. You can't do that. But there are other things to do to his balls, you know."

"Oh yeah?"

Please—not the electricity again.

"Kenny, get me the clothespins."

Ken went to the counter, pulled the correct drawer. He kneeled and offered the velvet bag of clothespins to Carolyn; She took one from it.

"Go to Jennifer," She said. "Stand in front of her."

Ken approached the other woman, his erect cock at her eye level.

Jennifer leaned away.

"Oh, wrong attitude, dear. I *adore* this thing. You've just got to claim it as your own, not his."

Carolyn stood next to Ken, Her arm on his shoulder. She leaned Her weight against him. She reached down and attached the clip onto his scrotum. Ken arched his back; it was all he could do.

"Spread 'em, dear."

Dear? Ken spread his feet.

"Give the bag to Jennifer."

Jennifer's face lit up. She took a clothespin out of the bag.

"Make sure you only get skin," Carolyn told her. "An actual testicle will be too much. Men are so weak, aren't they?"

Jennifer grinned, not looking up. She pinched a section of Ken's skin, and applied the pin.

Ken fidgeted, but kept his place. Another. And another.

"How many can he take?" Jennifer asked.

"As many as there's room for."

Soon Ken's balls were covered in the torturous little clips; it took everything he had to hold still. But he had been through this before.

Jennifer looked up at his face. "He doesn't look so calm, now," she said.

"Watch this," Carolyn said, and turned to Ken.

"On your hands and knees."

Ken dropped; he had to keep his legs spread wide to accommodate the mass of clips. His balls were like a porcupine, bristling with clothespins in every direction.

"Face Jennifer."

Ken kept his head held high. He grimaced as the whip fell across his already sore ass. He hadn't yet had time to recover from Jennifer's beating. Another. This was going to take some concentration, some serious self-discipline, to get through.

Jennifer leaned to the side, inspecting.

"How does he keep his hard-on like that?"

"Ken thinks about this aaaaaall week. This is his ultimate fantasy, being whipped by two beautiful women. Isn't it, Ken?"

"Yes, Mistress."

It was.

"We are beautiful, aren't we?"

"Yes, Mistress."

"Do you find Jennifer beautiful?"

He looked up at Jennifer's face as her eyes flickered to wherever the whip landed.

"Yes, Mistress. She is very beautiful."

"Who is the more beautiful?"

Ken's entire backside was beginning to seriously hurt. His mind raced through the many permutations of answers to such a loaded question, and their consequences.

"You are two of the most beautiful women I have ever seen in my life, Mistress. I would have to think about it."

"Good boy. It's hard to see what Jennifer looks like, in those business clothes." He suspected a look was exchanged between the women.

"What would you say to her, if you, say, saw her in the gym?"

"Nothing, Mistress. I'd be scared to talk to her."

"And me?"

"I was too scared to talk to you, Mistress," even though She'd stared at him from the moment She first saw him, for weeks. "You talked to me first."

"Hmm. That's right." Another painful crack of the whip.

Jennifer lifted Ken's chin. The pain was beginning to show on his face, he knew, and she was enjoying it.

"How you doing, sweetie?" Carolyn said—to Jennifer.

"I am so totally fucking turned on right now."

"He can help with that."

"Kiss my feet," Jennifer said.

Ken lowered his face, and as he was doing so, a pair of black panties fell across her shoes. He kissed the panties.

"Kenneth, make our guest feel welcome."

Ken rose to the level of the chaise's cushion and was staring at Jennifer's pubic hair, so dark and mysterious. She was sitting with her knees far enough apart to accommodate his head. As he moved forward, Jennifer pulled herself closer to meet him, spread her thighs. The various smells of her body—the evening's perspiration, her perfume, her pussy—were intoxicating.

"Get to it, boy," Jennifer said, leaning back to further expose herself.

Ken kept his hands on the floor, leaned forward. He extended his tongue and went to work—he was very good at this. He'd been trained by the best, or at least the most demanding.

Ken tilted his head to the side, and ran his tongue between the parted labia. At this first contact, Jennifer drew in her breath, then moaned almost imperceptibly. He did it again, running his tongue up and down along the outer edges of her pussy. Her very wet pussy. He explored a little deeper with the tip of his tongue. He gave her the slightest of touches on her clitoris, just hinting at it before his tongue caressed her inner labia, then back to her outer.

A little more pressure. He teased her clit—he flicked at it with his tongue, then left it again. Returned to it. He teased her inner lips, merely suggesting that he might enter, then went back to the clit. Back and forth, never committing. He pressed his tongue deeper into her, as deep as he could go. She shuddered. He was learning what she liked.

"I've never…done this in front of anyone," Jennifer said.

"Would you like me to leave?"

"No. I would like you to whip him."

Ken groaned as he felt the whip across his ass. Carolyn knew this sound, that it was getting to be too much. She switched to his back—She was showing some mercy. She waited between strokes, allowing the tension to build.

He concentrated on Jennifer's clit. He pressed harder onto it, rubbed his tongue back and forth like sandpaper. Jennifer rocked her hips.

Carolyn moved behind Ken and started whipping the backs of his thighs. The clothespins on his balls were adding to his agony—they overwhelmed. He needed to pull them off, to put more on. To jerk off.

Jennifer was getting close, her hips grinding, her pussy soaked by his saliva and her own juices.

"Whip his ass," she told Carolyn. "I know he's sore. Whip his ass." And Carolyn, never the one to take orders, obeyed.

Ken groaned at the pain and worked even harder. He lapped at her clit as fast as his tongue could work. Carolyn increased the speed of the lashes, and Ken wanted to wriggle away, but only lifted his ass higher. The pressure in his tormented balls was unbearable. He wanted to explode.

But only Jennifer did. Grasping the loops of his collar, she pulled him closer, crying out in a long, deep moan. Carolyn increased the whipping, timing each stroke with the rocking of Jennifer's hips.

Jennifer cried several more times; she was convulsing. She was making her orgasm last, milking Ken for everything she could. He worked hard to finish strong. What else could he do?

Carolyn stopped. Ken's entire backside burned with pain, real, searing pain. He was near tears as Jennifer gripped his head in her hands and moved it up and down against her. He licked up and down, lapping her up. He was very good at this.

She moaned and flopped back onto the chaise. Ken backed off, but kept tickling the outer lips as she twitched with pleasure. He risked a glance up the length of her body—breasts still held in place by her bra, smooth chin above the white collar of her blouse. Her skirt was hiked up to just below her navel. She brought her arm up over her face, covered her eyes in the crook of her elbow.

Was she embarrassed? New guests often were.

"I want…" she said, still panting but beginning to calm down, "I want to fuck him."

"Are you sure?" Carolyn asked. "You're free to do whatever you want, but I can tell you he won't last very long. He's about to pop. Besides, are you sure you want to give him the satisfact—"

Jennifer raised her arm from her face and lifted her shoulders off the chaise, supporting herself on her elbows.

"That's not what I meant."

❖

Ken was bent over the back of the chartreuse chaise at an undignified angle, his hands fastened behind his back with rope and his ankles tied to the legs of the furniture to keep his legs spread. Jennifer was down to her underwear, applying lube to the strap-on dildo that she had found in the playroom's cabinet drawers. She slowly stroked it in anticipation.

She had already applied a healthy dab to his anus, after a very cruel removal of the clothespins from his balls—pulling each one off his scrotum without squeezing them open, each time repeating "He loves me; he loves me not…" (He did not end up loving her.)

"You realize what an incredible privilege I'm giving you, allowing you to do this," his Mistress said. She was seated on the chaise with his head resting on Her lap.

160

She still wore Her skirt but had stuffed Her panties into his mouth.

Jennifer circled the chaise.

"Oh, yes. And I thank you. You really do understand what I've been going through at work." She never took her eyes off of Ken. "You're a good friend."

"Thank you." Carolyn finished Her wine, swirled the empty glass. Ken could tell She wished She'd sent him for another round before bending him over and binding him. "I don't get told that, very often."

He'd never seen Her so maudlin—She *was* getting drunk.

"Well it's true." Jennifer was behind Ken again.

Ken felt the slippery tip of the dildo press against him. She swirled and soaked it in the lube as he tried to relax. He could feel the roundness of its head as she centered it. She braced one hand on his hip, his very sore hip. He grunted helplessly.

"Easy, dear. Don't hurt him. That sounds silly. Don't damage him. He's my…"

Your what?

Carolyn didn't finish the sentence.

"Oh, I know all about anal sex, don't worry," Jennifer said. "I had a boyfriend who was way into it. You know what he did when I said I'd had enough?"

"What?" Carolyn asked.

"He fired me."

"Oh no. Sweetie, you have to start asserting yourself with these jerks, I keep telling you. Athertiveness…" She giggled, drunk—"Assertiveneth… Damn it! *Assertiveness* lessons begin at eight o'clock tomorrow. In my office."

Jennifer laughed, too. "Yes, Ma'am!"

The dildo was inside him. It slid easily, the head of the cock inside Ken as he relaxed to accommodate it.

His Mistress sighed as She ran Her fingers through his hair. Which took him by surprise. It was such a…tender thing, to do. His Mistress had been behaving oddly, lately—showing far more tenderness than usual, then acting angry at Herself for doing so and taking it out on him. The word "tenterhooks" came to mind, as did "eggshells." He was never sure where he stood with Her, anymore.

And now She wanted another redhead?

"You've made some questionable choices, I have to say," Carolyn said.

"Think so?" Jennifer pushed the dildo farther into Ken, pausing to test his reaction. For once, Ken was hoping that *Carolyn* didn't piss someone *else* off.

"Well, you just told me one."

Jennifer paused, perhaps in thought. She withdrew the phallus, only its head still embedded, but Ken knew what was coming.

She thrust her hips forward.

"*Unnnng!*" Ken groaned, his mouth full of his Mistress's underwear.

"*Ssshhh,*" Carolyn said.

She caressed his temple, which confused him more than soothed.

"I tend to be taken advantage of," Jennifer said as she slowly pulled back.

Ken could only brace.

"Only *you* can let people do that to you," Carolyn said.

"People? Men," Jennifer said, thrusting her hips again.

Ken shuddered as the chaise creaked from the force against him.

"Men, then. I understand your frustration with them. They *are* pigs,"—She ran Her fingers through Ken's hair once more—"And I'm not saying you can win every battle. But sweetie, I'd never let a boss do me in the ass, and put myself in the position of being at *his* mercy when I tried to end it. I'd have him on sexual harassment faster than he could zip up."

Jennifer was no longer pausing between thrusts, but was slowly moving the dildo back and forth at a constant rate. At least she wasn't going so deep, so hard.

"That's easy for you to say, Carolyn—"

"Say? My friend, I've *done* it. Any time a male coworker, or at least a higher up—no, a *climber*—suggests we go out, suggests it might be in my interest, I start the documentation. I'm takin' video. I'm recordin' audio."—Her slurring again—"Hell, I'll lead him down the trail, set him up. He tries *anything*, I've got him."

"Wow."

Faster thrusts.

"You have to see it all as a game, Jen. You have to *play*. To win. You have to see people as the pieces, the boys as toys." She patted Ken on the back. "See?"

"Oooh," Jennifer said, like a light bulb went on above her head. "Boys are toys."

She gave Ken an extra deep shove, forcing her hips against his ass. He groaned again.

"Exactly. Usually, I get enough evidence to where *I* can manipulate *them*. Video, audio—did I say that already?—on every man I've worked with. Some are sweet and I'll never have to use it. Some, I've used to get what I want. You can *always* bet that the males will try to screw you, in every way possible…"

Ken didn't like the way this conversation was going. Jennifer was thrusting faster, pumping him. He felt the friction of the phallus as it slid in and out, felt himself filled and emptied, over and over.

"…so you *have* to be prepared, sweetie. At all times."

"You game *life*! I can't believe that you have surveillance tapes of every meeting at work."

"I'll show you my files. Most of them are so boring, work talk. As it should be. But I have a camera hidden in my office. I get called into the boss's office, my phone is recordin'. A few of them would knock your socks off."

"You're a goddess!"

"I'll play you a few tomorrow, before we go in."

"That early?"

"You're spending the night. You're not driving home."

"You *are* a warrior goddess, you know that?" Jennifer was now giving a Ken a good fucking, as if she were getting close to coming. "I guess it is possible to fuck them back," she said.

Ken tilted his head up and gave his Mistress an imploring look. She cradled his head on Her lap, still running Her fingers through his hair.

"You need someone to show you how, that's all. It's not like I never got screwed or taken advantage of. But I learned early. You're learning; you just need a lil' help. I'll teach you."

"You'd help me?"

"Of course. I def'nit'ly see potential. Def-in-it-ly."

"To be a warrior goddess?"

"A drunken warrior goddess."

They laughed together. Jennifer sped up.

She spoke. "Why don't you, uh…I know he's yours anyway, but can I offer him to you? I noticed you…removed your underwear."

"I wish I had another glass of wine."

"Want me to stop for a minute?"

"No. We'll make do."

Carolyn petted Ken, ran Her hand up his back. She leaned down over him, close to his face, and hugged his neck with Her arm.

"*You*," She whispered to him. "*What do I do about you?*"

Ken didn't understand, didn't answer. He smelled the wine on Her breath, Her scent in the panties stuffed into his mouth.

Carolyn leaned away and lifted Her legs and slid them under Ken's body, reclined back on the chaise's seat. She hiked up Her skirt, showing Her lower tummy, flat and muscular, Her shaved pussy.

"Get to work," She said, but Jennifer must have thought She was talking to her. She started fucking Ken even harder, reaming his ass as she thrust her hips against his. He could only moan in protest. He had already taken one of the worst whippings in recent memory.

Carolyn pulled Her panties out of his mouth and he started on Her clit, exactly how he knew She liked it. His Mistress was sleepy but slippery, and it didn't take Ken long to get Her off. She rocked Her hips, She turned Her head to the side, She grabbed his hair as She panted. He wondered what the Asian girl upstairs was doing right now, or thinking about.

"Wow," Jennifer said. "Just, wow."

She stopped her thrusting, the dildo implanted deep into him.

Both women were tired, and sleepy, and drunk. Carolyn simply stopped—talking, moving, anything but breathing. She let his head go, kept Her legs apart. Jennifer did not withdraw the dildo, but unhooked the straps holding it to her; the assembly hung between his spread thighs. She found her clothes on the floor and picked up her jacket and blouse but left the skirt where it lay.

Returning to the chaise, she pulled Ken up by the collar and lifted him to a standing position.

"Good boy," she said, sounding exhausted. "I think we've both had a little too…"

Jennifer sat on the chaise and reclined sideways, her head at Carolyn's feet. Carolyn didn't open Her eyes but slid to the side to make room. Jennifer settled in. She covered herself with her clothes like little blankets, and covered Carolyn with what would reach across them both.

The two women lay in a sixty-nine position, but only in Ken's imagination would they do anything exciting. They were both out cold in seconds. He stood motionless, his weight against the back of the chaise. With his hands tied behind his back and his ankles fastened to the legs of the chaise, there was nothing he could do until morning but hope one of them would get up to pee and have enough mercy to at least untie his feet. His cock was hard as stone.

All he could do was gaze at the two beautiful women lying before him, head-to-feet, hips touching breasts through their clothes. Jennifer began gently snoring.

Carolyn opened Her eyes.

"My…" She said, as if remembering something, and then She went back to sleep.

It was going to be a long night.

Ken wondered if his Mistress really wanted another red-head, and why.

Chapter Ten

Another hotel? Seriously?

The same chain as in Lubbock, even; not a good omen. At least this one was here in town, although it was clear out by the airport, forty minutes away through traffic.

She had started to feel a little pimped out when Jon called her, which maybe should have bothered her more than it did.

But she had to admit, she was curious about this Dmitri.

"Turn left," her phone said. "You have arrived at your destination." She pulled into the hotel's parking lot.

Once again, it had been a few weeks since she'd seen Jon or anyone else. But at least he'd called a few times, texted fairly often. She'd gone to work, gone out with friends, gone on with her life. Her normal, boring life.

She wanted to be dressed professionally, today, as she walked by the front desk—maybe some kind of art dealer, since she was, apparently, meeting with two artists. She was wearing a black skirt and dark blue top, because it brought out her eyes, and a short black jacket that was maybe a little warm for June.

High black heels; she hoped not too high, as she nodded at

the desk clerk. Black stockings and garter belt. Janet knew what Jon thought of her light complexion with her black hair; this outfit would *really* highlight that. Plus she had a few surprises for them.

Room 745. Top floor, she noticed as the elevator rose. She looked down into the receding courtyard through the glass walls—the little indoor forest they'd made; waterfalls, paths and bridges over the little fake stream. People seated at tables outside the bar. She looked up at the roof, which was all translucent skylight, and the elevator came to a stop.

It was the last room on the floor, down a little hallway that extended off the big square balcony that ringed the vast empty space over the courtyard.

Very secluded, as far as hotel rooms go—only one neighbor next door, one downstairs. A maintenance closet across the hall. She passed the ice machine at the corner of the hallway, took a very deep breath, and knocked on the door.

It opened quickly—Jon, in a black suit with white shirt and no tie.

"Janet! Right on time. My God, you look beautiful." He looked her up and down. "Please, come in."

"Hi, Jon. You look great, too."

He gave her a little kiss on the cheek. She scanned the room as he shut the door behind her. It was identical to the room in Lubbock—green and tan, small kitchenette/bar on the way to the bedroom, small living room up front with a sofa and two chairs across the room from it. Even the floral art was the same.

On the sofa sat a man in another black suit, with a graying crew cut that had become tousled and slightly mussed. He had the look of someone who'd had a wind-burned youth but could now afford skin care. He surveyed her with dark eyes that took in a bit more than she felt comfortable with, and his posture was somehow both relaxed and tensed like a compressed spring. His tie was beside him on the couch, still looped from being pulled over his head. She had a mental image of her wrists being bound with it, whether behind her back or in front of her she wasn't sure. He was stockier than Jon, though certainly not fat. Janet had doubts that he spent much time in the gym.

Jon turned Janet's shoulders toward this man, stood behind her, and ran his hands up and down her arms.

"Dmitri, this is Janet. Janet, Dmitri."

Janet stepped forward to meet him, hand extended.

"Hi, Dmitri. So good to finally meet—"

But Dmitri took her hand and pulled her downward, onto her knees, before she could realize what had happened. His stout fingers completely engulfed hers.

"Of course the challenge here in a hotel room is to maintain a strict discipline, have creative fun, and use her to her full potential, all while enforcing an almost complete silence."

He was speaking to Jon, not her. He had a foreign accent—Russian?

"Hotel walls are very thin," he said.

"I—I agree!" Janet blurted out, shocked but glad to find an ally in hotel-room silence, and wanting to somehow appease him. She looked over her shoulder at Jon.

"I can see she has not been so thoroughly trained," Dmitri said, his English a little awkward.

Dmitri opened an attaché case on the sofa beside him.

Janet glanced in—*uh oh*.

There were no papers within it. She saw white ropes, leather cuffs, lots of chrome. She saw two dildos, one large and black, one smaller and blue that narrowed and widened again at one end, a steel loop at its base. She understood its use. Another white one. Straps with buckles; a stern rubber gag shaped like a horse bit.

As usual, this was all happening faster than she would like. She also hoped there was no saddle waiting in the bedroom.

He took out a blue ball gag with black strap and held it up

in front of her face. This was new for her, but she opened her mouth, swallowing first.

"You really are new to this, aren't you," he said.

She nodded.

"Pull your lips back from your teeth. If you don't, they will likely get pinched between the ball and your teeth, and would probably bleed."

Janet pulled her lips back into a grimace, and he pushed the ball into her mouth, behind her front teeth, and fastened the buckle behind her head. The straps pressed against her cheeks, her lips were pulled back. She felt a surge of wetness in her loins along with her nervousness. This was so *wrong*. It felt…undignified. Demeaning. It was also difficult to swallow.

"Go stand by Jon."

She stood and obeyed, turned to face him again.

"Strip her, Jon," Dmitri said.

Janet's heart skipped a beat. So *fast*. She thought there'd be drinks, chat. *Then* this.

Jon moved close behind her and carefully removed her jacket, pulling it off her shoulders and tossing it onto the chair behind him. He reached around her, unbuttoned her lovely blue blouse, slowly worked his way down to each button before pulling it off.

She was wearing no bra, and she felt the cool hotel air on her breasts.

Jon unzipped her skirt from behind. She was wearing no underwear, either.

"I'm impressed," he whispered, as she stepped out of the fallen skirt.

"What do you think, Dmitri—stockings, too?"

"No, no. Leave them. Very nice, the way they go against her skin so white. Leave her shoes on too, very nice."

Janet looked at the art above Dmitri, and saw her own re-flection in the glass that covered the framed print: her small black triangle of pubic hair was perfectly framed by her stockings and garter belts. Seeing the reflection of the glaringly obvious blue ball in her mouth, forcing her jaw into such an awkward position, made her blush even more than the feel of it alone had. All surrounded by the simple steel frame of the print. She considered the irony of trying to look like an elegant art dealer when she had selected her outfit.

Dmitri leaned back. He said to Janet, "Where's my respect, hm?"

Janet thought it sounded as though he had said "respekt." She dropped to her hands and knees, crawled to lower herself to kiss his feet.

With her mouth pried open by the ball gag, she was unable to kiss Dmitri's shoes, Tanino Criscis, they looked like—very expensive. She touched the gag against them, careful not to drool.

"I'm not so sure about this one, Jon. She doesn't seem to understand the manners and the proper etiquette; the postures, the protocols. She came in like we were all equals, hm?"

"She's very new," Jon answered. "She does understand the concept of being punished for inadequacies."

Janet shut her eyes tight.

"We'll see," Dmitri said. "There's vodka on the bar. *Real* vodka. Get Jon and me drinks, on ice." Janet stood and nearly ran.

She stood at the bar and cracked open the bottle, and pondered the moment as she found the tongs and reached into the ice bucket—there wasn't much ice left. Being so obviously gagged, her mouth full and spread so wide open, gave her a surreal feeling. Was it simply a precaution in a public building? Or was it a silencing humiliation—a signal that, as a woman, a naked one at that, she was just tits and ass, to be seen and used, but not heard?

There was a small, shameful thrill in that.

She carried the glasses to Dmitri. He pointed to Jon, seated across the room.

"This is my house, so you will serve my guest first."

No one corrected her when she kneeled for Jon, then again for Dmitri.

"This is incredibly smooth, Dmitri," Jon said.

"Yes. Stay," Dmitri told Janet, as she was about to get up.

She waited as the men sipped their drinks in silence, watching her. She heard voices outside as someone loaded their buckets from the ice machine down the hall.

Dmitri reached out and felt her breast, cupping and lifting it. His free hand was warm, and calloused—not what she'd expected, dressed so well. He ran his fingers where breast met ribcage, then felt the other. He seemed to approve. He reached into his attaché case.

Dmitri smelled good—time in the sun, time in offices; some kind of lotion applied in the morning, hours ago. He turned toward her before she could look away, and kept her gaze. He was staring into her eyes with a purpose.

No—he was staring *at* her eyes. He smiled with what looked like satisfaction. Unable to stand the scrutiny, Janet looked down at the floor.

"You were extremely accurate in your description, Jon," he said.

He had a little black box, from the attaché case. A little jewelry box. He opened it in front of Janet's lowered face.

Inside were two earrings, rounded teardrop sapphires mounted on the ends of thin silver stems about two inches long. The sapphires, if they were real, were nearly a half-inch in diameter, multifaceted and sparkling in the light. The stems were connected to—

—these weren't earrings. At the other ends of the thin rods were clips, small and silver, with shallow recesses between the little spring-loaded arms. Janet had read enough, seen enough, to know what they were.

He picked one from the silk lining of the box.

"These are for you, Janet. Yes, they are real. Nearly five carats each. Even if I never see you again, they are yours to keep."

Janet was stupefied—they must be worth over twelve, fifteen thousand dollars. Worth more than her car. What was he expecting, for these? He took one of the ice cubes from his glass, as the bauble dangled in his other hand. She winced as he pressed the ice cube against her left nipple—it was already erect, from his touches, but it elongated further, hard and tough. He did the same to the other.

He pinched it harder than she thought he needed to. He squeezed the tiny clamp open, and held her nipple taut as he released it onto her.

She nearly screamed. The pinch was excruciating against her already freezing flesh. She had never had this done to her. It was not what she thought it would feel like at all—it felt like Amanda or Hannah cruelly pinching her, but not letting go. Sharper, too.

He placed the other clip onto her opposite nipple. She shuddered, wanting to rip them both off. How long did she have to endure these? And why would any sane person allow anyone to do this to them?

"Stand up, show Jon," Dmitri said.

Slowly, Janet stood and faced Jon.

Jon was entranced. He wore the same expression he'd had when he first saw her naked body, at her house. He was marveling.

"Dmitri, you got them exactly right. They *perfectly* match her eyes."

"Based on your description, my friend. A minor collaboration, yes?"

Janet wanted to shrink away to nothing. She wanted to pull these goddamn things off, was what she wanted to do. Couldn't they just whip her, like she was starting to get used to?

No—she was getting what she'd hoped for, in this hotel: silent torments.

"And of course the blue gag instead of the red," Jon added as an afterthought. Dmitri grunted as though this were obvious. Janet bit into the ball of rubber filling her mouth.

She felt hands on her hips. Behind her, Dmitri began feeling her curves, under the garters. His hands moved lower, his thumbs gliding along the tops of her stockings. She tilted her head back to swallow. His thumbs went up the crack of her ass; he kneaded her buttocks.

"Spread your legs," he said. "As wide as possible."

Janet, nearly trembling, did so. She wished she had worn shorter heels.

"Wider. Grab your ankles and stay there."

This was a shocking order, but Janet's main concern, besides the sheer mortification of all this, was keeping her ankles from giving out while perched atop her stilettos. She grasped both ankles, hoping to strengthen them, and looked up at Jon, sapphires spinning in little circles from her hanging breasts. He was mesmerized.

She could feel Dmitri's warm breath on her ass, her exposed sex. His hands continued their roaming. She had nowhere to move when she felt his thumb against her clit—and she could only squeal, when without any more foreplay, he thrust two fingers deep inside her wetness.

She looked down, away from Jon. Dmitri was feeling her insides, getting to know her. He rotated his hand, twisting the fingers, all the while toggling her clit with his other hand.

Janet moaned audibly, a gurgling sound in her throat that she couldn't help.

"Quiet," Dmitri said, with enough authority for her to try.

But she couldn't stop. With his next thrust she came, helpless and red-faced, as Jon leaned forward to watch her eyes.

He watched her spinning sapphires, orbiting her nipples like crazed little satellites as she panted and groaned. Jesus—this guy was *good*.

"She needs more control," Dmitri observed. It was clear from Jon's expression that he disagreed.

Dmitri continued his stroking, but he started running his fingers higher—to her shamefully exhibited anus. His very wet fingers. He was still plunging into her sex, every thrust a new shock, a new ravishing, a new rapture, and then running his wet fingers up again, to her tight and tingling hole.

Oh, no no no no. But he plunged his stout fingers into her sex once more, and she came—again. She hadn't been made to come, by anyone other than herself, since…*that* night.

"*Mmmph!*" she said to Jon. She was drooling onto the carpet and there was nothing she could do about it.

Sound of rattling—the attaché case. She tried to gather herself, catch her breath. She looked up to Jon for clues, but he only shifted in his seat. A wet thumb entered her asshole almost effortlessly, and something new—one of the dildos—was pressed into her sex. She shook again, tried to keep quiet.

Both were removed, then she felt the dildo, soaking wet from her own juices, pressing against her equally wet anus. She shook her head and moaned at Jon.

But she didn't let go of her ankles, now, did she? She stayed in place, knowing she would, and felt the phallus enter her, slowly, as Dmitri allowed her time to adjust and relax.

It felt huge. She'd never had more than someone's thumb inserted there, and that was at her dinner party. The dildo was smooth: she knew it was the smaller blue one, the butt plug. Good God, what would the big black one, veined and enormous, feel like? Or a cock?

She waited, pressed back against it, as Dmitri pushed it into her.

"Good girl," he said, her first praise from him. Her anus

tightened as the plug narrowed, and she felt the two small extensions on either side of its base nestle between her cheeks.

"Stand up, legs together," he told her, and she straightened with care, getting used to this feeling of impalement. It didn't hurt, she just felt…filled. She wanted to *wriggle.*

Dmitri brought her arms back behind her, grasped her wrists in one hand. She watched Jon's enraptured expression as she felt cuffs being tightened onto her wrists, heard the buckles—it occurred to her that she had never been *bound,* in her experiences with these people, until now.

"Arch your back."

She bent backwards as he fastened her cuffs together, and then onto…the plug inside her. This was the loop she had seen, at its base. She tried to raise her bound arms, but it only pulled the phallus upward, deeper into her. Pulling her arms downward far enough to dislodge it was out of the question. It was too long and she was already bent backwards to accommodate it.

She was stuck.

Dmitri pulled one of the leather straps from his case, and wrapped it around Janet's elbows. She was now pretty damn immobilized, from the waist up, anyway.

"Knees together," he said, and Janet brought her feet in and closed her legs tight. He wrapped and fastened another strap above her knees.

"Walk to Jon," Dmitri said.

Janet could barely stand upright, let alone move. Her back was flexed far back, in an unnatural posture. Her legs were bound together, and she was regretting her choice of shoes. She couldn't even use her arms to balance herself. And her nipples ached.

Her first step was the worst. She nearly toppled, and caught herself by sticking the other foot out sideways as she almost fell that way. She stopped. It was hard to look down, with her shoulders bound so far back. She tried again, and figured out she would have to walk with her lower legs extended out to the sides, toes pointed in.

She looked ridiculous and she knew it. She was clumsy, but able to totter across the room to Jon, the painful little jewels swinging wildly from her nipples as she wobbled toward him.

"On your knees," Dmitri said, behind her. "Look at the state you've got him in. He's all worked up, poor fellow."

Dmitri was right. Jon's cock was pressing hard against his black pants; she could see the outline of its head through the fabric, a tiny stain from its drop of moisture. She had no idea how to kneel all bound up like this.

"Dmitri, this is your project," Jon said. "Sure you don't want her first?"

"My house, my rules. Serve my guest, Janet."

Janet fell forward, onto her knees, after she'd lowered herself as far as possible. Jon's cock was already out.

Jon's cock. She remembered it well—every rib and vein along its shaft, its perfectly rounded head. It was like he had designed it just for her. She remembered its feel in her mouth, her sex...okay, her cunt. That seemed like a better word at the moment, as she stared at the erection in his hand. It had been in her soaking wet cunt, there on her floor in the middle of everyone.

Bending forward was difficult—her back was so arched that all she could do was fall forward against the chair's cushion, her head in his lap. Jon unbuckled her gag and guided his swollen dick into her mouth.

She remembered his taste, too: rich and musky, everything male. She sucked ravenously, penetrated at both ends, two orgasms to her name so far tonight. She moaned louder than he did, her mouth full of his cock.

He came quickly. He held her in place as he released into her mouth, and she struggled with the flood of come and cock against her tongue and throat. She moaned at the joy of it, swallowed as fast as she could.

As he softened, she licked it clean within her mouth, and then without as he withdrew.

Jon lifted her chin and gave her a sip of his vodka. It *was* smooth, hardly burning at all as she swilled it around in her mouth and swallowed.

"Good girl. Dmitri's turn."

She thought maybe Jon would help her stand, but he watched her struggle as he zipped up, then he reclined back.

The hard part was getting her shoes straight first. It took all her muscles in her legs, but once she was up, easing the pull against the plug inside her, life was easier. She tottered back to Dmitri, a little faster this time, and kneeled between his legs, before his fully erect cock.

As with the rest of him, his cock has stouter than Jon's and a bit shorter. Pink and hard, his head was larger, too. She had to open her mouth wider for him. She dove against it and devoured it, taking in nearly every inch.

God, she had to admit—she loved giving head.

She took it as a compliment that he came so fast as well. He held her head still as he filled her mouth, and she struggled to swallow with his cock so far into her. He gave her no vodka.

In fact, once he'd caught his breath, he stood and went to the bar to pour himself another, leaving her kneeling. Probably because her hands weren't free, she guessed.

Janet turned around on her knees and faced them.

"Look, um, could we at least take these clamps off?" she asked. "They're really starting to hurt."

Both men stared at her.

"How much training has she had, Jon?"

"None. I told you."

"You said she had good instincts."

Janet lowered her face, as much as her forced posture would

allow. Why did disapproval bother her so much?

"Stand up, Janet," Dmitri said.

She tried against all odds to look graceful as both men watched her struggle to raise herself. The men looked like they were appraising her, with her chest forced forward and her bound legs accentuating her hips. They exchanged glances. These two *were* aestheticians, she knew, even if she wasn't sure what medium either worked in.

Dmitri refilled his glass, then looked into the ice bucket and poured its water into the little sink in the bar. He brought it around the bar with him.

"We're out of ice," he said.

She wasn't sure what that had to do with anything, but it gave her an uneasy feeling.

"You've broken a major rule, Janet, talking out of turn. It makes me wonder about you as a possible subject."

"A what?"

She'd done it again. She shut her mouth. Her nipples *were* starting to hurt, a sharp pain, worse every minute.

"A rule."

That wasn't what she'd meant. *Subject?*

"I'm sorry, it won't happen again, Sir," she said.

Dmitri held the ice bucket up, in front of her face. He walked behind her and placed the plastic bucket into her bound hands. He opened the door.

The door to the outside world.

Janet stood paralyzed, staring out into the hall. These things were supposed to be kept *secret*—wasn't he an ally in privacy?

"You broke a rule, now I do too," he said in his accented English, answering her unspoken question.

"Get us more ice."

Janet swallowed hard. The word "consent" passed through her mind. So did "blue"—she would never forget her safeword again. She looked at Jon, who had the same look he'd shown when Carolyn was beating the hell out of her—waiting to see what she would do.

"Do you want to gag her?" Jon said.

"No. We'll see how she behaves without it. More of a test, yes?"

Okay then.

She peeked out into the empty hallway, then stepped forward, slow and barely coordinated.

The ice machine was some twenty feet away, near the corner where this isolated little corridor widened into the cavernous space over the courtyard and the surrounding walkways. It was as private as you could hope for, except for the straight-shot of the walkway that it aligned with, some eight or ten rooms along the same wall as Dmitri's. As long as no one came out of those, she could make it there and back without much chance of detection.

Dmitri closed the door behind her.

She was alone in the hallway, sounds of children playing in the pool seven floors below.

She had several options:

Beg to be let back in. Not move, and hope this wasn't actually happening. Shout for help (no). Or walk, slow and hobbled as she was.

She walked.

This possible exposure was everything she'd hoped to avoid, ever, in her entire life. *Do NOT drop the bucket*, she told herself. She stumbled along, toes pointed inward, back arched, plug up her ass, praying no one would come out of a door or around the corner. How the hell would she ever explain this?

Or the resulting phone footage, uploaded to the Internet? She tried to hurry, but hurrying nearly caused her to fall, heels catching on carpet.

She'd made it. She turned her back to the machine, shoved the bucket into the recessed dispenser. She looked over her shoulder and found the button; pushed it. Loud rattle of ice hitting hollow plastic: *sshhhh!* she thought.

Please, please please please. The machine stopped. She listened. She looked out at the rooms across the hotel, then looked away in case someone was looking at her. She fumbled for the bucket, which pressed the tight blue plug deeper into her. She caught the bucket's upper edge and managed to grab it.

She heard voices—but not the echoey ring of guests down in the courtyard. Someone near. She started back and almost tripped onto her face, forgetting the band around her knees was even there.

One step at a time. One step. One more, one more. She felt the wet bucket, now heavier, starting to slip out of her hand.

The voices were getting louder. A laugh, though muffled—still around the corner. But she could tell they were young voices, boys. Teenagers, probably.

Oh, God.

She knocked on the door with her forehead, three times. Again. Oh, this was just mean. She couldn't kick it, or she'd lose her balance. She turned around, facing the hall, the machine, the approaching pair—or three?—teenagers talking trash about some girl, she could hear them clearly now.

She fought to keep the bucket in her grip with one hand, and knocked hard against the door with the other.

It opened. She practically fell in as the bucket slipped from her hand.

"Dude—did you see what I just—"

Dmitri closed the door behind her. She was panting, and Jon held up the bucket that he had caught behind her. They were laughing.

Janet was not.

"What did I tell you?" Jon said. "Is she a good girl, or what?"

"You are right, Jon, I must admit. I think she might very

well do."

Dmitri evaluated her, calm as she panted in exhaustion and panic.

"Where's the gag?"

◈

What was it with these people and their coffee table fetishes? She lay down on her back on the glass and steel table like they told her to do. She let them bend her legs, bind her wrists and ankles to the legs of the table with rope. Human furniture, like something from an old Betty Page photo shoot. Dmitri rummaged through his case.

"Damn it," he said. "I have forgotten my clothespins. We are in a *hotel room*, and I have forgotten my clothespins."

The large blue butt plug was still inserted into Janet's ass, and she couldn't quite relax, couldn't quite rest her behind on the table. She had to keep her hips elevated to keep it from twisting inside her.

"I could use a drink, Jon," Dmitri said. "How about you?"

"Sure. This vodka's wonderful, could you bring me a bottle, next time?"

"Of course. But the bar downstairs has one red worth trying. I thought we could perhaps talk in the bar, away from prying ears." He looked at Janet.

"You know, they say never to mix grain and grape," Jon said.

"Yes. Well. You Americans really don't know how to drink, do you."

Janet had the feeling she was going to be here a while.

Dmitri pulled the white dildo she had seen earlier from his case. He turned the knob at its base, and it began to buzz. That wasn't just a dildo.

Janet's legs were spread as wide as the table, her legs hanging over the sides, ankles bound to the corner legs. He inserted the vibrator into her with no resistance—she was still wet, to her embarrassment.

The vibration was intense. She bit into her gag and moaned loudly, too loud for a hotel room. Dmitri shushed her as she rocked her hips at the double penetration. She couldn't relax her thighs—she would have to keep her hips raised as long as he decided to leave the buzzing intruder inside her. She looked up at him, pleading.

"Good girl," he said.

Both men were standing above her, looking down, enjoying the spectacle. She was wriggling, writhing, trying with all her might to stay quiet.

They watched as she came, her face red and she knew it.

"Wonderful coloration," Dmitri observed. "Well chosen, Jon."

"Told you."

Dmitri crouched down near her face.

"Janet, we are going downstairs for a little while to discuss things. To discuss you. I want you to enjoy this little gift as much as you like. But listen."

He pulled the vibrator from her, and she moaned at its absence. He placed it on the surface of the table between her legs. Rattling against the glass surface, its hard plastic made an incredibly loud, growling, mechanical roar.

"This table amplifies, yes? Imagine what that sounds like downstairs, the sound coming through the floor, their ceiling. Imagine! They might have to call the management."

She imagined. She nodded. He inserted the vibrator back into her, and she moaned again, now at its presence. Her hips rocked at the intensity. Yet she would have to hold it there, clamp her muscles around it until they returned.

"Ready, Jon?"

Dmitri stopped, turned back to Janet. He bent over her,

183

and removed one of the bejeweled silver clamps from her nipple, then the other. Janet felt an immense sense of relief even more intense than the two plastic cocks invading her. She whimpered a thank you.

He placed them in her navel, and out the door the men went.

❖

When Janet got home, the next morning, her legs quaking so severely she could hardly walk (she'd set the cruise control every chance she'd had, driving home, too weak to push the accelerator), she bypassed the wine glasses in the kitchen and went straight for the half-empty bottle on the counter. She went into her bedroom, and pulled the bottom two drawers of her dresser open. Her porn collection.

She had to lift a few volumes high enough to see the cover art or the blurb on the back, but most she remembered well. She went through them A-Z, taking a few swigs from the bottle, early as it was. Her legs were too shaky to hold her weight, so she sat cross-legged on the floor.

She picked out every smutty book she could find featuring dominant males with East European accents, some half-dozen, at least. Where was he from? Latvia? Lithuania? She found four more in which the cruel or strict men had Russian accents, close enough.

She gathered them together in a neat little pile, and put them on the bed stand, the little table beside her bed with her reading lamp on it.

The "For Immediate Reading" pile.

Part 3: On-Ramps

Chapter Eleven

All right. The first thing Janet had to do was go ahead and admit that she liked all of this. Why was that so hard to do? She sat on her front porch swing sipping a Bellini, enjoying the warmth of the evening but becoming annoyed at the neighbors' fireworks while she was trying to think. They would only get worse over the next few days, until the Fourth was over. But someone launched some kind of big pretty starburst down the street that exploded into pink, yellow and green streamers, and she decided to just enjoy the show.

Of *course* she'd been terrified, that first night, and ashamed. Who wouldn't have been, lifelong fantasy realized or not? She hadn't exactly been eased into it, no gentle scarf around the wrists and a light spanking. And that bitch Carolyn...

But let's face it: sure, she'd wanted to slap Jon when she saw him in that bookstore, but she also wanted to strip off her clothes right there. And that night in the hotel was the most exciting thing to ever happen to her. *Ever.*

What she didn't like—well, besides nipple clamps, even if they were $20,000 nipple clamps—were these weeks-long periods between phone calls. Literally waiting by the phone, to be called up for service like some call girl, only without getting paid. Not that she'd want that, either. Or were those clamps a payment? *Was* she a call girl?

No, and she needed to stop thinking like that. These were *her* choices.

Jon called the next day, this time, and sent her funny texts, but she *was* sort of feeling like she was at their disposal. Maybe she should be more aggressive, in her subservience? Call *them* and say, "Use me—now"?

What an odd thing she'd gotten herself into. And did Jon live with Amanda or not, anyway?

At least Dmitri had a reason not to call; he'd left for Europe the day after she'd met him. "Met" him.

Well, what do you know: her phone rang and it buzzed against the wooden slats of the porch swing, amplifying it. Some long, unidentifiable foreign number. Could be a spammer.

"Hello?"

A scammer, maybe, but it was no spammer.

❖

Janet saw Dmitri in the back of the hotel's bar, in the corner booth conversing with a waiter. Nice and private. His eyes gleamed when he saw her approach; he told the waiter something and dismissed him. He stood to meet her.

"Janet! Darling." He kissed her hand, a slightly different greeting from the last time. His thick fingers still enveloped hers. "Sit, please."

Janet sat across from him, smoothed her blue and black patterned sundress.

"Hello, Dmitri."

"You've been good?"

"Depends on what you mean."

"I'm sorry I have not called." His accent.

"That's okay. You've been overseas, yes?" Now she was picking it up.

"Mostly. I've been in town a week. I needed to make preparations."

The waiter brought two glasses of red wine.

"Wonderful *Garnacha*, they serve here. Try it. I took the liberty, I hope it's not too early?"

"It's almost sundown, isn't it?" Janet took a sip. Nice. "Why, will I be driving home soon?"

"I am afraid so. My plane leaves in two hours, but I wanted to speak to you about something before I'm gone for another week. I'd like to get things started."

"...Started?"

Dmitri nodded, excited like a schoolboy trying to hide a secret he didn't want to keep in the first place.

"Jon has told you about me?" he said. "What I do?"

"Actually, no. Everyone,"—*everyone!*—"has been a little vague. You're some kind of artist?" Janet felt a little uneasy. What if he wanted to take pictures?

Dmitri placed his hands flat on the table. "I want to put you in a film."

Janet was taken aback, and felt a deep wave of disappointment.

"A porno?"

"No! You can of course leave anytime, but please, hear me out."

Janet crossed her arms. *Be assertive, take charge.*

"Okay." She was not *about* to appear in some bondage video to be spread around on the Internet. "You want me in a video."

"No! Again, please listen. I'm sorry. I should have begun with more small talk, yes?" He looked a little worried. "My passion...it is not a hobby...is making short films, twenty to twenty-two minutes long, featuring women that I find especially…"—he searched for the word—"…compelling."

Janet gave him the best dead-fisheye stare she could muster.

"They are filmed under very strict circumstances, very controlled." Well, that didn't exactly surprise her. "Only a minimal crew sees it made, and a minimum of people see it afterward."

"So why do it? Why so few people?"

"It is an intensely private activity."

"It's not a business?"

"No. Not at all. They are very expensive to make, and I make them only for myself. I have small screenings for friends. And when I show my films, almost always only once, there are no cell phones allowed, no cameras. Eyeglasses are checked to make sure no cameras are in them. Pens in pocket, buttons on clothes, even. Sometimes, viewers have to agree to strip naked to watch, funny huh? Only twelve people have seen my first film. Another, at most, maybe fifty or so. I flood the room with jamming devices, no electronics will work inside room, but the old light bulb and motor in projector work just fine. See?"

"Uh…seriously?"

"Yes."

"Actual old film? Do they still make that?"

"Of course. Listen: after I shoot the film, there are only two copies—the original, which I keep in a vault in Vilnius"— Janet wondered where exactly Vilnius was—"and the copy in a vault somewhere else. Closer to you. Only I have the keys to both. If I should die, the keys to the Vilnius vault are lost. Only I know where they are. They are literally buried. The other key is sent, by attorneys, to you. They will find you. Maybe next year, huh? Maybe when you are an old lady."

"Why couldn't I just have a key?"

"Because of the contract." Janet leaned back at this.

"The contract says, $50,000 is put into escrow account in the United States. If the film makes it to the Internet, the escrow goes to you. So, then, it might be in your interest to put it on the Internet. Yes?"

"No."

"For fifty thousand dollars? Many would say yes."

"Yes." Janet still didn't understand all this. "So...how *do* you make any money at this? Charge some crazy admission at the screenings?"

Dmitri was maybe losing a little patience.

"It's not a business. It's my...*art*. For me. Only for me, and I decide to show it to a few friends. Trusted friends."

"What do you do for a living, if I may ask?"

"I am an attorney. International corporate law. I make a great deal of money, putting together deals for men with far more money than me. But do not think these men—these... oligarchs, huh? Do not think that they will ever see a film of you. I wouldn't let those pigs near it."

"So...what exactly would I be doing in this film, this art film?"

Dmitri started to speak, but she interrupted.

"A little bondage film, me being a sex slave? Filming what we did last time we met? Tied up, a bunch of guys fucking me? I've seen a few of *those*, and they are not—"

"No!"

Dmitri looked pained. Janet watched him for any signs of anger, losing his temper. She had actually found his rather cold matter-of-factness at her sufferings last time somewhat appealing, despite herself, but she wanted to make sure that he hadn't been covering up something darker.

"I am not explaining well," he said.

"Why don't you get professional bondage models or actresses? There seem to be more of them every day." She had been looking at a few sites, lately.

"No, Janet. First, many of those models are very damaged people. Not all, but many need the drugs to get through shoots, made to do humiliating things as a business. Not a good…milieu, yes? And more important: I don't want professionals. They act. They know what's coming. They are…jaded, is the word. I want women who are not jaded, not needing the money—but will do it because they feel a *need* to do it."

He paused and leaned back, looked at Janet far more knowingly than she liked. She blushed again, damn it. She had told herself, tonight on the porch, that she was done blushing.

"They are not narrative films. No one plays a character like in a bad porn movie. I spend weeks, months, constructing a set, setting up lights and sound with professionals. Very few of those people will see you—dressed, even. I make endless sketches first. The films are carefully made, but never, ever rehearsed. They are very…*stylized*." He held an imaginary object in his hands. "Very heavy on visual style. They are unique."

Janet took a sip of her wine. Dmitri wasn't proposing to pay her for being in his film. He wanted her to *want* to be in it.

But she didn't, really.

"I have made six films, featuring three women. One woman was in three films. One in two. The other girl only had one movie in her, as she said, but it is magnificent." Dmitri paused. "Jon has seen three of my films, more than anyone. He is quite an aesthete, you know."

"Yes, I know. How did you two meet?"

"At a gallery opening, of course."

"Of course."

"This is why he introduced you to me. He thinks you should be in a film. After meeting you last time,"—he gave her a satisfied smile, almost smug—"I completely agree."

They sat staring at each other. *Don't look away, Janet. Be strong.*

"If you are at all interested, I have set up a projector in my room. No hidden corner room, this time, it's right by the pool—see the children? You will be free to go at any moment."

Blue

The mere presence of a camera or phone at Janet's house that first night would have been the one thing that would have made her send everyone packing, even if it had come out of a pocket or purse while she was, to say the least, distracted by Jon's solid fucking. *"Out,"* she would have said, *"Blue."* Without hesitation. Even to Carolyn, whip in her hand or not.

But what exactly *did* this guy do, that had Jon so obsessed, and had compelled Jack to pursue Hannah to the ends of the Earth? She looked across the hotel's courtyard, saw the row of rooms mere yards away from a half-dozen urchins splashing and screaming in the water.

"...Okay."

❖

Janet and Dmitri sat in his room in the pair of chairs with a low table between them, an old-fashioned film projector set upon it—an actual metal, *ticka ticka ticka ticka* machine, two big reels with film strung through it. He had removed the hotel art from the wall above the sofa and was adjusting the focus. Janet remembered seeing herself being stripped naked in the glass reflection of another such print—the exact *same* print. Same one as in Lubbock, come to think of it.

"Comfortable?"

"Yes. Thank you."

"Drink? I will bring to you, this time."

"No thank you."

Dmitri turned the room light off. "Each film is twenty-two minutes long, because a canister of sixteen millimeter film is eleven minutes," he said, returning to his seat. "We shoot straight through, no breaks, no rehearsals, switch *cameras* halfway through, no time to change canisters." He rattled off something about film speeds, apertures, something called an "Arriflex," which was apparently a camera.

"Sometimes, things are not quite ready at the beginning,

I have to cut a little off. Sometimes at the end. I keep the title sequence short. Ready?" He started the projector. There was a black rectangle darker than the wall around it.

Words in white letters appeared:

EYE OF THE STORM (RED)
A FILM BY DMITRI CORSO

Janet wondered how many colors of *Eye of the Storm* there were; Hannah was in *(Yellow)*.

The title faded to black, and in a few seconds the frame was perfectly square, concentric circles within it. Circles of people.

"Oh," Janet said.

The camera had been placed high, looking straight down. At the very center of the image was a spread-eagled young woman, a fair-skinned redhead, stretched—very tightly—into a perfect X. Cuffs on her wrists and ankles were fastened into the floor on which she lay, her limbs pulled taut and wide. There was a bare circle of black floor around her, reaching just beyond her hands and feet, and outside of this circle was a far wider circle consisting of writhing human flesh.

"Oh!" Janet repeated when she realized what she was looking at.

There were at least fifty or sixty people, all redheads, arranged in a perfect ring from just beyond the girl's reach to the four edges of the square image; a band of flesh maybe six feet wide, everyone engaging in various sexual acts, too many to take in all at once.

Janet's eyes wandered around the circle of bodies. Viewed from above, they laid or kneeled on black cushions and pillows, fucking, sucking, fondling, kissing. There were all combinations—men with women, women together, a few men sucking each other. There were threesomes of all combinations. People were being fucked from behind, from above, from below. The scene was evenly lit, in neutral colors. They were definitely redheads—white skin, pink skin. The color of their heads and pubic hair ranged from strawberry blond to an almost reddish brown, but their skin was uniformly pale, which the white lighting accentuated.

Janet listened. The sounds of so many people having sex blended into a strange sort of white noise—there were so many high pitched sighs, deep grunts, and overlapping cries of orgasm that it was impossible to pick any single person out.

She tried to focus on individuals in the crowd. She started at the top of the screen, the twelve o'clock position of the circle: directly above the spread-eagled girl's head was a beautiful woman on her back, her spread body exposed to the camera. Her arms were splayed above her head, and she was getting fucked by a man on his knees, her hips atop his, her legs wrapped around his back. Her breasts bounced with each of his thrusts. Above them, at the very top of the screen, there was a threesome: a woman on all fours, the swell of her hips contrasted against the dark pillows. She was between two men, sucking one, receiving the other from behind.

More threesomes: a man on his back, one woman straddling his face, the other riding his cock, writhing up and down. Nice to see the man's body laid out and used like that, Janet thought. She could not imagine getting naked in front of that many people, having sex in such a public environment. Not that she would have been invited, to this one—how did he find all these redheads?

At the three o'clock position, a woman on her back sucked the cock of the man kneeling beside her, while another man was between her spread legs orally servicing her. Janet saw one woman pinning another's wrists to the floor as a man fucked her. Two women were sixty-nining each other; so were two men, lying on their sides, cocks thrusting into mouths.

It was all too much to comprehend, a big mass, not individuals. Janet's eyes followed the circle of this orbiting orgy until she was drawn once again to the woman in the center, her white skin contrasting so strongly with the dark floor to which she was bound.

Even with the camera far enough away to take in the entire scene, it was clear the girl was having a tough time of it. Her face was barely discernible at this distance, but she was rocking her hips as much as her bindings would let her, her triangular red bush a focal point, moving from side to side and up and down. Her long red hair was spread across the floor around her face, and her head was rocking back and forth as she watched those closest to her. She wanted to participate, but no one would come to her. They were all *just* out of reach.

The camera began slowly zooming in. The outermost participants began to disappear off the edges of the screen, oblivious and preoccupied. Bodies now filled the corners of the square image, and Janet's eyes darted from them, now in closer detail, back to the woman in the center. The writhing bodies radiated off the screen, their faces more clear—a woman leaned back in ecstasy; a man wore a satisfied, dominant expression as his cock was being sucked.

But the main attractor was clearly the woman in the center, her lonely bare circle taking up more and more of the screen. Janet could finally see the features of her face—she was young, early twenties or maybe even late teens. She was in agony, her desperation overwhelming. She could watch everything going on around her, the nearest bodies, at least, but she could do nothing about it. She watched two women right above her head in a tense 69 position, then looked away only to find a woman licking a very handsome man's large balls. Even viewed from above, it was clear this woman was looking over at the helpless girl as she did this, taunting her, teasing her as she stroked the cock with her hand.

The central redhead looked away. Looking down the length of her own body, a broad-shouldered man had a small-framed woman pinned on her back, her knees up by her head, fucking her without mercy. The muscles in his ass clenched at each thrust; her mouth was open in a perfect circle of pleasure.

Janet felt herself become aroused, her breath short. She looked over to Dmitri, who was absorbed in the film.

The girl was desperate to join in with someone, anyone. She tried to grasp with her hands, her feet. She closed her eyes, unable to watch more, then reopened them, equally unable not to.

The camera continued its slow zoom, and the closest participants began to disappear off the screen. The last to go were those in the very corners, and the final bit of flesh to vanish was a rounded white breast, inches away from the girl's outstretched hand.

The perfect X of her body now filled the square screen. She had been *so* tightly stretched before her cuffs were fastened to the floor, bolted, Janet could see. Her muscles struggled for release, but she was afforded no movement except her hips, which were not fastened to the floor—but they were still restricted by the very wide spread of her legs and the tightness with which she was bound.

The girl's stomach flexed as she panted and writhed, and Janet could not help but stare at her bright orange pubic hair, and taking a voyeuristic peek at the lips beneath them, a slit of pink visible. She must have been *so* fucking wet, Janet thought. The girl's red bush stood out like a beacon against the sea of white skin, whiter than Janet's. Soon it too disappeared off the bottom of the screen, and then the curves of her hips, and Janet was left looking at breasts, shoulders and the girl's pained face.

The girl continued to look from side to side, all around. Her chest heaved again, and this close up Janet could see how tightly the muscles in her shoulders were being pulled. She could barely move.

Janet swallowed hard. The screen was filled entirely by the girl's face, a very intrusive act, for some reason. She rested her head back onto the floor, and soon the red of her hair was gone—her green eyes and full pink lips took up the entire square. She closed her eyes again, then opened them, staring right into the camera, at Janet. Janet winced at her intensity.

The girl was silently pleading with the camera, but was also incredibly determined. She struggled; bit her lip. She wanted to say something, but didn't, couldn't. Were there no words allowed in this film? Janet was held captive by the fierceness of her gaze, so close, so intimate. Her green eyes were looking straight into Janet, asking her for help. Janet was torn between wanting to help her and wanting to watch her suffer so exquisitely.

The camera, which had been still for some time—Janet had lost track how long—began zooming out, backing away. The girl's expression did not change, and her red hair again became visible—but it was different. Her hair was no longer in a swirl around her head, but was lying straight down along the sides of her face, as if she were now vertical.

The camera moved slightly farther away, and Janet heard the sounds of sex in the room fading in again—she hadn't realized that they had faded out. She wasn't sure when the dense din had quieted to silence, but it had certainly contributed to the intimate, intrusive feeling of the extreme close-up.

The slow zoom out continued, and Janet saw that the girl's hair *was* hanging down—she was standing! Her red hair hung with the slightest curl around her straining shoulders, her arms still outstretched upwards from her body. She had beautiful hair, Janet thought. Janet took in the girl's flexed deltoid muscles, her tensed and smooth armpits. She could see a certain darkness behind the woman's head that was no longer the painted floor.

Janet was seeing into the darkness of the room behind her. The girl was still staring directly into the camera, but no longer looking from side to side—because everyone was now below her, fucking on the floor.

"How did you—"

"*Shh.*" Dmitri with his hand raised, never taking his eyes off the screen.

Janet would have to think about this later. Either they had spliced the film while it had been close to her face, moving her between shots, or the camera had somehow been moved from the ceiling to eye level on the floor, *while* they tilted her body with it. But she had seen no change in the girl's face, no edit.

It was too much to think about at the moment.

The girl *was* standing—her breasts were visible again, gravity pulling them downward in a natural curve. Full and round, they still heaved with her labored breathing. Her eyes began to wander. She glanced downward, at the mass of bodies off-camera but still surrounding her, and a new desperation took over her face—she could now see far more people than only those next to her.

The camera backed away to reveal her thighs, spread as wide as before. The girl was still in a radically taut X stance, spread-eagled vertically. She was almost hanging by her wrists, but the camera backed away wide enough to show her feet touching the ground, her ankles still cuffed and bolted to the same spots as before. They had lifted her upright somehow, her wrists pulled by long cables reaching up to the ceiling.

How did they do that? The camera stopped its retreat as the X of her body precisely filled the square screen.

A pale and muscled man stood up behind her, sweaty and with a glistening erection jutting up from his red pubic hair. He wore a dark red mask across his eyes. He stood to one side, his body evenly lit, as was hers. He held a whip, a black flogger with many long leather tendrils. Janet squirmed in her seat. She knew what was coming.

The man stretched the tendrils of the whip between his hands, then stepped nearer to her. With a very sure movement, he raised his arm straight up, and in a flash made a forceful windmill motion, like a softball pitcher, and struck the girl upward, from below, between her spread legs.

Janet grimaced at the force of it, the sharp sound of leather on soft flesh above the din of the room. The black tips of the whip came up from the girl's crotch and across her lower stomach; the main force of the blow had hit directly onto her exposed sex.

The girl had not expected this at all—she had not known the man was there—and her eyes and mouth opened wide. She tried to buckle over, but she was being pulled too taut. She cried out as her hips rocked, and she ducked her head down, her hair falling around her face, hiding it, then she flipped her hair behind her and looked up to the ceiling. She clenched her teeth.

Janet did too, in sympathy, waiting for the next blow.

But there wasn't one. She watched the muscular man smile at his work, his hips involuntarily thrusting, cock pointing upward, then looked at whatever partner was beneath him, and lowered himself onto her. Or him; they were nothing but a mass of blurred moving bodies.

The bound girl shuddered; her thighs quivered. She tried to pull her arms toward her but couldn't. She tried twisting her shoulders, to little success. All she could move were her hips, and she twisted; rocked them forward and back.

As Janet watched, the girl's struggling face turned from pale white to bright pink to crimson. She grimaced again, tried to close her legs, but failed. After a tense hesitation, face still red, her mouth rounded and she let out a harrowing cry: "*Ggggaaaaaaaaaaaa! …aaa ah ah ahd.*"

"God," is what Janet thought she heard. The only word

uttered so far. She had just had one of the most intense orgasms Janet had ever witnessed, ever *imagined*. And she clearly wasn't acting.

The girl moaned, quieter, but still desperate. She was still quivering, her whole body shaking. She made another moaning sound, "*Huhn...huuuuuuh.*" Her face turned red again.

Janet leaned forward in anticipation as the girl gritted her teeth and tried to close her legs. Janet looked down at the girl's open labia, still reddened from the whip. The flogger had likely struck her clitoris, her inner lips. It was the only touch she had received through her entire ordeal of watching, hearing, and denial.

She came again, not quite so violently as before. She whimpered, then moaned as she looked down at the people surrounding her, no one coming to her to touch her. If only a hand would slide up one of her thighs. The girl struggled against the cables, against the cuffs holding her feet apart. But she was immobile. She rocked her hips again in frustration. Her thighs shook, and her chest heaved, and she raised her face, a deep crimson once more, and cried out with a long, sorrowful wail. Did she come *again*? Was this why Dmitri chose her? She shook with the aftermath of this last one, making tiny, high-pitched sounds.

She hung her head low, exhausted, her beautiful red hair falling about her face. Janet could tell that she wanted to collapse, but couldn't. All but her head was held rigidly in place, perfectly vertical. The young redhead hung there, spread and panting, and the screen faded to black, as did the room Janet was in.

Janet's own breathing was labored as well. She waited for Dmitri to say something. Would he order her to her knees, use her now? She was willing. *Eager*. But she waited.

"Well?" he finally said.

"Well what?"

"I can smell you from here, my dear. I can almost taste you."

Unlike last time, she had worn underwear, but they were soaked, she knew it. Wasn't the point of being a girl that your excitement wasn't always on display?

Be aggressive, Janet. Not on call.

She stood, reached behind her and unfastened her dress, let it fall. She rolled her wet panties off and stepped out of her clothes.

He must have heard her. "Janet, we don't have much time."

"I know."

"Will you do it?"

"What."

"Make a film with me."

No.

"Yes."

"There is paperwork—a contract."

Janet let her bra fall to the floor and she walked in front of the projector to Dmitri, seated in the other chair in the dark. She was going to lean over him, kiss him full on the lips, but he found her hand and pulled her down, though much more gently than the last time, onto her knees.

"Sign," he said, and handed her a sheaf of papers that she couldn't see, nor did she care. He placed a pen in the hand he held.

Janet scribbled her name without even seeing, took the initiative and kissed him as she'd planned.

Dmitri grasped her hair and pulled her away. The darkness made it all the more thrilling.

"Good girl," he said. "Tonight, you may make as much noise as you wish."

Chapter Twelve

"Would you like to come up and see my etchings, little girl?"

Jon, on her cell phone at work. It took her a moment to figure out what he meant; she wasn't concentrating very well these days. Perhaps because she had signed a contract to star in a porn film, a few days ago?

"Your alphabet?" she said. She looked around to see if any coworkers had heard. As if they'd know what she was talking about.

"Yes. Would you like to come over and see it?"

She looked over at Julie, typing away at her computer, then Dawn, shaking her head and looking very confused at some form or another.

"It's etchings?"

"It's a figure of speech. An old joke."

"I don't get it."

"An old pick-up line. From like, Vaudeville."

"How do you even know that?"

"I know many things. How 'bout it?"

"I'm at work."

"I know that, too. After work."

Janet thought a moment. Here she was again, on call for these guys. She wondered if Amanda was ever going to call her and say "Come on over," as well.

"Okay. Six?"

"Perfect. Bye, doll."

Janet looked around at her coworkers, typing or on their phones, trying to chip away at the endless strata of the American health care system. Besides Ron's office—and she wasn't in the mood to hear about fishing—there was no privacy here in Medical Records, no cubicle in which to hide and gather her thoughts, just the two rows of desks in the big gray room. And she *really* needed to gather her thoughts. Which of course meant "obsess on things."

What in the hell had she done? She'd signed an agreement, without reading it, without even being able to *see* it, to appear in a pornographic film. *If these people only knew.* She was such a fool.

Were Dmitri's safeguards really all that airtight? She had searched *Eye of the Storm* on the internet, both *(Yellow)* and *(Red)*, and found nothing but Doppler radar images on weather sites; she added such qualifiers as +movie, +film, +video, +erotic, +porn, +bondage, +BDSM... She'd found nothing. The only references to Dmitri online were his professional pages—his law firm's website in English and several other languages, a nice picture of him; legal records. She'd downloaded his picture.

Was that contract even legally binding? Like everything else, couldn't she safeword out of this?

"Hey—you okay?" Julie said, turning around at her desk in front of Janet's.

"Sure, I'm fine."

"You look a little pale. And when you look pale, you look *pale*."

"No, I'm good."

"Some of us are getting together for drinks after work. You wanna come? You've seemed a little tense."

Drinks with the girls. It sounded so good. Release a little tension, talk too much…

She held up her phone. "Thanks. I'd love to, but I've got plans."

"Ooh! Excellent. Date?"

Janet tipped her head left and right, not a big enough smile to be decisive. "Don't really know."

"I understand. Well good luck then! You deserve it."

"Thanks." Now Janet smiled. Or tried to.

❖

Janet found the address Jon had given her easily enough; it was surprisingly close to her own house, on the same side of Oakdale's joke of a "downtown," where Jon's office was. (Everyone in Oakdale pronounced "downtown" with finger-quotes, as opposed to the City's downtown.) It was the same kind of tree-lined neighborhood as her own, slightly newer since it was slightly farther west: the Ranch houses were built in the early '70's, probably, rather than the late '60's as hers was.

She had to park in the street because there was a little Honda in the single-wide driveway, older and rougher than her own. Jon's huge old Buick was nowhere to be seen. She parked under a big oak and walked up the drive.

She was met by an attractive young man in a hoodie and loose jeans, a bit taller than she; ruddy red hair under his hood, a few years younger. The old Honda must have been his.

"Hello," she said.

He stopped short, looking nervous. He'd been staring at the ground.

"Oh. Hello, Ma'am," he said. So polite! Janet wasn't used to being *called* "Ma'am."

"Is…is this Jon's house?" *And is it Amanda's, too?*

"Yes, Ma'am," he said, sizing her up like most of the men in her life lately, but without the entitlement. He looked back at the ground, at his feet. "Yes, he's inside."

Janet recognized the humility, and felt goosebumps up the back of her neck. He was Of Her Tribe. What was he doing here? Should she introduce herself, or was there some rule about that kind of thing?

"Thank you," she said, and walked on while the young man started his car and left. Had he felt it too?

She rang the doorbell.

"Janet! Come in, come in."

"Hello, Jon." The kiss on the cheek.

"Dmitri told me," he said, holding both her hands. "I can't believe it's going to happen. It's going to be awesome, I know it." He looked down her body as he closed the door behind her. "Take off your clothes."

Well, at least he waited until he'd shut the door.

"Seriously? Right here?"

He beckoned her into his living room.

"Yes." He leaned against the back of his sofa; Janet was barely out of the entryway. He crossed his arms to watch her.

You'd think I'd be getting used to this, she thought. She hesitated—she was trying to get *away* from this kind of behavior, to be a bit more in charge of her out-of-chargeness. But she dropped her purse and began unbuttoning her shirt while she kicked off her shoes. Well, did she really think she'd come over just to discuss art?

"So where are these 'etchings' of yours?" she said, trying to make conversation. But Jon put his finger to his lips, shushing her.

She stood naked. She stretched her shoulders, not yet out of work/commute mode. Jon beckoned her to follow with the same finger, and he led her through the living room.

She looked around as she left her clothes behind. The house was so…normal, a model of precise, traditional homemaking, and it had a bit of a woman's touch around—flowers in a vase on the buffet table near the door, subtly patterned furniture that didn't reek of masculinity. Smell of Lemon Pledge. None of it seemed to reflect the choices of a devoted aesthete. Did Amanda live here after all? Had she in the past?

Janet wasn't sure what she'd expected, in a house possibly owned by a kinky artist and/or a former dominatrix, but what she was seeing was the house of an insurance salesman and a caterer—what the rest of the neighborhood knew them as. The curtains were pastel, the carpet beige. Beige! Thomas's favorite. There was an outdated chandelier, bordering on the gaudy, in the center of the living room with its slightly higher ceiling, far too ornate for such a pedestrian space.

She felt the cool air across her body as she followed Jon—to where? He stopped by a doorway and gestured for her to enter: stairs. His dungeon? Maybe she wished Amanda were here after all.

He followed behind as she descended, and they walked into another carpeted room, cooler down here.

But this room was different, and it was no dungeon. The space was long and narrow, the walls painted a dark umber, with an undertone of brighter orange—fiery, vital. It contrasted with the off-white carpet, and with the entire upstairs, frankly. Looking around, Janet could see an adjoining room through a doorless entryway, its walls a cool light green with a darker green undercoat—creative but calming. Down here was where the color and life happened.

The room they were in was lit by track lighting from the ceiling, and there was one piece of furniture, in the very center: a padded bench, like what you would find in museums. Because hanging on the entire length of one wall was a neat row of black and white images, matted in neutral white and framed in thin black metal. She looked back at Jon, who motioned her toward them.

The first image in the row was a photograph of a woman, naked and bound, full-frontal. Her body filled the square frame of the image, nearly two feet high and wide, the background behind her a contrasting black. She was blindfolded and gagged, her arms stretched above her head, bound there. Her legs were spread wide and held by a spreader bar between her knees, not her ankles. The bar was wide, and white, as were her gag, blindfold, and bonds. She was blonde and shaved, her nipples barely visible in the flat, neutral lighting—no shadows.

"Okay…" Janet said. She walked to the next photograph with her arms crossed. She felt a little self-conscious, naked in new surroundings, looking at nude art.

In the next image a woman was bound to a large black spool of some kind, viewed from the side—a big round drum or something, somehow suspended or floating. It was painted flat black to match the dark background. Her body was curved backward around it, so that her backside was against the rounded shape. Her torso was roughly vertical, with her arms bound above and behind her head, her legs curving back under the spool. Her face was in profile, partially hidden by her upraised arm, and she wore the same white gag and blindfold the other woman had worn. Her breasts were small, barely protruding.

"That's an 'A', and this is a 'C'," Janet said. "This is your alphabet?"

Jon nodded, beaming with pride.

"Where's the 'B'?"

"I haven't figured that one out, yet. Think about it."

"Hmm. That would be sort of complicated. It'll take more than one person, maybe?"

"A few do." He motioned her down the row.

D: two women, one standing straight, her arms bound

behind her back so that she was just a vertical column; another woman bound to the round spool in a half circle. The standing woman was in front, her head hidden in a black leather bondage hood to shorten her height to match the bent, curved woman—she'd been reduced to mere object, vertical line; a component. She was unshaved, her pubic hair platinum white, and her breasts were fuller than the others.

"Are these professional models?"

Jon gave her a devious look.

"None of them are. Like Dmitri, I like to use people who want to be in them. Or whose…" He left the thought hanging.

H: two women stood, blindfolded and gagged, holding another horizontal woman between them. The woman in the middle had her knees bent back behind her to shorten her length; there were ropes across her thighs. Her head, which extended beyond the hips of the woman holding her, was covered in a black hood to keep the lines consistent. Janet looked closer and saw that the two standing women weren't so much holding the third as *supporting* her—a network of ropes ran from their shoulders and necks to the body of the woman bridging the gap. Their hands were behind their backs, probably bound. She was hanging, there.

Janet felt a little thrill at their ordeal, ordered to stand still once they'd been bound, while Jon took the photo. She could see sweat gleaming on their skin.

"They each look different, so far. Do you photograph any of them more than once?"

"Nope."

"Even in the groups…"

"No, just once, each."

"Even Dmitri will use them more than once." "*Them?*" "*Us?*"

"Dmitri has his perfectionisms. I have mine."

Janet felt a slight uneasiness creep up on her, but she

couldn't quite put her finger on why. It wasn't simply that she was supposed to model for Dmitri, even if that was her *greatest fear*.

Next to the *H* was the *I*, a simple image of a brunette standing straight, her arms bound behind her, her dark bush cropped into a vertical line that matched her body. Her eyes and mouth were covered in the white bands, her dark hair pulled back tight.

"All women, I see."

"Take a look at the other wall," Jon said, pointing to the narrow wall at the far end of the room.

She walked by the other photos on the long wall, quickly noting the letters: a woman on her back with her legs lifted by a rope: *L*; *two* women wrapped around the black cylinder, their wrists and ankles bound to each other's in a big *O*.

On the far wall, partly taken up by a closed door, were three photos of nude men. One was standing straight, bound, gagged, and blindfolded as the female *I* had been. His cock was stiff, vertical, and perfectly centered: a miniature representation of the number.

"One," she said.

Another man kneeled, bound and bent over, his back arched forward—painfully, she thought, with his head bowed lower yet, pulled down by a dark cable around his neck.

"Two?"

Jon nodded.

Another was bent over at the waist, his arms bound against his sides, suspended by ropes because his legs were at a diagonal that couldn't have supported his weight.

"Seven," Janet said.

Jon bowed his head, honored.

"Who was that, out in the driveway?"

"Oh, you met him? That was my 'four'."

Janet tried to picture the pose.

"Who was he? The redhead. How did you find him?"

"Well, actually, he was sort of 'volunteered'. Carolyn sent him over. Which makes it kind of hot in a different way, you know? That he was ordered by his Mistress. Because he was less than thrilled."

Janet didn't want to talk about Carolyn. She looked at the *T*: a woman standing tall, her head hooded black, arms outstretched and bound to some kind of beam.

"But he obeyed. Perfectly," Jon said.

"Hmm." Janet clasped one hand in the other and brought them up under her chin, covering her breasts with her forearms.

It was while looking at the *V*, the last in the row of women, that she began to realize some inkling of what was bothering her. The woman was suspended upside down, hanging by her ankles, her legs spread wide. She had wide, white cuffs around her ankles, and the ropes or cables were black, leading diagonally up out of the frame. Her wrists were bound to her thighs with rope, her hands pressed flat against them. Her medium-dark pubic hair—a redhead?—had been trimmed into an *upside-down* triangle—so that the peak pointed toward her navel, matching the V-shape of her body. Gravity pulled her smallish breasts downward, toward her shoulders. Her light nipples were barely visible.

As with the others, the woman wore white bands over her mouth and eyes, and her hair had been styled into a peak, making a sharp point that hovered just above the bottom of the frame. Janet looked closely, and saw that her face was turning dark—red, no doubt, from the blood rushing to her head, and it not only matched her hair, but she also saw that the blindfold and gag were darker than the fresh white in the other photos.

Good God, the sheer perfectionism of the image. The lengths to which Jon had gone to ensure that perfection, the focus that would have been necessary. Janet felt a tightening in her chest and her wetness starting deep within her. The attention that this woman had received, to be made into a mere letter, one of many.

Janet still wasn't quite sure what was nagging at her. It wasn't jealousy, exactly…

She looked again at the *T*. The woman, a brunette judging from her bush that had been trimmed into a tiny "T", stood hooded—to keep her head from protruding above the top bar of the letter—and her arms were bound with white rope to the wide beam at her wrists, her elbows, upper arms and shoulders. Her neck. She had waited, submitting to the click of Jon's camera, after standing very still while he'd tied each rope one at a time. It must have taken hours. Janet longed for that experience, and yet feared it, face hidden or not.

She felt dread at what she'd agreed to do with Dmitri, but she finally realized what else was bothering her:

Up until now, whenever she'd been with Jon, she could see the adoration in his eyes. In the hotel, in her house, at the bookstore.

She thought she'd been the center of his attention. His aesthetic, if not emotional attention.

But here was evidence to the contrary. All these weeks he'd gone without calling her, while she waited by the phone—she knew he had a life, sure—but here it was. He wasn't her own personal fantasy Dom, gazing at her longingly while still disciplining her. He was photographing women, bound and gagged—lots of them—focusing on them with that goddamned sexy concentration and methodicism, that sense of knowing exactly what he wanted and how to get it. So…*thorough*—while she was at home reading porn and masturbating. And waiting.

Why did this jealousy—no, this…*denial*—get her even hotter?

"Janet…"

"Yes?"

"I'd like you to be my 'X'."

"I thought maybe Amanda was your 'ex'."

"Funny. The 'X' is the hottest letter, don't you think? Spread-eagled, pulled tight"—Janet felt her wetness beginning to seep—"Your hair down around your shoulders…"

"No hood? Shouldn't I be covered; anonymous?"

"I'd make an exception. Blindfold and gag."

Janet pictured herself bound and pulled taut, spread wide for the world to see like the redhead in Dmitri's film.

"Are you going to show these publicly?"

"I hope to. I'm pretty sure I can get a show. I'd also like to make a book of them."

"Really? They'd be pirated, you know. All over the Internet."

"Cool. Fine by me. I hope people start writing letters in them. Printing business reports."

Janet looked again at the *V*, the woman hanging in so much discomfort, forged by him into art.

"There's no 'Y'," she said.

"You could be my X and Y." He moved closer to her. Could he smell her arousal? From the look in his eyes, she thought perhaps so. She could.

"Twice? Isn't that breaking the rule?"

Maybe she *did* matter to him more than these other girls. She turned to face him, lowered her arms to her sides, presented her body for his perusal. He was looking.

He placed his hands on her hips, and slid his foot forward between hers. He pushed one shoe against her naked foot, and she slid it outward, spreading her legs. He ran both hands up her ribs, and when he reached her armpits he pushed her arms up and ran his hands along them to her wrists, placing them exactly how he wanted them. She was posed into his *X*, and she felt incredibly exposed. Wonderfully exposed.

"Maybe some rules," he said as he leaned toward her mouth, "are meant—oh, hello, dear."

Janet turned. Amanda was standing at the bottom of the carpeted stairs, dressed in her white chef's uniform. A few food stains graced her abdomen, yet she looked as precise and together as the first time she'd walked through Janet's door.

Janet's jaw dropped.

"Amanda." She brought her arms down across her chest and brought her legs together. "I, uh…"

Hell, they'd *shared* her, last time—why was she so nervous?

"Sampling Jon's arts, are we?" Did she say "art", or "arts"?

"No. Yes. I mean, I hope I'm not—I mean I—" She looked to Jon for help, but he didn't seem to want to give her any. Maybe he was in trouble, too.

Amanda's eyes narrowed, an expression Janet couldn't quite place.

"Carolyn was right about one thing—you *are* a little trollop, aren't you?"

"I'm…I'm so sorry. I didn't know—I still don't know if—"

Amanda stepped into the center of the room, ignoring the photographs.

"And you *still* haven't learned proper respect, have you, you little wench?" She was cool as could be, no signs of temper.

"I'm so sorry! I didn't know you were—or I was—Ma'am! I'm so sorry, Ma'am!" Janet felt as foolish and panicked as she had that first night.

Amanda pointed down to the carpet at her feet, snapped her fingers, and Janet dropped to her hands and knees and crawled, fast and humble, to the woman who so intimidated her merely with her calm tone of voice. She kissed her shoes. Sneakers, she was wearing; probably on her feet all day.

"Up on your knees."

Janet wanted to run upstairs, gather her clothes, make a run for it. She could dress in the car. She kneeled up. How did this woman always make her feel like a child in trouble?

"So," Amanda said, looking straight down at her, "you

think you can come into my house—"

"*Your* house?" She looked over her shoulder at Jon, standing with his arms crossed over his chest.

"Eyes. Up. Here," Amanda said, and Janet focused on her like an anxious puppy.

"Just what do you think you're doing here?"

"I'm so sorry! I didn't know!"

"Didn't know what?"

"That you and Jon are…are…" *What?* "Look, are you and Jon—"

"Jon and Dmitri are also right about one thing, you little scamp. You do need more training."

Janet's jaw dropped again, her mouth a perfect "O" to match the two women in the photo.

"But I—"

"*And* you still don't know how to show respect."

"I'm sorry, Ma'am! I—"

"Well, as long as you're here. Jon, you don't mind if I…?" She pointed upstairs.

"Not at all, my dear."

Janet wanted to look back at Jon, but she was already down kissing Amanda's shoes again.

"Come on. You sneak into my house, intending to use it for your pleasure—"

"But I was invited! Jon invited me! *Ow!*" Janet felt a stinging slap on her ass as Amanda bent over her.

"My God, you disrespectful little minx. You think you can interrupt and talk to me like that in my own house?"

Janet wasn't sure, but she thought Amanda sounded more amused than angry. But she lowered her face, her ass raised high.

"I asked you a question."

"No, Ma'am. Please forgive me!"

"I was going to say…" she waited for Janet to interrupt

again, "…that if you think you can use *my* house as you please, the least you can do is clean it for me, yes?"

Janet raised her face to look up.

"What?"

"We'll start with the kitchen."

Janet froze, unsure of what to do. She was going to have to *work*?

"Up the stairs, come on. What are you waiting for?" She bent and slapped Janet again, on the other ass cheek, and Janet cried out in surprise.

"Go. Go go go go go go *go!*"

Janet stood and ran up the stairs as fast as she could, her forearm across her breasts to keep them from bouncing. Climbing, she looked back at Jon, and thought she saw the slightest of smiles on his face.

❖

Janet kneeled on the hard kitchen tiles at the sink as Amanda filled the bucket with water. She could barely see over the counter. She looked around the kitchen: tile floor, slate counters (lots of maintenance), high-end appliances; a breakfast nook in the bay widow at the far end, lots of glass—and visibility. Everything was placed with precision—a row of utensils arrayed by function above the counter, knives in a thick wood block arranged by size.

"I should have you do this," Amanda said, "But I want the temperature *exactly* right."

She shut the water off and dropped the plastic bucket onto the floor in front of Janet; it made a loud thud and the water splashed up onto her chest and stomach.

"Feel that water. Remember the temperature for next time." *Next time?* "Here's your scrub brush. You will scrub every inch of this kitchen floor, perfectly."

No "or else"; none necessary as Janet bowed her head. Amanda handed her the brush and a towel.

"You'll mop it dry after every few feet. I want it *spotless*, do you understand?"

Janet could not believe this was happening. A few minutes ago she was in Jon's arms, ready to break her rule about being photographed (not that the rule meant what it used to, now that she'd literally signed on with Dmitri); an hour before that she'd been at her desk sorting failed insurance claims with the government.

"Yes, Ma'am," she said. She shook her head at her own malleability. She wet the brush and started scrubbing.

Amanda stood over her and watched.

"No, child. We're going to have to work on your postures, I see. You're on *display*, understand? Do you really think I'd bother having you scrub my floor naked if I only wanted it clean?"

"…No? Ma'am?"

"Spread your knees. Keep that little ass of yours high. *Higher*. Make a show for me, dear." Now she said it: "Or you'll pay later."

"Dmitri said he doesn't want me marked for my shoot!" Janet ducked her head as Amanda sighed in resignation.

"You *do* need some serious training, don't you child."

Janet heard the few tones of Amanda's speed-dial on her phone.

"Jon. When you come upstairs—yes, I know. Do they look good? Are you happy with the shoot? Excellent. When you come back up, could you bring a ball gag for our guest? She has a little problem with speaking out of turn."

Janet cried out as she felt two fingers being inserted deep into her sex with remarkable ease.

"Hear that? No self-discipline. Better make it the penis gag, Jon. Yes, the big one."

Amanda twisted her fingers inside Janet, and Janet struggled to stay quiet. But she couldn't help moaning in pleasure, arching her back, wriggling her exposed backside as Amanda so casually worked her magic.

"She also can't seem to do two things at once. She is easily distracted from her work. We have a lot of work to do on her, don't we. She's certainly eager, I'll give her that. What did you say to her to get her in such a state?"

Janet started scrubbing frantically but without focus, unable to concentrate. Amanda was getting her so…close…

"And Dmitri is insisting we don't mark her? That is so inconvenient…" She withdrew her fingers, stepped in front of Janet, and held them in front of Janet's lowered face.

"Clean them," she said. Janet took the fingers into her mouth and sucked on them like they were a stiff cock, tasting her own obvious excitement, sticky and tangy.

"You mentioned she has an aversion to nipple clamps," Amanda said into the phone. "Yes? Likes to express her displeasure? Good. Bring a pair up. That should be an interesting combination. We will honor Dmitri's request. Mm-hm. Thank you, dear." She ended the call and pulled her fingers from Janet's mouth.

"Work, you lazy little vixen," she said. "Work!" Janet began swinging the brush back and forth across the tile. "And thank me for the opportunity."

"Thank you, Mistress!" Janet said, desperately missing Amanda's fingers, anywhere.

Amanda had turned toward the cabinets above the counter, but stopped and looked down at Janet.

"What did you call me, child?"

Janet hesitated. Every time Amanda addressed her, it had been in the diminutive—little this, little that, child, girl. It was ridiculous, but it was having an effect, down on her hands and knees like this. She still felt like a total newbie.

Janet wanted to sit and talk with Amanda, ask her questions about her dominatrix past, her catering present, sympathize with her for being tired after work. But it was getting harder and harder to picture herself doing any of that.

"Thank you, Ma'am, for the opportunity to acquire some discipline. I know I need it."

"Good girl. Now clean my floor. And when you're done, you may wash my windows."

Janet looked up in shock.

"Outside?"

Amanda opened a cupboard above the counter and took out a little foil bag of some kind of snack. From the look Amanda gave her, Janet knew she'd made another mistake, speaking up.

"Ma'am?"

"Just the insides. But you'd better hurry with the floor. Once it gets dark, and the lights are on in here, it'll be much easier for aaaall my neighbors to see you."

Janet lowered her head.

"Now, as for these little outbursts of yours..."

Amanda ripped open the bag, and a shower of bright orange particles rained down in front of Janet onto the floor—popcorn. That nasty, cheesy, convenience-store popcorn that she'd always hated. So awful and fake-tasting. Popcorn should be *popcorn*.

"Oh, no," Amanda said, oh-so sadly. "Look at this mess. I guess we'll just have to keep your mouth occupied until Jon brings us the gag."

Janet looked up as Amanda walked to the little breakfast nook, dropping a trail of the vile little treats in her wake.

"Ma'am?"

"You know what to do. *Spotless*, Janet."

Janet had no doubt that Amanda's kitchen floor was probably the cleanest surface in the entire Metro area. But eating off of it? And eating *these* foul little things?

Amanda flopped back onto the bench of her breakfast table, and crunched one of the few remaining bits still in the bag. Why did a chef even have these in her house?

"What are you waiting for?"

Janet lowered her face to the floor, and took one of the horrible little kernels into her mouth with her tongue. Crunchy, faux-cheesy; awful. Plasticky. She gave Amanda a pleading look from as low to the ground as she could.

"Don't try that with me," Amanda said. "And you had better finish the floor before Jon comes up. He's in his studio, looking over his photo shoot from today. But I'm sure he'll want to see you framed in the windows, like a lovely artwork."

His studio, her house, her neighbors—no "our." Janet didn't understand. She also didn't want to wash the windows in the nude, but she took another wretched little piece of popcorn into her mouth and chewed and swallowed as quickly as possible.

She wanted to see the picture Jon had taken. Would she be allowed to? How had that redheaded boy been contorted into a "4"? *That* would be quite an artwork. But she knew better than to ask, right now.

"Don't forget to scrub, dear. This isn't only snack time, you know."

Amanda must have seen Janet's crestfallen face.

"*Attitude*, Janet. Buck it up, when you come into someone else's house. It's not all about *you*."

Janet was learning this, today. She scrubbed the spot where the popcorn had shed its disgusting orange powder on the tile. She bent down for the next piece as she slowly crawled toward Amanda.

Amanda kicked off her shoes. "If you do a good enough job, I'll let you give me a nice foot rub. Would you like that?"

Janet pictured herself with Amanda on the terrace of some bar or in some coffee shop downtown after shopping—chatting, laughing, having a girls' night out. Equals. Talking about men. Talking about Jon? No—she let the thought go.

She bowed for another piece of the nasty popcorn and took it into her mouth and grimaced as she crunched it. She scrubbed the thin line of powdery, artificially flavored cheese-food product out of the grout between two tiles. Her naked breasts swayed with the effort.

She had given up drinks with the girls for this.

"Yes, Ma'am," she said. "I would like that very much."

Chapter Thirteen

Ken was on the 147th Street overpass, calming himself by making lists, figuring out permutations in his head. Traffic was moving at a slow but steady rate. He checked the dashboard clock anyway—no problem there, at least.

He was feeling that particular Friday tension that was both comforting and full of anxiety—what kind of mood would his Mistress be in? It was the unexpected, with Her, that always made this drive so filled with both dread and anticipation, a deep, deep urgency that made his face hot and his hands cold.

He was visualizing sexual power structures, mentally drawing grids and maps. Simple enough, at least at first. When the relationships were between two people, there were only four possibilities as far as gender (until you got into transgenders, etc., which he hadn't, in his experience) and power: woman dominates man, as was the case in his life (or that was his ideal; that's where it got complicated); man dominates woman; man tops man, woman tops woman.

What fun. With three persons, it should be quite simple. There were six possible triangles for one person dominating two

others: F/mm, F/ff, F/mf; and M/mm, M/ff, M/mf. Then, six
for two people topping one submissive: FF/m (as had been the
case when Jennifer had been over), FM/m (more than once in
his life, with various male friends She'd brought over), MM/m
(not yet, at least). And then of course with a female submissive,
there would be FF/f, FM/f, MM/f.

All pretty hot combinations to think about. But what
about when these pairs of Doms or subs weren't really equal?
When Jennifer had been over, yes they both dominated Ken,
very much so; but the women weren't equal. His Mistress was
still very much in charge even though She shared him almost
equally—almost. It was more like F>F>m, or would it be written F>f>m?

There really needed to be some kind of proper notation
for this. Written out, it would be FEMALE>Female>male. All
caps, one cap, no caps. Yes.

But when four people were involved, good God, it got
complicated. You could have one topping three others, two
topping two, or three topping one. He'd been involved in all
three basic structures, but if he were to break it down into gen-
ders, how many possibilities were there, and how many had he
been in? *Let's see…*

Seventeen, off the top of his head. And, thinking, he had
been in nearly every possible combination, except of course for
the four that involved only one female sub: MMM/f, FFF/f,
MMF/f, and MFF/f. Oh, and the three using two female subs:
MM/ff, FF/ff, MF/ff.

He'd served with both another man and a woman for his
Mistress and another woman as well as male friends of Hers, so
he'd been in FM/fm, FF/fm, FM/mm and FF/mm situations.
Jesus, who *hadn't* he had sex with/been whipped by?

But again, it got more complicated once the different levels
of power were factored in. Yes, he'd once submitted to three
male friends of Hers—and it was not a fun night. He'd been

sore for days, and in more ways than one. So while it was technically the MMM/m option, She was on top of them all. But then we're getting into *five*-person permutations.

And that big night during Training Week? That five-on-one orgy? (Or one-on-five, more accurately.) How the hell would that be charted out? His Mistress on top, definitely; then three females and two males mid-level; then him on the very bottom. The *very* bottom. So: FEMALE>FFFMM>m? But She had taken one of them to bed, he'd had to rank higher than the other four.

Oh—he was here already, at Her house.

And there was another car in the driveway, a beat up old Honda.

❖

Ken entered the secluded little courtyard entryway and stripped, placed his clothes beside someone else's—hoodie, jeans, expensive sneakers—in the bench that doubled as a chest. His collar was still there, as usual. He padlocked the bench shut, locked his collar and rang the doorbell, waited on his knees.

His Mistress opened the door and said, "Come," and he was relieved when She gestured for him to enter. At this house, that could have meant one of several things.

"Crawl."

She seemed happy today, excited. He crawled. He glanced *ever* so briefly at the Asian girl in the alcove, exact same pose as always; briefest of glances back at him.

"Do not look at her," Carolyn said without looking back, but also without urgency. He passed with his head ducked down, eyes to the floor. His Mistress stepped into the living room and waited as he followed, Her hands clasped demurely in front of Her.

He stopped at Her feet, but his attention was drawn upward: standing on the table was a naked man, a redhead like himself.

Just like himself.

She'd done it.

Ken forgot to kiss his Mistress's feet in greeting as he gawked up at this new person, who was looking back at him with what was probably the same baffled expression. The guy was fair-skinned, and had the same ruddy-red shade of hair as Ken. He had a similar build, and he worked out, but not insanely so, same as Ken. Unlike Ken, his cock was fully erect. He stood on the coffee table at perfect attention, no electric torture devices attached to him.

"Kenny, this is James. Jimmy, this is Kenneth." She tilted Her head to the side, all very proper. "Isn't there anything you'd like to say, Kenny?"

"Hello, James," he said. Who *was* this? Clearly not a "Sir."

"Jimmy, anything to say to Kenneth?"

"Hello, Sir," Jimmy said. James.

"Kenneth is not a 'Sir,' Jimmy. He is my slave, just like you."

"Hey, Kenneth."

"That informality will cost you."

"Hello, Kenneth."

"Better. I thought it was time you two met," Carolyn said. "James is new. I've only had him a few weeks, now," She told Ken. A few weeks? Ken hadn't seen any sign of anyone new. Usually he could sense *something* different when She had a new toy—a scent, something.

She'd finally got Her other redhead.

"Jimmy, Kenneth has been with me for over a year. I adore him so much I wanted another one. You're it." Jimmy's cock stayed rock hard, and Ken could see the indecision in his eyes, wondering if he should say something. He wisely stayed quiet, stayed at perfect attention.

"Kenny, James is so beautiful I had him photographed today."

Ken looked up, unsure of how to feel—that She found his near-twin beautiful meant She found him beautiful as well, but not enough to photograph, apparently.

"You remember my friend Jon? You've sucked his cock once or twice."

"Yes, Mistress."

A tall Dom, brown hair, some kind of history with Her. Fond of holding Ken's head in place while he fucked his mouth, often while continuing his conversation with his Mistress.

"He's doing this little art project. Photographing people shaped like letters and numbers or something. He said he needed a boy, a pretty one, asked if I knew any. I said, 'Do I!' and sent Jimmy over. I think I'll have it framed when I see it; wouldn't you like to see that, Kenny?"

"Yes, Mistress."

People shaped like letters? What the hell did that mean? What kind of new mind-fuck was all this? He waited on his hands and knees but felt a pang of jealousy—no, insecurity.

"Do you notice anything a little off, though, Kenny?"

Ken looked up again at the pale man on the table.

"He's not shaved, Mistress," he said. Carolyn had always demanded meticulous grooming from Ken, usually doing it Herself: balls shaved, and everything between his legs back to his asshole, which was waxed or—

—She handed him the roll of duct tape. He knew the duct tape well; poor man's wax job, not that She was poor. She just enjoyed the spectacle. He kneeled up to take it, and She gestured for him to rise. She then signaled Jimmy to come down from the table.

"Follow me, boys," She said.

❖

Ken kneeled in the bathroom, Jimmy's stiff cock in his face. A tiny drop of moisture had gathered on its tip. Ken had lathered the shaving cream onto Jimmy's balls as well as behind them, and his Mistress handed him the razor, an expensive cartridge type—his. He detested sharing the razor more than having to shave Jimmy.

Carolyn had turned on all the lights in the room, to make it easier for him to see. It gave the space a very harsh, clinical feel, nothing hidden.

"Get to it," Carolyn said. She was matter-of-fact but smirking a bit, one of those moods when She simply enjoyed knowing She was boss.

For all the practice on himself he'd had, Ken wasn't sure how to start. He was backwards, facing the cock; it was like trying to tie a necktie from in front. He started at the base of Jimmy's shaft, shaved downward, but that was awkward. So he grasped the top of the scrotum and squeezed, making Jimmy flinch, and shaved the tightened skin upward, first one side, then the other. Jimmy gasped with every shift of Ken's grip.

For all their superficial resemblances, Ken felt he and Jimmy looked nothing alike, and it was especially true for their members: Ken's was ramrod straight, with a rounded, bullet-like head, while Jimmy's was...well, it was larger and thicker. It also had a slight upward curve to it, and its head was not smooth and convex like Ken's but more conical, a sharper point.

Ken reached up to rinse off the razor in the sink that Jimmy was leaning against, then returned his attention to the balls in front of him. He continued to bare one side, making it all nice and smooth, then concentrated on the bottom, shifting his grip to stretch out different parts of the skin.

Jimmy moaned as he did this, arched his back.

Blue

"Hold still," Carolyn said.

Ken was surprised She had tolerated this much hair on him for several weeks, if that really was how long he'd been around. She was *such* a stickler for neatness.

"Yes, Mistress," Jimmy said. *Mistress?* Had She formally taken him in? Usually She demanded "Ma'am" from mere playthings. But She didn't correct him. Ken risked a quick glance up at Her. She was watching his hands on Jimmy's cock.

Jimmy was beginning to rock his hips at Ken's touches. Ken didn't know how to calm him down.

"Haven't you ever been shaved, Jimmy?" She said.

"No Mistress," Jimmy answered, his voice quivering. He reached behind him and gripped the sink with both hands.

"Hold *still*," She told him. "And spread your legs wider." He whimpered as Ken lifted his balls and ran the razor back between his legs.

"Wider, lean back," Carolyn said, and he did. Ken was worried about cutting him. But then again, no he wasn't. He smiled a little at the thought.

"Hold. Still."

"Yes, Mis—"

Jimmy's cock twitched as Ken ran the razor back again, farther this time.

His—their?—Mistress handed Ken the roll of gray duct tape.

"Turn around, Jimmy."

Jimmy obeyed, and braced himself against the sink while Carolyn pulled at a thigh to separate his legs.

"Bend over a little."

Ken pulled a few inches from the roll, tore it off. He made a crease down its length, and inserted the folded tape into the crack of Jimmy's ass. Jimmy leaned forward and said "Oh, no," as Ken pulled the tape, as hard as possible.

Jimmy shuddered, gripped the bathroom vanity. Ken tossed

the hairy tape into the trash, and tore another piece from the roll. *This* was fun. Disgusting, but fun.

Again. A tiny screech emitted from Jimmy's mouth.

"Mistress?" Ken said, asking for Her approval.

But She was preoccupied with Jimmy's face. He looked up, and saw that She was cradling his jaw in Her hand, forcing him to face Her.

"Kenny, you've almost made him cry," She said. "Look at him." She turned Jimmy's head back as far as it would go over his shoulder. From his low vantage point, Ken could see Jimmy's eyes watering. *Fucking amateur.*

"Aw," She said, stroking Jimmy's face. "I think you should make it up to him, Kenny, don't you think?"

Ken did not think so at all.

"Yes, Mistress," he said.

Carolyn turned Jimmy around by the shoulders, and he was once again confronted with Jimmy's erect cock.

"Yes what, Kenny?"

"May I please be allowed to make it up to Jimmy—"

"That's James, to you."

"May I please be allowed to make it up to James for hurting him, Mistress?"

This burned. This really, really burned. Who *was* this? He'd interacted with other slaves dozens of times, males even, certainly—but always at parties, and never *Her* others. And never someone selected to make *some* sort of statement, to him, whatever it was. Or about him, maybe?

"Why yes, Kenny. I think that would be the least you could do." She gave him that devious look. "Only *I* am allowed to make my slaves cry. Unless I tell you to, which I did not."

That meant that there would likely be punishment in addition to this, which already felt like punishment at the moment.

She looked at Ken, then at the rock hard cock in front of his face, then back to Ken.

"Well?"

Might as well get it over with. Ken exhaled, and the cock flinched at the mere current of air. *This shouldn't take long, at least.* Ken licked his lips and let Jimmy's pointed head penetrate them. He took it in a reasonable depth and held it, then backed away, then moved in again. No finesse or teasing. *Let's just do this.*

He sucked the hard dick methodically, hands at his sides.

"Better enjoy it like it was your own, Kenny," his Mistress said. The playfulness in Her voice was gone; She was making a point. "Because this weekend, it is."

Ken marveled at Her ability to know exactly which buttons to push. His cock would not be touched, this weekend. Jimmy's would substitute for his. He closed his eyes in resignation as he sucked, and as his own cock began to swell in size.

There was something about the *denial* of his own organ that always added a new layer of shame and complexity to this. And She knew that he both hated it and yet somehow responded to it.

There were different categories of cocksucking, each with its own attendant levels of humiliation. There were his Mistress's friends, some of whom he disliked intensely (thank God the Smirking Man hadn't been over in a while), but many of whom he felt a certain satisfaction, almost a pride in serving his Mistress by perfectly servicing. Then there was performing with other slaves; sometimes female but often male. He was always rock hard for these encounters, usually with a small crowd watching, as he was splayed out in some living room or playroom or old-fashioned dungeon—sixty-nining, being made a slave's slave, whatever the Masters and guests wanted. There was something about being the naked center of attention, the spectacle itself, an entertaining object, that he had to admit he found thrilling.

But he had never interacted in any way with any of Her

other slaves, the people who came and went during the week when he sat at home watching TV and trying not to think about it. Barring any parties, he was Hers alone on weekends.

Until now. He didn't understand it.

What *was* all this? Was he sucking his own possible replacement's pale pink cock? And why did he automatically assume Jimmy was his replacement? He was filled with jealousy, and jealousy was something a person in this kind of life couldn't afford. This Life could destroy a jealous person.

He could feel the blood rush to his face, and to his own throbbing cock, useless and untouched. He wanted to grab it, stroke his own balls, jack off. Ease the tension and distraction and try to figure all this out.

Ken glanced up as he sucked, and saw his Mistress still holding Jimmy by the chin, staring into his eyes.

Ken adjusted his posture to get a better angle, and bobbed his head up and down on the dick, sucking on its pointed head. He raised his hands and jacked the base, the wet, slippery base. He squeezed the newly smooth balls, released them, stroked them. *Come on.*

Jimmy moaned. Ken could feel the tension building in Jimmy's cock, the tightening in his balls. And in his own, aching for release that would not come.

But Jimmy was about to. He was thrusting his hips as he gripped the sink, and Ken sucked and jacked up and down the slick shaft. Jimmy cried out as his first shot filled Ken's throat, then Carolyn moaned as She covered Jimmy's mouth with Her own.

A kiss?

Ken was in shock as Jimmy thrust his hips forward, filling Ken's mouth with his hardness and semen. Carolyn reached down and pulled Ken's head back by the hair. He kept jacking, and now Jimmy was coming onto his face, his bright red embarrassed face. She held him there, inches from the tip of

Jimmy's pink cock, the white fluid ejecting toward him. He kept jacking, knew this was what was expected. Ken kept his mouth shut, although he knew it was also expected for him to kneel with his mouth wide open, tongue extended.

He didn't. Jimmy shot onto Ken's forehead, both cheeks, and one last massive load across his entire face, from one cheekbone to the opposite side of his chin. He leaned forward to catch the last few dribbles with his tongue; better than having to lick them off the floor.

Everyone settled down, although Ken's cock was still erect. Ken swallowed the foul come in his mouth—especially foul because it was Jimmy's, this other redhead—and jacked the wet cock. He looked up at his Mistress, who was no longer kissing Jimmy but still held him in place, watching Jimmy's eyes. Watching his face as he came. She liked to do this with Ken, too, sometimes. Or She used to.

She smiled with deep satisfaction.

"Don't you think you should thank him?" She said. "Kenny?"

"Thank you James," he said, seething. Would he be allowed to wipe off his face, or not?

He would not.

"Did I tell you to stop?" Carolyn asked him.

"No, Mistress."

"Suck him hard, again," She said, and watched him do it, as did Jimmy. This *was* a new level of humiliation, both faces looking down like that.

He ran his fingers not only over Jimmy's balls but behind them, back and forth, felt the newly shaved smoothness. Jimmy responded, his cock firming up and regaining its upward curve.

Ken's head bobbed until Carolyn was satisfied.

"Good job, Jimmy," She said, ignoring Ken.

"Stand up," She told him, and he stood next to Jimmy, his

face still covered in come.

"My boys," Carolyn said, smiling proudly. "Look at you two. Kenny, run down to the playroom and get me something. Actually, don't run; walk. Take your time."

He was most disappointed when She told him what it was.

❖

Ken came up from the basement holding the dildo in his hands like a revered samurai sword. It was nearly as long. Black, and, what he dreaded most, both ends were rounded with prominent cock heads. He had the lube in one hand, as well.

He rounded the corner to the living room, and saw that Jimmy was on his hands and knees in front of his Mistress, head bobbing and swirling—he was pleasuring Her. Ken felt another stab of jealousy—like a stubborn demon, he wasn't going to be able to exorcise it, today.

Ken had decided early on to use these feelings—jealousy, envy, possessiveness (yes, he wanted to possess Her, or to at least be Her only possession)—to add to the intensity of this insane experience, this Life here. Actually, it wasn't so much a "decision" as what always happened, so he accepted it. Like when She had taken that man to bed, that big night of Training Week. It had hurt so much to watch Her go, to be able to do nothing about it—an even more complete form of powerlessness, only sweetened because it was imposed by Her. And he had obeyed Her. There was an intense desperation to it that made him suck the Smirking Man with total devotion to his task, hate it though he might.

He knew it made no sense.

Ken's jaw dropped when he was close enough to see that She was completely naked.

She was reclining far down into the chair, Her favorite

leather chair, Her legs spread wide, watching Jimmy as he licked Her clit—*and Jimmy was watching Her.*

Her face! They were looking into each other's eyes, as She allowed him to perform this most sacred act upon Her. And Jimmy was gazing at Her perfect face; She was allowing him to look up and down the length of Her body. Her naked body.

Ken felt nauseous. He wanted to tackle Jimmy and rescue Her from what must have been a mistake, an assault. He wanted to run to the bathroom and throw up, the smell of Jimmy's drying semen on his face not helping. His Mistress hardly ever let *anyone* see Her entirely naked, slaves at least. As far as honored guests that She allowed into Her bedroom, he could not know. But this was most unusual. *Most* unusual. It was such a shock to Ken that he couldn't even pinpoint the emotions, other than a stab to the heart.

He had been blindfolded while She was naked many times, but he'd only seen Her completely nude on two occasions since he'd been with Her.

Neither time had he touched Her: She'd teased him once, dressing in front of him like it was no big deal, casual lovers enjoying the weekend together, chatting. And there was one time he'd served Her breakfast, She sitting at the table in nothing at all while he kneeled to pour Her coffee, serve Her eggs and toast. He'd sneaked every glance he could at the perfection of Her lean and fit body—Her muscular thighs, Her flat and muscled stomach, Her breasts which were not overly large but so, so firm.

And here was this…fucking *punk*, who apparently looked like him, licking Her pussy and staring right at Her. *Right at Her tits.* At Her *eyes.*

Ken wanted to take a swing at him. His erection fell with each heartbeat.

But he kneeled down, beside Jimmy, and held the long evil dildo high, in offering. He closed his eyes to shut out the scene.

"Thank you, Kenny," She said, not taking Her eyes off of Jimmy, who was definitely enjoying his work.

"Kenny, apply the lube, and shove that dildo right up James's ass."

Jimmy's eyes widened but he didn't stop.

Ken wanted to say "With pleasure, Mistress," but did not. He'd been trained to obey in silence. He squirted the lube onto the dildo, though not much. He did not rub any onto Jimmy's asshole.

He shoved, enough to push Jimmy forward.

"Easy! Both of you. Jimmy, hold yourself steady. If I feel the mere *presence* of teeth, I will whip you so fucking hard…"

But She didn't finish Her sentence. Jimmy braced himself and went back to work, licking, lapping. Ken thrust the dildo deeper as Jimmy grunted in what he hoped was serious pain.

"Now, you," his Mistress said. Ken applied a much more generous amount of lube onto the other end, especially its wide head. He knew it was not proper protocol to reach back and smear it onto his own anus; such a maneuver and posture was viewed as awkward and unseemly by his Mistress.

"You know what to do."

Ken got on his hands and knees and moved behind Jimmy, facing away. Facing away from the both of them, from what they were doing. He reached behind him, found the big black cock, and placed it against his asshole. He pressed himself back against Jimmy, not too hard, or he would shove him into Her again, and he did not want those consequences once he had been warned.

It was thick, and long. He smiled, since his back was to Her, at the thought of the discomfort his rude shove had given Jimmy. He slid back.

He cringed as his own ass cheeks pressed against Jimmy's. There was some sorting out to do of shins and calves and feet. Once pegged, he could feel Jimmy's motions through the dildo and their flesh: he was licking, swirling, moving his head, lowering his body for a better angle. His Mistress moaned.

She gave Ken no new orders. He merely felt and listened, while his Mistress moaned repeatedly, louder, until he heard Her come. Jimmy's motions slowed but did not stop.

God damn it—only Ken knew every nuance, every tiny movement to *truly* make Her come. Sure this guy could lap away until She got there. But it would never compare to his tongue. How long would it take Her to see that? Or would this jerk figure it all out before She did?

"All right, you two," She said. "Fuck each other. With it." She was sounding a little incoherent. But Ken, and Jimmy, both started moving, on their hands and knees, shifting forward then back.

"My gorgeous boys."

Ken realized the error of his earlier decision to deny Jimmy the lube—the dildo was firmly implanted up Jimmy's ass, stable, while it was sliding well into and out of Ken's more lubricated hole. He actually might get the worst of it. But at least Jimmy would hurt like hell.

"Harder, boys. I want to see those asses slam against each other, I want to hear your balls slap together." Ken moved faster; forward, back.

"Faster, Kenny."

Ken grunted as the dildo slammed into his ass and his cheeks backed against Jimmy's.

"You too," She told Jimmy, in a softer, gentler tone.

Ken swore he could feel, through the shaft of rubber between them and the contact of ass to ass, his Mistress running Her fingers through his new adversary's hair. His new enemy.

"And don't you dare look up at my art project in the alcove, Kenny," She said.

Ken glanced up. The Asian girl was standing still, as she always did, beautifully lit and radiant in her recessed nook, heavy steel collar and thick rope hanging from her, all so precisely arranged. As always, her hands were behind her back, and she did not look up.

But Ken did look. With his back to his Mistress so naked and spread, and Her new boy, a pale copy of *him*, Ken kept his head lowered but his eyes up. He didn't glance, he stared. He thrust himself back and forth, limp cock swinging with each stroke, dildo jamming farther and farther up his own ass until it hurt so bad he was almost crying.

His Mistress was groaning, and on any other day She would have been attentive enough to *know* that he was staring at the beautiful girl in the alcove. He was *leering* at her, goddamn it.

In his mind he was fucking her, from behind, his thick cock buried deep in her little Asian pussy, then her tight little ass. She was screaming, begging for mercy. What would her voice sound like? In his mind, he would come on her face.

His Mistress came once again, as he impaled himself on the dildo, harder and harder, and before he knew it his cock was very, very stiff.

Ken hated himself for being such a fool, such a…well, he couldn't very well call himself a cuckold. This was what he'd always pledged to do: whatever She wanted.

This was what Obedience *was*: the giving of yourself to another. You don't always like it, what She wants. And part of the thrill might *be* that you don't always like it. You do what She says. You are free from decisions—you just *do*. She wants a cock in your mouth, you take a cock into your mouth. She wants a dildo up your ass, you take a dildo up your ass. You follow the Rules.

But Ken couldn't help feeling that things were slipping beyond the Rules, or maybe the Rules were changing, and not for the better, and not in an orderly way. Things had never been entirely pleasant here, but that was all right, that was what he wanted. To serve Her. To be the center of Her attention, even when She was making such a *point* of ignoring him that he knew he was still in Her mind. To be punished, sometimes, let's face it. But this was all new, today; too many changes at once. Everything was sliding around, out of place, becoming unstable. He didn't understand what was going on, and though it wasn't his place to, he felt like something was definitely changing, and not for the better.

He didn't like it. Not one bit.

Chapter Fourteen

"I wish we could put the top down."

Jon shrugged. "It's *your* hair."

They were barreling down the freeway, or at least they had been; traffic rarely barreled so near downtown. The wind whistled through the loose seam where the old canvas top of Jon's '68 LeSabre locked into the windshield, but she couldn't feel any airflow from it. And the massive car's ancient air conditioner wasn't keeping up with the last of the day's heat. She cranked—with a crank—the window down a bit. She didn't want to sweat.

"Maybe on the way back?" he said.

Janet crossed her arms and looked out the window. Downtown meant they were almost there and yes, she was nervous. She was wearing a loose T-shirt, a soft knee-length skirt, and nothing else. Dmitri didn't want to waste time waiting for the lines from any elastic to fade away. She had her tiny bag with her, nothing but the minimal (except for the bright red lipstick) makeup Dmitri had sent over (via courier!), which she'd already applied. And of course those accursed, infernal *things* he'd told her to bring. She kicked her flip-flops onto the floor.

She looked down over the streets between the skyscrapers as they passed them by. There were surprisingly few cars in the deep asphalt valleys. Rush hour was already over; people were about to start coming in looking for restaurants and entertainment.

"I saw in the rag that there's some kind of Fetish Ball down here next week," Janet said. She'd seen the big ad in the local cultural weekly, which wasn't really local, some corporation out of state owned it but it was the best they had. It was a full-page ad, photos from last year probably, people dressed in latex and PVC and black leather, or barely dressed at all. People leading others on leashes, some bound and gagged, lots of very, very high heels. Crowds of them. "Do you ever go to those?"

Jon didn't say anything for a long time, pretending to watch a truck overtaking them in the mirror.

"Not anymore," he said. "We're not really…welcome, downtown. Anymore."

Janet turned to look at him.

"What? Why not? Who? Who says?" This was news.

"Me, Amanda, Carolyn. We sort of…I don't really want to talk about it."

"Oh come on. Jesus, look what I'm about to do. It can't be that bad. Tell me. What'd you do?"

"It's a different crowd. We sort of burned some bridges." And he said nothing more.

Janet watched him. She felt small on this incredibly wide bench seat, seat belts only, no shoulder straps.

"This car is huge," she said. "It's like you're cleeeear over there, and I'm cleeeear over here."

Jon smiled, gave her a sidelong glance.

"You are, doll."

They were leaving downtown behind, the city's little skyscrapers giving way to huge old warehouses and abandoned train tracks snaking between them. Those closest to downtown were being converted to lofts, the ones farther out still looked worn and beaten and vaguely dangerous.

"Here's our exit," Jon said, and he eased the blue behemoth into the turning lane. Janet shifted nervously in her seat.

"Thank you for coming with me."

"It's my pleasure. Besides, Dmitri told you *someone* would need to drive you home."

❖

Jon took the exit that descended into the Warehouse District—hundreds of metal or tarred roofs as far as Janet could see. The car sank below the rooftops, and into a canyon of large storehouses and old factories. Three more turns, and she was completely lost.

They pulled up to an old brick building, several stories high, some kind of empty factory that hadn't produced who knew what for who knew how long. Janet could see nothing in the many tall windows, just the last of the day's sunlight coming through from the other side. There were several cars lined up in front, and a cargo van. They pulled in between two small foreign cars, and Janet smiled at how big Jon's car really was. He started to come around the car to open her door, but she had already let herself out. She took a deep breath, and looked up at the huge facade of the building. They climbed up the steps to the big old wooden doors.

"You okay?" Jon asked.

"Yea."

She had expected the entire building to somehow be hollow, a big shell. But once inside the big doors they walked through a small, old foyer with a sagging drop ceiling, with cheap doors that appeared to lead to offices. It smelled musty. They came to another door at the far end of the space. It was locked; Jon knocked.

A young man dressed in jeans and grimy T-shirt opened it, looked at them both, and said, "Come in!"

Janet secretly hoped she would not be appearing with this man. His clothes were filthy, and he had a smell of sweat, of work in small spaces, about him. Wispy beard, not particularly handsome.

But friendly: "I'm Jake. I'm with the camera crew. We're just leaving. You must be the lead?"

Janet nodded, her throat a little tight.

"Pleased to meet you," he said. "Good luck, tonight."

Janet expected him to say, "*You'll need it*," but instead he pointed to their left, down the length of the long hallway they were now in.

"Mr. Corso is that way, around the corner."

Janet cleared her throat; she was going to have to talk sooner or later.

"Thank you very much. Nice to meet you, Jake."

Jake sort of bowed, and Jon and Janet walked the length of the hallway, passing what looked to be a movie camera stuck into the wall, until they came to a corner leading to the right. Attached to that corner was some kind of complex system of cables, pulleys and a motor, reaching from the floor to the ceiling. They had to step around it.

They were looking down another hallway, this one wider. There were old couches along one wall and electronic equipment that Janet could not identify along the other. There were no windows or doors; they were somewhere in the center of the big warehouse. The walls were covered in cheap, decades-old paneling, and the floor had very old, worn carpet that had once been green but was now a dingy gray. It all smelled faintly dingy, as well. The hall was dark, lit by a couple of bare light bulbs and the lights from the equipment. She saw another movie camera, again fastened to the wall, pointing through it. There were several people near what looked like some kind of sound mixing board.

"Janet! Jon!" Dmitri shouted from the group, and walked toward them. "Right on time. Welcome, Janet. Welcome." He took both of Janet's hands into his, shaking them. He kissed her hand.

"Hello, Dmitri."

He released her, then shook Jon's hand.

"Welcome, Jon! It's good to see you again. Thank you for bringing our Janet to me safely."

"It was my pleasure, Dmitri. I look forward to the evening."

"Yes, I'm sure you do. It will be quite a time we'll have." He looked at Janet and pressed the palms of his hands together, thinking.

"Yes, well. Most of these people are leaving, as soon as they pack. Everything is set up. I like to have everything prepared, then use a very small crew. This prevents anyone shooting unauthorized video, yes? I always think of music studios, some asshole, you know? Working in the studio, making a copy of a recording someone is working on, releasing it ahead of time. A bootleg." He pointed to a tiny security camera mounted to the ceiling, then another, pointed at the movie camera fastened to the wall. "Here, everyone is watched while they work. Nothing escapes me. We film the filmers."

Several crew members passed them as Dmitri spoke, pushing large black cases on tiny wheels that struggled through the old carpet. The crew went around the corner and the hallway was quiet, only three other people left near the equipment.

"Come," Dmitri said, gesturing for them to follow.

"Janet, Jon, this is David, my lighting expert; Susan, sound; and Serge, my equipment manager. Everyone, this," showing her like a fine automobile, "...is Janet."

"Hello, everyone," Janet said, trying to look casual. "Nice to meet you."

"And my friend Jon. He introduced us," pointing to himself and Janet. "He is responsible, in certain ways, for this project." He paused. "Well, Janet, why don't you go ahead and take your clothes off."

It took her a few seconds to register what he had said.

"What? Oh, okay. Now?"

"Yes. Now."

Janet felt the twinge of embarrassment and surprise that always came when that first command came. Why was she always surprised? She glanced at the crew members, who were watching, though barely.

As always, she wanted to stall. This time, it wasn't going to be private. Or even a matter of a hotel guest or two seeing her. Or just this crew. This was a commitment. She would be preserved on film, shown to strangers and locked away in vaults, foreign and, apparently, here in town. There would be a definite "before" and a definite "after," today; no going back.

Do I really want to do this? She had thought of little else since Dmitri had proposed it to her, since she'd signed the contract.

She'd thought of the redhead in the film she'd watched, how intense that would be, to be that girl. That part had thrilled her. But it was the aftermath, the consequences, that had nagged at her nonstop.

She could still back out, even while they were shooting. After that, her image would be owned by another. Was that how she wanted to be remembered, generations from now? She pictured future archaeologists, dressed in skin-tight silver jumpsuits, coming across the reel of film in a buried vault hundreds of years from now, unspooling the film and holding it up to the light, eyebrows raised.

Oh, why the hell not? Nothing in her life had ever thrilled her to her core like these last couple of months had.

"Second thoughts?" Dmitri asked. "If so, please tell me

now."

Everyone was still watching her, professionally, not ogling. She put the pressure of the situation out of her mind, the expense Dmitri must have gone to for this. He could always find *someone* else if she had to back out later.

But no. She wanted this.

"No," she said. "Sir."

Janet dropped her bag onto the sofa, pulled her T-shirt over her head and tossed it onto the couch too; unzipped her skirt and let it fall to the floor. She kicked off her flip-flops. She stood naked, hands pressed against her sides. She knew her face was bright red, but she didn't want to look down at the floor. She looked the crew in the eyes. Hell, people do this every day.

"Good," said Dmitri, evaluating. "No lines. Turn around, please."

She turned, feeling the eyes on her backside.

"A few lines where you were sitting. Not bad. Gone in a few minutes."

She turned back around to face everyone.

"We'll start soon. Do you need anything? Restroom?"

"No, I'm fine."

"Remember, it's a twenty-two minute shoot, no breaks. Possibly…invasive. Are you sure?"

"Yes. Thank you."

"Water?" Dmitri pulled a small plastic bottle from a carton by the sofa.

"A little, yes, thank you." Janet took the bottle, cracked it open, and took a sip to wet her throat.

Dmitri lifted Janet's chin with his hand. "Your makeup is perfect. Excellent. So is your hair, Janet. Your beautiful hair."

"Thank you."

"Do you have them?"

Janet looked at Dmitri, confused.

"Did you bring them?" He held out his hand.

Ah. Yes. Janet reached down for her bag, unzipped it, and pulled out the tiny box containing the sapphire nipple clamps he had given her the night they met. She handed the box to him with an irritated, pleading look.

"Serge, you have the cuffs?"

Janet nearly choked on her water as she took another sip. The man named Serge held out a handful of buckled black leather straps, with metal loops sewn into them. Dmitri took the bottle from Janet's hand, and traded Serge for the cuffs.

Dmitri kneeled in front of Janet, on both knees. He bent forward and fastened the first cuff around her left ankle, feeding the strap through the steel buckle and pulling it snug, but not painfully tight. He fastened it and wrapped the other strap around her right ankle.

Janet watched her own feet being shackled, then looked up at the others. Jon watched with fascination. The other two men, and Susan the sound woman, watched with a more professional nonchalance. What did these people do when they weren't doing this?

Dmitri stood. "Your wrists, Janet."

She extended her arms for him. As he locked the wide cuffs around each wrist, Susan pretended to check a piece of sound equipment, perhaps giving Janet a moment of relative privacy. *What sounds will Susan be recording?* Janet wondered.

She was now cuffed, and her nakedness felt different. More thorough.

"Follow me, Janet. I'll show you the set. Jon, do you mind staying here?" Jon had started to follow, but stopped.

"Oh. Okay." He seemed less than pleased. "I'll get to watch the filming, right?"

"No, Jon. I am sorry. I trust you, of course, but a rule is a rule. You should understand that."

"Oh, yea, sure. I'd love to see the set, though, at least…"

"Jon. Don't make me tell Amanda, hm?" He smiled genially.

Jon laughed, more of a snort.

"All right. All right. I'll just make myself comfortable on the sofa, here."

"Thank you, my friend. Crew, please follow me."

Janet, feeling the worn carpet beneath her bare feet, followed, the others behind her. They walked down the dark and old hallway towards another corner, yet another turn to the right. Janet looked back at Jon, disappointment and envy on his face.

They turned the corner, where another of the pulley and cable systems reached to the ceiling, and the hallway was gone, opened to the vastness of the empty warehouse. One high wall was still to their right, with yet another camera fastened into it. The left wall and ceiling had simply ended, to open, empty space. The last glow of sunset faded through the rows of windows of the far side of the building, yards and yards away, and the air was much cooler, odd considering the summer heat outside. Janet could feel her nipples tighten, goose bumps on her skin. It was an immense space, five or six stories high.

The high plywood wall to their right towered at least two stories high, Janet figured. She began to understand that they had been walking around the outside of a large square, a big cube, or room—the set, with cameras poking into it from the halls that surrounded it. They had *built* this big plywood cube, inside the cavernous space of the warehouse. What on Earth was in there?

They came to a door, before yet another corner to the fourth wall of the cube. Again the big pulley/cable system. Dmitri opened the door, held it open for her, and Janet was covered in bright white light.

She stepped in, Dmitri behind her, followed by the three members of his film crew. The musty smell was gone, replaced by fresh paint and newly cut plywood—pristine, inorganic. The mildew had somehow been more comforting.

"We do not rehearse, I have told you this. I want every-thing you experience to be a surprise."

Oh, it has been, she thought.

"But I have brought you in here so that you can see it first. I do not want your eyes wandering around the room the entire film, seeing it for the first time." His voice echoed in the huge space.

"What do you want my eyes to be doing?"

"Whatever you *feel*. I will perhaps tell you to look directly into the camera, or not to, but I hope I won't have to say any-thing."

"You'll be here with me?"

"No. You have seen the other film. I will be outside, run-ning the cameras."

Janet hugged her shoulders. She was standing near the cor-ner of a large and perfectly white room, maybe twenty feet square, and almost as high. A big, white cube. The room was nearly featureless, no windows and only the one door they had just stepped through. Janet gazed up at the high ceiling. It was white as well, with a row of lighting all around, where the walls met the ceiling. The lights were behind some kind of screening that smoothed out the light, a solid bar of soft illumination all the way around the room. Similar lighting lined the edges of one wall, ceiling to floor. The wood floor was also paint-ed white. In the center of all four walls were circles cut waist-high—with camera lenses, all aimed directly at the center of the room. Smaller holes below them were perhaps for micro-phones?

Janet took a few tentative steps in, and nearly bumped into a thin steel cable coming horizontally out from the corner near-est the door. She ducked, touching it, and her eyes followed where it led.

The room was completely bare, an empty space, but for one thing: four thin, black cables, each leading straight at eye level from a corner to the center of the room, where a wide black ring, four or five inches in diameter, was suspended by them at shoulder height. Her shoulder height.

A collar.

It was fastened to the four cables that held it there by metal rings welded to its outer surface. Janet felt a knot in her stomach. She looked at Dmitri, who motioned toward it. She walked, slowly.

The collar was wide, its top ridge curved. One side's top edge was lower, the band narrower than the other; it widened with a graceful curve to the opposite side. Janet approached it. It was made to hold the head, her head, in one position, the narrow side fitting under her chin, the curves following the jawline back, holding it, and the wider side gripping the back of her head. It was flared out to fit her skull. The collar had a thick metal clasp on its widest spot, and, she saw, a hinge on its front, opposite the clasp. She peered inside the floating collar, then touched it. It was soft, padded in black suede.

She tried to move the collar. She could lift it just slightly. It had a slight amount of up and down motion, gravity pulling against the tautness of the cables, but she could not budge it side-to-side. No matter which way she pulled or pushed, there was a cable holding it fast to the wall. It was *tight*. She looked back at Dmitri.

"The collar will keep you facing that camera there," Dmitri said. "You will not be able to turn your head, once locked into it." She ran her fingers around the inside of the ring. "It will fit tightly, but you will be able to breathe naturally. Although the only way you will be able to open your mouth"—Dmitri reached up and grasped Janet's chin between his thumb and finger—"will be to tilt your head back. You will not be able to lower your jaw. The collar is made to keep it in place." Dmitri looked into her eyes, holding her face to him. She looked back at him, then turned her head to free herself from his grip.

Her eyes followed the cables away from the collar. The cables were not fastened to anything stationary in the corners, any kind of metal ring or hook, but instead disappeared into tall, narrow, vertical slots in the very corners that ran up and down the walls several feet. She looked around; all four were the same. She remembered the complex pulley systems outside in the hall. Touching a cable, she walked to its corner. The thin slots ran from about a foot above the floor to well above her head, some eight feet high.

She looked at Dmitri in confusion, then to the others, then back at Dmitri.

"Yes, Janet. Motors behind the walls will raise the cables together in perfect unison, raising and lowering the collar as I see fit, while you are locked in place. It will of course raise and lower you with it."

Janet looked up at how high the slots went.

"Dmitri. That sounds *really* dangerous," she said. "This could hang me! I don't think—"

"Janet. Calm down. I would not hurt you for the world. But as you know, I *am* fond of restraining you." He smiled, lips closed. "It *cannot* lift you off of the floor. This has been thoroughly tested, on a model your exact size and weight."

Janet looked to Susan, who raised her eyebrows in surprise, shook her head and made a silent, exaggerated "*Noooooooo*" shape with her mouth. Susan left the room, looking amused.

Her relaxed air had calmed Janet. Janet was now the only woman in the room, and there was a subtle change in mood. She saw something beneath her feet, and when she looked down, she saw two small platforms, rectangles, directly under the collar. They were barely larger than her feet. They were made of metal, with textured pads on top and straps across them, steel loops on the sides. To fasten her ankle cuffs to, no doubt. There were also narrow slots in the floor, which ran straight out from the center, to either side.

She looked up to Dmitri, and he nodded confirmation: they would mechanically move as well, moving her feet with them. He went to the trouble of installing cables and pulleys under the floor?

"Um, do we have some kind of safeword, or something? If this,"—Janet gestured up to the slots in the corners—"gets to be too much?"

"Yes. As I said, you can call off the shoot anytime. But try not to, Janet. I've gone to a lot of trouble." He made a sweeping motion across the whole room.

"As long as you are still able to speak, simply yell 'Stop'."

As long as I'm able to—

"If you are no longer able to speak, just snap your fingers. You can do that, yes?"

Janet tried to snap the thumb and fingers on her right hand, but it was shaking too much. She tried again. The snap echoed through the room.

Dmitri, standing behind her, took and pulled both of her wrists behind her, clasping them together behind her back.

"And now?"

She'd known she was going to be bound when he'd cuffed her, but it all didn't truly hit her until now.

She snapped her fingers again, louder than before. He released her wrists, but the brief feeling of being gripped, held, sent a new surge of helplessness through her. That feeling of being at Dmitri's mercy, once again, hot and sexy and scary all at once. How was it she kept feeling *more* naked?

She turned around, taking in the space, and stopped. A neat row of whips, floggers, crops—and canes!—hung on what would be the rear wall. Her eyes widened. She'd walked right past them. There were eight or ten of them, arranged like a xylophone of torments, all black and contrasting starkly with the pure white. They were hung precisely, perfectly spaced from each other, their tops at the same level but increasing in length from a short band—a gag—to a long, single-tail whip. Janet had never felt one of those, but there was one in every novel she'd read, every fantasy she'd ever had. And yet…

She took a step back, pictured herself running out of the room. Pictured herself huddling in the far corner. She looked from the wall to the men. They were all watching her. Serge focused on her face, looking quite satisfied, searching her expression. Janet remembered: he was the equipment manager. This was probably his work, the elevating collar, if not the toys as well. The lighting guy—David?—was looking over her body, perhaps figuring light readings or perhaps just having fun. Dmitri, nearest to her, watched her eyes.

She steeled herself. "Okay, then."

She would take whatever Dmitri gave her; he hadn't disappointed her before. She brought her shoulders back, stood straight and proud. Hands at her sides, she looked to Dmitri for instruction.

But, she wondered, *who is going to* use *these things?*

"Good girl, Janet. You look ready to start."

"Yes, Sir. I am."

"Excellent, my dear. Come, follow me. There is someone you need to meet before we begin." He headed toward the door and Janet followed, two steps behind. Serge and David slipped out of the room behind her, and walked down the hall toward their work.

Janet turned. Standing before her was a man, over a foot taller than her, dressed entirely in black. Entirely: covering his head was a black leather bondage hood, with holes for his eyes—piercing, authoritative, dark eyes—but no opening for a mouth and only tiny holes for his nostrils. He wore a black suit of expensive fabric, black shirt and tie, tight black leather gloves, and black shoes, suede, not polished—too reflective of the rows of light?

Janet took all this in as a way to avoid his eyes.

"Nice suit, eh? Hugo Boss." Dmitri said. "I chose it, of course."

The man was powerfully built beneath the suit—a domineering and, quite frankly, frightening presence. He said nothing, only stared at her.

"Janet, I cannot introduce you to your costar, because I do not want you to know his name. He will not exceed the instructions I have given him. As with the room itself, I wanted you to see him before we start, so that you are not surprised by his presence, but by what he does."

Good God, what was Dmitri planning? Would this guy be fucking her? She lost her earlier confidence; her shoulders slouched.

"Am I safe, Dmitri?"

"Yes, Janet. You survived the hotel room, yes? And I'm guessing you've thought of it often, and quite fondly, once you got over the initial embarrassment. Remember, Jon is here as well. You know *he* will let nothing bad happen to you."

Janet looked into the stranger's eyes, dark and penetrating. She tried to think of other words besides "penetrating." His eyes bore no cruelty, just...that damned authority. Which Janet seemed unable to resist.

"He knows my name?" she said.

"Your first name, only, but if the two of you ever pass each other in the street, he will of course recognize you, all of you, but you will not know him. This is true. It's unfair, yes?"

Why did unfairness get her hot?

"What do I do?" she asked. "Sir."

Dmitri took a thin collar, a simple black leather strip with a buckle and one metal loop, and brought it up around her neck, fastened the buckle.

"You are my perfect, porcelain object. A precious beauty; such pure white skin."

Janet appreciated the little confidence-booster but felt *so* not perfect.

He arranged her black curls, freeing any strands from the collar. He clasped a black leash to the loop at her throat, and handed the other end to the man in the suit and mask. He then handed the box with the semi-precious nipple clamps to him. The man put the little box in his pocket.

Dmitri turned her shoulders toward the door.

"You will follow this man in black, and you will accept what happens to you." He fastened her cuffs together behind her back. "You are very good at that. And remember, Janet, there are no words in my films."

Janet nodded, heart pounding, hands sweating.

"Prepare to roll cameras!" Dmitri shouted down the hall.

The man gently pulled on the leash, and Janet followed him through the door into the white cube.

Chapter Fifteen

Jon held her hand in his and supported the small of her back as Janet slowly wavered down the concrete steps; her other hand gripped the industrial steel handrail.

"Are you sure you're okay?" he asked.

"Yea. Yea," was all she said.

"You're sure you don't want to rest a while longer?"

"On those couches? All the way back in there? Just take me home."

"Okay. You're sure you're—"

"I'm fine, Jon. I'll be fine."

They reached the bottom of the steps. There was no curb here, just the decaying old street in front of the warehouse's porch/loading dock, one distant streetlight barely illuminating the entire block. Jon stayed at her side.

She stopped in front of the car.

"Oh," she said. "You put the top down."

"It's a beautiful night. I thought you might enjoy it?" He opened the Buick's heavy passenger door for her. "I can put it back up, if you like."

"No, no. It's good. I could use the air." Janet slid into the wide bench seat, sucked in air through her teeth when her behind made contact with it. She lifted her weight off the seat and made a pained sound.

"Damn," she said.

Jon walked around the car. "You wanna lie down in the back?"

"No. I want to sit up here with you."

"I should have brought…"

"There's nothing you can do," she said. "I'm okay."

Jon slid the key into the ignition, but looked at Janet before starting it.

"Dmitri carried you out of that set, Janet. You'd passed out. I'm wondering if I should take you to the hospital or something."

"Do you really want to explain these to them?" She lifted her skirt to just below her crotch and showed him her thighs, once a bright red but already turning purple.

Jon inhaled sharply, his mouth open. He looked up at her face, then back down at her legs.

"I saw them, inside. I saw all of you."

Janet could see he was trying to calm his breath.

"It turns you on, doesn't it," she said, almost an accusation.

"Yes."

She lowered her skirt to cover them.

"I don't know how I feel. Sore. Sore as hell. But I'm…"

Jon waited for her to finish, then started the car when it was clear she wouldn't. He put the gearshift into reverse and the massive car backed into the street like an ocean liner leaving port.

He put it in gear and the suspension rattled over the potholes but she didn't feel any of them, thank God. Jon made a turn, and after passing a few warehouses, frighteningly dark, he made another.

"I thought the on-ramp was that way?" she said, but she had no idea.

"It is. There's a ball game, tonight."

"Oh, no."

"It'll be packed downtown. I thought we'd take the old State highway south, then 98 back west. We'll dodge the mess and it'll be just as fast, and less crowded."

"Okay."

They sat in silence as Jon drove them out of the maze of the Warehouse District. They met no one but a few slow-moving semi-trucks making late deliveries until he found the empty highway headed south, nothing but a beat-up stop sign to mark it. He accelerated and soon they were in a dimly lit older residential neighborhood, all tiny houses.

Janet gathered her hair, blown in every direction as the car sped up, and held it in her hand by her neck. Jon left her to her thoughts as he drove.

"Did you see it?" she finally said.

"No. All the cameras were remotely controlled by Dmitri. He was the only one able to see them all. No one saw but him."

"Not just him."

"Oh. Well, yea. Who was that guy?"

"I have no idea."

Jon seemed to be thinking that over.

"I heard it," he said.

It took her a while to answer. "How'd I sound?"

Jon didn't seem to have an answer for that, either.

"Agonizing," he finally said.

"Agonizing, not agonized?"

She looked down at the crotch of his jeans, saw the fabric stretched tight. She shook her head and looked out at the passing houses.

She'd never really been to this part of town, south of the warehouses, all the houses so small and run down, all heavily fenced with dogs that barked as they passed. She wished the road was a bit wider, away from the dogs, away from any pedestrians in the dark. Away from people.

"I have a gift for you, of sorts," he said.

Janet held up her little makeup bag and swung it back and forth between her thumb and forefinger.

"Please tell me it's not nipple clamps," she said.

Jon smiled, gave her a sideways look. She could see the concern in his eyes, something else as well.

"No."

"What is it?"

"We'll wait 'til we get out of this neighborhood," he said.

That was okay with Janet. She turned to look out the window, which was still up, probably to keep the wind level down within the car.

It was a beautiful night. The day's heat had subsided, and the evening was warm but the breeze was cooling. Perfect night for a margarita on a terrace, somewhere. Not to be…

She put it out of her head. She opened her bag and found an elastic hair band, pulled her hair through it into a rough ponytail. The air felt wonderful on her neck.

She felt grimy. She'd sweat quite a bit in there. She'd—

She covered her mouth as she burst into tears. She looked at Jon, feeling ashamed of her outburst, but needing to cry at *somebody*.

"Sorry," she said, then felt another wave of tears roll down her cheeks. She didn't think she had any left.

"It's okay, it's okay," Jon said. He took a handkerchief out of his pocket and handed it to her.

"Men still carry these?" she said.

"This one does. Especially when he's going to be taking a woman home from what is more than likely going to be a pretty intense introduction to the film arts."

Janet laughed and cried at the same time.

The truth was, she didn't know how she felt. She hurt—all over. She would for days. *Welts.* She'd already scheduled the first two days of next week off from work. She was ashamed and embarrassed. As always. But she was also in some kind of...*zone*, some strange place that wasn't entirely negative. She couldn't say she "regretted" it. She just needed time to...to sort it all *out.*

She didn't remember passing out. She remembered coming to, on the sofa in the hall, Dmitri and Jon both leaning over her, fussing over her, pressing a wet washcloth onto her forehead and trying to get her to take a sip of water. She was naked, and severely welted, and was still wearing the cuffs on her wrists and ankles. The old sofa felt *so* soft...

"Better?" Jon said.

She'd stopped crying, without knowing it. She was looking at the little houses passing by, wider apart, now. They must have demolished the more run-down ones between them. There were fewer streetlights, as well, and Jon was making slow swerves to dodge the potholes.

"It's like we're almost out of town," she said.

"We are."

The texture of the road changed—fewer potholes, but the evenly spaced cracks in the newer pavement produced a *tha-thunk, tha-thunk, tha-thunk* sound as the tires rolled over them.

"Technically we're still in Southdon," he said. "But see? Here they come." He pointed past Janet and she saw a mass of orange streetlights illuminating a horizontal strip of jagged beige, a cookie-cutter housing development all alone beyond the empty field they were passing.

"Does anyone live in those?"

"Hell if I know."

The rough road smoothed at the intersection that led to the new development and the streetlights were orange now, not the bluish glow the older neighborhoods had. They blocked out the stars, which Janet had just noticed.

They were passing cultivated fields, and the summer smells of moist earth and green—something growing in these fields, even if they were soon to be covered in crappy houses and strip malls—gave Janet a feeling of peace. Escape from the city; hope. She looked over her shoulder and saw the glow of downtown as they sped away, the lights in the taller buildings, people still working late.

"Let me see your markings," Jon said.

She turned to face him.

"You said you already saw them. On the sofa."

"Let me see them again."

The streetlights were becoming more regularly spaced but farther apart, civilization imposing itself on the darkness, even though there was absolutely no one out here.

"Jon, I—"

"Take off your clothes, Janet."

She knew she could refuse him. And he knew she'd been through a lot; he would understand.

She hesitated. It had been a long day.

But he persisted: "Do it."

Janet considered telling him to fuck off. It wasn't like Jon was her Master, able to tell her what to do at any time. They played, right? They had no agreement, no Contract.

She was exhausted; he had to know this. But there was a shininess in his eyes as they reflected the glow of the streetlights, something playfully devious or teasing—but not cruel.

She managed a tired, crooked smile.

"Yes, Sir. Of course, Sir."

She pulled off her T-shirt and gingerly slid her skirt down her legs. Her flip-flops were already off. She sat naked on the huge bench seat, and turned to let him see her body.

Her breasts had been heavily whipped, as had her stomach. Her thighs were a mass of blotchy purple. Her entire torso was a mass of red welts turning to bruises—almost.

Jon leaned toward her in the dim light, looked down at her lap.

"They didn't touch your…"

"Oh, they touched it," Janet said.

Jon was staring at the only unmarked spot on her front, a perfect square of neglected white skin surrounding her pubic hair.

"Turn around."

Janet turned, scooted toward Jon and leaned forward, gripping the door. She didn't know exactly what she looked like, but knew that she was sore. Her ass had taken the worst of the beating, her thighs too.

"Jesus."

"It's still not as bad as what Carolyn did," she said over her shoulder.

She felt the chaotic breeze ripple across her torso as Jon looked.

"I want you to assume a position for me."

She dropped her head. Seriously? But she just didn't have the will to argue, right now.

She sighed.

"All right."

She slid down onto the floor between the seat and dashboard, reddened breasts pressed against the seat. She reached for Jon's zipper. He *was* a mouth man. She felt resigned, more than anything.

"No, sweetie. Up on the seat. Lay down on it."

Janet climbed back up, confused. She started to lay face down, her head above his crotch.

"No. On your back, your head against the door. Get your clothes, use them as a pillow. Make yourself comfortable."

What was all this? Janet just wanted to sit, to *think*.

She slid her legs under her, toward him, and leaned back,

reached down to pull up her clothes. She wound them into a tight roll and placed them behind her head, on the door's armrest. Her shins were tucked awkwardly against Jon. Her welts ached anew against the vinyl seat.

Jon looked down at her. She looked away, up at the sky. The streetlights had ended and the Milky Way was out; there was no Moon so the stars were especially bright out here in the middle of nowhere.

"Spread your legs."

"Jon, I—"

But he was staring at her, not backing down. She still knew she could stop this—*Nothing you don't want to do,*" he'd once said.

She let her right leg fall, foot to the floor, and lifted her left knee against the seat back.

"Wider."

"Jon…"

Janet obeyed, not especially enthused. What did he *want*? She pulled both legs farther back, her arms supporting her on the huge bench seat. The seat of the LeSabre was long and wide and flat, almost a tiny bed. But this was embarrassing, more than fun, and she'd had more than enough embarrassment for one day.

A massive semi-truck, speeding in the opposite direction, roared by in a flash of headlights and shocking turbulence. Janet flinched, suddenly aware of her visibility to the world, if the world could look down into the car. She looked up at Jon.

"Wider."

"Jon, please."

"Come on."

This was getting irritating. She considered finally using her safeword, after all these weeks, but that seemed extreme, at the moment. He wasn't being forceful, just persistent, like some high school boy.

Looking toward the windshield, Janet arched her back as she pulled her knees back to her armpits with her hands.

Jon was barely even glancing at the road. He looked down at Janet's abused body, illuminated by the dashboard's lights, all the red and purple lines crisscrossing her skin.

More streetlights: the lights cast moving, diagonal shadows from the windshield's frame across her chest and stomach.

"Jon, I'm not really—"

"Yes I know, you want to go home. I'm taking you home. This is my present to you."

"This is my present?"

"Let's see you touch that clit," he told her.

"What?" She was surprised, more than anything, though she didn't know why at this point.

"You heard me. Masturbate it. Touch that clit. Pleasure yourself."

"Jon, I'm—I'm kind of sexed out, to tell you the truth. I really don't—"

"Do it, Janet."

Janet hesitated. She was tired, and no doubt looked it. She was still in a daze that she couldn't define. She wanted to think, not play games. She considered another protest, or just getting up. But she released her right knee and lowered her hand down to her sex. She touched her outer labia with her fingertips.

"You're not too sore there, are you?"

"No. Not…there, anyway." Deeper, was a different story. She slid her middle finger to her clitoris and touched it. "Are you seriously going to make me do this?"

"I can't 'make' you do anything, doll. But do it. Rub one out. Let's see it."

This was a "gift"?

She began moving two fingers over her clit. She circled it with her fingers, pressing it from side to side. It started to harden up a bit, but not much.

"You weren't faking in there, when I heard you, were you?" Janet laughed and she shook her head in resignation.

"No."

She didn't want to talk about it. Was he going to want to talk about it?

"Then tonight, I am giving you control. Of you. I want you to enjoy yourself at your own pace, however you want. My only condition is that I want to see it."

Janet, still just wanting to go home, looked up at Jon but continued her motion.

"Enjoy," he said.

Janet stroked her clit, but she was doing it for him, not her. She wondered how she would feel about all this tomorrow—the filming itself, in that white cube, and then this, whatever this was. She didn't even know how she felt about it now.

"That's my gift to you. Control. No one telling you when or if you can come, no one forcing it out of you. I don't know what they did to you, in there, but now I want you to give yourself one, at least one—your thoughts are your own, your body is your own. After all that. Reclaim it."

"But you're *telling* me to do it."

"And you're allowing it, or you're not."

Janet relaxed, at this. He wasn't being an asshole about it.

"But…you?" She glanced down the length of her own body to Jon's swollen crotch.

"You take care of yourself, and I'll worry about me. You don't worry, about me. Don't worry about anything. You think about whatever you want to think about."

Janet took a deep breath. She was still wet inside, from the shoot, despite herself. She was able to reach down and bring up a little of that wetness with her fingers, though her inner labia were still tender to the touch.

She was *so* exhausted. Horizontal on the big seat, she let her mind shut down, instead of trying to force it to think the evening through.

Her brain was happy to comply. It had been through a lot, too. Soon she wasn't thinking of anything—she just felt. She closed her eyes, and sensed the turbulence across her bare and sore body, heard the roar of road noise and wind and the big old engine. She jiggled her clit with her fingers, stroked it like no one else quite knew how.

No pornographic scenarios, no abstracted perfect men, no Jon, no Dmitri. No Jack. Certainly not that horrible man in the black suit. She simply *felt*—and it felt pretty good.

"I'll give you another choice, too. We have about five minutes before we hit 98 and go back into the city, or...I can keep going south, farther into the country. We can circle around the whole city, and head west on county roads. I drive out here sometimes, I know my way. It'll take about an extra thirty minutes or so." He looked down at Janet, spread wide before him. "It's a beautiful night for a drive."

The car passed into near darkness, the streetlights ending again as civilization withdrew. Janet looked up, as Jon did too, and saw the stars so, so clearly. She cocked her head around to look at the sky from different angles. She aligned her eyes with the Milky Way, then turned her head ninety degrees so it looked like a big vertical column. Jon took it all in as long as he dared before looking down the road at the brightly lit intersection several miles ahead—even down on the seat, she could sense its glow.

Janet, keeping her knees wide apart, released her other hand and brought it across her stomach. She ran the tips of her fingers along some of the less painful welts. She continued her masturbation with her fingers, using some wrist motion as she became more energetic. She was too sore to insert her fingers, even though she sort of wanted to. But her fingers on her clit did feel pretty good, she had to admit, with the wind whipping over her body instead of actual whips. It felt freeing, soothing, cooling.

Jon watched as she stroked her stomach, her breasts. She massaged a nipple. They were sore to the touch, too, but she squeezed one hard anyway, and felt the hurt again but now she could stop whenever she wanted. It became as hard and erect as her swollen clitoris was. Her other nipple hardened sympathetically in the cooling air.

She arched her back and wriggled her hips. Jon watched as her mouth opened, her eyes closed. She said goodbye to him in her head. *So sorry, Jon, it's my trip now.*

She opened her eyes and stared up into the stars, very determined—she was close. She'd never had an orgasm under the stars, like this. Her jaw jutted forward, and she rocked her hips. She was going to town on herself, but which way would she want to go back to town? She moaned quietly to herself, just herself. She was getting *very* close…

Janet opened her mouth wide and screamed in ecstasy at the moment that the car passed under the first of the bright sodium lights that illuminated the intersection with Highway 98. Jon slowed the car as he watched her face, lost in her own interior illumination. She rocked her hips again, her spread and elevated feet moving up and down, her sex on full display. She didn't care. She gazed up at the lights as he watched her. Her body was fully lit; her mottled skin glowed under the next streetlight.

She was out of breath, and she felt suddenly drained as the endorphins or dopamine or whatever surged through her body.

"Jesus Christ, I'm shot," she said. She started to laugh as her eyes teared up again; this whole day was just too much. She covered her face with her hand.

Jon stopped the car.

She raised her hand, shielded her eyes from the light directly above her. "Why did we stop?"

"It's a stop sign."

Janet held her spread position. She was spent and euphoric, ashamed and ecstatic, and still very confused about…everything.

"Is…anyone coming?" she asked in the bright light, trying to see out of the car but not able to see over the dash without lifting herself, which she had no desire or energy to do.

"Just you, doll."

"Oh that was so ridiculously cheesy."

Jon laughed. He was lit up as well, orange lights behind his head like a halo. He was totally aroused by the sight of her. She liked that. So far, he was sticking to his word about this being only for her.

"West or south? It's up to you. South is serious country roads, no lights. Feel like a drive?"

Janet leaned back and looked up toward the sky, the stars obscured by the glare. She closed her eyes, caressed the underside of her breast, touched the welts. Everything hurt. But the summer air smelled so good, out here in the country—flowering plants in the ditches, tilled earth, just…air.

She moved her fingers from her stomach back to her sex.

"Take the long way," she said.

No "Sir," for him, not tonight. No "Sir" for anyone.

She slid her calf over his shoulders and behind his neck, dropped her other foot to the floor.

Jon pressed his foot on the accelerator, and the huge old Buick lumbered straight ahead into the darkness.

Part 4: Traffic Jams

Chapter Sixteen

Janet had to laugh at the irony.

"What's so funny?" Jon asked.

"See that girl who just came in? I was just thinking her dress was a little too revealing."

Jon stroked her back. "You'll be fine."

She sighed.

"I feel sick to my stomach."

There were twenty-five, maybe thirty people in the room, with a few more coming in. Most of the men were older than Janet, most of the women younger, although there were plenty of exceptions to both. Everyone was wearing black: the men in suits, a few hipster-slovenly, and the women in dresses, ranging from slightly slutty to an almost matronly elegant. Janet had considered wearing a nice blue evening dress, the whole blue-eyes thing, but was glad she wore simple black. She didn't want to stand out.

Dmitri wasn't kidding about security: everyone, including her and Jon, had been searched and felt up, metal-detecting devices waved over their bodies, cell phones taken and placed in a lead-lined box. They were in a conference room in a down-town hotel, one that had occasional clients who valued security. Rumor had it there were electronic suppression devices in the walls, probably irradiating everyone with deadly radio waves of some kind.

The servers were two young women, dressed in shiny, skin-tight black PVC from neck to toe, stiletto heels, and both wore wide leather collars around their necks designed to keep their postures enforced. You couldn't see a single inch of them below the chin, and yet you could see everything.

"Sir? Ma'am?" one of them said, and Jon took two glasses of champagne from her tray and handed one to Janet.

"I don't know anyone here," she said.

"Is that good or bad?"

The other girl was carrying a tray of hors d'oeuvres, which Janet waved by.

"I wonder who does the catering?" Jon said.

"Oh, look—there's Jack." He was standing at the door, watching with pleasure as Hannah was being quite thoroughly patted down by the security guard, a very butch woman in a man's suit with a severe expression on her face.

"Janet! What are you doing here?" Jack said as they approached. "Hey, Jon. Thanks for getting us invites."

"You didn't tell him?" Janet whispered to Jon, who gave her a mischievous look.

"Janet, you remember Hannah?" Hannah was dressed in a short cocktail dress with subtle black sequins that sparkled in the bland overhead lighting. It was rather low cut and she wore no bra, bedazzling.

"Well yes, of course. How are you, Hannah?"

"Good, thank you. You?" Hannah seemed friendlier now, maybe because Janet wasn't hanging around anymore.

"So have you seen any of Dmitri's films before, Janet?" Jack asked.

"Well, I've—"

"I know Jon's seen one or two."

"Three," Jon said.

"This'n'll be my third. I've seen *Eye of the Storm (Yellow)*, of course. That's how I met my Hannah."

"Yes, I remember."

Jack patted Hannah on the ass, just loud enough for them to hear. "It was pretty damn hot—have you seen it?"

"No."

"Oh that's right—you haven't even met Dmitri yet, have you."

Janet started to speak, but—

"The invitation said this one's called *White Cube*," Jack said. "I wonder if it's anything like that one?"

Janet shrugged.

"We really need to introduce you to Dmitri," Jack said. "Oh look, there he is."

"Later, maybe, Jack," Jon said. "He looks a little busy."

"All right." Jack looked thoughtful. "The only other one I've seen is *SissyPuss*. I wonder if this 'n's anything like that one."

"Sissy? Puss?" Janet said. "Are you sure that's not pronounced—"

"Yea. One of Dmitri's first. One gal. He'd built this ramp, this big, steep slope. Made her roll this huge boulder up the ramp, naked of course, with her hands cuffed together in front of her, and every time she got up near the top, it would tumble back down. She'd have to start over. That's it—that's all there was to it. But it turns out he'd built the entire ramp thing on a big…rocker, of some kind, and when she'd get close to the top, the whole thing—the camera too, so you didn't know it was rocking—would tilt back, making it roll back down no matter what she did. She couldn't win."

"You know, that's based on a Greek—"

"Now, this gal was *fit*. She had some muscles, but they were girl muscles, you know? Not big scary bodybuilder muscles. She worked up a *sweat*, Janet. All shiny from it. More and more through the film. Muscles all tensed up, flexing. God, those thighs. By the end of it, it was maybe twenty minutes long, she was in tears. On her knees, at the bottom, every time. Sweaty body, breathin' heavy, she couldn't win. It was all so unfair. God damn, I'm turned on right now just thinkin' about it."

Jack was lost in thought again. He placed his hand on Hannah's ass and squeezed.

"I wonder if this one's anything closer to that one," he finally said.

Janet decided not to bother explaining the Greek myth of Sisyphus—it just wasn't worth it.

Jack walked away with his arm around Hannah.

"Janet! Jon!" Dmitri crossed the room.

"Hello, Dmitri."

"Are you having a good time? Enough to drink? Eat? Meeting anyone interesting?"

Janet nodded.

"Jon, is Amanda not here?" He looked disappointed.

"Working, I'm afraid. She's very busy."

"Ah. Too bad. I adore her, you know." Dmitri paused, looked around the room. "No one knows it's you, Janet. Unless you've told them. Isn't that interesting?"

"I haven't told anyone," Janet said. "I'd rather keep it that way."

"You won't be able to for long, I'm afraid," Dmitri said. "Ah, step aside a little, please."

The two serving girls were making their way through the crowd with armfuls of plush cushions, taking them off a rolling cart and laying them on the floor in neat rows. They worked stiffly, their posture collars preventing them from bending their necks. People were stepping out of their way, falling into lines that the cushions plotted out.

Four rows of eight cushions, Janet counted. No more than thirty-two people here. Thirty-two people who would be seeing her—

"Please, you two. Sit here. Right here in front and center, yes?"

Janet had planned on sitting in the very back row, watching everyone else rather than being watched. But she sat, Dmitri taking her hand and helping her down to the floor. She sat with her legs tucked underneath her.

"More champagne?" Dmitri asked. Jon sat cross-legged on the cushion next to Janet, and Janet finished her glass in one gulp. She handed it up to Dmitri.

"Please."

Dmitri handed the glass to one of the shiny serving girls, who handed a full one to Janet. An older couple sat next to her. They exchanged pleasant greetings, but not introductions.

"Everyone, please!" Dmitri shouted, hands in the air. The crowd stopped their chattering; most sat down. "Attention please. It is time."

The last few standing had to search around for an empty spot.

"As most of you know, this is my seventh film. Each one has been very different, each one designed around a particular woman. *For* her. Her beauty, her personality. In this regard, this one is no different. I have a new actress, even though as you know there is no 'acting' in my films."

Janet held her breath, hoping he would not ask her to stand up.

"Those of you who have seen my previous work, you know I use one camera, one shot, two canisters of film. For this film, I tried to do something a little different. I used four cameras, not just one. Four different angles. I was prepared, for the first time, to *edit*. Such a beautiful subject, one point of view was not enough."

He shook his head. "But I was coward. I love the purity of image, to match the purity of subject."

Jesus, Janet thought. *He must be joking.*

"I could not bring myself to embrace this change, not this time. So I have kept that purity. I wanted to make a rigorous film."

You got that *right.*

"A film about…permutations. An exercise. What is possible, with curves against straight lines? A particular color palette against pure white?"

He stopped to think.

"Ladies and gentlemen, *White Cube.*"

Dmitri walked along the wall to the back of the room as the lights went out.

The projector started. As with his other film Janet had seen, the screen was black, then white letters faded in:

WHITE CUBE
A FILM BY DMITRI CORSO

Here we go, Janet thought.

The title faded out, and the screen was black, then eased into white. There was nothing on the screen but what looked to be a very flat, thin, horizontal 'X', with a small black oval in the crux of the X. The collar; and two little black squares under it, close together on the floor of the empty, featureless room. The foot pedals.

Under the cables, to the right, were the row of torments that resembled not a xylophone, as Janet had thought at the time, but a cruel Pan flute of pain:

Each device precisely tuned to produce a different tone of sorrow from Janet.

The hooded man dressed in stark black entered from the left, and behind the leash he pulled was Janet, her skin resplendent white. Both had to duck under one of the cables suspending the collar.

"Oh. My. Gawd," Jack said from somewhere near the back of the room. Jon laughed, and gently nudged Janet in the ribs with his elbow.

Janet couldn't watch. She turned away—this was not like looking in a mirror. The woman onscreen was bound and collared and completely submissive to the man in the suit. Did she really look like that, eyes down and shoulders slumped, going wherever he led?

Hell, her eyes were down *now*, in this room. She forced herself to look back up, to see what everyone else in the room was seeing.

She didn't look half bad, at least. Under Dmitri's, or David's, smooth lighting, all the body issues that Janet lamented daily were washed out—her tits looked pretty awesome, really; her stomach almost flat and her rounded hips were not nearly as wide as she'd convinced herself they were.

The man unlocked the suspended collar, the cables slackened as its hinge opened, and he gestured for Janet to step forward.

Janet hadn't expected that the washed-out lighting would make her already-pale skin look almost as white as the walls behind her. She looked like a ghost, the black of her hair and bush standing out, the pink of her nipples and that garish red lipstick. Janet tried to remember who that artist was in the '60's, who painted nude women reduced to silhouettes and these details.

The man unfastened the collar he'd led her in with and locked her into her new one. He pulled any hair trapped in the collar out; let it fall over her shoulders. He stooped down behind her and guided her feet onto the little platforms, buckled the straps across her toes and locked the tiny hoops into her ankle cuffs. Then he stood and disappeared off the side of the screen.

Janet watched her own blue eyes as they rolled around in her head, waiting. She remembered feeling very alone and unsure of what would happen.

Onscreen, her eyes widened as the cables and collar, and her neck, rose—those pulleys and motors hidden behind the corners of the walls. It was terrifying—the feeling that she could very well be lifted off of the floor, hung by the neck, or stretched so tight with her feet locked in place that it could pull her head right off. The collar was so stiff that it didn't choke her, but the feeling was one of near-panic. She'd braced herself to shout, or if she couldn't, snap her fingers. She stood up on her tiptoes as it kept rising.

But it stopped, right at the tipping point of discomfort and panic. Janet struggled to stay on her toes, her entire body stretched in tension. There was fear on her face as she waited.

Then the collar was lowered. She relaxed, but it kept moving down—and down. There was nothing she could do to stop it. She had to follow, but having her feet locked in place meant that she couldn't kick her feet back to kneel. She was forced into an awkward squat, the collar just a few feet off the ground. Then it got worse: the platforms under her feet moved, outward from each other in their slots in the floor, straight to the sides. They moved slowly, but there was no fighting them; they were powered by motors and steel. Her feet were forced apart so that she was squatting with her legs spread wide, her sex exposed. The even lighting showed it all, her pink clitoral hood and inner labia, there for the whole world to see.

The Janet watching covered her eyes with her hand. She waited until she knew the next position was underway to look back up.

The machine lifted her again. Now to a more comfortable height, but her feet were still spread. The machine was putting her through all the positions that it could, showing the audience how she was nothing but malleable flesh. The collar pushed her downward again, and she was again forced into the splayed squat, very unladylike.

The man walked into the frame, to the far wall. He selected the shortest item from the end of the row, which was no whip, but a black ball gag—unusual since everyone seemed to love her in blue. He walked to her, reached around her head and placed it in front of her face and she tilted her head back and opened her mouth and drew back her lips. He pulled it in and buckled it, and her movement was even more restricted—the collar did indeed hold her head and jaw still, and her skull was forced back with her mouth jacked open by the offending black orb. Her bright lipstick made an obscene red circle around it. He then lifted her wrists higher on her back, and with a short chain from his pocket he fastened them to the collar, far too high to be comfortable. Her breathing was suddenly more difficult.

He then went back for the next item on the wall. This one *was* a whip. Or at least an object for abuse: a short leather strap.

He walked to her side, just behind her, and after a poignant pause, bent forward and hit her on the ass, quite forcefully. Janet's eyes were as round as her mouth, all such perfect symmetry. Immobilized, legs spread and so exposed, with her ass extended out behind her, it was perhaps the most humiliating moment of Janet's life—all caught right there on film, for all posterity. Or at least this roomful of people.

Her gagged squeals didn't exactly add to her dignity. Janet thought about all the unused film from the other three cameras, over an hour's worth of footage. Had Dmitri destroyed all that? The one behind her would show her ass beaten redder and redder until it was nearly purple, and the next implement was even more cruel:

A tawse, Janet would later learn it was called. And it hurt like hell. It was another short leather strap with a handle, but the strap part was split in two, and there were two layers of leather sewn together to make it heavier.

He walked back to exchange the tools as Janet's collar was raised. Her legs were also brought together by the pedals, and she was stretched up onto her toes again. He began on her calf muscles, and hit her higher with each blow. He worked his way up the back of her body, calves, thighs, ass, back. She screamed and jerked with each blow, but could do nothing more about it. Her entire backside was on fire.

The collar lowered, and she could finally relax—but only for a moment. As the man walked back to the row of whips, Janet's legs were spread by the platforms under her feet. The cables tightened as her neck pulled the collar down, and again she could do nothing but stand there, legs spread, face red, immobilized.

She heard footsteps, and a buzzing sound.

The man returned from the wall with what looked like a billy club, but wasn't.

It was a vibrator, loud and long, full of batteries. Lots of batteries.

Janet didn't cry in pain, but moaned loud and sharp as the man stood behind her and slid its length between her spread legs. Her eyes were wider than when the straps had crossed her skin. It was powerful, and so *personal.*

He slid it back and forth, and with a deft touch: he picked up on her every sound, her every movement as he rocked it between her lips, her very wet lips (which had embarrassed her to no end). The black rod emerged gleaming as he rotated it, and he played her like a cello with his magic bow. He angled the vibrator up, then straight out, feeling her out—driving her insane.

She was panting as he pressed it against her clit, never stopping his back-and-forth motion. She rocked her hips what little she could, which was not much. But the camera caught her efforts; the microphones heard every moan.

He slid it deep inside her. She nearly screamed—she *did* scream—and he held it there, far too intense to be simply enjoyable, until she came, which did not take long at all. Incredibly red face, on both the Janet on the screen and the one watching.

The man removed it from her and returned it to the wall

wet and shiny, and came back with the next item, a long black leather flogger. He whipped her front as she flinched with each strike—her breasts, her stomach, her thighs.

Her skin was reddening. Her face was still red, and now her torso was too, and then the man stepped behind her and started in on her hips, from behind.

But he didn't whip her ass. Instead, with admirable precision, he struck her flanks, the tips of the flogger extending the same exact distance around her hips with every blow. He adjusted his swing each time, and in effect painted a straight line of red down each side of her pelvis—he was leaving the skin around her pubic area white. He was painting a nice little box around her bush: Dmitri's palette, with a tiny black triangle inside a white square inside the red curves of her hips inside the white cube.

She remembered the bizarre feelings of agony from the flogger combined with the odd absence of sensation closer to her sex—like he'd somehow neglected it. She hadn't realized it was for visual effect. She just thought it was a new torment. The man returned to the wall, and came back with a crop.

She screamed as he hit her on the ass, red lips tight around the ball gag, and she came, with no contact on her sex at all. Merely from the combination of absence and touch, longing and pain. She remembered the embarrassment at knowing how this spectacle would look to an audience, and she'd been right. She was shuddering, no control at all over herself, only the tightness of the collar and footholds keeping her from writhing in absolute ecstasy, even as the crop continued to fall against her red-hot ass.

Then he made it worse: the man ducked under the cables, and lifted the box from his pocket that she'd brought Dmitri. He opened it and took out the two dreaded little sapphires, squeezed the clamp of one open, and fastened it to her erect right nipple. She squealed. Her breasts were already in agony from the flogging, and she hated those expensive little things to begin with.

She tried to twist her body away, but he grasped her left breast, lifted, and applied the other one.

She moaned in a loud, pained voice as he walked back to the toys. The sapphires sparkled in the studio lights, danced as her chest heaved and breasts jiggled. They did match her eyes, which were now tearing up. Add black streaks of mascara to that color palette. People in the audience inhaled as the first blackened drop fell upon her breast.

Next up: what Janet had been whipped with her first night in this twisted world—the three-foot long braided whip known as a quirt. (She'd looked up the term in one of her books.) The main attraction here seemed to be his fluid motion, alternating seamlessly from backhand to forehand, whipping her front, back, front, back. The whip made lovely figure eights in the air, off-center and asymmetrical. She could only wail in agony. She hated quirts.

He returned with the next-to-the-last item, a cane, long and black. He gave Janet three painful blows across her ass, each time waiting for her gagged screams to subside before administering the next blow. The tiny blue spheres circled her nipples in frantic orbits as she squirmed.

The foot pedals separated and spread her legs. The collar pulled against her neck as her height was reduced, but the collar was not lowered. She could barely breathe. She waited for the man to return, but he did not.

She heard a sound, a motor; but it was not the buzz of the vibrator. She couldn't look down because of the collar and gag that pried her head back. She would have to wait.

Janet now saw it for the first time. She glanced around. The audience was mesmerized.

A tiny pair of doors opened in the floor, directly underneath her. From the small square hole emerged what looked like a small white missile, like old footage of nuclear warheads launching from their silos.

It was rising, and it soon became clear that it was spinning. It was a long, conical tube, a missile indeed—pointed, and heavily ribbed. But the ribs spiraled around the tube, threaded, like a screw. The threads were smooth and rounded, yes, not sharp like those of a real screw or bolt—but as it rotated, the spiral ribs were moving upward, round and round and round, spinning, spinning, spinning. And it was heading for Janet's spread and exposed sex. The whirling phallus was mounted on a long steel rod that continued to propel it upward. She was literally going to be screwed.

In this position, Janet had been restrained and pulled so taut she couldn't even rock her hips. She felt the collar rise higher yet, and she had to stand on her toes with her legs spread. She struggled to breathe. She began panting in panic, but she was already exhausted and she just didn't have the energy to fight. She tried to relax, to submit to Dmitri's will.

The audience held their breath.

Janet could feel it against her spread outer labia. The tip was smooth, and she didn't yet know it was spinning. She thought it was another vibrator. Frightened yet eager for it, she adjusted her posture to give it easier access to her depths.

As it rose, it split her inner lips, and as soon as she felt the first of the spinning ribs, her eyes widened in near-panic. But it was too late. She couldn't raise herself off of it. She was impaled.

Impaled by a whirling, threaded dildo—what could she do?

Nothing, it turned out, but accept it or call the whole thing off, ruin the shoot, and, well…deny herself.

The dildo widened out as it entered her; it had a rounded, zeppelin-like shape. She bit down on the gag, clenched her eyes shut. It was overpowering, the sensation within her. It would have been intense without the crazy ribs spinning against her

Blue

inner walls, fast-moving bulges pushing undulating waves deeper at an amazing rate, even as the missile as a whole was slowly plunging in.

Finally its climb stopped, the bottom of the white device barely visible inside her red and plumped labia, but the spinning continued. It drilled her. She shuddered, grunted, tried to shake her head. She wriggled her shoulders, to no use. Her face was a deep crimson, and her breasts heaved and jiggled; sapphires spun. She screamed as she came. It was too much. *Way* too much.

The man returned. He held the final instrument from the wall, the long single-tail whip.

Braided black leather, the epitome of cruelty in all the books she'd ever read. She'd always wondered what one of those would feel like, in real life.

She found out. Helpless and impaled and quivering, shivering, shuddering, Janet felt the first harsh lash from the whip as the man struck it against her ass. She screamed, gag or no gag, and it was a terrifying sound—audience members leaned back, away from the screen.

He whipped her ass again, then her thighs, each stroke feeling like it was tearing into her skin, she must have been bleeding, she was sure.

But she wasn't. The man whipped her across her front as she tried to shake her head no, but she couldn't move. All she could do was try to look toward him, pleading with her eyes, and scream and scream again.

And come.

The rounded auger bored into her, throbbing against her insides, and it was more than she could take. Her hips quivered nonstop as one orgasm ran into the next, beyond her ability to keep track of them, tell one from the next. And the whip—it was excruciating, searing. She had never felt anything as intensely painful as this before—nor anything as intensely pleasurable, over*whelmingly* pleasurable, as the multi-ribbed helix within her.

Her face was beyond crimson, into purple, her torso red from the whips (all but her pristine and accentuated pubic area), her every nerve on fire. And within all these radical changes of color the blue dots of her eyes widened, shut, rolled, and begged, and the little oscillating sapphire orbs swung beneath her pained nipples with every movement.

Screaming, crying, coming. Janet couldn't breathe; she didn't know how to make herself breathe again, she didn't know how to stop not breathing. With one final, shattering, rapturous wave, she came again, harder than she ever had, and as if it were a wave, too high to swim against, she submitted, let herself drown, let herself go under.

It was the last thing she remembered.

The Janet on the screen went slack within her bonds, unconscious, but the man did not realize and gave her one more fierce lash of the whip. When she did not react at *all*, even considering her inability to fall or bend over or move much, he stopped. He stood still like a robot deactivated, and the image of her spread and impaled body slowly faded to black.

The lights came on, and the audience exhaled as if they were one collective entity. There was silence, and for some reason Janet felt she had let them down—but then the thirty-two people in the room exploded into a roar of applause.

What they did not see was that as soon as Dmitri had seen her collapse, he had pushed the switch that stopped the penetrating phallus from spinning, reversed its supporting axle, and told the man via speaker to unfasten Janet's collar, wrists, and feet as he ran around the hallways and into the set. He scooped the limp Janet up from the man's arms and carried her out into the hall, onto a sofa where Jon was already standing.

The next thing she knew, they were above her, bent over, urgent looks in their eyes and smiles and sighs of relief when she acknowledged them. Sips of cool water.

"Ladies and gentlemen, the star of the film—please welcome Janet!" Dmitri held out his hand and pulled her up. Thank God he didn't give them her last name.

She was surrounded by an onrush of people.

"Oh my God, you showed us so *much*!" one woman said.

"Well, yea," Janet said, embarrassed. No denying *that*.

"I mean, your soul. You showed us your *soul*. We saw it." Janet backed away a little.

"*That?*" she said, pointing to the empty screen with her thumb. The woman put her hand on Janet's cheek.

"Wow," an older man said. "Wow." He handed her a business card.

"God damn! You rock!" one of the serving girls said, her neck still locked into the stiff posture collar. She handed Janet a glass of champagne. "Have one on me."

"Thank you." She took a grateful swig.

Another business card, and a man held his fist to his cheek, thumb and pinky extended. *Call me*, he mouthed as he walked away. Janet turned to Jon, but he wasn't there. He was standing outside the circle, the mob of people wanting to talk to her, just her.

"What were you…what were you *feeling*, up there?" a woman asked. "I wouldn't have the nerve to do that."

"I…"

More cards were placed into her hand. Jack winked and nodded his approval from across the room. He didn't want to fight his way to the center of the little mob. Hannah made a thumbs-up, waved, and they walked out of sight.

Janet fielded more questions. "How did it *feel*?" again, and "How could you do that? I mean, not judgmentally, just *how* could you *do* it?"

Invitations to parties, invitations to model. To be in other films, which she politely turned down.

The crowd began to disperse as people started conversing with each other, but someone was always waiting their turn to speak to Janet.

"Hell of a thing, wasn't it?" Dmitri said.

Janet looked down at the stack of cards in her hand.

"Yes," she said, not knowing what else to say. "Yes it was."

"So. You'll be in another, yes?"

Janet looked up. She'd been dreading this opening too much to think beyond it.

"Not such an elaborate set, for my next idea. Your bruises are healed, aren't they?"

"Um, yes." Dmitri had said several women had made two or even three films with him. How much had they gone through before they quit?

"We could get started as soon as next week. I have someone else to schedule along with you of course."

Janet wasn't so sure about this. She hadn't signed on to be a—a what—film star? Porn star? Art star? What *had* she signed on for?

A young woman she hadn't talked to yet came up to her, almost bowing.

"That was incredible," she said. "I've been scared to talk to you. You're amazing. Can…can you teach me?"

"Teach you what?" Janet asked.

"How to be amazing?"

Janet just looked at her. The woman seriously seemed to be expecting an answer.

She looked at Dmitri.

"Well?" he said, "What do you think?"

She nodded.

"…Okay."

Chapter Seventeen

Liberated.

That was how Janet felt.

So. What.

So fucking what—*that* was how she felt. It was out there, in the world. Dmitri had engineered the most intense experience of her life, and a roomful of people witnessed it.

So fucking what.

How many times had she masturbated to fantasies of being whipped in front of a roomful of people, live; not just on film? Never mind that she'd never known how bad it would actually *hurt*. For *days*. Or who those real people who saw the film were...

Maybe she *had* shown them her soul, or at least a part?

Everyone at work told her how good it was to see her so cheerful and carefree for a change, and she was still laughing in the car, singing along with the radio while waiting at a stoplight.

She'd even sent Jon a text: So am I in this club or not? Hm? I think we need another dinner party but I want to be guest not host.

Be careful what you wish for, was his reply.

She texted back a laughing-face emoticon— :D.

She felt like celebrating. She'd invited the girls from work over to her house later, even though she'd have to be careful about what she said; she couldn't get *too* effusive. And she knew the appropriate drink for when it occurred: that *Garnacha* that Dmitri had ordered for her at the hotel. She'd called there, to find out what it was, and then called all over town to find it. No one in Oakdale stocked it; she had to call clear over here in Carlton to find it. A quick detour to Mr. Booze Emporium on her way home, and then just enough time to shower before everyone showed up.

Damn, she felt good. Ten feet tall. She could almost tell the world. Almost.

Her phone rang.

Oh no—the one person who knew how to dampen her enthusiasm about *anything*. How did she always know when to call?

"Hi, Marj."

❖

Ken was never all that into porn. His life *was* porn. Before he'd met his Mistress, he'd looked at a fair amount online, of course. But now, during the week when he was not at Her house, porn would drive him insane, unless She had given him permission to masturbate while alone. Which She rarely did.

But he'd been reading a little novel, an erotic science fiction novel, *The Stars All Point to You*. He'd read a dirty book or two when he was younger, passed on to him by some friend or another, but they were never what he was looking for. But while perusing one of the science fiction websites he frequented, he'd encountered a discussion about the book after one thread had inevitably veered toward *Barbarella* and meandered from there.

It was about a married couple who owned a smuggling spaceship (so many smugglers in SF), and their submissive female pet/slave to whom they did incredibly obscene things, but who in reality ran the show—always getting them out of jams with the Empire, etc.

The book also followed their main pursuer, a cruel female Commander determined to catch and punish them. However, the very strict military culture in which she lived also punished failure quite severely, and, well, she never did quite catch those miscreants, and so she suffered heavily at the hands of her all-male superiors. In the nude, of course.

Nevertheless, the smugglers did get separated during a pirate raid on their ship, each sold into slavery, and all three had to endure very humiliating and painful hardships on their way to—

Oh, wait. Traffic was moving up. Ken was stuck in the turning lane at the always fucked-up 25th and Esprit intersection. No one *ever* moved, especially at rush hour. He had sat in the left-turn lane through three cycles, and he knew there'd be no way he was close enough to speed through the next one.

So anyway he was thinking about this novel, and how pretty much every gender is dominated or tormented by every other gender. He was trying to match up the pairings, and three-ings, and four-ings in the book with all the permutations he'd mapped out last week. But the new problem was one of point-of-view. Figuring out the same relationships he'd thought about before, but adding on the additional requirement of who is telling the story, makes things even more complicated. The simplest pairing, two people, was one easy diagram, M/f, F/m, etc., but each now had two possible points of view. This was going to grow almost exponentially. He'd have to make a chart tonight. It was Thursday; he'd have nothing better to do.

The arrow signal turned green, and he inched forward behind some kind of small SUV. Everyone started accelerating, as fed up as he was. Yes! He was almost to the intersection, if the guy ahead would just *go*, speed up, speed up, go for it, come on, come on, and now—

The SUV stopped. *On a fucking yellow light.*

Oh that asshole! Ken was almost home, but he would never get across this goddamned street.

He tried to peer into the SUV to see what kind of idiot he was dealing with, but he saw only tinted windows. He looked up at the rush of cars passing by in front of him, going left, going right in conflicting stampedes of gray and silver.

He saw a car heading west on Esprit that he recognized. A late-model Lexus, so dark green that it appeared black. In the driver's seat was a shockingly beautiful woman with her brown hair pulled back into a severe bun, wearing a gray business jacket and sunglasses.

In the passenger seat was someone else, a male.

A redhead.

❖

"Hey, sis! How are you?"

"Fine, Marj. You? The kids? How's David?"

"Everyone's wonderful. How have you been?"

"Good, good. What's up?" Marjorie never called without a reason. And the reason was usually—

"I just wanted to see how you were doing." She meant "*what* you were doing."

"I'm doing great! Just working, mostly. I've finally got the house pretty much how I want it, so I've been taking it a little easy."

"Oh that house. It's so sad about you and Thomas. You two had such a nice house together." *Here we go.* "I just don't under-stand what you've done to your house. It was so *comfortable*."

"Yea. It's more comfortable now."

"Do you ever hear from Thomas?"

"No. Why would I?"

"Well…I thought maybe, if you—"

"It's been two years. There's no money issues, no kids, no—" *Sssshit.* Why did she say that?

"Oh, I know. And I'm so sorry."

"I'm fine without kids, Marj."

"Yes but—wouldn't it be so wonderful if you'd—"

"Be a single divorced Mom? No, Marj, that wouldn't be wonderful. I'm fine. Someday, maybe." It was amazing how fast these conversations spun out of control.

"Well you haven't got forever."

Janet held her tongue.

"He was such a nice guy."

"Yea."

"Well, are you seeing anyone new?"

"Did Mom put you up to this?"

"You haven't called them lately."

"I will, I promise."

"So?"

"What."

"Are you seeing anyone new?"

"…Sort of."

"Oh really! What's he like?"

"Very sweet."

"As sweet as Thomas?"

"Different. Very different."

"Oh. Treats you well?"

"Of course."

"What's he do?"

"He's a realtor. And he sells insurance."

"That sounds nice and stable. You know, with that job of yours, you could probably use someone with a little better income, if it gets more serious. Is it serious?"

"Not…really. Yet. I don't know."

"Well, real estate goes up and down with the economy. Maybe you should find a doctor, at that hospital. Or a lawyer, an attorney. They could always provide a—"

"Well, I'm sort of seeing a lawyer, too." *ShitwhydidIsaythat?*

"You're seeing two men? Oh, Janet, that's not good. That's not good at all. This isn't high school. Remember Jason and Brent, in high school? When you tried to date them both, and they found out? What would happen if your realtor and lawyer found out about each other? Hm?"

Well since they made me suck both of their dicks with my wrists fastened to a dildo up my ass, sent me into the hall naked to fetch ice, and fucked me all night, yes both of them, all night, I really don't think that'll be a problem.

"I don't know."

"Well you think about that."

"Okay."

"You've got to find someone who'll take *care* of you, Janet. The way Thomas did. The way David takes care of me. In fact, Sunday, after church, he told me that I should thank—"

"I've got another call, Marj."

"What?"

"I've got another call coming in. Bye."

"But I—"

"Bye, Marj. Love you. I'll call Mom and Dad."

Janet hit End Call and looked at the number of the call coming in.

Shit.

❖

Where the hell did She go? Ken was weaving between lanes, cutting people off, trying to move ahead of the slow-motion traffic. It was like everyone was on rails. He always hated jerks who did this, and now he was one of them. He was really only gaining a few seconds, and still *just* missing the yellow lights. Maybe all those guys had a reason—they were chasing down their Mistresses and their own replacement slaves?

His eyes searched ahead, and he used the time stuck at lights to search the parking lots. Why the hell was She even in Carlton? There was nothing here. And why was Jimmy with Her?

Carlton was notorious for consisting of nothing but strip malls and cheap apartments. On the map it was a thin stripe reaching north from Downtown like a "landing strip" on a woman's pussy; they'd pretty much just filled in the space between the two existing suburbs on either side and named it after the developer. It followed Boulevard d'Esprit de Corps all the way from the city limits to Sweetwater, and was pretty much the City's crotch. The whole town smelled of spilled beer, rotting Masonite, and loneliness. Ken lived here because it was cheap, but boring. No late-night shootouts, just…white guys with no lives, living alone behind the strip mall, waiting for their turn to go to their Mistress' houses on weekends.

Green light, and Ken shot out ahead of everyone else and changed lanes again, ready to pass the next light's stragglers. He knew better to waste time and inefficient effort searching the fast food places—his Mistress wouldn't be caught dead at those.

Where could She be? What was She after, in this part of town?

And why the fuck was Jimmy with Her?

❖

"Hello?"

"Janet?"

"Yes?"

"Carlotta Janski, from the Neighborhood Association."

"Oh, hi, Carlotta! How are you?"

"Fine. You?"

"Fine, thank you."

Carlotta—*not* Carly—lived entirely too close to Janet, not that physical proximity mattered. She was the Little Empress of Oakdale, and had a spy network to match any empire. She'd probably traced everyone's license plates, that first big night, obtained drone footage of the evening.

"We've been watching you, you know."

"What?"

"Yes, we've been keeping an eye on you, Janet. All the wonderful things you've done with that house."

"Oh—uh…"

"It was nice before the—well, you know. It was nice! But what you've done—you've got such an imagination!"

Janet breathed a sigh of relief. "Yes. I guess I do. Thank you."

"We thought maybe we could put that imagination to good use."

"What can I do for you, Carlotta?"

"Well, I hear you're quite the hostess."

"*What?*"

"And baker. You can make quite the drizzled rum balls?"

"What?"

"Sandra Jennings told me. Last year, when her father was ill?"

"Oh, right, right."

"So…you're interested?"

"Oh, sure! Of course, of course. …What are we doing?"

"The bake sale! You're up for it, right?"

"Ooooh, the bake sale. For the—"

"For the park, yes. You *did* read the letter I sent you? It's been a while, now."

"Yes, yes, of course. I'm sorry." *The letter I've avoided like the plague for a month.* It was about a bake sale?

"You could do some baking, right? It's for the children. Even though you don't have any?"

"Oh, yes, okay."

"We're having a dinner, too."

"Oh, okay. Is it catered? You know who'd love the business?"

"Well, it's volunt—"

"Amanda… Amanda…" Janet realized she didn't know Amanda's last name. It wasn't the same as Jon's. She'd seen it somewhere…

"Amanda Martin?"

…on the blood tests Jon had sent her, before her dinner party. "Yes, that's it."

"You know Amanda Martin."

Long pause. Very long pause.

Too long. "Well, yes."

"…How well?"

"W—uh, wha? Pretty well." *Pretty* darn *well, in some ways.*

"You think she'd cook for us?"

"Well, she's a caterer. She lives close by. I'm sure she'd love to."

Another long, long, silent pause.

"Okay. You arrange that. That would be great."

Jesus. What just happened? Janet turned her blinker on and pulled into Mr. Booze Emporium's vast parking lot.

"Carlotta, can I call you back? I'm sort of running some errands."

"Yes. Yes, that would be fine. And you're recruiting Amanda Martin for us, right?"

"Yes. I'll see what I can do," Janet said. "Bye."

Whatever this was all about, Janet realized she was not yet ready to tell the world about her new film career. Not that she would have *ever* told Carlotta, anyway. She really did need to keep this to herself when the girls came over.

She put the car in Park and opened the door.

❖

Where, where, where, where, where? Where was She? Where did She go? Ken looked around frantically while stuck in the center lane at the stoplight. He could now jump left or right; he was first in line so he could—

There. Black/green Lexus. The Mr. Booze Emporium parking lot. The car was parked, and someone was in the passenger seat. Short hair…red.

But the store was behind him. Ken would have to go all the way to the next stoplight, or he could just…

He ran the red light, turned hard left across the turning lane, and made a U-turn while the oncoming traffic was clear.

…To many honks and middle fingers. He checked the mirror; no sirens, no flashing lights. Half a block, and he turned in as soon as the jam he'd just been in front of moved out of his way.

❖

"Excuse me, I called about a *Garnacha*? It's…I'm sorry, I forgot the vintage. She said she'd hold it back for me."

The guy behind the counter searched the shelf behind him; shook his head.

"Sorry, must not a' got done. They're over in the next to last aisle, sign says 'Spain'? Sorry I can't take you, I've got people checking out, here."

"That's okay. I can find it."

Janet headed down the length of the huge store.

❖

Ken knocked on the car window. Jimmy turned, surprised, his eyebrows raised behind gold wrap-around sunglasses. Carolyn had rolled the window down a few inches for him, like he was a puppy, before leaving him in the car.

"Oh. Hey. What up, dawg?"

"What are you doing here?"

"Waiting."

"Why are you here?"

"She wanted to get some fancy wine, you know? They only have it here I guess."

"I mean, what are *you* doing here?"

"She told me to come with her. Do *you* ever tell her no?" He laughed.

"What are you—what you *doing* here, with Her?" This didn't make any sense. Ken had never seen Her out of Her house, not since they'd first started out and would meet at restaurants. Riding around with Her was inconceivable; there was a definite order to things. Was Jimmy the only other one She took around?

"I told you, man. What the fuck do you want?"

"Where do you go with Her?"

"Wherever she says. You know how it is, man."

"Do you talk like that to Her?"

"Yea right. Not that it's your business. It's not your night."

"When are your nights?"

"When she says. Look, man, this is gettin' old. You know her: ya do what she says. It's her way or the fuckin' highway, right? Get over it or get out." He pointed his thumb behind him.

"You need to go."

"Go where, man? I live in Blue Sky. It's my night. She's cookin'."

"She's *cooking*? For you?"

"I dunno."

"Has She cooked for you before?"

"Yea. So what. So fuckin' what. Look, man, get lost. I'll see you tomorrow, man. 'Til then, fuck off." Tomorrow? That was *his* night.

"No, *you* fuck off. You need to go. I don't mean now. I mean, you need to get lost. Leave. Tell Her it ain't"—now he was talking like Jimmy—"tell Her it's not working out. You need another Mistress."

"Yo, fuck you, man. *You* move on, you don't like it. We do what she says. That's the gig. That's all there is to it, you should know that."

"I am telling you to move on, man. Move. On."

"She's in there. Don't like the arrangement, go tell her yourself. Otherwise, you can suck my dick—oh wait, you already have."

Ken wanted to punch him. He was *this* close. But he'd have to punch into the little slot above the partially opened window, or try to pull the door open, which he saw was locked. He clenched his fists. Jimmy stared back behind his sunglasses. He flipped Ken off.

Ken flipped him back as he headed into the store.

This was it. He was ready to stand up to Her, lay it all out. Tell Her it was Jimmy, or him. He would do whatever She said, but he would not be *replaced*. Not without a fight. The powered doors to the store slid open for him.

❖

Janet knew it had to be around here somewhere. The Spanish wines were tucked in near the end of the aisle, the far end, almost the farthest spot from the counters. She wondered if there was much shoplifting here, with these high shelves like grocery stores had, rather than the low ones in most liquor stores. But Mr. Booze Emporium was always an oddball place.

They could find you anything, but you never knew quite what was going to happen when you got there. Like forgetting to reserve your bottle. Or they'd be packed one minute, practically empty like this the next. She looked up, and saw the security camera at the end of the aisle.

She found the Argentinian wines, the Malbecs that she liked so much, Portuguese...here. Spain. Ah, *Garnachas*! But she didn't see the one she was after. She looked up and down the rows, ran her finger along the labels. No...no...

She leaned over and saw them. They were stacked lower than they deserved to be; didn't they know how awesome these were? She got down on her knees to look at the bottom rows.

❖

He couldn't find Her. He'd gone by all the aisles to the right until he'd run out of the wines, and even past them to make sure She hadn't already picked one out and gone over to the hard liquor; She did have guests with varied tastes. God, did She.

Did he really want to do this? What if She told him "*Fine, go*"? He couldn't imagine living without Her, without Her structure, Her order. Her achingly beautiful face and body. Her will. But he was ready. He was going to tell Her. *Him or me.*

If She'd intended to buy very much, She'd have brought Jimmy in, right? To carry it. He turned around and headed the other way, to the other half of the store. He glanced out the front windows as he passed the front counter—"Help ya find sump'n'?"

"Just looking." Her car was still out there.

Ken was almost to the end of the store; he was running out of aisles. He was up to the next-to-the-last row, all red wines, when he heard the distinctive sound of his Mistress's fingers snapping, just once.

❖

Janet turned.

Standing above her, dressed for work in a tight gray skirt and jacket that accentuated her thin waist and worked-out shoulders. Severe heels (neither scuffed), severe bun. Goddamn perfect cheekbones. She was holding a bottle of some red with a boring label, which meant expensive.

Janet couldn't say anything. Her throat was too tight.

"Well look who we have here," Carolyn said, in a way that reminded Janet of certain girls from grade school. Mean girls.

She started to get up.

"Stay on your knees."

Janet hesitated; stayed.

Carolyn scanned Janet up and down, evaluating her with a slight sneer.

"I hear you've become quite a hot little commodity. A celebrity, even."

Janet opened her mouth.

"Did I say you could talk?"

Janet closed her mouth.

"Now I asked you a question."

Janet cleared her throat.

"No."

"No what?"

"No, you never said I could talk."

"Try again. How do you address me?"

Janet's jaw clenched tight. This couldn't be happening.

"No. Ma'am."

Carolyn smiled. She waited a long time to speak again.

"Your eyes are fully dilated, and you're short of breath. Your hands are shaking, I can see. And you're whiter than your usual white. Is there a problem, Janet?"

I hate your fucking guts, if that's what you mean.

"I asked you a question."

"What—what do you want?"

"I wanted to see the big film star on her knees in front of me, where she belongs. So obedient, so subservient. Just about perfect, some people think. I have my doubts."

"How did you find out about the film?"

"How do you think?"

Jon.

Carolyn stepped closer to Janet, towering above her.

"Kiss my feet."

Janet was shocked. Here in the store? *Any*where, really. No way in hell was she going to lower herself for this bitch again, especially here in public. She looked up and down the aisle, but saw no one who could help her.

"It's the least you can do, since you destroyed my other pair."

"No. I said I was sorry about that."

Carolyn managed to lean forward without actually moving. "Do it, Janet."

"I won't."

Janet was trembling almost violently. She wanted to punch Carolyn in the gut, she was right at that level. But she pictured her weak little fist not having any effect, and then what? Carolyn tightened her grip on the neck of the bottle of wine she was holding.

Janet took a deep, shaky breath. She looked behind her, then behind Carolyn, this time to make sure no one was looking.

She bent down and kissed Carolyn's shiny black shoe.

She hated herself.

"Both of them."

Janet kissed the other shoe, and rose back up to her knees. She looked down at the floor, wanting to fight this bitch but not able to look her in the eye again.

"Good girl. Good little slave girl."

Just. Go. Away.

"You know, I like to make films, too."

Janet clenched her fists in humiliation.

"Stand up."

Janet shook her head no.

"I said stand up."

Janet shook her head again, but grabbed a shelf and pulled herself up. She kept her face down, her red, red face.

"So shy! How did they ever get you to appear in front of a camera? You'll have to get over this shyness, if you're going to become the little slave girl you think you are. Not quite like the books, is it?"

Silence.

"Hm?"

"No."

"No what."

"No, Ma'am."

"Let me see your markings."

"I don't have any."

"What?"

"I don't have any. Dmitri doesn't want me marked for my next film."

"*Next* film, you say! Well aren't you the little *star*. Hmm…" Carolyn tapped her chin with her finger, deep in thought. "Well, then. We'll have to think of something else for *my* little film project."

Like hell would I ever make a film for you!

"Turn around."

Janet stood still, face down.

"Turn. Around."

Janet slowly turned, away from Carolyn.

"Lift your shirt. Show me your back. I can't believe no one has marked you lately, you little whore. I'll bet you're searching all over your neighborhood for someone to whip you."

"No!"

"Show me. Lift up your shirt. Show me your tits."

"No."

"Do it."

Janet looked toward the end of the aisle and shook her head, as if that could make this not be happening, and lowered her arms to raise the hem of her shirt. She lifted it a few inches.

"Higher."

A few more inches.

"Take it off."

"What? No!"

She could smell Carolyn's expensive scent as the bitch leaned in behind her. She could feel heat from Carolyn's face as she rested her chin on Janet's shoulder.

"*Take. It. Off*," she whispered, almost a growl.

"No."

Janet felt the heat of Carolyn's hand on the small of her bare back.

"*Don't make me hurt you.*"

Janet lifted her shirt over her head. She kept it bunched up in front of her breasts.

Carolyn reached around Janet and unzipped the fly of her pants. With the lightest of touches, she loosened them around Janet's hips and let them fall past her knees.

"Drop the shirt."

"N—"

"Drop it."

Janet was ready to cry. But she let the shirt go, and covered her chest with her arms.

"You *don't* have any markings," Carolyn said, surprised. Janet was standing in her underwear, back to Carolyn, facing the end of the aisle.

"See that camera up there? Look up into it."

"…No."

"Do I have to pull your head back by the hair? Look up. At the camera. This is my film, I'm making."

Janet swallowed and looked up. The video camera was pointed right back at her, its beady little lens cold and cruel. *Can't you see I need help?*

"Unfasten your bra, drop your panties."

"Carolyn, please."

"Ooh, 'Carolyn', now, is it? Are we friends?"

"No."

"Then a.) take off your bra and panties for the camera, b.) do not address me by name again, and c.) if you disobey me again I will make that little beating I gave you at your house feel like a tickling with a feather duster. Now. *Do it.*" Her voice hardened at this last command, and Janet felt a chill of genuine fear.

She reached behind her, her hands shaking too much to wrap around the hooks in her bra. Janet fumbled until the straps were opened. She crossed her arms and lowered the bra down her arms, and finally let it fall to the floor. She stifled a sniffle. She would not let Carolyn see her cry. She slid her fingers underneath the elastic of her panties, and slid them over her hips.

"Happy?" *You cunt. You fucking cunt.*

"Getting there. Someone's getting a show, aren't they? I wonder if anyone's watching the monitor. Are they male? Female? You seem to like to please both. Maybe a crowd. Maybe some assistant manager is making sure to record this for the Internet. What do you think? Hm?"

Janet lowered her head in shame, couldn't look up.

"I said look at the camera. Eyes up. *Up.* Look your audience in the eye. Lower your hands to your sides."

Janet brought her arms down, her clothes wrapped around her ankles. This was easily the worst moment of her life. She looked up at the camera.

"Good girl. We'll make a proper little slave of you yet. Don't Dmitri's films always have some exact time limit?"

"Twenty-two minutes."

"Well, I'm not going to pretend that you'll stand here for twenty-two minutes. Because I'm leaving. But here's the thing: you *will* stand there until I leave. When you no longer hear my shoes stepping away from you, hear my laughter, then you can pull your little panties up and get dressed."

There was a long pause.

"Understand?"

Janet was crying, still looking up at the camera. She shook her head yes; she didn't want to let Carolyn hear her voice quivering.

"I asked you a question."

"Yes, Ma'am," she whispered.

"Good girl. I'll see you around, won't I, Janet. Tell Jon hello for me."

Janet stood still, too afraid to move, feeling the store's cold air conditioning against her naked, sweating body. She heard the familiar click of that fucking bitch's heels click away into the distance, down the aisle behind her, around the corner. She bent over and pulled up her pants and underwear in one motion.

❖

What the hell was *that?* Ken turned around and hid behind the shelf's end cap before his Mistress turned around and saw him. She was heading this way.

Shit.

He turned and ran. Slowed to a fast walk as he neared the counter, but he really, *really* needed to get out the door before his Mistress rounded the corner of that aisle.

"Aw, hey, were you looking for that *Garnacha* back there? Everybody is. We've moved them up here, to the front. Hey… hey can I help—?"

But he was already out the door.

Who *was* that? That brunette, with the black hair? He remembered Her telling him about going to see one the last time She'd put him into Deep Storage, but he hadn't heard anything about her since. The girl didn't seem very happy about the whole thing, but his Mistress did. He could tell from their postures, even though he only saw their backs. He couldn't hear anything they'd said. Just his Mistress's cool cooing.

He ran past his Mistress's car. Jimmy flipped him off again, and Ken made the "I'm watching you" gesture by pointing to his eyes with two fingers and then pointing to Jimmy with one. Lame, he knew. There would probably be hell to pay tomorrow, after Jimmy told Her about the encounter.

Why was he going back to Her house at all? He should just *not show up*.

God, he thought as he reached his car. *I am one fucked-up individual.*

❖

"You told that fucking cunt from hell about my movies? What goddamn business is it of hers? Why are you talking about me to that fucking cunt in any way shape or form?!" She was gripping her phone so hard she thought she'd break it. Good.

Jon waited for her to finish.

"Doll. Janet. Please, what's going on? What happened again?"

"That fucking bitch! God I hate that fucking bitch! That cunt! How could you?"

"How could I what? What did she do?"

"Oh! Jon!"

"Janet, calm down."

"Do not tell me to calm down!" Janet was still in her car, still in the Mr. Booze Emporium parking lot. As far she knew, no one had seen her standing there, in person at least, though on camera who the hell could know until she turned up on the Internet.

It wasn't until she was safe in her car, doors locked, that she allowed herself to break down, to wail like a baby, to punch the steering wheel. Oh, that fucking cunt.

She remembered she still had friends coming over later. Shit.

She could still go back in there, talk to the manager, ask to have it deleted. That would be an interesting conversation, though, wouldn't it? And would the police get involved? How would she explain *that* to Marj and her parents?

"How could you trust that bitch with *anything* to do with me?"

"What do you mean?"

"You told her I was in a film?"

"Why wouldn't I?"

"Because she'll use it against me. She *did* use it against me. I might be on the fucking Internet! Why do you have anything to do with her?"

"Janet..."

"What!"

"Stop. Carolyn and I, we go *way* back, even before..."

"Before what?"

"Never mind. Look. We used to top, together. We'd compete. Go after the same people, who weren't even in the Scene. 'Capture' them. We'd *hunt*, and keep score. Show up at each other's houses once one of us caught someone."

"That's sick."

"Careful, now. Like your film wasn't? Your dinner party? Your fantasies?"

Janet tried to slow down her breathing. She thought she was going to hyperventilate.

"We can take care of this."

"What is *wrong* with her? Besides being the asshole of Satan, I mean."

"I don't know. She used to be fun. Hard, but fun. Consensual, at least. But yea, I have to admit, she's kind of going off the rails. Even when I talked to her today, she was all buggy and distracted. Like someone's topping *her*, and she doesn't like it."

"Who the hell would try *that*?" Janet almost laughed.

"You got me. She was jumpy. Something's bothering her, all right. She's always been so controlled."

"Her soul, that's what's bothering her. Her lack of one."

"Now, stop. Where did this happen?"

"I told you. In Mr. Booze Emporium, in Carlton."

"This can be taken care of. You're not thinking like a Top."

She started to calm down, a little at least.

"Why would *I* think like a Top?"

"Because…" Jon said.

"What?"

"You might need to start doing that, thinking like a Top. A switch, at least."

"What? Why? Wait a minute. Why were you talking to her *today*?"

"Well, you were agitating for another dinner party. To be a guest, not the hostess. I found the perfect girl. Out in Westbrook, looking for something different, just like you were. She's into it."

"…And?"

"Carolyn's going to be there."

Chapter Eighteen

Two cars?

Ken had to park in the street, because not only was Jimmy's junk pile in the way, but so was another little car—some souped-up black Mazda with day-glow green highlights, orange rims, and a giant spoiler fin stuck on the back. The neighbors were going to *love* that. He wasn't late and he was dreading going in, but he ran to the walled-off entryway to undress, anyway.

He was shocked to see what his Mistress was wearing when She opened the door: a black leather corset/bustier assembly that accentuated Her hips and pushed Her smallish breasts upward; tiny black panties that, when She turned around, were disappointingly not a thong. Very shiny black leather knee-high boots with incredibly high heels, and a black military-style officer's cap which She wore at a jaunty angle, Her hair in a ponytail underneath it.

"Crawl," She said, already halfway down the hallway.

His Mistress never wore dominatrix regalia, except at certain parties, usually Halloween, with him naked and leashed in tow. On such rare occasions, She would ironically dress the part of what She already was, yet wasn't—control was simply Life, for Carolyn, no point in getting flashy about it on any other day.

Ken crawled past the Asian girl in the alcove—his Mistress didn't even tell him not to look at her—and they exchanged glances. She looked worried, not her usual serene, which did not bode well at all. He crawled into the living room.

Not only were there two cars outside, there were two naked redheads standing in the room, both of whom looked remarkably like Ken. Both were at perfect attention, and unlike Ken, their cocks were as well.

"Kenny, you know James. Say hello to Robert."

"Hello, Robert," Ken said on his hands and knees.

"Bobby, say hello to Kenny." No "Kenneth," this time, for the others? Only he was to use the more formal names, tonight?

"Hello, Kenny."

Bobby's voice was deeper than Ken's, but he looked even more like Ken than Jimmy did. How did She even *find* these guys, around town? Submissives, even? Both men stood perfectly still, shoulders back, about two feet apart. Both of their genitals were shaved clean, same as Ken's, the red hair above their cocks trimmed short. Bobby's cock looked more like Ken's than Jimmy's—ramrod straight, no curve. Perhaps a few more veins along its length. He wondered if Jimmy'd had to shave and suck Bobby. He hoped so.

Jimmy glanced down with an arrogance on his face that made Ken recall the Smirking Man. Had he told Her about the parking lot?

"Stand between them, Kenny." He took his place in the center of the line. "Kenny, you don't seem to be as happy to see me as these other boys are. Are you not happy to see me?"

"I'm very happy, Mistress."

"Then why aren't you showing it?"

He didn't have an excuse. He just wasn't feeling it. At all.

He'd always known that Obedience didn't always equate with arousal, like in people's fantasies. Often this Life meant hours of boredom, as long as orders were obeyed and submission shown. But until now, he'd almost always *been* aroused, by Her mere presence. And by the lack of masturbation during the rest of the week, when She ordered him not to touch himself—even at home, he obeyed. But today, he was feeling different. Blank.

"I…"

He couldn't read Her face. It was an expression he'd never quite seen on Her—not anger, not the usual disappointment in a failure of his (though this particular failing was rare). It was as if She wanted to say something, without all the formalities that these situations required to keep the game going.

"Well, then. All right."

There was an awkward moment before She regained Her composure. She looked down, away.

"You have some atoning to do," She finally said. "I understand you were rather rude to James yesterday."

Ken waited for a command or a question.

"Well?"

"I am sorry, Mistress."

"Explain yourself."

I love you, I'll never know why, and I want all these jerkoffs out of our Life. I want things how they were before they started to change. Before you said you wanted another redhead. That was when the changes started, these awkward moments of uncertainty, or increased emotional cruelty (as opposed to the mere physical). Or was it before then, that night She'd put him in Deep Storage because some black-haired woman had spoiled Her plans with him? And was that the girl in the liquor store?

"I spoke to another slave outside of playtime, Mistress. I knew it was one of Your rules but I broke it. I am sorry."

She looked down at his cock, still limp, and crossed Her arms. She looked back into his eyes, probably wondering why the impending punishment wasn't arousing him as usual.

He wondered as well. Most days, the overwhelming tension of knowing some extreme activities were coming to his body—*his* body, from *Her*—was enough to speed up his heart and engorge his cock with blood until it hardened like stone. It was Her full attention that got him going, even if others were around, watching. Maybe that was the problem—it wouldn't be his Mistress doing the punishing, he knew already. It would likely be *them*, whoever these guys were. This was Her new game, and it wasn't arousing.

"Tell James you're sorry. It was he you were rude to."

"Sorry, James."

"No, look him in the eye. In fact, get on your knees when you do. And mean it. Did I just see you shake your head?"

"No, Mistress."

Yes. Ken kneeled. He was already standing shoulder to shoulder with Jimmy, so when he kneeled to face him, he had Jimmy's now-familiar stiff pink cock in his face. He looked up to meet Jimmy's eyes.

"I'm sorry I was rude at the store," he said.

"Jimmy, how could Kenny make it up to you?"

"Aw, I think he should suck my dick, Mistress," Jimmy said, staring Ken in the face. He moved his hips forward.

"Kenny?"

Ken held still.

"Why aren't you sucking? You offended James, and now he's told you how to make it up to him."

"It was Your rule I broke, Mistress. I am waiting for You to tell me what I should do."

"I'd kinda like to whip him too, Mistress," Jimmy said. *That was pushy, moron.* "If it pleases you." *Damn it.* For such a dullard bro, Jimmy was learning the language.

"Would you, now. We'll see. And you'll be punished for speaking out of turn, Jimmy."

Ken felt a little satisfaction at that.

"Suck him, Kenny."

Ken opened his mouth to let Jimmy enter it.

"Naw, you do the work, dawg," Jimmy said.

God, Ken hated this guy.

"Jimmy, you speak out of turn once more and you'll get it worse than he will."

"Yes, Mistress."

"But you're right. Kenny, *suck* James. He shouldn't have to work at it. It was your offense."

Ken didn't answer. He leaned forward and took Jimmy's cock into his mouth, glaring up at him once more before lowering his eyes. The satisfied smirk on Jimmy's face angered him too much. He heard his Mistress take a deep breath and moan her approval. She settled into Her favorite chair to watch.

"Kenny, turn your body this way, with your head still turned to James. Bobby, turn to face Kenny." Ken kept the hard cock in his mouth as he rotated on his knees; now his Mistress got the full frontal view of him.

"And use your hands. On both of them. Grab James's cock, and grab Robert's as well. Jack them both off as you suck James."

Ken sighed, mouth full of dick. He could hear Her heavy breathing. He reached up and grasped each cock at the base as he bobbed his head forward and back on Jimmy's.

Then he saw and heard something he never had before, in this house: a flash, and the sound-effect click of the camera in Her phone. She had never taken pictures. Ever. Allowed none of Her guests to, either. There was surveillance video in every room, who knew what She did with that, but no pictures.

"Oh, yeah," She said. "Suck him, Kenny. Jack those cocks." She sounded like a porn director. "*Suck* it, boy."

Usually, servicing a male at parties, Ken would begin to harden despite himself, the eyes of Her fascinated friends upon him shamefully arousing. But not today. He rolled his eyes as far toward his Mistress as he could, but She was still out of his vision without turning his head. Yet he could detect motion, rapid, back and forth—Her hand, in Her black panties.

What? She *never* did this either—never ever ever—in front of slaves, especially multiple slaves, during a performance.

Never. Her breath was ragged, desperate—which itself was another first, in his experience. She prided Herself on Her self-control, at least until She came.

Ken could tell by the rhythm of Jimmy's body that he was close. Their Mistress—no, damn it, *his* Mistress—could tell too: "Yeah! Come on his face, Jimmy. Wouldn't you like that? Would that make up for his rudeness?"

"Y—yes. I still want to—to whi—whip—"

Jimmy pulled out and his come erupted onto Ken's face. Another flash and camera click. Jimmy grabbed Ken by the hair and held him still, while Ken, to his own chagrin, kept jerking him off. Jimmy shot hot come onto Ken's cheeks, lips, forehead. Jimmy finally grabbed his own cock and jacked; Ken wasn't doing it quite right. He spewed a few more spurts onto Ken's chest.

"Yeah! Now Robert, Kenny. Suck him. Suck him off."

Bobby didn't take long at all. He was new to all this, probably. Ken sucked his cock as his Mistress took another picture, and when Bobby pulled out and came on his face as well, She took two more. Bobby's come had a heavier viscosity, stuck to him even more. He was covered in it. He held both dicks, neither gone fully limp, and faced his Mistress. She took one more shot of him, very humiliating.

"Get them both hard, then stand up." Ken stroked both of their balls and leaned one way to suck Jimmy to full hardness, then the other for Bobby. He stood up and they were all in a neat row again, shoulder to shoulder.

"Oh, God. My boys," She said. "Stand up straight." She took another shot of them, three nearly identical men, the two on either side with hard cocks, the one in the center's face dripping with semen.

"Jimmy, you may go to the playroom and select a whip. We'll get this boy hard if we have to beat it into him."

❖

"Bobby, you said to me that you really want to top more than serve," She said. She was pacing, impatient; restless. Dissatisfied.

"Yes, Ma'am."

Ma'am, not Mistress. He wasn't a full slave, just a guest? Ken was grasping for any information about what was going on.

"Well, today you'll get your chance. But not completely, now, will you?"

"No, Ma'am. You're the boss lady." He smiled agreeably.

Carolyn nodded slowly, barely tolerating his idiocy.

"Yes. Well." Ken watched as She ground Her teeth, Her eyes flickering around instead of the usual steel concentration. "You may begin."

Ken, kneeling, watched with satisfaction as Bobby gave Jimmy ten harsh strokes with the whip, a nasty little quirt that Jimmy had selected in the playroom because he thought he'd get to use it on Ken. But he had forgotten he was due for punishment as well. Jimmy stood straight, his arms raised, and bowed his head and grimaced as Bobby left ten crisp red lines across his body. That quirt hurt like hell, Ken knew. He tried to suppress his smile.

"What's the lesson, Jimmy?"

"I will not speak out of turn, Mistress."

"Good." Heavy sigh, still impatient, as though She had something else She'd rather be doing. She didn't even tell Jimmy to thank Bobby: "All right, Bobby, hand the whip to James."

He did so.

"Jimmy, Kenny offended you, which reflects badly on me. On my training. Would you prefer to whip me, or Kenny?"

"Oh, Kenny, Mistress. Kenny." He was fighting back some tears from his whipping. "If it pleases you, of course, Mistress."

"Good answer, Jimmy. Kenny,"—She kicked the leather ottoman away from Her chair, out into the middle of the furniture—"Bend over it."

Well, this wasn't exactly new. How many times had he been bent over this piece of furniture, for Her, for Her guests to whip or use? This was where She'd once whipped him to bleeding. He got onto his knees and lowered his stomach onto its cushion.

"No, all the way over it. Up on it."

Ken lifted himself onto and across the ottoman, enough that his face was over its edge. Which, considering his face was still dripping with come, meant he at least wouldn't be punished for soiling it. Just for soiling the carpet, probably.

"Jimmy, how many strokes do you think Kenny deserves for insulting you?"

"Aw, as many as you think, Mistress." He was learning. "Ten? Naw—twenty!"

"Ten will do. Place them across his ass. This is good practice for you."

Jimmy didn't need any practice. He hit hard, and placed the blows perfectly—as Ken faced forward, only occasionally glancing over at his Mistress sitting in Her chair, he could see Her satisfaction as Jimmy whipped his upraised ass in a neat row. Ken could imagine the perfectly spaced horizontal stripes.

He gritted his teeth and kept his face high, as She would want.

"Now, Kenny—how many do you think you deserve for insulting *me*? For breaking my rule about speaking to other slaves outside of my home?"

"As many as you see fit, Mistress."

"Oh come on—answer the question."

"Twenty, Mistress. Insulting you is easily twice as unforgivable as insulting another slave." *Especially this idiot.* "Easily," he said. Despite his hatred of this situation, he knew how to answer, and how to please. And he still wanted to please Her.

Carolyn nodded at Jimmy.

"Twenty," She said. "And place half across his back, the other half on his ass. Remember to avoid the kidneys, like I told you about."

Ken heard the crack of the whip across his shoulders before he felt the sting. This bastard hit *hard.* Another blow. Each felt like a blade.

"Aw, look at poor Robert, Kenny." Ken looked over his shoulder at Bobby, who was still at full attention. He looked anxious. Hungry. His cock was at full attention, red and swollen.

"He can hardly stand this. Bobby, what would you like to do, if I were to let you do anything?"

"Fuck him. Ma'am."

"Mm-hm. Mm-hm. Well, since you're still a guest, not my slave, I will allow this. I trust the mouth will do?"

"Oh God, yea. Ma'am."

"All right. Kneel in front of him. Don't be in any hurry. I want to enjoy this moment." Bobby got onto his knees in front of Ken, which blocked his view of his Mistress. Ken opened his mouth.

"Suck it. Up and down," Bobby said.

"Don't get ahead of yourself," Carolyn said. "Who calls the shots, Bobby?"

"You do, Ma'am. My bad."

"You heard him, Kenny."

He sucked the dick in front of him, gliding his lips up and down the shaft. He flinched as the whipping shifted from his back to his ass again, which was already sore from the first ten.

"Learning your lesson, Kenny?"

Ken released the cock from his lips. "Yes, Mistress."

He sighed—he knew this trick, and what was next: "Did I give you permission to stop sucking Robert's cock?"

But he hadn't started again yet, which meant only one violation, not the two of having to stop again.

"No, Mistress." Only then did he resume his sucking.

"Twenty, Mistress," Jimmy said, Ken's ass in pain.

"And how do you feel Kenny should make it up to you, for his insult? He's been punished, but not made amends."

"I'd like to fuck him, too."

"Ah. Well, that does sound lovely. You may proceed." She was tapping Her foot, so fast and nervously Her heel sounded like a drumroll.

Ken heard the sound of a tube of lube landing in the palm of Jimmy's hand—his Mistress had tossed it. He felt it injected into his anus, squeezed like a syringe, and felt the tip of Jimmy's cock press against him.

He moaned, muffled by the cock in his mouth, as Jimmy entered without much preliminary ceremony—or charity, for that matter. He saw another flash and heard a click as he held still for the two men, so identical to him, fucking him in both ends. His Mistress stood and moved to the side of them, phone held up in front of Her.

"Bobby, start fucking his mouth," She said, and Ken realized She was filming this on Her phone, not just taking still pictures. Something else She had never done, never permitted any guests to do. Couldn't She just watch this on the surveillance video, or was the *act* of Her filming it to make it more humiliating for him? She crouched down, to his level, and held the phone still.

"Come on, boys. Let's see some effort."

At least Jimmy had lubed him better than Ken had lubed Jimmy the week before. But Jesus—Jimmy's cock was big, bigger than his own. This was tough. Jimmy had done a good job with the lube, but he was thrusting pretty hard. He tried to stay relaxed, but it wasn't easy. Bobby was fucking his mouth harder, and going deeper, probing into his throat.

"Oh, yeah!" his Mistress said, like a fashion photographer. He couldn't see Her; he couldn't see much but Bobby's stomach inches from his face. She was directly to his left, getting that symmetrical, side view: two men kneeling, both fucking the one in the middle, all nearly identical.

Quite a visual: they'd managed to coordinate their timing so that they were both pumping in unison. Ken moaned with each simultaneous assault.

"Like that, Kenny?"

He could only nod and moan, cock still embedded deep in his face, even though he did not like it at all. It felt like a punishment, for something far more serious than insulting Jimmy. But for what, he couldn't fathom.

"I asked you a question." She waited for an answer, but Ken couldn't back away from Bobby's thrusting cock to speak.

"Spank him, Jimmy. He's failed to answer my question. You may spank him hard."

"Yes, *Mis*tress!" And Ken felt the sting of Jimmy's hand on his right flank.

"Don't acknowledge commands, Jimmy. Just carry them out."

"Yes, Mistress. I mean—"

Another blow, and another. Jimmy was clearly enjoying this as he started fucking faster; his timing with Bobby was getting all out of sync.

"This side, James. The camera side."

Jimmy started hitting Ken's left flank.

Ken wondered if he'd have to watch that video, later, or if was just for Her enjoyment. Or if She would post it onto the Internet, the ultimate disgrace. Or send it to Her friends;

maybe as an advertisement to sell him to someone else? Did She sell slaves? He'd heard Her mention something about that once, to some friend of Hers or another.

Why was he even thinking that was a possibility?

What was he doing wrong? What more could he *do*?

What kind of fucked-up individual am I? he thought. What kind of loser would *do* this, endure this, merely to please another? Even if it *was* Her. Yes Her, capitalized. There had never been another spelling, not since She'd approached him that day at the gym nearly two years ago with that knowing smile, wiping the sweat off of Her face, and then his as he sat at the weight machine. He could smell, feel Her perspiration in the towel as She pressed it against his forehead, taste their mingled sweat as She stuffed the towel into his mouth, right there in front of everybody. That was the first time She ever spoke to him, after She'd watched him for weeks and then gagged him with their own salty fluids: "You're buying me dinner tonight."

Ken had outlasted every one of Her other slaves; they came and went. He was the most devoted slave She had ever had—She'd told him so.

But for the first time, he wasn't sure he could outlast this.

She sighed, and he got the feeling She'd turned the phone's camera off.

"Kenny," She said. "Ken…"

He waited, both orifices getting a pretty good pounding. Jimmy kept hitting his ass with his hand, but even he seemed to be losing interest.

"Ken, I'm thinking of taking away your name. I'm thinking of calling you 'Slave number three', after these two. If I make Robert a slave, of course. Or maybe…six." She drifted off.

"Would you like that, Ken? Slave Number 6?"

"*Mmph*," Ken grunted.

There was a silence, except for the sporadic slapping of Jimmy's hand on Ken's ass and the sliding of wet cocks into Ken's orifices.

His Mistress pulled Her leather cap from Her head, and ran Her hand cross Her forehead. She massaged it as She stared down at the floor. She closed Her eyes. She was quiet for an awfully long time, Her mind elsewhere. She took a very deep, unsteady breath. Ken could swear he heard Her stifle a sniffle, but that was impossible. His Mistress did not cry.

Then She raised Her head, refocused, as stern as ever.

"Bobby, how's your control?"

"Ma'am?" Bobby slowed his fucking.

"Are you close?"

"Oh. No, Ma'am. I could be, if you want."

"I do not want. Come here."

Bobby withdrew his cock, to Ken's immense relief, and turned around to face Carolyn. He was only a couple of feet from Her chair.

Ken's Mistress stood up, and pulled Her skimpy black underwear over Her hips and down Her legs—She did this Herself! She stepped out of them and handed them to Bobby.

"Fill Kenneth's mouth with this and sit down. Here." She pointed to Her chair. *Her* chair. No one else sat there. *No one.* *Nothing* was making any sense, tonight.

Bobby poked the panties—wet, aromatic, the tastes of the best nights of Ken's life—into Ken's mouth, pushed them in until his mouth was filled with Her musky taste. Bobby sat on the chair.

"Knees together."

And then She straddled him. Ken's sore jaw dropped. Jimmy pushed him forward with each thrust into his ass, but he hardly noticed. Carolyn straddled Bobby's legs, facing away from him, Her naked ass right there in front of his stupid face, so like Ken's own, and She grasped his hard cock and lowered Herself onto it.

This could not be happening.

She didn't moan, but audibly exhaled, like She was sinking into a hot bathtub. She put Her hands on Her knees, Her spread knees, and raised Herself up, then sank down onto it again. Bobby stayed perfectly still as She slowly repeated. The muscles in Her thighs flexed and Her eyes closed and reopened. She looked right at Ken.

Ken looked down; away. Not out of proper respect, it was technically none of his business who She fucked. She'd fucked plenty of men and women with his full knowledge, he'd even heard Her moans from the next room, or from behind a blindfold, but never right in front of him, where he could see. It was a show She denied him.

But now, he couldn't watch Her even if She wanted him to. He just couldn't.

"If you come before I say, Bobby, you will get the same treatment Kenneth is getting. Understand?"

"Yes, Ma'am. No, I'm good. I could do this all night."

"You might."

Ken looked straight down, and noticed that several drops of the semen that covered his face had dropped onto the carpet, Her expensive, esoteric, and incredibly complicated antique Turkish rug. Such complex and changing patterns. How fitting. He stared down at the growing mess; could not look up at the other, the mess his life had become.

Jimmy must have been watching. His fucking and slapping were both becoming faster and more forceful.

"Watch me, Slave Number 6. Watch your Mistress fuck another."

But he couldn't. He looked down, down at the floor. He glanced at the tall heels of Her boots but could look no higher.

"*Watch*, Slave Number 6."

No.

"Ken."

He looked up. Her legs were spread ridiculously wide over

Bobby's lap, Her hands on his knees. She was doing squats on his cock, a lap dance, almost. On his wet cock. Wet from Ken's mouth, wet from Her pussy. For the first time in a long, long time, he considered getting up and walking out. But he had committed, so long ago, to do whatever She said. Whatever She said.

"Watch all of me. I never let you look upon my open cunt, but you will now. Watch my face in pleasure, watch my cunt being penetrated by this fat cock."

Ken looked away, shook his head no. He had never said no, not ever. *Whatever She said.*

"*Watch*, Kenny."

Chapter Nineteen

Trapped.

That was how Janet felt. And ashamed.

Small and weak and insignificant, but not insignificant enough—she wanted to disappear completely, but couldn't.

Any minute, she expected a text, an email, from someone she knew—Marj, someone at work, a neighbor—with a video attached, the thumbnail a tiny video still of her standing naked in a liquor store aisle, subject titled "Is this you?" Or worse yet, it would be from that bitch who'd made her do it: "Got your contacts list," the text would say. "Thought they might all like to see this."

The worst part was, she'd let it happen. Carolyn had physically threatened her, yes, but they were in a public place—Janet could have walked away, run even, just told her to *fuck off*. Carolyn had used nothing but words, and Janet had done what that fucking bitch told her to. *Exactly* what she'd told her to. Janet hated herself. With a vengeance. It's one thing to be sexually submissive, another to be *weak*.

Then to top it off, while she was home last night, worrying, the doorbell rang, scaring her out of her wits. Dmitri's courier. A pretty black cocktail dress and stiletto heels; skimpy black underwear, another makeup kit. And a note:

Tomorrow. Be at the warehouse at 6:00 pm, wearing this. Drive yourself there, alone. Love, D.

He'd included directions to the warehouse, smart on his part.

She didn't want to do it. At all. Not *now*, especially. The timing could not be worse.

Yet here she was, *stupid, stupid, stupid.* Dressed to the nines, driving her old car past downtown, almost to the Warehouse District off-ramp. It's also one thing to be sexually submissive, and yet *another* to be a pushover. And Janet knew she was both weak *and* a pushover.

"Take this exit," her phone said.

❖

No one was there. No cars, anyway; no cargo vans full of film equipment. Was this even the right place? Her phone said so, and it looked familiar, but she was too nervous the last time to pay much attention when they'd arrived, and incapable of doing so while leaving. She got out of her car and looked up and down the deserted street.

She started up the concrete steps. Those were indeed the same heavy doors, up on the loading platform that passed for a porch. She pulled one open.

"Hello?"

No answer.

The worn old doors to the side offices were closed, as was the door they'd gone through to the hallway last time. She knocked on it, then turned the doorknob when no one answered.

The hallway to the left, which they'd followed around the giant white cube, was now closed off—blocked, with drywall, like it had never existed. She could only go to the right, a hall-way she hadn't even noticed last time, preoccupied as she was.

It was darkly lit, like the other had been, only more so. Just one bare, low-wattage light bulb hanging from the ceiling from a wire, all the way to the end of the hall at what must have been the far wall of the building. She smelled the familiar mildew, heard only silence.

"Hello? Anyone? Dmitri?"

She headed down the hall, tip-toing in her heels, trying not to make the floors creak. There were no windows, almost no light in the long hallway. Why was she trying to stay quiet?

Halfway down the hall, she could see that it would lead around a corner to the left, deeper into the building. She thought she heard a click behind her—a door opening? But she looked back and saw nothing.

It gave her the creeps anyway. Part of her wanted to turn and leave, but she hadn't liked the sound behind her. Better to find Dmitri?

A louder thunk behind her, still nothing she could see, and she walked forward a little faster. Didn't this always go badly in the slasher movies, the stupid teenagers ignoring all logic and plowing ahead when they should have known better? There was a creak, just as she was about to round the corner, and she stopped. But there was no one there.

She saw an "Exit" sign—but the corridor ended, just up ahead. However, there was a door—an elevator door, she could see, worn-looking like an old freight elevator. A bell dinged, and the door slid open. Thank God.

She walked quickly up to the elevator, ready to greet Dmitri or Susan or whoever that smelly film crew guy had been, when—

—she screamed, high-pitched and at full-volume, as she was grabbed by the wrist and pulled into the elevator as the doors opened.

She was surrounded by hooded, black-suited men, five or six of them, standing around the walls of the tiny space, all huge and tall and looking down at her through the eyeholes in their leather bondage masks. The same as the man who'd whipped her silly, intense and mean and—two of them grabbed her arms with their gloved hands, and she screamed again, although they weren't going for her clothes or hitting her or—

"Wonderful, Janet, wonderful!" a voice said behind her.

Heart pounding, she screamed a third time, wrenched her arms free and swung her fist at the person standing in her way as she turned to run out of the elevator. Her fist landed square on his jaw, making a loud smacking sound, and she stumbled out of the elevator into the hallway before her heels caught on the old carpet and she fell to the floor. She looked over her shoulder as she tried to scramble up in her tight dress.

Dmitri.

"Janet!" he yelled, bent over, holding his jaw, and she struggled to stand on her impractical stilettos and run.

She fell with her back against the wall, adrenalin pumping fire through her veins, and she stumbled two steps away before she stopped.

"What the hell was that!" she screamed.

"Janet, please," Dmitri said, still holding his face, making a downward motion with his free hand. "Calm down."

Janet backed away, looking to the elevator door, but no one was coming out after her. She was completely disoriented, her survival reflexes on full alert.

"Fuck you, calm down!" she shouted. "What the hell!"

"Janet please, it's okay," he said. "Is film!" His English was decaying in his excitement. "Susan!" he shouted. He was bent over, rubbing his jaw. Janet's breath was fast but slowing, her heartbeat still racing.

Susan came around the corner.

"Did you get that?" Dmitri asked her.

"Yea. Oh yea. Perfect," she said. She looked at Janet leaning against the wall, bent over with her hands on her knees. "You okay, kid? It's okay. You're okay."

"What—what the *fuck*, Dmitri?"

Dmitri straightened, lowered his hands.

"Janet. Please. It's okay. Susan is here. I am here. Everything is okay."

"You scared the *shit* out of me," Janet said.

"Yes, I know. That was my plan. There is no acting in my films, remember? I needed you scared, not pretending to be scared. Is important."

Janet let out a deep breath. "That is manipulative as hell, Dmitri," she said. "I really don't need this shit in my life, right now."

"Janet. I am—"

She turned to Susan. "You knew about this? You were okay with this?" Some support from another woman, maybe?

But no: Susan shrugged, made a "money" gesture with her hand, thumb rubbing across fingers.

"You're fine," she said. "No one was going to hurt you."

Janet pushed off from the wall, stood straight.

"I thought I could—" What—trust him?

"You can," reading her thoughts. "Janet, please. I—mmm." He rubbed his jaw again.

There was noise coming from the elevator, which she realized was still full of men, and a short man in jeans and a T-shirt came out, holding a black movie camera.

"It's ready to go," the man said, and walked by Janet as he carried the camera around the corner.

"Thank you," Dmitri said. "Janet. Camera is out of elevator. Only small security cameras up in the corners now."

"And?"

Did he seriously expect her to get in there with those men? Did he seriously expect her to keep going on this stupid project at all?

"Please get in. I need you on the roof. We will pretend you didn't escape from elevator and punch director in face."

"I thought you said there was no pretending."

"I need you to be nervous on ride up. On *the* ride up." He was regaining his bearings, correcting his English. And his authority: he stood straight, ignored his jaw which was beginning to swell. "The film takes place on the roof. I need you to stand in the center of those men, and let them cut your clothes off with knives. I tell you this ahead of time, which I never do. But I have to admit," he said, raising his hand to the side of his face, "maybe I should have.

"I need you to look nervous while they do this. Do you think you can do that without acting?"

Like *that* would be a problem. Janet shook her head, thought about telling him to fuck off. She was thinking a lot about telling people to fuck off, these days, but never doing it.

But he was staring her in the eye, like he had that first night they'd met, like when he'd shown her the inside of the white cube. She put her hands on her hips, and breathed deeply while turning away from him. She stopped.

"All right. Give me a second." Deep breath. Two.

She decided not to think about why she was stepping into the elevator as Dmitri yelled "Cameras!"

The tiny space was painted red, adding to its eeriness, and the men were lit from directly above, each under a small yellow light that hid their hooded faces in even more frightening shadows. Janet's heart was still racing and she could practically hear the six larger male hearts surrounding her beat as well.

The door rolled shut and she felt the elevator rise, the slightly sickening vertigo. She closed her eyes, and smelled the odd combination of weathered wood and old grease, cologne and leather and six males who'd been waiting in a small space for her to arrive in order to scare her witless.

She let the men turn her around and grasp her upper arms again, and she felt twelve gloved hands fall upon her. No one said anything. She held perfectly still as she heard the sound of six sharpened steel blades slicing through fabric.

◈

The sky was the brilliant blue of early autumn as she was pushed out the elevator doors onto the roof. She felt the breeze on her skin, that September breeze that's still warm but with an edge of change on it.

She was naked but for her tall shoes; she hugged her arms as she looked around. The tarred surface on which she was standing had been painted a clean white. She couldn't see beyond the roof; there was a wall, a fence, of corrugated steel taller than her around the edge. She was in a sort of narrow walkway, between the fence and what looked like a corrugated metal shed, some two stories tall, set on top of the bigger roof of the warehouse. Maybe it held the winch and pulleys for the elevator?

Two of the men stepped out behind her. They were holding long poles with pointed tips, though hardly knife-like. Plastic props. One of them pointed forward, and when she hesitated, he touched the pole to her flank and she felt a sharp shock, a jolt of electricity, and she screamed as she jumped away from it. Not props!

Damn that Dmitri. She did not *need* this shit right now.

She rubbed her hip. She had seen these toys, these zappers, in pornos online, just not at the end of a long pole. The man pointed again and she walked.

Until she couldn't. Around the corner, where the space widened, she was stopped, her way blocked. She looked back to the men to make sure they wouldn't zap her again for stopping, and to see if they thought what she was seeing was as unbelievable as she thought—but of course she couldn't read their hidden faces.

Strung across the space were ropes, white ropes. *Lots* of them, strung back and forth in a grid between steel poles in the wall and the shed, through stanchions in both. Many ropes met in the center, many wound around that center in a widening spiral.

A spider's web. Two stories tall on the shed's side, and as wide as the walkway, at least fifteen feet. It tilted diagonally away from her.

One of the men pressed his pole to her ass and she flinched even though he didn't activate it. He pointed. Up.

She stepped forward and tried pulling apart the ropes, the vertical and horizontal rows of it, trying to make a hole to crawl through. They were tied tight at every juncture. She felt the zapper against her ass, and the man pointed again.

She looked up. There was a square hole, an open window, near the top of the metal shed, where the upper regions of the huge web joined the building. It was nearly twenty feet up there, but it was her only way out. At least the web's slope meant that it would be underneath her.

She grabbed the net with both hands, lifted her leg, and placed her shoe over a rope at knee-height. She could hook the rope in the arch of her shoe; it worked pretty well—the high heel caught it securely.

She stepped up. The web gave a little under her weight and shifted toward her, but it was very sturdy. Of course it was— look who was in charge. No doubt tested by a model exactly her size and weight. She shook her head in disbelief that she was going to do this. She lifted her other leg, carefully hooked her shoe onto the rope, and pulled herself up. She looked back to the men, who stood at attention, watching.

Another big step up, and another. Janet's adrenaline high from downstairs was wearing off, and she was suddenly crashing, tired. She stopped and looked around.

This was ridiculous. She was climbing a rope web, naked, on a rooftop, after being startled practically shitless. *And was still going along with it.* Foolish, submissive, yet again. None of this was real, none of this was reality. It was just…silliness.

She'd wanted to play sex slave for years, and here she was in this ridiculous set, making an idiot out of herself once more. She wanted to climb back down, call this nonsense off. Fuck Dmitri. Fuck his stupid movie. She couldn't see any cameras; they must all be hidden, probably so she wouldn't look into them. She thought of the liquor store camera. She thought of it all the time, now—she had actually stood there and stared into the little lens, just as she'd been told.

And here she was, naked again. Janet thought of actresses—*real* actresses, in Hollywood, and actors. Not porn stars, not idiots like her doing it because someone wanted her to, or even coerced her to (that *bitch*), but people starring in science fiction movies, fantasy, historical dramas. Climbing up the rigging in pirate movies. Did they feel stupid too? Or did they enjoy it? At least they got paid for their silliness.

Janet thought of one of her filthy novels, one that takes place on a pirate ship. *Stowed*, it was called. In that one, a young redheaded lass was crossing the Atlantic from Ireland on a sailing ship, which was boarded by pirates. They killed the crew, stole all the passengers' possessions—and the redhead. She was stripped naked and made their sex slave, in particular the handsome but strict Captain, who adored her. But her defiant nature was at odds with the also handsome First Mate, who maintained a firm hand on the crew and was fond of wielding the whip.

Quite a little novel, that one. All alone on the high seas, always naked, with all those rough men. The girl was frequently tied to the masts, hung by the wrists from the rigging, bound and bent over the handrails for the crew's use, facing out to sea.

Complete nonsense; it would be horrific in real life. And

yet she'd read it. Three times.

Oh, what the hell. Janet climbed. She wondered if there was a camera behind her, getting the full view as she lifted her leg for each step, her thighs spread wide against the web for stability. Knowing Dmitri, there'd be a camera for every angle. He really had gone to town on this—it really did look like a giant spider's web. White lines radiated out, jagged circles spiraled wider and wider; every intersection was tied tight.

She stepped up and could see over the metal fence. She could see much of the city, from here. Could anyone see her? Not unless they had one hell of a telescope, wherever they were. She looked toward the skyscrapers downtown; tried to see past it to her home on the other side. She felt a long way from Oakdale. She climbed.

She stopped short. She was halfway up, near the tight center of the web. But as she looked ahead, into the dark window cut into the metal building above her, she swore she could see…

…two yellow eyes. Yes. Glowing, almost, in the darkness. She wanted to call out, but remembered she was supposed to stay quiet. She was tired, and skeptical. She grabbed the rope, and climbed another step.

The eyes moved. Toward Janet, toward the light. A head emerged, dark and nearly shaved—a woman. Focused and severe, she looked like Grace Jones in her heyday, but for the eerie yellow eyes.

Moving with incredible smoothness, the very, very dark-skinned woman, compact and muscled and wiry, crawled out of the window and onto the ropes. She was dressed only in a black leather corset and a thin black thong, but she had a fanny pack across her belly and a small backpack strapped to her shoulders, all matching black. Her feet were bare, her toes clinging to the ropes as she crawled quickly—*very* quickly—down the web toward Janet. Spiderlike! Her yellow eyes stayed fixed on Janet with an incredible intensity.

Okay, Dmitri had left his Minimalist phase behind, and was moving into Surrealism.

This strange woman was used to all this. An acrobat? A dancer? Her chest, arms and legs were incredibly muscular despite her thin, graceful frame. Her skin was as dark as Janet's was white, a perfect ebony, nearly as dark as the black leather corset that held her small, firm breasts in place. Janet wanted to back up, climb down, but she was slow, and a little afraid of heights. She looked down, saw that the men were gone.

The woman did not take her eyes off Janet as she neared—her frightening, yellow eyes. Contacts, obviously—they had vertical pupils, reptilian—but they were still scary. Janet could not help but stare back, transfixed.

Janet realized she was to be the prey, in this film.

She tried to step down, but the woman—the spider—pulled a piece of rope from the black pouch at her waist, and wrapped it quickly around Janet's wrist and fastened it to the web.

"Hey…" Then the other.

The woman climbed behind Janet—right over Janet's body; she weighed next to nothing—and down to her legs, and tied her ankles firmly in place, then her knees. She worked *fast*—elbows, next—how was she able to do this so easily? Pulling short pieces of rope from her pouch left and right. Janet was spread-eagled to the web, hanging askew with two limbs out straight and two bent.

Without a word, the spider woman maneuvered effortlessly behind Janet. The woman smelled of sweat, female sweat. She opened her mouth as if to kiss Janet, but hissed, and showed her a mouthful of sharp fangs. Janet recoiled and turned away. *Seriously?*

Who has this life?

Janet felt hands feeling up and down her torso. She tried to raise up, but she was pushed forward. She felt arms reaching around her, through the net. Rope—she was being tied to the web. She felt several coils of rope slide and tighten against her back and stomach. She was being forced against the web, her breasts protruding through two of the irregular rectangles. She felt hands tying the rope against her back.

The climbing position she'd been in, one leg raised, one straight down, meant that her legs were spread, her sex exposed. More new ropes coiled around her thighs, immobilizing her further, and the woman climbed back upward and fastened Janet's shoulders to the web, running the twine under her armpits. Janet could not move except for her head. She watched open-mouthed until the woman ran the rope between her teeth, twice, making a gag.

Now her captor climbed over Janet's shoulders, climbed all the way above her on the net and rotated around in place, just as a spider would. She locked herself into the net with her knees, face to face with Janet. Janet could only look up at her, amazed.

The woman kissed her full on the mouth—two sprawled figures, diametrically opposed, touching only at their mouths, even though Janet's lips were pulled back and restricted by the rope gag. The woman's mouth tasted sweet, fresh like strawberry bubble gum, which she did not expect. The spider woman backed up to survey her work.

Well, there was really no going back now, was there? She might as well see what happened next. But Janet had a very unsure feeling—this *was* Dmitri's film. And sure enough, the spider woman pulled a black leather flogger from her pouch; it matched her skin and corset beautifully. She slinked down over Janet's body and positioned herself behind her.

Janet moaned into her impromptu gag as the whip cracked across her ass, that now-familiar, wide burn of a flogger. She could barely move. Dmitri hadn't talked about how to safeword out of this, but then, they'd been interrupted and distracted.

Could she still snap her fingers?

The athletic woman whipped hard, a good fifteen or twenty strokes, and it was impossible to stay quiet. Janet could feel the slight swing in the web when each next one was coming, but could do nothing about it but tense up and clench her fists, shut her eyes and gasp at the burning sting until she cried out—unless she decided to call this off.

Janet looked down at the bright surface of the roof—so reflective, perfect for lighting her from below. She wondered where the cameras were, then stopped wondering anything as her ass truly started to burn. What embarrassing facial expressions must Dmitri be recording? What cries were the hidden microphones recording?

The whipping stopped, and Janet waited for what was next, which was worse than the beating. Not being in charge, it was always that anticipation, when facing away and unable to see, that was even more intense than the whipping itself. Knowing it was going to hurt, but not knowing *when*—it made her feel even less in control. Or, wondering if it might not be something painful…

Fingers. Fingers everywhere, caressing Janet's torso, squeezing breasts, pinching nipples until she whimpered. Fingers in the crack of her ass, fingers lower. Janet shook her head no, but to no avail: the woman's fingers found their way to Janet's labia, so opened by her position, and then zeroed in on her clit.

Janet had *not* been in the mood for this. This whole stupid day, her stupid life, the surprise downstairs, punching Dmitri in the face. *Yea, well, sorry Dmitri.* He had it coming, scaring and manipulating her. She did feel a little satisfaction at that punch, as the woman behind her continued to massage her clit, right here in mid-air, tied to a fucking spider web. Janet nearly giggled. What a fucking day.

The woman's fingers were very adept. She knew the exact way to caress, massage, tickle. Janet rocked her hips as the woman hit a sweet spot, her bindings unable to stop their movement. The entire web shook and bounced.

The spider woman continued masturbating Janet from behind as if she knew exactly what buttons to push, until Janet felt something building within her. She was still groaning, grunting, wanting to throw her head back but keeping it humbly bowed where the woman had placed her. She could *really* use a little relief.

She was unable to stop it—she was almost there, almost there, almost, almost—

—and then it stopped. Janet cried out in longing. *Damn this day!* She was sure the expression on her face would be satisfying for Dmitri, or for any heartless, perverted viewer watching this film who had no idea the stress she'd been under.

The whip returned. Across her ass, across her shoulders. Janet tried to duck against the ropes as she screamed, hoped for talented fingers afterward.

The whipping stopped, and she heard the sound of Velcro.

Fingertips grasped her hips. Now what? Something was pressing against her spread, wet labia, and not nimble fingers.

In an instant Janet's entire vagina was filled with something long and large.

"Oh…*Gog*," Janet's gagged mouth unable to close.

She was filled to her cervix with a huge phallus, totally taken by surprise. The woman held it there for a moment, for maximum effect. She withdrew it, not all the way out, then thrust it deep again. Janet could feel the head, every rib on the dildo. She lost all control of her breathing. She threw her head back, the only thing she could move, but the woman pressed it down, humbling her again.

Janet felt hips against her sore ass—the woman was wearing the dildo, not handling it. Janet had heard her strap it on.

She backed out again, then in. This evil Spider Woman was fucking her. This was so embarrassing, so ridiculous. But *so* good. Janet tried to rock her hips back to meet her, offer herself. Would she stop at the moment of ecstasy again?

The woman behind her developed an elegant rhythm. She was rocking her own hips with each thrust, making a rolling motion that matched Janet's involuntary movements. This woman could *fuck*.

Her pace increased. She knew exactly how to play Janet, when to speed up, when to hesitate. She began fucking her harder as well as faster. Her hips were slamming against Janet, against the ass she'd just whipped so hard, and Janet was moaning with every thrust, her fists clenched tight around the ropes of the web. Once again, she was getting close.

And then the whip was back. The flogger cracked across her back, and the woman raised her own torso to gain access to Janet's bare ass. *Smack*. Again. Again. Again across her lower back; her shoulders.

Janet bit into the rope crossing through her teeth. She was trapped between the pain and the intense pleasure, giving herself to this woman, the cameras taking her emotions and this silly humiliation into them. She was beyond caring. The whip only brought her closer…closer…

This time, the spider woman did not stop. Janet erupted into orgasm as the whip continued its work. She screamed her muffled screams; her body convulsed involuntarily. She saw sparks, the bright blue sky began to go dark. She was growling, full-throat, as the woman continued fucking and whipping her, but she was now timing her thrusts and blows with Janet's cries.

The whip and the dildo began to slow as Janet started wearing down. The Spider Woman finally stopped her whipping altogether, and gave Janet a few deep, grinding thrusts, holding each one there as Janet milked it for all she could, her inner muscles gripping that fucking dildo.

The woman pulled out. Janet, exhausted, could do nothing. God what a day. She collapsed, her body limp but bound in place, suddenly vacated. She released her fingers from the web and hung loosely, held only by the ropes. She was covered in sweat, the fall breeze cooling the skin that the Sun and the whip had just warmed.

Janet was spent. She had nothing left to give Dmitri. If he or this arachnoid abomination had any more plans for her, they were going to be cinematically disappointed. She would endure the whip again if she had to, but they wouldn't get a very satisfying reaction.

Janet turned her head, and saw that the Sun had moved enough across the sky that her shadow was now in her field of view, on the roof below her. The Sun would be dropping below the tall rooftop shed soon, and she would be in shadow. But these films only lasted twenty minutes, right?

The shadow of the creature behind her was pure spider—arms and legs bent in un-human ways, the only giveaway the shortage of limbs. She watched the shadow spider reach into its backpack, its huge arachnid abdomen. It began pulling something out—a thin whip? No: more rope. A *lot* of rope. Like a real spider spinning its web, the shadow spider was extracting line from its body, reaching towards its shadow prey—Janet.

Janet felt an arm reach under her, between her legs, and up. A knot being tied across her belly. Her captor strung the new rope between her tingling labia, pressing against her clitoris. She brought it up through the crack of her ass, like a thong. Pulling more rope out from her backpack, she laid a line up the center of Janet's back, and looped it over her head. She fastened it around her neck. Janet groaned in protest.

The woman pushed Janet's face downward, but then pulled it back by the hair.

"Hold your head here, exactly here," the woman whispered into her ear, the first words she'd said. "This is a gift." She had a foreign accent that Janet could not identify.

Janet obeyed and held as still as she could.

The rope was strung down her back again, then she felt a knot being tied at the small of her back. Looking down, she saw yard after yard of slack rope dropping below them towards the rooftop.

Then the rope was around her waist. Again, all the way around her; across her stomach, her back. Another. She now wore a belt made of four strands of rope. Then five, then she lost count. Each strand was placed next to the last, held in place by interweaving them with the web and the new ropes up her back. A wide, solid band of rope was covering her rib cage.

Janet was being cocooned.

The woman brought the ropes around under her body, leading it with one hand and reaching around her to grab it with the other. She ran the rope below and then above Janet's hanging breasts, leaving them exposed. Of course.

When she was covered from her waist to her armpits, the woman stopped. Janet was wearing a pure white corset to match the spider woman's black one—one of rope, one of leather.

The woman crawled up around Janet's immobilized body, turned upside down once again above Janet's head. She stared hard into Janet's eyes, yellow meeting blue. Janet was too exhausted to offer anything back.

"After I leave, lean your head forward," the woman whispered into Janet's ear, too quiet for any microphone. She gave her earlobe a little nibble that Janet couldn't avoid if she'd wanted to. Then the spider crawled backwards up into her window, her lair, and disappeared.

How long Dmitri would leave her hanging there, Janet could not know. Would he film her suspended against the blue sky until the stars came out? He would have to change cameras a few times, not his usual plan.

At least now she could rest, she hoped. And she had to admit—at least she hadn't been thinking about *that bitch* for the last half hour, for the first time in a week.

Remembering what the Spider Woman had told her, Janet tilted her face forward, what little the cocoon corset would allow. She felt the long rope from her neck tug, just slightly, up her back and ass and press against her clitoris as she pulled. She shuddered in pleasure. She tilted back and felt it loosen, then leaned forward again.

Maybe this wouldn't be such a boring wait after all.

Chapter Twenty

Three cars.

There were three cars in front of his Mistress's house tonight. Jimmy's beat up Honda, Bobby's ridiculously souped-up Mazda, and now a rounded nondescript gray something or other, no telling what it had brought.

Well actually, he knew exactly what it had brought: another redheaded man, looking remarkably like himself. One more pink cock to have to suck, 50% more come on his face as his Mistress would proceed to have him punished for who knows what, and then ignore him.

Ignore him while She fucked them. *Fucked. Them.*

He had always been able to stand the guests; that was part of the bargain, painful as it sometimes was—and fun as it sometimes was. And maybe, yes maybe, that knowledge and denial somehow made things even more intense. He was, he'd come to admit, a fairly fucked-up individual. But *this*—he looked at the three cars in front of Her house, two in the driveway, one in the street, right in front of his own car—this: it was too much.

This was no whipping him in front of guests, making him

cry, making him suck dicks and eat pussy with tears in his eyes. She was always showing him off, in Her strange way, when She did that; demo-ing Her trophy to amazed and jealous friends. Speaking of him with tenderness and pride while beating him as he crawled to the next guest. He didn't mind all that—hell, tears were part of the fantasy, right?

But this was a grinding of his soul into the ground. She must not want him around, anymore. She was *trying* to drive him away. And if this was how things were going to go, he wasn't sure how much more he could take.

Ken looked at the clock in his dash. Five minutes before he would be punished for tardiness. What would it be, an extra round of facials? He looked down in shame, and not the fun kind. Still gripping the steering wheel with one hand, he shifted the car into Park and reached to turn off the key.

❖

"Thanks for staying late, Janet. I really appreciate it. You've helped us get caught up, and I owe you one. God, what a mess."

"I'm glad to help, Ron."

She'd stopped by his office before going home, the claustrophobic space decorated with mounted taxidermied fish, fishing trophies; photos of him proudly holding up larger fish than his companions, goofy smile on his face.

"Well, you are *very* highly valued around here," Ron said.

"Thank you. That's so nice to hear." Everyone else had left. Janet imagined them out having drinks without her. It was Friday after all, but no one had said anything or asked her to go.

Which worried her—did they not like her so much anymore? Did anyone still like her? Did they find out what a pervert she was, and were now distancing themselves? Did they find out she'd been fucked by a Spider Woman on a web, suspended over a rooftop? Or did they hear about what a pussy she'd been in the liquor store, letting that bitch make her—"make" her—kiss her fucking feet and strip naked for the video camera. Janet had felt, every day going into work, like they had surely seen it. Someone had uploaded the video to the Internet, put her name on it, and emailed notices to everyone she knew.

But anytime she searched her own name, nothing obscene came up. There must be some kind of code word, that they all knew meant "Janet's naked onscreen again." She'd searched "liquor store naked," and while she found far more videos than she thought she would, she wasn't in any of them.

She sighed. Everyone was still friendly to her; she hadn't detected any change in anyone's attitude. Or had she? A smile disappearing a little too fast, a back turned after an attempted joke.

"No, really. Truly. You are a trooper and I appreciate it so much. Everyone does." Ron sat at his desk; he'd asked her to check in before she took off to go home. Home alone, to think her thoughts, to dread this fucking party coming up next week.

"Thank you, Ron."

"Are you okay, Janet? You've been a little distant, this week. You seem worried. I'll be frank: someone thought they heard you crying in the bathroom, more than once."

Shit. She had been a bundle of nerves since the liquor store, since Jon said he'd scheduled this second dinner party. She didn't want to go, not one bit. She had even asked him to cancel. But damn it, *she'd* been the one demanding the party, as he reminded her. But how could she go? Face that fucking cunt again?

"You haven't looked happy at all. And you've been working so hard. If it's not my business, tell me, but is there anything I can do? I want this to be a decent place to work, you know. It's dry work, but I try to make it fun or at least tolerable. I'm a little worried about you."

Janet really didn't want this to go where she knew it would. As much as she didn't want to go home and start her cycle of thinking, of worrying, she didn't want—

"Have you ever considered fishing, Janet? It's *so* relaxing."

"No, Ron. Thanks, but I really don't see myself—"

"Out in nature, just you and the fish, and maybe a friend. The moving water, the breeze, the *preparation* all paying off. It's—"

"Yea, it's relaxing, I'm sure. But I—"

"It's all about the knots, you know."

"The what?"

"*That's* what makes it all worthwhile—you don't just show up and fish. I make my own lures, all of them. I'll spend weeks."

Janet furrowed her eyebrows in confusion.

"There are dozens of knots you have to know. Intricate knots—Rapala knot, Palomar, Spider Hitch."

Janet flushed—*How does he know about the Spider Woman?*

"What?"

"I gather the materials, beautiful little objects, scraps of cloth, fur; and arrange them on my vise, on my workbench. I bind them—into the most beautiful little shapes, so seductive, so perfect. One knot to bind rabbit hair, another to tie the whole thing together. Round and round their abdomens, like flies. My little lures are so vulnerable, so…so…"

"Knots."

"I am an expert at knots. They come in handy, for so many activities. In fact, after work—"

Janet backed slowly away, toward the open office door.

"I have to go, Ron."

"Oh. Okay. Are you sure? You know, don't get me wrong, but I've always felt like maybe we've shared a certain—"

"Bye, Ron. I'll see you Monday."

She made sure not to bump into the little wooden fisherman statue on the bookshelf.

Blue

❖

Ken sat with his hand still on the key. He looked at the clock—ten after; he was already late. Of course his Mistress hadn't called; it was his job to report in late, not Hers to check on him. He'd been staring at the tachometer for fifteen minutes now, not really looking at it, not really able to concentrate on anything. 725 rpm.

The driver of the third car would no doubt be called Billy, whom Ken would have to address as William, before sucking his cock and licking the jizz off his own lips, and then watch Billy fuck Her as his own ass was worked hard by Jimmy. She seemed to enjoy watching Jimmy fuck him—would She film all three of them fucking him, tonight? He only had two fuckable orifices—it would be quite a night.

Why did She want another one? Another him? *Three* more? At first he'd thought it was just one of Her kinks, one of Her bizarre aesthetic decisions to endure, like the tempting Asian girl in the alcove, whoever she was.

But it clearly wasn't. It was something else, something he couldn't understand.

Something he could no longer abide, if it was all going to go downhill from here.

Ken lowered his hand from the key, placed it on the gear-shift.

If only She would just...

If She would just...

But of course She wouldn't. No matter what he tried to imagine, he knew She wouldn't. Be reasonable? Uh, no. That was never what attracted him to Her, anyway. Talk? He wasn't even allowed to speak, without prior permission.

This was all so ridiculous, these pretend Rules. Who says he couldn't talk?

Oh yeah—*She says.*

He brought his hand back up to the key to turn it off.

Why couldn't they just talk—like, you know, people?

Because, to Her, he wasn't a person. He was a slave. A toy. *Boys are toys.* Less than human. It could be exciting, being less than human, a mere object. For a while. For quite a while, even. But when it spilled over into real life, it could hurt. More than he'd thought.

Maybe this Life wasn't life after all. It really was just a game, that She always won. A very stupid game, if you're one of Her pawns. And he was Pawn Number 6. Who She was now pushing off the board.

He imagined himself going to the door, right now, and ringing the doorbell. Dressed; standing.

Ha. It would be ugly. Very ugly.

He imagined himself doing what he did every Friday, ringing the doorbell naked, on his knees, collar locked.

Late, with three more redheads inside.

Ken lowered his hand from the key again. He gripped the gearshift tight.

He shifted the gear into Reverse, backed just far enough to clear the little gray car in front of him.

He shifted into Drive, and pulled out into the street.

He drove the two streets to the first corner, past straight streets until they turned into the winding maze of newer curves and cul-de-sacs, and then he hit the gauntlet of convenience stores and strip malls on the frontage road that faced the freeway.

He took the on-ramp.

But not the West ramp that took him back to Carlton, to his shitty little apartment behind more strip malls, where he sat alone every weeknight waiting for his nights, his *turn*, with Her—his Life.

No.

He took the freeway East.

Away.

❖

"It's all taken care of, doll."

"Oh thank God, Jon. Thank you. Thank you." Janet lay in bed, third glass of wine half finished on the bedside table, her newest erotic novel unread. She just hadn't been in the mood.

"Don't thank me. It was Amanda."

"What? What did she do? Not you?" She thought surely he'd be her Knight in Shining Armor, if anything could be done.

"If I'd gone in, it would have escalated—'Sorry, buddy, store business.' They'd have checked it out for sure, maybe called the cops if I got too aggressive. Amanda's one of their better customers. She orders a lot of wine and liquor from them. And... she has a certain way, with certain types of men."

"So she...?"

"Carrot and stick, let's say."

Janet breathed an immense sigh of relief.

"Tell her thank you."

"You can tell her yourself, at the dinner party."

"Oh, Jesus..."

He had to remind her, just when she was finally feeling good about something.

"It'll be fine, doll. You'll be fine. She's got nothing on you."

"Yea, right. Are you kidding?" Janet's stomach had hurt for over a week now, with another week to go.

"For what it's worth, it was pretty awesome."

"What was?"

"The video."

"You *watched* it? Jon! Where, at the store?" She covered her eyes with her hand. These people really *were* a bunch of cruel motherfuckers.

"We both did. Here at home. It was on a DVD, their system records over it every few days, so they said. Amanda got it from them anyway. The only copy. She'll give it to you at the party."

Great. Carolyn would probably demand to show it to everyone.

"It looks kind of like one of Dmitri's," Jon said. "Low resolution, but it's all symmetrical and everything, looking down the aisle, your body in the center. Very Kubrick."

"Jon."

"Cruel woman whispering in your ear."

"Shut *up*. There was *nothing* erotic about it. It was horrible. The most humiliating moment of my life."

"Yes. Well, Dmitri makes some pretty cruel films, too, you know."

"Yes. I know." Her ass still smarted from the Spider Woman's flogger, a full week later. "But I *consented* to those." How could he and Amanda find that video hot?

"It'll be all right, doll. You just need to stand up to her. She can't make you do anything you don't want."

"Yea. Thanks." *Sympathizer. Collaborator. Traitor.*

"Janet, I—"

"Bye, Jon. Thank you—and Amanda—for taking care of that for me."

"Anytime, doll. You know I—"

Janet ended the call. She tossed the phone onto the table, picked up the glass and swilled it down before turning off the light and burrowing into the covers.

Stand up to her. If only she could. Janet shook her head in defeat—already.

Janet knew she didn't have a dominant bone in her body. She couldn't imagine forcing her will on anyone—didn't even want to. She was a sub, through and through. Usually it was hot, sexy. She was thrilled to be submissive. Her body and will were supple, pliable, and that was what the people she found sexiest were searching for. But sometimes, when it spilled over into real life...

There was only one person in the world she wished she could dominate, who she would love to see suffer, and that was Carolyn. Yes. On her knees, naked, tears running down her perfect little cheeks. Her arrogance and meanness whipped right out of her.

But Carolyn would never submit to anyone, especially someone like Janet. She would see right through her, use Janet's submissive nature against her and turn the situation right around, and make her pay for the attempt.

No, Carolyn would have to be taken by force, tightly restrained, and then coerced into obedience by a very unpleasant training until she relented. But Janet would never be able to overpower Carolyn; she was too strong. She worked out. Janet flexed her arm, under the covers. The arm she'd punched Dmitri with. Skinny little arm.

She would have to trick Carolyn, slip her a drug or something. Or get a man's help. Then they would have their way with her once she was tied up and helpless.

Wait a minute—was she actually fantasizing about recruiting a man to help her kidnap, brutalize, and rape another woman?

Yes. Yes she was, and she was okay with that.

They would overpower and kidnap her, tie her hands behind her back, and bend her over the furniture—a sofa, maybe—and tie her ankles together. Then Janet would whip her perfect little ass until it was bleeding and Carolyn begged for mercy. That would be a nice start.

No—better: no sofa. They would tie her hands behind her back, with a cable running up to a pulley on the ceiling. Janet would pull on the cable until Carolyn was forced into a bent-over position, her arms pointing straight up. And her legs would be spread wide, kept apart by a long spreader bar fastened to her ankles. Very long. Yes. And she would be gagged. With a thick penis gag—no, then she couldn't beg for mercy.

Janet would whip her hard, harder than Carolyn had ever whipped anyone, especially her. Revenge of the submissives! Carolyn would no doubt call Janet every name in the book, until her ass would be so thoroughly thrashed that she could take it no longer. Then she would cry, tears falling from her perfect face onto the floor just inches away.

"P—please stop," she would say. "Please."

"Please *what*?"

"Please stop, Ma'am."

"Nope. Not good enough. What do you say?"

"Please stop, Mistress. My Mistress. Please."

But Janet wouldn't stop. Now that she had begged, Janet would insert a thick dildo into Carolyn's mouth, and order her to keep it there, and if she let it go she would learn what pain *really* meant. And then she would whip her some more anyway, just for fun. What could Carolyn do? She'd be trussed up like a pig.

Then Janet would take another big dildo—no, better: she would buckle on one of those strap-ons, like the Spider Woman had, around her waist. Wait—why was Janet naked in this? No matter. Janet would strap on the dildo and fuck Carolyn hard, like a man would.

In the ass, maybe? No—save that for later. In that perfect little cunt, as Carolyn liked to call it. Yes. Hard, making her keep that other dildo in her mouth, as Carolyn would struggle to keep her balance.

Oh, but here comes Jon, who helped subdue her. No— Jack, who would enjoy this much more than Jon. Jon was far too forgiving of Carolyn. What did he *see* in her? Why was he so tolerant? Almost entertained… They went back, apparently, but so what? Back to what? Oh, that *bitch*.

But anyway, so here was Jack, with his stiff cock thrusting out from his pants. Wait, why isn't *he* naked? No matter. He would stand in front of Carolyn, watch her take *such* a harsh fucking from Janet.

Janet would tell him to take the dildo out of Carolyn's mouth. And Jack would do it, yes. And then she would tell Carolyn—order her—to beg Jack to *let* her suck his cock.

"Please let me suck your cock," Carolyn would say, without hesitation. Because Carolyn would be in pain.

"Why don't you tell me—exactly and precisely—why I should let you do that?" Jack would say, staring down at her with glee. "Darlin'?"

Now Carolyn would hesitate, and Janet would slap her *hard*, on the ass, her red and bleeding ass, blood splattering. Carolyn would cry out, and Janet would reach forward and undo Carolyn's stupid tight bun into a ponytail, and pull it hard to lift her head to face Jack's erect cock.

"What did he say?" she would demand. She would thrust her hips hard against Carolyn's ass as she pulled her hair back toward her, forcing the dildo deeper into her cunt until she hit her cervix. Oh, Janet couldn't wait to fuck that ass next.

Carolyn would struggle, sobbing, gathering her thoughts.

"P—please let me suck your cock, Sir. I will suck it however you like. Please let me lick your balls first. Or you can fuck my mouth, if you like, as hard as you want. Fuck my throat, please!"

Should she make her swallow Jack's come, the way Janet had done for him every morning in Texas? No—better:

"Don't forget to come on her face," Janet would tell Jack. And Jack would do it.

Yes.

And, slowly, Janet began to drift off to sleep, feeling kind of warm and fuzzy inside.

Part 5: Off-Ramps

Chapter Twenty-One

Janet tried to keep her hand from shaking as she pushed the doorbell button. She'd insisted on driving herself here, into these acres of identical cookie-cutter houses, each with their own little stick tree staked into the center of their small yard, miles and miles of them, in four rotating colors: beige, tan, blue, gray. Westbrook, the very outskirts of the west side. Beyond it lay empty frontier, small towns slowly growing until the day they're engulfed by the City as well.

She wished she'd paid more attention to who'd driven what to her own house back in May. She recognized Jon's awesome blue LeSabre of course, and Jack's new black Cadillac. There was only one other car here, dark—was it *hers*, or did Amanda drive herself? Or was there someone else here she didn't know about? Dmitri was supposedly in Europe, this week, not that he was a formal member of this "club."

The door opened, and a pretty, petite young blonde smiled at her nervously.

"Hi!" she said, friendly and eager. "Are you…?"

"Janet," she said, and walked in as the girl held open the

door. She should have let her finish—would she have listed the unarrived names?

"So nice to finally meet you, Janet." She extended her hand, and Janet shook it. Her hand was tiny, cold and clammy. This woman was terrified. "I'm Kylie."

"Hello, Kylie. Nice to meet you. Relax, okay? We're all friends." *Lie.*

"Thanks." Kylie wrung her hands together. Her hair was cut into a short bob above the shoulders much like Amanda's, but not as expensively. Janet searched for roots: none. Kylie was dressed in sweater and jeans, as was she. Her amber eyes were very nervous.

Janet looked around. A stairway leading downstairs right in front of the door (she hated that feature in mass-produced housing, a cheap shortcut); living room to the left. Gray carpet, white walls with no art, no photos. She neither saw nor smelled any sign of children. The room was nearly bare, but unlike Janet's it was likely unintentional: Kylie had no money.

The furniture, mismatched, was arranged in the same pattern as Janet's—sofa, on which Jon and Amanda were seated, along one side of a coffee table. The coffee table was plain, brown, fake wood, but it was loaded with appetizers and decanting wine—Kylie was trying, and Janet's heart went out to her. There was the chair at the head of the table, and two odd chairs along the other side, one of which was filled with Jack.

"Janet! Blue eyes!" Jack said, and stood.

"Hello, Jack. Hello, Amanda, Jon."

Jack took her hands in his, surrounded them, kissed one. "It's been ages, darlin'. How've you been?"

"Good! Good." *Not so good.* "How's Hannah?"

"Behavin' herself. You starrin' in any more pitchers?" Had he always pronounced it "pitchers"?

"Well, y—"

"Ha, ha! I know—I heard about it. I cannot *wait* to see this one. When's it gonna be ready?"

"A while. He has to actually edit, with this one, I guess."

"Awww—so he's movin' on, artistically."

"I guess so, yea."

"Kylie, darlin'. D'you know Janet here is a bona fide film star? An artiste—is that how you say a female artist, Jon?"

"Well—"

"Jon, we should introduce Kylie here to Dmitri, sometime."

"Well, yea, maybe so, Jack."

"You haven't already, have ya? You got me good, on that, last time."

Jon laughed. "No, Jack."

Janet felt a small twinge of jealousy, or maybe it was that more complex, arousing sense of being denied, at the thought of all three male tops in her life focusing their energies on someone new—even though she knew she wasn't anywhere as close to the center of their creative universes as she liked to think.

"Can I get anyone anything to drink?" Kylie asked.

"Not until everyone is here," Amanda said. She was sitting with her legs crossed at the knee, her arm across the back of the sofa—calm and elegant in her pinstriped jacket and skirt, like a photo from Hollywood's Golden Age.

"She's not here, yet," she said to Janet.

Janet walked around the coffee table, ignoring Kylie.

"Amanda, I want to thank you for—"

"You volunteered me for the Bake Sale," Amanda said.

"What?"

"The Bake Sale. And the dinner afterward? You told them I would cater them, *gratis*, without even asking me?"

Ssssshit. She'd forgotten all about that.

"Amanda, I am so sorry! I told Carlotta that I would speak to you, I never told her you would *do* it. Honest! I'm so sorry. Can I help you get out of it?"

"I'm afraid it's too late for that." She looked up at Janet, calm but clearly peeved. "Turn around."

"What?"

"Turn around."

Janet turned, facing Jack across the table. Amanda ran her hand up the back of Janet's thigh, squeezed a buttock in her jeans.

"Yes. I *will* take that out of your hide. And you'll help me with the dinner, of course."

The old feelings of wanting to drop to her knees and grovel to Amanda came welling up.

"Yes! Of course I will!" she said. "I'm so sorry."

So much for being equals at the new dinner party.

"It's all right. But you will owe me."

Janet couldn't tell if she was kidding or not. Probably not. But she didn't seem especially angry, either.

Amanda dug into her purse.

"Here," she said. "I have something for you."

She pulled out a square plastic case with a silver disc inside it. The DVD. She held it up to Janet, but pulled it back so that Janet had to lean in to get it.

"There are no copies," she whispered, when Janet was close. "But I watched it. And I was very turned on."

Janet didn't know what to say.

"I know it was non-consensual, cruel, even," Amanda whispered. "You are clearly not happy in it. You look like you've been captured—kidnapped, for *real*, and put up on an auction block for sale. And there's nothing you can do about it. Nothing. No way to know who'll buy you and take you; could be a real creep. It's all out of your hands. But you know that to run away would bring even worse punishment."

She leaned back, still holding the disc up for Janet.

"I was as wet as the ocean," she said out loud.

Janet took the disc, and Amanda smiled a sweet little smile as Janet backed away and sat down next to Jack as he and Jon watched.

She cleared her throat, and looked at the remaining chairs. The only two left were next to each other, next to her. No matter where she sat, she was going to be next to—

The doorbell rang.

Janet's heart sank and bile rose as Kylie nearly ran to the door.

"Hi, I'm Kylie," she said. "You must be Carolyn?"

Janet stared at her own hands. She stuffed the DVD into her purse before Carolyn could see it.

"Hello, Caro—" Jon stopped mid-word, and when Janet looked up to see his and Amanda's faces, she turned and did the same double-take that they had.

"Carolyn," he finished.

This was not the same tight bundle of restrained discipline and intense focus that had entered her house so many months ago. Janet wasn't even sure it was the same cool, mean creature from the liquor store. The intensity was still there, yes, but Carolyn looked wild, desperate—almost feral. She wasn't dressed in her perfect pencil skirt and matching jacket, but an average denim skirt with a short-sleeve lavender top—maybe it was casual Friday at work? Brown pumps that matched neither. She clutched her phone in one hand and her small purse in the other. Her hair was pulled back in a ponytail, not the disciplined bun, and it had lost its sheen.

But her eyes—her eyebrows and cheekbones were still perfect, but it was the space between that had changed the most. Her eyes were swollen, bloodshot, with dark circles under them, and they wandered from guest to guest, stopping slightly longer on Janet.

She looked around the room.

"Huh. Nice," Carolyn said sarcastically of Kylie's house. "Get me a drink."

"Oh. Okay. Yes Ma'am," Kylie said. "Um, wine?"

"Hold it, dear. Stop," Amanda said, and Kylie promptly stopped. "Carolyn, you're throwing her off. No drinks until she's undressed? There are rules, remember?"

"Don't start with me, Amanda," and Amanda's eyebrows rose. "Jon just made up this shit before he brought *her* in, anyway." She pointed her thumb at Janet, and Janet looked up at Carolyn. Carolyn looked back until she burst into laughter. Janet leaned away.

Jesus. Janet felt like Carolyn might explode into total, unpredictable violence at any moment. She glanced at Jon and Jack, who seemed to be feeling the same way. Everyone was leaning away.

"Yes, well, perhaps we should get started then? Kylie, you remember the procedure? The line you need to recite?"

"Get me a *drink*," Carolyn said.

"*Not* until we follow procedure," Amanda said, and the two women stared at each other.

Janet's jaw dropped open—the men were speechless, too. Amanda tilted her head slightly to the side, her eyes locked on Carolyn.

Carolyn looked at Kylie.

"Fine. Strip," she said, and plopped down next to Janet. *Great.*

"Um. Okay?" Kylie said. She looked terrified. But she took her place just where Janet had, at the open end of the table, and slowly began to take off her clothes. She avoided eye contact with Carolyn, avoided it with pretty much everybody, for that matter. Janet remembered doing the same.

Kylie pulled her sweater over her head, unzipped her jeans. She had only been wearing socks, no shoes, and peeled them off along with her jeans. She stood nervously in tan underwear.

"Um, do I...?" But everyone sat silent, watching.

"You're doing fine," Janet said.

"You're doing fine," Carolyn repeated, behind her, and Janet clenched her teeth.

"Okay…"

Kylie's body was compact but generous. Thin waist, stomach muscles—she did crunches to pass the time. Her hips were beautifully rounded, her thighs and calf muscles toned and well developed; she likely did some jogging. Janet realized this woman was recently divorced as well—the empty, cheaper house, the yard-sale furniture, a new body. She must not have won the old house in the settlement. Or maybe she'd just left. She'd been getting herself in shape, because it's cheap and she was looking for something new.

Well, she'd certainly found it.

Kylie fumbled to unfasten her bra, and her large breasts relaxed into their natural shape, which was not far off from their supported shape. She slipped her matching, tan panties off her hips. Her pubic hair was gone, shaved smooth.

"Welcome to my home," she said. "How may I serve you?"

"You can get me a fucking drink," Carolyn said. She looked at her phone.

"Wine all around, dear," Amanda said. Kylie reached for the bottle as everyone grabbed their glasses; she began the elaborate kneeling and pouring procedure that Janet remembered so well.

Janet felt the same thrill at watching Kylie kneel for her that she'd felt when Hannah had done the same at Jack's house. The view from the other side—the served, not the server. It felt wrong, out of place, but she could see the appeal. Kylie gave her a nervous look and Janet smiled.

The wine was awful. Not awful, maybe, but not especially good. Sweet; cloying.

"Jesus," Carolyn said, and gulped down her entire glass in one swig. She clanged her fingernail on the glass and held it out, and Kylie poured her another, glancing at Amanda and Jon. She moved across the table before Carolyn could demand another refill and empty the bottle.

Everyone ate, everyone drank, except Kylie, of course. That was the point. She was kept running around, naked, exposed. Learning her place, apologizing. Kneeling. Janet was surprised at herself for keeping a mental tabulation of errors and breaches of etiquette.

Despite her lack of knowledge regarding wine, Kylie had done a great job with the food. Spanish *tapas* was her theme—*pinchos morunos* with skewered lamb and chicken, stuffed *empanadillas*, *croquetas*. *Chorizo* sausage *al vino*, delicious despite the questionable *vino*. She was *trying*, bless her heart, and mostly succeeding. Janet wondered if she herself had looked anywhere near so adorable, or if these cruel motherfuckers only saw a victim, a body and soul to exploit. She wanted to hug Kylie. And then make her beg for…something.

Kylie was kneeling at the end of the table, panting, finally able to take a bite of her *croqueta*.

"Now," Jon said. "You were told how this works. Clean this up, and we'll gather and discuss your conduct and service. You'll be inspected, and we'll decide if we're interested in this property"—that same confusion on Kylie's face as had been on Janet's: Jon was Kylie's realtor as well—"and then we'll add up your failings for punishment."

Kylie swallowed hard. "Yes, Sir."

She shoved the last of the *croqueta* into her mouth.

"I saw that," Amanda said, and Kylie started picking up plates. "And we'll need more wine, darling. Do you happen to have any other vineyards we could sample?"

"Yes, Ma'am."

Right on cue: "Where's the bathroom?" Carolyn said. She had been distracted the whole meal, checking her phone more than anything else.

"Through that doorway, to the right, Ma'am."

Carolyn stood.

"Brief break," Jon announced. "Clear this all up, sweetie. You still have work to do."

❖

Janet was in the kitchen with Kylie. Kylie was at her sink, rinsing off the dishes but leaving them there. Janet leaned back against the counter and folded her arms.

Kylie's ass was rounded and firm; fairly large, but it added to her short and curvaceous stature.

"So how did Jon corral you into this?" Janet asked.

Kylie shut off the water but stayed leaning against the counter. She was hiding.

"He—"

"Face me when you speak to me," Janet said, and felt another thrill when Kylie obeyed. She turned around, clearly resisting the urge to cover herself.

"When he was helping me move…"

Janet laughed. "He saw your books?"

"Yea! I've got a few. He saw one. I'll admit, maybe I kind of left it out?"

Janet laughed again. That book of hers hadn't been left out by accident, either. Was this a common tactic?

"Which book was it?"

"*Paraded*," Kylie said.

"Oh yes. I have that one. Is that your fantasy? Tell me about it."

Kylie nodded. "I sort of confessed it to him. That one is *so close* to the fantasy I've had my whole life."

"Which is?"

Kylie looked flustered, so naked in her own kitchen. Janet remembered the feeling.

"Tell me."

"I'm…I'm a peasant girl, some little kingdom. Soldiers

369

come through, capture me."

"Mmm, yes. And they…?"

"No, no—not yet. I'm still a virgin, never left the village. No, I'm prime property, as Jon would say. Spoils of war. I'm put in a cart with a cage on it, along with several other young girls. We're all naked."

Kylie wasn't *that* young, anymore, but Janet understood.

"The soldiers make us serve them whenever we camp for the night, entertain them. But they have to keep us virgins."

"Okay."

"Then I'm put on a different cart to be paraded through the capitol. A flat platform, with a pole. I'm tied to it, like this," Kylie stretched her arms above her head, wrists crossed, "and the people laugh and point at me."

Janet was starting to get aroused.

"I'm brought before the king, in the big court, and I'm whipped for the amusement of everyone."

Janet knew this fantasy.

"Then I have to service everyone, the whole roomful—every courtier, male, female, generals, captains."

"Wow. Servants, too?"

Kylie's eyes widened, her mouth open. "I hadn't thought of that! That's good!"

"Anyway…"

"So then, only if I've suitably impressed the King—and I do, I'm *very* good—does he take me to his chamber and…"

She hesitated.

"Say it."

"Fucks me. Over and over. Every which way. But unknown to me, the whole court is watching."

Janet thought it funny that it would be unknown to her if it was her own fantasy, but she understood how these things worked.

"But he doesn't keep me. I tried so hard, gave him everything, and I do mean everything, but he sends me off to be sold. Discarded."

"Ah." Was this how the book went? She would have to find it when she got home.

"So I'm put up for auction, against my will, and there is nothing I can do about it. Who knows who'll buy me? Could be a real creep or something. But there I stand, not even tied up, because—"

"Because trying to leave would bring even worse punishment," Janet said. Had Kylie heard Amanda's whispering?

It's just not as fun in real life, Janet thought as she pictured the liquor store video.

She thought of Kylie's fantasy, then the novel she'd just reread (again), *Stowed*, about the pirate ship. In real life, that would be the worst thing *ever*, the only woman on board, denied clothes. But in thought, in fantasy, good God it was hot. But why ruin Kylie's fun?

"Tell me more," she said.

"Jon said he couldn't quite give me that, but he could get me as close as possible here in the suburbs," Kylie said.

Janet nodded. Indeed.

She was surprised Jack hadn't wandered into the kitchen as he'd done at her house, everything else was following such a familiar pattern. Janet looked up and down Kylie's body as she stood naked, and Kylie blushed.

"I don't—"

"*Ssh*," Janet said. She stepped nearer to Kylie and placed her hand under her chin, as Jack had done to her. Kylie looked at Janet, looked away. Janet held her chin.

The girl was terrified—of Janet!—and it was adorable. Her breaths came quickly; she was trying to control them. She opened her mouth to speak, but decided better of it.

Janet looked down at Kylie's small but curvy body again, and for the first time, she pictured herself not *on* an auction block, at the mercy of cruel potential buyers, wanting to see more, wanting a demonstration—but in the crowd, considering whether to bid.

And Janet would most definitely bid on Kylie. Her effort, her eagerness to please. Her exposure, her abandonment, her newfound, humbling poverty—such unfortunate circumstances. Her big, naked tits.

This was quite a feeling. She felt that dark surge of…she didn't know *what*, that she had felt when Kylie kneeled to serve her, when Hannah had done the same. It was an unfamiliar feeling. But a powerful one.

Janet lifted.

Kylie raised her head, and Janet lifted higher. She was taller than Kylie, and Kylie strained up onto her toes to obey Janet's hand.

"Ma'am?" Janet couldn't get over being called "Ma'am," "I've—I've never been with a woman."

"No? But it's in your fantasy."

"…Yes. Am I going to have to—"

"Trying to claim her for yourself?" Carolyn said, in the doorway. "She's community property, tonight."

This was some serious déjà vu.

Carolyn had no razor, this time; none was necessary on Kylie's hairless groin. Janet expected her to head to the living room, but Carolyn walked in and stepped right up to Janet, stared her in the eyes. Inches from Janet's face. Janet was taken aback.

"Show me your tits," she said to Janet.

"I'm not the sub. She is." Kylie stayed up on her toes.

"We both know who is. Show me your tits. Now." Carolyn's eyes were crazy, aggressive.

"No."

"You'll do it, slave girl. You think you're so perfect, always distracting everyone."

"What? I don't."

"I think you're a fake, a pretender, certainly no Domme. Show me your tits like you did in the store."

She leaned closer to Janet.

Kylie's mouth dropped open. Janet let her chin go so Kylie wouldn't feel her fingers beginning to shake.

"I said no."

"Do it, you little bitch. Show them. Show them to Kelly, here. Show her you're no top. Lift your shirt."

"Kylie."

"Shut up, you. Was I speaking to you?"

"No, Ma'am. I'm sorry."

"Now, Janet. Show. Me. Your—"

Carolyn's phone rang. Janet was shaking, the same fear she'd felt in that store. Carolyn turned her phone upward—it was already in her hand—and after looking at the screen, said "*Damn* it," and ignored the call.

But Janet was already gone.

❖

Kylie was inspected, thoroughly. Probed, penetrated, licked, sucked, pinched; by all but Carolyn, who sat in her chair sulking, drinking, staring at her phone—and staring at Janet as she made Kylie lick her own juices off her fingers after probing her. This was what Janet had been dreading for the last two weeks, this unwanted attention from Carolyn.

Kylie was whipped with a flogger for her shortcomings. She took it remarkably well—standing up and fairly quiet, from Jack, and on her hands and knees on the coffee table and not so quiet, from Amanda. Carolyn wanted no part of it, which no one understood, especially Jon, her old friend. He tried coaxing her, tempting, taking command and handing her the flogger. But she became more and more irritated, temperamental—and fixated on Janet. Damn it, just when she was beginning to see the joys of being a Domme. Janet was torn between her fear of Carolyn and this thrill of having someone obey her will, this darling, soft creature groveling at her feet. *Her* feet. It was all very unsettling and confusing. She pressed her fingers deep into Kylie's mouth once more before taking her seat.

"Now, dear," Amanda said, trying to maintain some semblance of order despite Carolyn's increasing outbursts, such as:

"You're all a bunch of…of fucking pretenders," pouring herself another glass of wine, rather than demanding it from Kylie—most out of character.

Amanda waited patiently, though less and less so, and continued.

"Kylie darling. You're doing well. Are you all right?"

"Yes, Ma'am," wiping away a tear. Her body was streaked in welts.

"No fixin' 'er makeup," Jack said.

"Yes, no fixing your makeup, Kylie. Stand straight, arms at your sides. You do know what's next?"

Carolyn grunted, laughed. "Fucking joke."

"Carolyn, sunshine, will you kindly shut the fuck up?" Jack said. He had been surprisingly silent until now, compared to all the bickering and antagonizing of Carolyn he'd done at Janet's house.

"I've been trying to be nice," he said. "I've been hoping you'll calm your shit down. But I've had enough. I came here to relax, see this beautiful young thing strip naked and dance for us—so to speak, darlin', you don't really have to dance—I came here to get off. It's my fun. Jon put this together out of the kindness of his—"

"Oh, don't give me that country-boy bullshit, Jack." Everyone froze, especially Kylie, who was standing at the foot of the table, ready for orders, not expecting any of this. "I have had it with you, I have had it with Miss Perfect over there,"—she pointed to Amanda—"You too, Jon, we all know what you are, and I have especially had it with little Miss Raven-haired, Blue-eyed, Center of the fucking Universe, here."

"Carolyn, what the hell are—"

"What do you have against me?" Janet said, looking at her for the first time since the kitchen. "I've never done *anything* to you."

"Oh, you. Listen you little—"

"Carolyn! Shut the fuck up!" Jack yelled. *Finally*, Janet thought. *Backup.* "You pretty much have to ruin everything, don't you."

"Um," Kylie said, "Are we still—"

"You," Jack said to Kylie, "Get on your knees, crawl over here. Open my pants. It's time to get to work, girly."

"*You*," Carolyn said, pointing at Janet, but her eyes wandered. "I'll get back to you."

She waved her finger accusingly at everyone in the room. "I am sick of all of you."

"Then perhaps you should leave," Amanda said.

"You are all nothing but a bunch of fucking poseurs," Carolyn said, not even hearing her. "You all know *nothing* about The Life, the commitment it takes. Nothing."

"Carolyn, shut up," Jack said. "We all came here to have fun. I came here to watch this little filly—"

"Oh, shut it, Jack. You're from *Chicago*. You didn't even have that ridiculous accent until your 'granddaddy' left you that land in Texas. And *you*," she said, pointing at Jon, "Where shall we start?"

"Carolyn…"

"Or you," she said, now staring at Janet.

"*What*," Janet said, not looking away.

She would not look away, this time. Her heart was racing.

"Kylie," she said. "Me first. Get over here." Kylie was on her knees and had unfastened Jack's fly.

Kylie looked up at Jack, who shrugged, always up for something interesting, and he gestured toward Janet. Kylie crawled, kneeled between Janet's legs. She reached for her zipper.

Whatever had surged into Janet's bloodstream earlier was still there, some vestige of it, anyway.

"Why do you hate me, Carolyn? I've only ever tried to be nice to you. I only try to be nice to everybody. Why are you so nasty? To *me*?"

"Why?" Carolyn said. She paused, her eyes roaming around to the others. "Because you keep taking me away from… Because every time I…"

Now her eyes focused, the old steel, disciplined and mean: "Because I can."

"I *knew* it!" Janet shouted. "You think you know how it's done, how to be a top. But *real* tops give a shit about their subs. You're not a top, Carolyn—you're just a *bully*. I pity all those slaves of yours. They deserve better than you, I *know*, and I don't even know them. Jon's a real top. Amanda. You're an *abuser*. If you were a man, they'd have kicked you out of this stupid club a long time ago. Probably beat the hell out of you. But because you've got those perfect sexy eyes and that perfect little ass, they let you walk all over them. And me. Why Amanda puts up with you, I have no idea."

Janet realized she had Kylie by the hair; Kylie had undone Janet's fly and pulled her jeans and underwear to her ankles—Janet must have raised her hips to let her do so while she was shouting.

Janet's heart was still pounding as she kicked off her jeans. She was shaking like a leaf in the wind.

But so was Carolyn.

"I should beat the holy hell out of you," Carolyn said. She clenched both her hands into fists.

Janet made a fist in her trembling hand, the one not holding Kylie's head between her spread legs.

"Go ahead." Carolyn could do no worse than she had that first night, that horrible beating. What was there to lose?

"I'd be careful, Carolyn," Jon said. "She nearly decked Dmitri when he took things too far."

"Yea, right."

"It's true," Amanda said. "Nearly broke his jaw, from what I understand." This wasn't true at all. She hadn't hurt him anywhere near that bad. But she *had* hit him, made him feel it.

Carolyn's eyes faltered, flickered away for an instant, then came back. Her jaw was quivering. She relaxed her fists.

"You little—" She shook her head. "You think Jon's a top?" she said. "A Dom?"

"Yeah. A good one. He respects me, even if he's…spanking me, or…whatever. *Get to work*," she told Kylie, and felt Kylie's tentative tongue enter her sex. Her cunt.

Kylie's lips and tongue were shaking as well.

"You think he's—"

"Carolyn…" Jon said.

Carolyn looked over at Jon, then at Amanda.

"She doesn't know," Carolyn said.

"Carolyn."

"Do you know, Jack?"

"Know what?"

"*Carolyn.*"

Janet looked to Jon and Amanda, both resolutely staring at Carolyn. Amanda was turning on her sternest glare but it wasn't working. Carolyn turned back to Janet.

"Jon's no top, you silly little fool. Not anymore, at least. He's under more control than anyone here, even that little slut between your legs."

Janet heard Kylie whimper, but her tongue started working faster against her clit. Janet felt a surge of her juices to match her adrenaline.

"What the hell are you talking about?"

"He's Amanda's *slave*, you idiot."

"Yea, right," Janet said. "He's her—" What the hell *was* he, anyway? "Why would you even say that?" *Jon?*

Carolyn leaned in, and took a long time before answering her:

"Because I'm the one *who sold him to her.*"

Carolyn stood, clenched both her fists again, and walked out the door, still grasping her phone. She left the door wide open, open to all those neighbors in their identical houses.

Janet looked at Jon, who was sitting with his head in his hands, and Amanda, arms crossed, legs crossed, lips asymmetrically pursed and eyes rolling as if to say "awkward." Janet looked at Jack, slack-jawed like herself and staring into space. His arms hung loose over the arms of his chair; he said nothing.

Finally she looked down at Kylie, nose buried in Janet's trimmed black bush, amber eyes as wide open as the front door. Clearly not what the girl had expected from the evening. Janet knew she was wishing someone would please shut the door.

"Why did you stop?" Janet said. "Did I say you could stop?"

Chapter Twenty-Two

"Hi, this is Ken! I'm sorry I can't answer my phone right now, I must be working very hard on something important. Please leave me a message or send me a text and I will get right back to you as soon as I can, I promise!" <beep.>

Friday, Sept. 14, 6:33 pm: "Kenneth, you are thirty minutes late. Ten strokes. From Jimmy. That should teach you."

Friday, Sept. 14, 6:46 pm: "Kenneth, you are now forty-five minutes late. Have you forgotten your phone at work again? You would have been in far less trouble just coming over late, rather than going back and getting it. Twenty strokes. Up to you."

Friday, Sept. 14, 7:01 pm: "Ken? You are an hour late. Twenty strokes plus the dreaded randomized electrical thing on your balls that you love so much. And don't you *dare* text an apology. That would be cowardly and you know it."

Friday, Sept. 14, 7:15 pm: "Kenny? Where are you. It's been an hour and fifteen minutes. You have never been this late. Call me now if you want anything resembling forgiveness. Your punishments are adding up, you're already going to be hurting tomorrow. Don't make it worse."

Friday, Sept. 14, 8:35 pm: "Ken, you have disabled your locator app, I don't know where you are or where your phone is. Turn it back on. Call me, let's get this straightened out before you're in real trouble."

Friday, Sept. 14, 11:06 pm: "Ken? You are five hours late! Everyone is still up, I'm making them stay up for you. You don't want to cause them too much grief do you, Ken? Jimmy and Bobby—and I have a treat for you, Kenny, her name is Tina—are all getting a little tired. They're in strict bondage, very uncomfortable. I know you don't like others to suffer, especially for you. Call. Now."

Friday, Sept. 14, 11:21 pm: "*Kenny!* Call. You are sinking into deeper and deeper trouble, mister. Yes 'mister.' Do you know how much it pains me to call you that? Call. Me. Now. Where are you, anyway?"

Saturday, Sept. 15, 12:45 am: "Okay, slave. The others are put to bed in their cages or sent home. I sent Tina home. I'll have you know she's beautiful, and you missed her. She's a gorgeous little redhead; she looks like you! But female. Not masculine, but a…a pretty version of you. I think you'd have liked her; too bad you missed her. I am going to bed, Kenny. Do not bother calling tonight."

Saturday, Sept. 15, 1:03 am: "Kenny! God damn it, where are you? It's 1:00 am. You are in such deep shit. *Deep* shit."

Saturday, Sept. 15, 3:10 am: "Jesus, Kenny, it's 3:00 am, and I am *up*. I need to know where you are so I can go back to sleep. Call me. Don't avoid me, I'm calm. Call me."

Saturday, Sept. 15, 5:45 am: "You prick, you've kept me up all night. Where are you? Why aren't you checking in? I am assuming something bad has happened, so I called the police. You would not worry your Mistress unless you had a good reason. You never have before, anyway. Call."

Saturday, Sept. 15, 8:30 am: "Okay, you called my bluff, I have not called the police. At least to report you. But I do have connections. No accidents on the freeway last night—that's my job, remember, I can find that out—no one dragged in for beating or raping redheads in the middle of the night. Where are you?"

Saturday, Sept. 15, 4:45 pm: "What are you trying to pull? Jimmy and Bobby are having to pull double duty, this fine Saturday. I am pissed, Ken, pissed. You call me, I am through calling you."

Sunday, Sept. 16, 6:00 pm: "You little son of a bitch, it's been two days now—forty-eight hours. If something has happened to you, they would say the trail of clues has already gone cold, on TV. Should I call the police? I mean it this time. Try to explain that one to them—yes, I'll tell them my little slave boy went AWOL. You don't want me to do that, do you?"

Sunday, Sept. 16, 10:47 pm: "Ken, I'm going to bed, I have work early tomorrow. Don't call and wake me up. The other redheads have gone home. Quite a weekend we had, without you. Too bad."

Monday, Sept. 17, 4:33 am: "Where the fuck are you? It's 4:30 in the morning! You are in such deep shit. *Such* deep shit."

Monday, Sept. 17, 10:07 am: "You called in sick? Your boss said you called in sick this morning. Yes I called him. Okay. At least I know you're okay. So where are you? What the fuck are you doing? Call. Me. You…you better call me."

Monday, Sept. 17, 7:26 pm: "Ken? I went by your apartment. Your car is not there. I don't know what you think you're doing, but it's not going to work. Are you avoiding me? You've *never* avoided me, Kenneth. I am ordering—*ordering*—you to call your Mistress. Now."

Monday, Sept. 17, 11:54 pm: "You are defying a command from your Mistress, which you have never done. You have been the best little slave in the world for over a year, and now you are becoming a very bad one. Do you want to remain my slave? Ordinarily, I would have released you, by now. I have no time for this shit. I have other slaves, remember. I have to maintain them, and I can replace you with any of them. Call me now."

Tuesday, Sept. 18, 5:55 pm: "All right, you bastard, you little prick. You are *so* in for it. Four days. Four days gone, you haven't been to your apartment once. I know. I've driven by. Yes I am thorough. What the hell do you think you are doing?"

Wednesday, Sept. 19, 6:17 pm: "You goddamn little bastard! What is this? I do not tolerate defiance, especially from you! Five days? Five days without even stopping by your apartment, your job? Your boss is really wondering what's happening, and so am I. We may just have to have a talk about you, you don't want him to know everything about you, do you?"

Blue

Thursday, Sept. 20, 10:37 pm: "Who are you staying with? Have you found another Mistress? Who is she? I know most of them, yes I do. I know it's not some girl, you don't need a girl, you wouldn't know what to do with one. You need a firm hand, Kenny. That narrows it down. If you're here in town. Have you left town? …Where the fuck are you!"

Friday, Sept. 21, 3:30 pm. "It's been a week and I am tired of calling you. Yes, Jimmy and Bobby, who look so much like you, are coming over again tonight. So is Tina, she rather enjoyed herself here last week. And the boys enjoyed her. You could have, too. She is very enjoyable. Very. God is she good. Do you hear me? We are all having far more fun than you are, so don't bother calling all weekend because we will be occupied. All of us. Busy. Sucking, fucking. Don't call."

Friday, Sept. 21, 5:07 pm. "I uh…I've got a thing, I have to go to, tonight. I'd forgotten all about it. Dinner party with some friends. 'Friends.' I've, um…put everyone in Deep Storage. Do you remember the last time I had to do that with you? Little black-haired… It seems like she keeps taking me away from… Like every time you and I…
I put them all three into Deep Storage until I get back. Which means it's up to Jimmy to free the others if there's a fire or something, there's only one release chain. But I've got my phone, okay? Okay? Call me if you need to. Okay?"

Friday, Sept. 21, 8:45 pm. "Kenny, I think I…I think I burned some bridges, tonight. With some people I've known a long time. And someone said something to me that's maybe… I'm pretty much alone, aren't I. Call me. Would you?"

Saturday, Sept. 22, 11:45 am. "*Kenneth!* God damn it, where are you? These boys say I'm a little rough—why don't you show them how it's done? How to take a whipping, hm? They don't have your stamina, your strength. Come back. Come home, while everyone is here. You get first shot at Tina, you'll love her. I got her for you, Ken. For *you*."

Saturday, Sept. 22, 10:51 pm. "You are in such deep shit. How many times do I have to say it? They leave tomorrow so call me now if you want in. You will have discipline to face, yes. You like that though, right? That's why you committed yourself to me, all those months ago? Committed, Kenny. Committed."

Sunday, Sept. 23, 9:45 pm. "Okay, they're gone again, happy? Another weekend without you. How does that feel? We did just fine. Oh, the things I made them do. Sick things. Debasing things. Miss it much? Hm?"

Monday, Sept. 24, 9:45 pm: "Are you going to come home or not, you prick? I do not understand this. What about your job? What about your Mistress? Those are the two most important things in your life, right? Your Life? Where the hell are you?"

Wednesday, Sept. 26, 5:06 pm: "You quit your job?! Kenny, what the hell? Your boss said you told him you were 'in the mountains.' What mountains? What does that even mean? You can't live long without a job! What, are you washing dishes in some greasy café? Flipping burgers? Call me, Goddamn it."

Thursday, Sept. 27, 12:26 pm: "I got your super to let me into your apartment. Your clothes are still there, your computer, your toothbrush, even. What are you doing? Is this about me? How can I do anything if you won't call me back? She wanted to know if she should kick you out, your rent is due. I said no, you were coming back."

Blue

Friday, Sept. 28, 5:37 pm: "I want you to know that your re-placements—yes I'm going to go ahead and call them that—your *replace*ments, Kenny, are going to suffer greatly tonight. Because of you. I am going to take all of my rage at you out on them. They are going to bleed. All of them. Jimmy, Bobby, and even sweet little Tina. Going to call the cops on me first? Go ahead. I dare you. I fucking dare you. You *know* how mad I can get, you bastard. So think about what they're going through while you go on some lovely hike or some spiritual quest in the mountains or whatever the fuck you're doing. You just think about that."

Tuesday, Oct. 2, 6:45 pm: "I went through your stuff. I got the super to let me in again and I went through your stuff. I didn't know that you… I mean, I, yes I did know. I have trouble say-ing the word, sometimes. Unless it's a joke. Right? You know? A joke. We've had a pretty good thing, you and me. Too bad you're blowing it. I've got two other redheads coming over and they look like you and they are a better you than you. Think ya love me, do ya? …Well show it and call me."

Thursday, Oct. 4, 4:30 pm: "Uh, hey Ken? It's Jim Bowers? Jimmy/James? Um, hey, look, I know we've had some words, in the past, I mean you kind of started that, but…hey, I'm sorry about that, anyway. And I'm sorry about the…well, you know. I mean, she told me to, right? That's what you and I do, right? I get it. We do what she says, that's our kink, man. But uh, hey, listen, you need to come back, man. Yea. She's uh…she's gettin' a little crazy? You know? I mean she showed up already pretty severe if you know what I mean—she's *made* that way, right? Well, yea, of course you know. But it's a-gettin' worse, my man. She's goin' a little off the deep end, not so fun, anymore. So uh, yea, could you at least call her maybe, dawg? I think it would help. I mean, she's callin' me at home, at work, all the time.

Call her, man. And, uh, don't tell her I called you? 'Kay? I got your number off her phone, she don't know. I'd like to keep it that way. Okay, cool, thanks, man."

Wednesday, Oct. 10, 3:15 pm: "I paid your rent. Did you hear me? I paid your fucking rent."

Tuesday, Oct. 17, 7:02 pm: "Hi, um, Kenneth? This is Tina Johnson. You don't know me, I um, I've been at your…your Mistress's house, for a few weeks now, on weekends? I think maybe you've heard about me. Listen, I hope I haven't stepped into anything too weird between the two of you, but I think maybe I have? I mean, I'd heard of her before—she's got a hell of a rep—so when she asked me over I said 'sure.' I mean I was expecting…well, if you're with her, it's obvious you're kinky, so I'll just say it. I was expecting some pretty good whippings and whatnot. I mean, whipping and fucking, it's what makes our world turn around, right? Our kind? But listen, um, she seems pretty hooked on you. Pretty, um…obsessed, I guess you'd call it. I guess you've kind of left her or something? I don't know what's going on. I got your number from Jim, he thought maybe we could all convince you to come back, or at least call her and talk things out? She's not just strict at her house, like I'd heard she would be. She's fucking *harsh*. But that's not it—I mean, I guess I keep coming back, right? But she's calling me at home, all day. She found me at work! She wants me to stay with her until you come back. I told her no, but she's kind of scary, you know? Anyway, please, if you could just give her a call, that would be so cool of you. I don't know what to do. I mean, people told me she's a fun top, if you like 'em hard. And I do. But Jesus."

Tuesday, Oct. 17, 8:45 pm: "I think this little game of yours has gone on long enough, Kenny. I am getting very sick and tired of it. I am thinking of hiring some investigators to search for you. Maybe *persuade* you? To come home? To fucking *call?*"

Tuesday, Oct. 17, 8:54 pm: "Call me, you asshole!"

Wednesday, Oct. 18, 2:15 pm: "Allisa's gone. My Monday nights girl? You've never met her. Beautiful little blonde, every other Monday. Great tits. She left me. Said I was getting too unstable. Unstable, Kenny! What the fuck does she know? Says yes she can take a good beating, then leaves me at the first sign of trouble. She was with me six months. Happy now, Kenny? Happy?"

Thursday, Oct. 19, 9:06 pm: "Now Justin's gone! My Tuesday boy! Rats on a sinking ship. And you are King Rat, Ken. King fucking Rat."

Friday, Oct. 20, 9:45 am: "Ken? Bob Higgins. You know me as Robert or Bobby or whatever the hell. Listen. Will you just call her already? You know who I mean. You, yes you, are personally causing me grief, physical pain at night, and harassment at work, which I cannot afford. I know you don't give a shit about me, but you're gettin' to be on my shit list, buddy, and I really need you to straighten this out with Carolyn. Whatever the hell it is. Your Mistress. Call her, dude."

Friday, Oct. 20, 10:07 pm: "No, he's…
(female murmuring.)
No, I said—I said get between them. On your hands and knees. Take 'em both, bitch. Yes at the same time. I'm going to text him the video.
(murmuring.)
You think I care? Take 'em both. Or I'll tell Jimmy to go up your tight little ass instead of your cunt. Shut up! You think I'm

joking? We're making a video to send to Kenny, so he'll—oh shit, it's on. Did I dial that? Did you guys hear it ring? Kenny? You there? You there?

Bobby, before you fuck her mouth, get me another bottle. And this time you *will* kneel when you pour it.

Kenny?"

Saturday, Oct. 20, 12:21 pm: "Kennnnnnnnny! (giggle.)
Kennnnnnnny."

Sunday, Oct. 21, 7:23 pm: "(cries of pain, female.)
Hear that Kenny?
(sounds of whip on flesh.)
She's suffering. For you. She loves the whip, don't you slave?
Yes, Mistress Carolyn, but I—*ah!*
(whip on flesh.)
Please!
(whipping.)
Do you like doing that to her, James?
Yes, Mistress.
(whip.)
Bobby?
Yes, Ma'am.
Mistress!
(repeated whipping, fast.)
Yes, Mistress, yes!
How about you, Kenny? Do you like doing this to her?"

Tuesday, Oct. 23, 8:45 pm: "(whispered): Mister…Ken? I don't know your last name. This is Tina. Please. Call her. I have to get out of this house, she won't let me out of the house until you get back. She's got so many pictures of me at all the bondage clubs she says the cops'll never believe my story. *Please.*

(squeak of a door opening.)
What the hell are you doing?
I—
(rustling.)
Kenny? Kenny are you there? Are you talking to Tina?
(silence.)
Who are you talking to? This is Ken's number. Are you talking to my Kenny?
No! I swear. I was trying to get him to come home to you! I was leaving a voicemail, that's all. I—no, please! Please! No, I—"

Wednesday, Oct. 24, 10:07 am: "Kenneth, Ken, Kenny, you gotta call her, man. This is Jimmy, yo? It's getting' *bad*, man, *bad*. I think, I think maybe she's got Tina somewhere in the house I don't know about? I dunno, man, our Mistress—*your* Mistress, I'm just playin' here, man, I know it and you know it too, I'm just a joke, to her—she's freakin' out. I mean *bad*. Should I call the cops or somethin'? I don't know what to do, I'm kinda new at all this. I ain't comin' back, I'll tell ya that. Just call her, you asshole! I mean, I can take a beatin', it gets me off, right? But *Jesus*."

Thursday, Oct. 25, 1:45 am: "Ken, where are you? I just can't… I can't. I…can't say it. I can't say it. I am getting really tired of this. Really really tired of it."

Thursday, Oct. 25, 8:07 am: "Am I going to have to pay your rent again, you little cocksucker? Am I? You're going to make me pay your rent again. Aren't you. Asshole. You are the asshole of the universe."

Thursday, Oct. 25, 10:34 am: "Call. Me. You motherfucker… …Damn it!"

Thursday, Oct. 25, 5:30 pm: "Okay, okay. I get it. I fucking get it. Don't like the others hanging around? Well tough shit. Who's serving who? If I'd'a known I was training a fucking deserter, a mutineer, I never would have given you the time of day…

Remember when I first talked to you, back in the gym? Hm? Almost two years ago. You looked so scared. I thought you were so beautiful. I watched you for weeks, you know. I had to have you. Don't you…don't you want…

Oh, fuck you, asshole. I am so fucking tired of this shit."

Thursday, Oct. 25, 8:14 pm: "Get me another bottle, my. What? *Yes.* Oh, you little bitch. You think you've got it bad now, my? Hungry for it, are you, my? Well, this'll be nothing. I will starve you for the rest of your life. You will die a virgin. And you know I could do it. Your father—

(sound of glass shattering.)

Oh, shit, Kenny? Kenny, you there?"

Thursday, Oct 25, 11:54 pm: "(sound of breathing.)"

Friday, Oct. 26, 1:21 am: "(sound of breathing, possible crying.)"

Friday, Oct 26, 11:57 pm: "(sound of breathing.)
(murmuring.)

Shut up! Shut up, I am listening. Shut the fuck up.

Bobby, whip her. Hard."

Saturday, Oct 27, 2:34 am: "Kenny, I… Kenny, I…
…call me."

Saturday, Oct 27, 3:17 am: "Asshole."

Blue

Monday, Oct. 29, 8:45 am: "I paid your rent. Again."

Friday, Nov 2, 9:02 pm: "I know I've been cruel, lately, Ken. I know I've been mean. To you, never mind the others. For a while now. I don't know *why*. You've always known I'm strict, harsh, even. That's why you like me, yes? 'Liked'…
It's…it's not my fault. I was abused as a child. Did I ever tell you that? My mother—she's beautiful, Kenny. You think I've got cheekbones? You should see her cheekbones—but she met a guy who—who abused me. Whipped me, raped me. My father, she said he was. It's not my fault."

Friday, Nov. 2, 9:06 pm: "Okay, actually I made that up. I had wonderful parents who were very sweet people. They still are. But it's so romantic, right? The cliché of the Damaged Top? Because how could anyone possibly enjoy whipping and controlling other people unless they were abused themselves, right? …Well, actually, I had a brother…my older brother. He *was* abusive. Not sexually, but sick. He would twist my arm behind my back, make me say things, make me kiss his feet. Sick fuck. Sadist. But I also had—have—a younger brother, and so I would do it to *him*. Terrible things. No, nothing sexual, you asshole. But I learned it was a lot more fun to torment than to be tormented.
Bye, Kenny."

Friday, Nov. 2, 9:11 pm: "No, I made that up, too. I'm an only child, my parents were sweet to me and they spoiled me. I had a great childhood. As long as everyone on the playground understood who was boss. And when the hormones hit? Oh my God I ran that place. I got my hips, I got my tits, and I could make any boy do whatever I wanted. Most of the girls, too, one way or another. You know who my favorites were? The little lost shy ones—like you—or the football players. Big tough quarterbacks, linebackers, in high school *and* college. Leader of the team, right? King of the field! I would have them naked on their knees, begging me to let them lick my cunt, just with a *look*. And I'd let them, and then send them home to the frat house with their dick still hard. And dry. They could call me a prick tease if they wanted, but I'd ask them back, and they'd show up. I'd just give it to them again—but make it worse.

Oh, Kenny, why don't—what?

(murmuring.)

What do you mean, she's out of her shackles?

(more murmuring.)

Well where the hell is she?

(murmur.)

Well find the little redheaded bitch, you little redheaded bastard! How did she get out? Did Jimmy unlock her? That's the only way she could have gotten out.

(shouts.)

Jimmy! You fuck! How did you even get in? Where the fuck is she?

(whip hitting skin, repeatedly.)

She is not *yours*, you fuck. Shut up! She is for Kenneth.

(*smack!* murmuring.)

You will call him 'Kenneth'.

(*smack!*)

She is my gift to Kenneth! She is to remain in Deep Storage until he sees her! Where is—her car is gone! Oh…oh. Both of you. Yes, welcome back, Jimmy. You're not going anywhere, now. Over here. Clothes off. Off! Hands and knees. *Elbows* and knees. Now. *Now.*

(murmuring!) (whip hitting flesh.)

Shut up!

(whip hitting flesh, repeatedly.)

(repeatedly.)

Shut up.

Shut. Up."

Sunday, Nov. 4, 11:20 pm: "Look, I've never... I've never been in... Oh, fuck it."

Monday, Nov. 5, 9:30 pm: "Where *are* you? Don't you give a shit? Don't you care? Can't you fucking..."

Tuesday, Nov. 6, 1:07 am: "Okay, dammit. Lissen. Lissen a me. D'you unnerstan' what a loss of control it is for me to fall in love, you asshole? D'you unnerstan' this? *Do you?* Because once it starts to go, it might never stop, get it? If I let it go, it might just..."

Tuesday, Nov. 6, 1:09 am: "*DO YOU UNDERSTAND THIS?*"

Wednesday, Nov. 7, 5:26 pm: "They're gone. Okay? The redheads. All of them. Bobby, Tina, and Jimmy—again, *that* fucking bastard. Gone. I fired them. Freed them. Whatever. Dismissed them. They're gone. Okay? Call me, okay?"

Wednesday, Nov 7, 10:45 pm: "(sounds of crying.)"

Wednesday, Nov. 7, 11:07 pm: "(sounds of crying.) Oh, you *fuck*, I hate you!"

Thursday, Nov. 8, 2:22 am: "Don't... Don't... (exhale.) Just—"

Thursday, Nov. 8, 7:00 pm: "Get me a red, my... I don't care which, just get me a red. Yes. The Cab is fine, my.
(sound of gulping.)
Kenny? Can't we... How can we talk if we...if you don't call me?
(sound of sloppy slurping.)

Pour me another. Shut up and pour me another.
(sound of glass shattering.)"

Thursday, Nov. 8, 9:50 pm: "(car door slamming shut, car starting.) Look. Look. Okay. Look.
I thought I could…replace you, somehow, but still 'ave you, the outside you. Unnerstand? Mm. Make you go, but keep the control. *That's* it. Hm? I mean *them.* You know. Yea. I thought I could make you go and keep a sort of you. I even thought if I put *you* on the film, or the camera, or whatever, but kept the almost-you, then…yes I know this is crazy yes. Have you never met your Mistr'ss, Kenny? Ima kinda fucked-up individual. And you drove me crazy. You drove me crazy. You juss…you juss…you're *you.* I don't unnerstan' all this. I have never been in love, not even wuh…once. Not even *once.* I've never said it. To anybody. *Ever.* Boys are toys. Boys are toys, godammit. Until… It…it *bugs* me, Ken. Kenny? Do—whoa."

Thursday, Nov. 8, 9:55 pm: " 'Kay I'm back. Do you unnerstan' this?
I'wz…gonna drive you away. That wz th' plan. But then I did! Fuck…
Oh shit, I'm—
(tires squeal, crashing sound.)"

Tuesday, Nov. 13, 8:30 am: "Okay. I'll stop. Please call me, Ken. Please."

Chapter Twenty-Three

Ken kept his hand steady as he rang the doorbell. The last time he had pressed it standing up—or dressed, for that matter—had to have been back before Training Week, flowers in hand, when they were still "dating." When he was still allowed speech, before any commitment had been made.

Commitment.

Carolyn opened the door.

"Come in," she said, and she held it open for him.

She looked like, well, a normal person. A normal, beautiful woman. He couldn't remember the last time he had seen her in jeans. Her hair was down, shimmering over her shoulders. She wore a soft gray Henley; the sleeve extended beyond her wrist and up to the knuckle of her thumb—one sleeve, that is.

As he entered, he saw that her left arm was in a cast, suspended in a sling around her neck and shoulder. That sleeve was pushed up over it, its fabric stretched, its cuff cut.

"How were the mountains?" she said.

"Cold. Are you…okay?" he asked. He would not call her Mistress, but the habit was hard to break.

She nodded as she closed the door. "Double fracture, both bones. Ulna and radius. Couple of broken ribs, too. I'm fucked. I thought…you might come and see me, in the hospital."

"I didn't know until you were out. I didn't listen to my messages for a very long time. I was afraid to." They slowly headed down the hall, both on their feet, side by side.

"What exactly happened, may I ask?"

"T-boned when I ran a red light."

"So you're lucky to be alive, then?"

"Yea. Please don't look at her," she said, as they passed the naked Asian girl in the alcove. His instinct and training were too strong to defy her despite the strangeness of her "please." He looked down at the floor. After the usual brief glance.

He waited for the "I said do *not* look at her," but instead she said, calmly, "It's to deny her, not you. She has not yet earned the right to be gazed upon by you."

Well. That was unexpected.

Carolyn gestured toward the sofa by her favorite chair; he knew she would not offer that. She'd only given that up once, that he knew of.

He tried to push the memory out of his mind.

"Please sit," she said, and she settled into her chair. He followed her example.

"Something to drink?"

This was too weird. "No, thank you."

She took a deep breath. Ken had never seen her like this.

"Look, Ken, I—"

"So are you in trouble?" he asked. She did not look angry at the interruption.

"DUI charges are pending until my court date. I cannot get out of it, my alcohol level was sky high."

He waited.

"I won't go to jail. It's my first offense and I was the only one hurt." She looked up at him. "Picturing me in a women-in-prison movie?"

He did not laugh. Actually, he had. She would run the gang that tormented the virginal, wrongly convicted heroine.

"Probation, quite a big fine. I've lost my license. I'm in need of a chauffeur, if you're still looking for a job." She smiled sadly. "Not that I have one either. Or a car."

"What?"

"Director of Traffic Risk Assessment Research, arrested for drunk and reckless driving? I was out before 8:00 am the next day. I don't have many friends, at work. I'm also being sued."

"I was asking about...the girl?"

Carolyn gave him a quizzical look. "Oh. Tina. Unlawful restraint and kidnapping. No, that went away weeks ago."

"The pictures of her in bondage clubs?"

"How did you know about that?"

Ken decided not to tell her.

Carolyn looked down, picked at a fingernail on her injured hand.

"Actually, I...apologized. Profusely. I've been doing a lot of that, lately. And *then* I showed her the pictures I could show to the cops. 'Couple-a kinky lesbos, havin' a spat,' the detective said. For once it helped to have a sexist, homophobic cop on the case."

She kept picking.

"Listen, Ken... Do you remember that time, oh, about a year ago, when I...I whipped you so hard you bled?"

"Yes, I definitely remember that," *Mistress*.

"I never said I was sorry, for that, did I."

"No, Mis—. No."

"Well, I was. Very sorry. I cried. Me. But I couldn't let you see. I am sorry I never said so. I think maybe it was because I..."

"...You what?"

"Look, I..." She nervously tapped a fingernail on her cast.

"Could we—? Look, I can't do this like this. Could you take off your clothes and get on your knees? It's the only way I know how to talk to you."

"No." *Don't say it, don't say it.* He didn't call her Mistress.

"Would you…at least kneel? Here, by my chair. Just come closer."

Ken slid off the sofa, and crouched down beside her. He kneeled, but not properly, not up on his knees. He sat on his feet and waited. "Okay."

"I need you to come back," she said. She wasn't looking at him; she was looking down, still picking at her nail. "I want you to come back. Not just for me, I want you to *want* to come back."

Ken said nothing.

"I know things… I know I need to…"

Ken stared at her, her head lowered, until she leaned back and then he averted his eyes as always.

"Would you like… I would like…"

He could sense her turning her head one way and then the other.

"Jesus, Ken, I don't negotiate, and you know it. Here is what I will offer, and nothing more. You can take it or leave it." That sounded more like his Mistress. "But please consider it." That did not.

"I would like you to move in with me."

Ken glanced up, only for a moment.

"Twenty-four seven." She hesitated. "Year round. Maybe… who knows—forever?"

Ken looked up and they finally made eye contact, both too determined not to be the one to look away first.

"Everyone is gone. All my slaves. Dismissed. Even the ones who hadn't left me already, I dismissed them as soon as I heard you were back in town. The redheads, definitely. Gone. I'm sorry about them."

"Am I still Slave Number Six?"

"God, no. I'm…so sorry."

"How many others were there?"

"You don't want to know."

"You should have no trouble finding more."

At this Carolyn actually looked worried, an expression he had never once seen.

"I don't want more. Just you. Full time."

She bit her lip—her *own* lip.

Ken looked at the girl in the alcove, who he thought might have been watching until he turned.

"I am obligated to keep my, for another year, of course. I made a commitment." She put a slight emphasis on the word "commitment." He sensed a little passive-aggressiveness, looked her in the eye, and she backed down.

"Your…?" he said, confused.

"No, not 'my'—Mai. M-a-i." She pointed at the girl. "She will have to stay until her Coming Out party, and then she will be on her way. It was going to be for four years, then three, now it looks like two; she's pretty amazing, really. But I made a promise."

Things were never normal, with this Mistress. He'd ask later.

"But no others. Ever, if you wish."

Wish? That was all he'd ever wanted. All.

"Will you accept this?" She was looking straight at him again.

This dance of their eyes was ridiculous; it used to be so simple. But she had just said something she had never said to anyone: I will change for you.

But he had one demand, one that he would not back down from.

"I want to hear you say it," he said.

"Say wh—" Then it hit her.

"Kenny, no. I can't. I *never have*. Do you realize that?"

"Why? It's so simple."

"It's…a slippery slope, you know? All my life, to do that, to say that—it would mean a loss of control. And once it starts… Let one person in, and it could all fall apart, the whole thing."

"Like it hasn't already? I've still got the voicemails."

Carolyn blushed. *Blushed.*

"And aren't you trying to let me in? To get me back in?"

Carolyn covered her face with her free hand.

"I'm afraid it's a condition," he blurted out, before he could change his mind. "My only condition."

Carolyn exhaled through her nose behind her hand. The Sun was sinking lower outside, and a sunbeam was slowly climbing toward her face, her hidden face.

"I'm not used to this," she said.

He waited.

"I love you," she said. "I love you, okay?"

She lowered her hand and stared straight at him.

"I said I love you… I've never fallen in love with *anyone*. 'Til you. It wasn't supposed to happen. You screwed things *all* up. Inside me. Damn it."

Ken felt goose bumps on his scalp, his neck, his entire body. The world rotated 360 degrees, in every direction at once (would that be 360 x 360, or 360^{360}? He couldn't think), and came back to where it started, the same but different; reconstituted.

She wasn't lying. He knew her tricks, by now—every tell on her face when she was pulling a ruse on him, the exact dilation of her green and amber eyes.

But no. Her skin was covered in goosebumps, too.

"You may have noticed your former Mistress is one fairly fucked-up individual," she said. Now it was her turn to wait. "Will you come back to me? Will you make this your home?"

He could only nod his head.

"Yes," he finally said. "Mistress."

She almost laughed in relief, and did something else She had never done: She leaned forward and She kissed him, full on the mouth—no biting, no tongue thrusting in, no gripping his hair.

Just a kiss.

She straightened in Her chair. He had placed his hands on Her thighs while they'd kissed, and She looked down at them.

"You should be punished for that, you know."

He ran his hands slowly down Her legs as he withdrew them, feeling the sculpted muscles underneath Her jeans.

"Yes, Mistress," he said. "I know."

She ducked Her head.

"I still…want to share you with friends, Ken. I *love* to show you off. God, that body of yours." She looked out the wall of glass and squinted into the sun. "Not that I have any of those left, either."

"I've never minded the parties, Mistress," he said. "They're thrilling. Except that guy who had that smirk on his face all the time. Can we—can we not have him over? Can I have the one exemption?"

"Oh. Yea. Kendrick. No, he's long gone." She stroked his face, then straightened again. "Not that you're allowed any say in the matter."

"No, Mistress. Of course not."

Ken looked again at Her thighs. He knew She'd normally say it was out of line, without permission, but he leaned down over them, laid his head on Her lap, and kept it there. He hugged Her hips, gripped them.

"Thank you," he whispered.

"Thank *you*," She whispered back, bending over and laying Her head on his back and feeling his muscles with Her free hand. She ran Her hand down his spine and back up again.

She leaned as far back in Her chair as She could.

"You're lucky I have a bad arm, bad ribs," She said. "That move deserves quite a whipping. Very forward of you."

"Yes, Mistress."

"Jesus, Ken, I am so ready, I am *so* fucking wet. You don't know how much I've—"

She looked away again.

"You've what?"

"*Missed* you, goddamn it. Now pull off my jeans, and suck your Mistress's clit until she begs you to stop."

...Begs?

Ken unzipped her fly as She watched, then peeled Her jeans and panties off together. Her scent was intoxicating, and so, so familiar. She slid down further in Her chair and laid Her free arm across Her face in the Sun. She spread Her legs and rocked Her hips in anticipation.

"I'll still expect complete obedience, you know."

"Of course, Mistress."

He would expect no less from Her.

Ken slid forward, and ran his hands along Her inner thighs like She had never allowed him to do before. He felt Her hips, Her stomach under Her shirt until he reached Her ribs.

He'd expected bandages. He touched Her gingerly, ran his fingertips up to Her breasts. She was wearing no bra. He squeezed them in his hands, which he had never done. Pinched Her nipples.

She arched Her back, exhaled.

"Next you can do something else for me. To me. Something I've never let you do, but should have. From the start."

Ken couldn't believe what he was hearing. She raised Her arm and looked down the length of Her body at him, a little more sternly now.

"Then you'll bathe me," She said. "And help me get dressed. We have a little party to go to. What you wear won't matter."

She tilted Her head back.

Blue

"Whatever You say, Mistress."

Ken leaned in as She raised Her hips up to him.

"*IloveyouIloveyouIloveyouIloveyou*," She whispered into the air, as if he wouldn't hear.

❖

Janet had hardly slept a wink, and her mind had been in turmoil for the last twenty-four hours. What did he want *now?*

Dawn and Julie and a few girls from the office had asked her out last night for drinks and laughs, and to compare fishing lure stories, of course. Poor Ron—those were always good for a laugh, and he'd just started up a new round of his little projects and outings.

All of her worries of shunning and being ostracized were put to rest. She was taking a sip from her second margarita—Dawn's fly-fishing convention story he'd told her had been the best so far—when her phone rang.

Dmitri. She excused herself and spoke to him in the restroom.

He called to summon her to the warehouse again—the next night, in fact; tonight. He wouldn't say for what, even though she asked him directly.

He told her to wear loose-fitting clothing, no underwear.

What on Earth could this be? She hadn't agreed to any third film, he hadn't even asked her. They hadn't "premiered" the second one yet—there was complex editing, this time, which he wasn't used to. What did he have in mind?

He just said to be there by six o'clock. He wanted her to drive herself there, which as she'd learned last time, was neither necessarily a good nor bad sign. She wasn't walking down any dark hallways alone, she knew that much. He did not send her a makeup kit via courier; he only told her to wear her highest, shiniest stiletto heels, or at least bring them along, and to look presentable, "beautiful, as always."

And to bring *those.*

She returned to her table, downed her margarita in one gulp, and ordered another.

So here she was.

Why did she so easily do what these men said? These *people*, actually, as she seemed to be obeying Amanda pretty thoroughly as well, lately.

She'd been inviting Jon and Amanda over more and more for dinner, the sexual tension thicker than the steaks she'd fed them the last time. Not only that, she would virtually offer herself as well, but her two guests wouldn't take the bait and allow her to strip and kneel for them.

Instead they teased her, hinted—they would be demanding, especially Amanda, now that it was known that Amanda was the one In Charge. She would reject wines, make Janet run to get another one, which Janet would do like an imbecile. A very horny imbecile.

And it had been evolving. Amanda would ask Janet for favors—to borrow a cup of sugar, and oh, she wouldn't mind delivering it, would she? Amanda was a *chef*, for crying out loud. She had sugar. Asking her over for dinner but teasing her more, demanding a shoulder massage, even a foot massage, once, then sending her home as Jon said nothing.

Janet's head was swimming in confusion, these days—a delicious, desperate, bittersweet confusion.

Meanwhile, she hadn't heard from Dmitri in weeks, until yesterday. Not since the last shoot—and, really, she wasn't too upset about that. That trick in the elevator…that was just kind of creepy, manipulative. So why was she driving back to the warehouse?

Jon had said, that time in the bookstore, that no one could make her do anything she didn't want to do. But it wasn't always so simple. Had she consented to Dmitri's creepy trick?

And she still dreaded ever running into Carolyn again, even if it had been weeks since the party. That bitch was *unstable.*

❖

There were a few cars in front of the warehouse, but she didn't recognize them. It occurred to her that she didn't even know what Dmitri drove. At least there was no delivery van being loaded with film equipment; there was no van at all. She thought she heard the sound of diesel engines idling, but she didn't see any trucks.

She pulled the heavy door open and was in the foyer. One of the side doors opened, the cheap old doors to the offices that she had pretty much ignored until then.

"Janet," Dmitri said. He gestured into the room behind him.

"Please come in."

The room was shabby but not dismal; an old sofa from the hallway, a desk, another door that led into what had once been the hallway surrounding the white cube. Worn paneling.

Standing in the room, aside from Dmitri, were five naked people, two men and three women. The men were beautiful, tall and toned and apparently waxed, their cocks flaccid but massive enough to garner attention (and respect). The women were slender and shapely and also beautiful. Two of them looked familiar but she couldn't quite remember from where.

Every mouth but Dmitri's and hers was filled with a black ball gag, and every naked body wore a black leather collar decorated with metal studs. The men were barefoot; the women in very high heels.

Janet proceeded to pull her sweatshirt off; why fight it. She'd agreed to come here.

"Good girl," Dmitri said, and held up her collar and gag.

She got into the line that the others had formed to the

door, the other door. As Dmitri took his place to open it, he picked up a stack of trays from the desk. Serving trays.

"Everyone ready?" he said.

All but Janet nodded.

Dmitri opened the door, and the first woman, the one she didn't know at all, took a tray from Dmitri and walked out. Janet tried to look around the people in front of her, but the men—and the two more familiar girls—were too tall. Then she remembered where she had seen the two naked women ahead of her in line: they were the serving girls at her film's opening reception; they had been covered head to toe in skin-tight PVC.

She could hear voices, out there. What *was* this? The men took trays and exited the room, and then the two slender women as well, and Janet could finally see out the door: the warehouse was now one vast, empty, space, as she'd imagined it the very first time she and Jon had pulled up in his car. The white cube was gone.

The warehouse was full of people, sitting around small round tables with dim little lamps on them.

Lots of people.

Janet wanted to say something to Dmitri; pull her gag out of her mouth, ask him what this was all about. But he pressed his fingers to his lips as she approached, shushing her.

"Do this, Janet. These people are all to be trusted. No one has a camera or even a phone, same security as all my parties."

He handed her the last tray, and—foolishly, she knew—she handed him the tiny box with the dreaded sapphire nipple clamps that he'd requested her to bring. He smiled as he opened the box.

"My God you're wonderful. The bar is right against this wall, at the back of the room. You will serve the row of tables farthest to the right." He took out a clamp.

Janet winced as he squeezed it open, pulled her nipple taut, and released it.

"You'll do well. You certainly know how to serve drinks." He winked.

Second clamp, and Janet's breasts were on fire.

"Don't be nervous. Or do be, if it's more fun. But don't let me down. You won't, will you, Janet?"

She shook her head no—she would do her best to please. Stupid submissive girl.

"Besides," he said. "From what I understand, this will likely be my last chance to use you without someone's permission, yes?"

Janet knew what he meant, but wasn't able to speak with her mouth filled by the gag. She wasn't sure what she would say if she could.

❖

Janet watched the other servers. They stood at attention to receive drink orders, then kneeled on the worn hardwood floor to serve the drinks. She had never waited tables, even in college when most of her friends did, had never had to memorize orders.

There were at least a hundred people in the room, probably closer to two hundred. The seated guests were all dressed elegantly if not formally, as at her premier, but quite a few of them had other people standing behind them—slaves, or submissives at least, many naked but a few gussied up in bondage gear. Most were leashed to their Masters.

Where were everyone's cars? Had he rented a bus to get them all here? Or two? Ah—the diesel engines. Were the cars the servers'?

Janet was to wait on eight tables, most with two people seated, some with three or four. She walked up to the table closest to the bar, in the back. Seated there was a very striking

African-American couple, the man dressed in an impeccable black suit with a red shirt and tie, the woman in an elegant red dress that showed *just* enough of her cleavage. They were each holding a red leather leash that ran up to the same red collar, worn by a standing white male who was slightly out of shape but—

"Wong?!" Janet said, or tried to say, gagged. Her eyes were so wide that her blue pupils were surrounded by a border of white.

Ron?!

Her boss.

"Ganget," Ron said, or tried to. He was gagged as well, with, of course, a bright red ball gag under his dark blond moustache. He obviously wanted to cover himself, but his hands were crossed and cuffed in red leather in front of him, bound at mid-stomach by a gold chain to his matching red collar.

Janet and Ron stared at each other, their faces phasing through increasingly dark shades of crimson, a wonderful accent to the black couple's motif. They tried not to look at each other's bodies, but couldn't not look. Ron went there first, glancing up and down Janet; his eyes lingered on the sapphire orbs dangling from her nipples.

As for Janet, she discovered that Ron was…well, exceptionally endowed. His cock, hanging straight down over sizable but tight balls, was longer than most men erect, a good eight inches, at least—*limp.* Funny how she'd never noticed, always dressed in loose khakis.

Fishing lure, indeed. His entire body below his moustache was shaved, all pubic hair absent, and his body was covered in precisely spaced horizontal markings that matched his red collar and cuffs.

The couple watched the little comedy/drama play out, understanding the gist of the spectacle if not the details, until the woman cleared her throat. Janet focused on her intense brown eyes and bowed a slight apology.

"Gin fizz," the woman said.

Janet looked to the man, broad-shouldered and barrel-chested beneath his suit.

"Jameson. Neat."

Janet walked toward the bar.

Then it occurred to her—how was she supposed to give the bartender her order? She was *gagged*. She stood at the bar, and gave the bartender one of her begging looks. He calmly spun a tablet to face her, and she saw that she was to type in the drink, and check the quantity. She breathed a sigh of relief, probably misspelled 'Jameson', and waited for the drinks.

He placed the two glasses on her tray, and a small plate of hors d'oeuvres, bacon-wrapped somethings that would have smelled delicious if her stomach wasn't in knots.

"Take them this," the bartender said. "Don't worry about busing the tables. Just keep the drinks refilled." Janet nodded, returned to the table, and kneeled.

Poor Ron got no drink.

God, Monday was going to be weird.

Janet noticed that most of the crowd was white. Most of her world was white, really, and apparently so was Dmitri's. She did see some darker complexions among the crowd, both the seated guests and the standing slaves—one couple near her looked perhaps Indian or Pakistani, another Latino. She saw one stunning black woman standing naked behind another black couple, and she saw—

Oh. It was the very dark-skinned woman who'd been in the film she'd made, the one who'd wrapped her in rope and fucked her hard in mid-air.

The Spider Woman. She was seated up front with a female companion, and Dmitri was leaning over their table, talking amiably, laughing, trying to hear them over the din of the room—and Janet was now certain what this was all about. But why was this woman front and center? That would be Janet's spot, right?

She tried to focus on her assigned task. Next table: simple. An older couple, no one standing naked behind them. Straight bourbon for both of them. Order typed, food and drinks delivered on her knees.

Next, nearly the same, another couple, younger and more attractive, a simple whiskey and some fancy vodka cocktail that Janet had to lean forward to get the woman to repeat. She typed in what she thought she'd said, and the woman looked satisfied when she brought it to her.

A table of three men, identical suits, touching each other's hands and slightly annoyed that she'd interrupted them with her presence. Deep-voiced, they argued over their orders, each trying to tell the next what he should or shouldn't be drinking. Janet waited. She had been taking in so much information so fast that she hadn't stopped to look ahead at the rest of the guests in her section. While the men argued, she took the moment to scan her other tables. It was better than dwelling on the pain in her nipples.

And there they were, three tables ahead. Jon and Amanda, in the glow of the little tabletop lamp.

It was actually reassuring to see them there, not embarrassing. What had they not seen, or felt, or done to her already? Surely they had spotted her, since they were seated more or less facing her. They were engrossed in conversation with another woman facing them, away from Janet, who had a naked male standing to one side behind her. He looked to be in better shape than Ron, at least from behind—pale skin, dark red hair, muscular shoulders and a nice, tight ass.

The woman was wearing a black cocktail dress, and had long, straight brown hair that hung around her shoulders. She had a cast on her arm in a sling, and Jesus God no no no no no. Jesus fucking God no no no. No.

No.

Janet wondered what would happen if she simply left. Fuck Dmitri. He invited *her*? Why would he invite her? Why would *anyone* invite her, to anything?

She was laughing, leaning forward to Jon and Amanda, talking and making gestures with her free hand. Telling a story. Amanda was watching her skeptically, almost warily—weighing evidence, it looked like. Jon was more open, of course. Why he liked and trusted her, Janet would never understand.

She'd *owned* him? He'd been her slave? Janet still couldn't believe it. She'd thought that they were all rid of her, after that party. But there they were, the three of—

"Hey. Hey!" Janet heard, dimly. She felt a solid, forceful pinch on her ass and she looked down at the three men staring up at her.

"I said, three mojitos!" one of them shouted. Janet looked ahead, to see if Jon or Amanda had seen her. She yelped as the man pulled on her sapphire.

"I. Said. Three. Mojitos."

She walked back to the bar like a woman condemned.

Mojts, 3, she typed.

"Three mojitos?" the bartender asked, but Janet barely heard him.

The next two tables were serviced at a remarkably slow pace.

She walked to their table and stood still and straight. All leaned back, their conversation interrupted.

"Well, it's you," Carolyn said.

Janet was breathing heavily through her nose, trying not to drool. She hoped more than anything that the other servers wouldn't come and grab her, tie her up on the stage, let Carolyn whip her in front of everyone just for kicks.

Wait—there was a stage? Yes, there was.

Carolyn took a long look at Janet without saying anything.

Janet looked her in the eye until she couldn't stand it any longer, then looked to Jon and Amanda for support. They seemed expectant, more than anything.

"You know," Carolyn said, "no one has *ever* stood up to me the way that you did, at that miserable little party. Not at work, not at play. Never. No one's ever…put me in my place. Not even Jack with his pathetic little put-downs."

Janet wondered if Jack was here; she could use a little backup.

Carolyn reached up to Janet's breast, before she could back away, and Janet braced for a painful pinch or a hard pull on the clamp. But Carolyn merely lifted the bauble with her fingers and examined it as it sparkled in the table lamp's low light.

"And I have to say," she said, "I respect that."

She let the sapphire go; it swung back and forth.

"Even if you did catch me at a moment of weakness." She leaned back and looked at Janet, but without the predatory, cruel expression she'd grown to expect.

Was that some sort of apology?

"Get me a champagne," Carolyn said. "And one for my slave. We're celebrating, tonight."

Janet looked up at the naked young man behind Carolyn, who looked back like he recognized her and wanted to say something—which of course he couldn't do. He was gagged as well, a large black ball gag stuffed in his mouth. She thought she recognized him, too—he looked like the boy she had talked to outside of Jon and Amanda's house, Jon's number "4." Yet he looked slightly different. They stared at each other a moment.

"Champagne all around," Jon said. "They're celebrating."

Janet took a step backwards; she still didn't trust Carolyn not to pull out a quirt and whip her all the way to the bar.

Janet's last two tables had already been served before she got to them. Would she be punished for that? Publicly?

Dmitri was taking the stage. He had a microphone.

"Ladies and gentlemen," he began. The crowd quieted.

"Servers, up on stage, with me," he said, and looked across the crowd, beckoning them whenever he made eye contact.

Janet swallowed hard. Her mouth was dry; for once she didn't have to worry about drooling with a ball gag in her mouth. She walked up the stairs on one side of the stage, behind one of the naked men. Dmitri gestured a line on the floor and told them to kneel side-by-side facing the audience.

"Ladies and gentlemen, every single one of you has seen at least one of my films, some of you more." He paused, looking out over the crowd.

"This has been the busiest and most creative period in my film-making life. Three films, in one season. Some of you were at my last premiere, for *White Cube*, yes?"

Janet blushed; there was a murmuring in the crowd among those who had either seen it (and would now recognize her), or those who hadn't been invited.

"That was the last of my old style of films. You might remember my remarks, I'd shot that film using four cameras? I'd intended to take the major step of editing the shots together. But I was still afraid. There is something so pure, so pristine, about one single camera, one shot uninterrupted. The possibilities within those limits."

Would Janet *never* stop being reminded of that video, that DVD? She had broken it into bits and thrown them away, after Amanda gave it to her.

Dmitri cleared his throat.

"But every artist must grow. This fall, I shot two new films."

Two? Janet thought, again feeling that sense of jealousy, of denial, of a man spending time with muses other than herself—even if she was a bit fed up with him.

"And they are both major artistic leaps forward for me," he continued. "Still choosing films and sets around a particular woman, of course."

Janet straightened her shoulders.

"I wanted to present these new works to you as a set, a double feature. As always, these people are not actors. What fun would be in that?" His English. "But there is a story, in these films, across them—one is a sequel of the other. More or less. Allow me a little artistic license."

There was mild laughter, and Dmitri gestured for the servers to return to work.

"Change sections. I want everyone to see each of you close up," he said to them, microphone lowered.

"Ladies and gentlemen," he said. "Eat. Drink. Please enjoy. I present *Black Widow, White Prey*, and *Marooned/Cocooned*."

From the sound of the titles, the ebony-skinned woman was likely in both films, but he didn't introduce her. But then he hadn't introduced Janet until after her film, either.

And the Spider Woman was seated where Janet should have been.

That last film had not been designed around Janet, but around the Spider Woman. It would be she, not Janet, who'd be applauded, a crowd gathered around her, offered cards and invitations and asked for advice on how to be amazing.

Janet probably wasn't even the only woman to climb that web. She was just an extra.

She was the Hannah.

Janet remembered Dmitri telling her that several women had made two or even three films with him. She'd supposed it was they who'd quit after not being able to take any more, give any more. But now she realized that maybe it was Dmitri who'd left *them*, moved on in his interests, his fascinations.

She'd been dismissed. He'd told her how wonderful she was, when he'd clamped these miserable little devices onto her nipples, but he was actually done with her. Was it because she'd punched him, stood up to him? He didn't like it when his women showed anything but total submission? Even if her punch was more from being startled than angry. (Or was it?) All that talk of asking someone's permission to put her in another film…he had no intention. *And how dare he think he would have to ask anyone—besides me—for permission.*

Well, at least she still had the sapphires—how's that for ironic? She hated the damnable, expensive things.

The lights in the warehouse dimmed as Janet and the others descended the stairs. It got very dark. The only lights were the dim glow of the tabletop lamps, the stars in the sky through the huge windows above them in the space, and the bright lamp in the big old mechanical projector behind the wall near the bar, *clickety clickety clickety*, much bigger than the one he'd used in the hotel room and at her premier. It sent a cone of light onto the big screen, which began as a black rectangle before the words appeared:

BLACK WIDOW, WHITE PREY.
A FILM BY DMITRI CORSO.

The image faded to white, and then a black-haired woman in a lovely cocktail dress driving an old Honda pulled up in front of an industrial warehouse, the one the audience was now seated within.

Chapter Twenty-Four

Janet heard the click in the darkness. Another, and another. She heard footfalls on carpet, felt a slight tug on her ankle. Smelled Jon's scent. Footsteps away, and more clicking. He wasn't talking much. He was concentrating.

She had an itch on her right side, where her breast met her ribs, but there was not much she could do about it. She certainly couldn't scratch it, and couldn't ask Jon to, either. Even if she could speak, he wouldn't want to leave a visible mark on her skin. Especially on such an interesting spot.

She tried to shift a bit to ease the itch, to lessen the stretch of skin for a moment. But she couldn't move at all—she was pulled taut, in all directions, by all four limbs. She was held *firm*. Her muscles were flexed just holding on.

She must have moved more than she thought: "Hold still, doll," Jon said. "Almost there."

She tried to relax, ignore the itch. She would have to stay still, submit to the process. There must be some meditative aspect to restrictive bondage that she would have to learn. She inhaled, tried to exhale through the hood and the gag.

"Oh, that was good," Jon said. "Breathe in again."

Janet inhaled.

"Stay like that as long you can. Your chest looks awesome, like that."

Click; click-click. Janet held her breath as long as she could, finally moaned for permission to let go.

"Okay. Exhale."

She'd offered to let him take her picture unhooded, even if her face was possibly identifiable behind the white blindfold and gag as in many of the other photos.

But no, he said beautiful or not, her head needed to match the background, disappear from the X. She was merely a body, an object, one letter among twenty-six.

And soon to be another. She would be his Y as well, the only woman in his collection twice. She smiled around her gag.

Jon pulled the hood off of her head and she squinted in the studio lights until he turned them off.

"Perfect," he said. "You're perfect."

She smiled as he unbuckled her gag and pulled it from her mouth.

"That's complete nonsense, but thank you."

"I wish we had time to shoot the Y," he said as he loosened the cables. She felt immense relief at the reduction in tension. "I know you have to help Amanda, today, but I've got a dead-line, damn it."

She lowered her arms, brought her feet together as the cables slackened. He kneeled in front of her, both knees, and unfastened her ankle cuffs. It was amusing to see him annoyed at himself for working so slowly for so long; now he was in a last-minute panic of his own devising. She also liked watching him kneel.

"Tomorrow, maybe?" she said.

He didn't answer for a long while. "Maybe."

She thought of him kneeling down for Amanda, for different reasons, something she still couldn't believe even though he'd finally explained over drinks one afternoon: Carolyn had won him in a bet.

"You were the prize?" Janet had asked. "Who did she bet?"

"Me."

Confusion on her face.

"It was more like a race. A contest."

"To claim submissives? Hunting?"

"And gathering. She was better. I mean, have you not seen her? I had to be her slave for six months. If she'd have lost, she had to be mine."

"I can't even imagine that."

"It was a fool's bet, on my part."

"How many did she get? How many did you get?"

"You don't want to know."

But Amanda, who already knew them both back then, had found out and bought out the remainder of his servitude four months in, with two months to go. Exactly what compensation or exchange was offered and accepted Jon wouldn't tell Janet, because he still did not know.

"How long ago was this?" Janet had asked.

"Four years."

Jon stood to take off her wrist cuffs.

"I mean—" Jon stopped. "Ah." He pointed up to the ceiling and looked at Janet. "You might want to learn to recognize that sound, if you're going to do what I think you're going to do."

She listened. A hum, a slightly rough mechanical buzz. She looked up at the ceiling.

"The garage door opening?" she asked.

"You should go up and see if she needs any help. Although I doubt if she has anything left to bring in."

She looked at Jon.

"You seem awfully confident of what I'm going to do."

"We all are, doll. It's been obvious for weeks, now."

She saw her pile of clothes, neatly folded, which seemed like the way to leave them, around here—neat, precise.

"Shouldn't I get dressed first?"

"I wouldn't make her wait, if I were you. Besides, you'll make a better impression."

❖

"I'm not going to ask you, you have to ask me," Amanda said. "You've been hinting and dancing around it since you found out about Jon."

Janet placed the box of display items on the counter. She was still naked. The garage was cold; goosebumps and nipples hard as pebbles. She was glad there wasn't anything else to unload. Just the big box of clear plastic platforms on tiny legs; round, all different heights so the pies looked like they were floating. She rubbed the sole of one foot across the top of the other, trying to warm it up from the cold concrete.

Amanda took a seat on the bench of her breakfast nook and leaned back. She extended one sneakered foot and said, "Foot rub."

Janet rubbed her hands together, kneeled and untied both shoes; removed one and then the other. Socks.

She wanted to make small talk. She wanted to ask The Question, the thing they'd all been hinting at, dancing around.

"So you sold every pie?"

"Yes. Word got out that I was making them."

"That says something. You're very highly regarded, you know."

"Thank you, sweetie. But it's nearly Thanksgiving. It's pie season."

Janet took Amanda's foot into her hands and started massaging it, gently at first and easy on the arch, where she knew Amanda was a little ticklish. Amanda looked exhausted as she ran her hand through her sandy blonde hair. For the first time, Janet noticed she had a few freckles along her cheekbones.

"I would have been glad to help," Janet said. "Since it's all my fault."

"I have staff." Amanda smiled with tired eyes. "They're very obedient, too."

Janet smiled but didn't blush. She was getting over her constant blushing. Almost.

"You were needed here," Amanda said. "Now that Jon has a gallery show scheduled, he's suddenly in a big hurry to finish." A glazed look came over her face as Janet massaged her ankle with one hand and squeezed her heel with the other. "Are you his X *and* Y?"

"Yes, Ma'am."

"That's unprecedented. *You're* highly regarded."

"Thank you, Ma'am."

She switched feet as Amanda lifted her other one.

"You'll help me here tonight," Amanda said. "As you promised. And I still need to take your debt out of your hide, you know."

Now Janet blushed. She was still dancing around the question.

"So how…how would it *work*?" she finally asked.

Amanda eyes rolled back into her head and she moaned. Janet was pressing her thumbs against the ball of Amanda's foot; this was the only time Janet ever saw her almost lose her cool and melt under someone else's control. For that alone, Janet liked rubbing Amanda's feet, she had to admit. She moved her hands to a less-favored spot.

"What do you mean?" Amanda said.

"I mean, would I have to move in? Would we pool our incomes? Would I have to sell my house, give you my money?"

"We're not a cult, Janet. You'd be my slave—bound by your word, your promise. And mine. You do keep your word, don't you?"

"Yes."

"Haven't you read all those books? I thought you were quite the scholar of erotic literature."

"There's a very wide range in the books, Ma'am. Some women—and men—are kidnapped, against their will, quote-unquote. Some sign contracts. Some—"

"You wouldn't move in. Full time, anyway. You'd spend weekends here, after work Friday to Sunday night or Monday morning. Initially, you'd spend one night here during the week, until your training was finished—a refresher night, so you wouldn't backslide. Sometimes more, if needed. But you'd always have a home to go back to. You have a wonderful house. Do you have pets? I don't recall any."

"No, Ma'am. And thank you, Ma'am." She did love her house. She thought a moment. "So how long would this be for? Like, forever?"

"Well, it's almost December…" Amanda grunted as Janet hit another sweet spot along the side of her sole.

"Thirteen months. Until the end of next year. We can all remember that, can't we?"

"And then what?"

"Then we'll see. We'll all three decide what to do next."

"Okay. I guess I don't understand how it would work with me, versus how it works with Jon?"

"Jon and I have a unique—oh, here he is."

Jon entered the kitchen carrying an empty coffee cup.

"We were just discussing you, my dear," Amanda said. She withdrew her foot from Janet's hands, but Janet stayed kneeling in front of her.

"Uh-oh. It's not true, whatever she says," Jon said, and walked to the espresso machine.

"Janet was trying to understand our relationship."

"Oh, God."

"Yes."

"Did you tell her I don't understand it, either?"

Amanda grinned. "Make me a cup, too, would you?"

"Of course."

Janet shook her head.

"See? I don't understand. No 'Yes, Mistress;' nothing. It's like you're married. Are you married?" She'd always been too timid to ask Amanda this directly, for some reason, but she had to know.

Amanda sighed, as though she were about to explain to a child why the sky is blue.

"Jon lives within the limits I set for him. We did not negotiate. Formally, at least. And our relationship has evolved. He has a top's instinct, a hunter's instinct. Which I indulge, as you should know by now. It's really none of your business, sweetheart."

"I know, Ma'am."

Amanda was admiring Jon, Janet could see, as he packed the coffee into the metal filter basket.

"He has nearly free reign, until he doesn't." She waited for him to rotate the filter's handle into the machine, and press the button to start the water running through it.

"Jon," she said.

"Yes, dear?"

"Strip."

Without hesitation, Jon began taking his clothes off. He took off his shirt first, and Janet rotated on her knees to watch, without completely turning her back to Amanda.

He folded each article and placed them in a neat pile on the counter. Finally he stood naked, waiting. Janet took in his body, familiar, solid but not over-muscled.

"Now get that beautiful cock hard for me."

"With my hands? Or just thinking?"

"Hands will be fine."

Jon started jacking off his limp dick. He wrapped his hand around its shaft while reaching down and stroking his balls with the other. Janet watched as it thickened in his hand, then grew, and she exhaled heavily as he brought it to full erection.

"Come here," Amanda said.

Jon walked to them, still stroking it.

"Masturbate into Janet's mouth."

Janet was shocked—this was all so sudden. Well, not really, but still…

Jon turned to her and started jacking faster, now that he had a goal. His cock was right in her face.

"What are you going to do, Janet?" Amanda asked.

Janet looked at Amanda wide-eyed, then turned to face Jon's stiff member. She tilted her head back, opened her mouth, and extended her tongue like they did in the porn videos. This made Jon stroke it even faster, and Janet stuck out her tongue as far as it would reach.

Amanda watched, as if this were nothing unusual.

Janet looked up at Jon's face as he watched hers. Her naked and humbled pose was clearly exciting him. She looked back at his cock, thick and dark, and waited, knowing there would be no *real* joy to this, or at least no getting off herself—just the satisfaction of pleasing Amanda as the warm fluid would shoot into her waiting mouth, probably onto her cheeks and tits as well. Not that that was entirely unenjoyable. She clenched her thighs with her fingertips and waited, a human receptacle. She was getting surprisingly wet.

And Jon? He'd get off, but he might as well be by himself, in the bathroom. There'd be no warm mouth, no cunt, just his own hand. Although the visual was probably pretty good, the situation certainly kinky. She tried to open her mouth wider.

The incongruous smell of coffee filled the room as Jon groaned and started jacking even faster, a furious rate. She saw his balls contract, his posture shift. He was getting close,

close...close—

"Stop," Amanda said.

And Jon, reluctantly but immediately, released his swollen cock. It was red, and throbbed with each heartbeat inches in front of Janet's face. A crystalline drop of fluid had accrued at its tip.

"You may get dressed."

Jon was panting from effort and expectation. But he did not even seem to consider arguing. "Yes, my love."

He walked to the coffee machine. "Your espresso is ready."

"Get dressed first, won't you?"

"Certainly." Clothes on, coffee served. He poured himself one. "Would you like an espresso, Janet?"

Janet realized she still had her mouth hanging open.

"No, thank you," she said.

He didn't have to ask Amanda's permission to offer her a drink, to do anything—to leave, even. He exited the kitchen without a word, probably to go downstairs to select and edit his new photos on the computer in his studio. Was he allowed to masturbate, down there?

"That, my child, is how it works, here." Amanda took a sip from her tiny cup. "You'd both serve me; you would serve Jon, as well." Janet thought of that big dick in her face, of spending every weekend with it. But nothing would ever be her choice. "But only within the limits I allow him." Nor would it be Jon's, apparently.

"I'm not going to ask you, you have to ask me," Amanda repeated.

"Do...do you *want* me?" Janet asked.

"Yes." Amanda did not dance around questions.

"Then, would," Janet took a deep breath. *Do it or don't,* she'd once told herself. "Will you accept me, as your slave?"

Amanda leaned back with a look of satisfaction on her face. Janet wondered how many clients had asked her that, back in her dominatrix days. But it was only business, with them, wasn't it?

"I want you to think about it seriously, Janet. It will be intense. I don't 'play'. It's Life."

Janet remembered Jon, in the bookstore so many months ago, telling her that some people, her and him included, just wanted to play, spend a few hours pretending, then go home. *Other* people Lived it.

He was clearly lying.

"I know, Ma'am."

"Do you really? I'm not sure you realize what this entails, Janet. Not just your weekends here. If I call you at work, and tell you to take your collar from your purse and put it on, you *will* do it, and text me photos. If I call you at home at three in the morning and tell you to come over and clean my toilet, you *will* do it. If I leave you in Jon's care for a weekend and he takes you out for a nice lunch and tells you to get under the table and suck his cock, you *will* crawl under there and suck him until he's come in your mouth. Or on your face, whatever he wants."

Janet's heart was in her throat, and her face was burning red. So much for not blushing anymore. She felt a trickle of wetness down the inside of her thigh.

"You will be whipped for every infraction, no matter how minor. You'll be whipped for fun. Bound for hours, and ignored; that's what dissuades most people. Being ignored."

Janet shook her head no, nodded yes.

"Are you going to appear in another film for Dmitri?"

"He hasn't asked. I haven't heard from him since the premier."

"If he asks, you will do so. No questions asked. Jon loves seeing you in Dmitri's films."

"Yes, Ma'am. I will."

"I understand you've never actually had anal sex? Except for a few toys and digits?"

It was true, despite reading it so many times in her books. Janet had always feared it, rejected suggestions from boyfriends in college. And of course her ex had never even asked.

"No, Ma'am," she said.

"You will."

"Yes Ma'am."

"If I tell you to strip in a liquor store, you will."

Janet bowed her head, nodded her assent.

She heard Amanda take a deep breath, tap her fingernails on the breakfast nook's wooden table.

"I had thought that he'd called you," Amanda said.

Janet's eyes wandered as she tried to follow Amanda's meaning.

"The DVD? He did," Janet said. "Ma'am."

"No. After your party. I assumed—stupidly, it seems—that he called you the next day, as any decent Top—any decent *person*—would do. I didn't find out until after he ran into you again, took you over to Jack's."

"Oh." Janet didn't know what to say—*Oh, that's okay?* Those seventeen days had been awful. Lonely, embarrassing, humiliating. Only toward the end were they oddly lustful.

"He was...punished, for that. Severely. Twenty lashes with the single tail, and then...I ordered him to give me twenty, for my oversight. He'd never whipped me, before. It nearly crushed him."

Janet's mouth dropped open; she looked up to meet Amanda's eyes.

"He spent the next two weeks in the green room, and I did not wear his ring for another two." She reached into the collar of her chef's uniform and slid her fingers along the thin gold chain, pulling the ring out. She let it dangle in front of her chest. "It's been forgotten, between us. I don't know how you'll feel about it. But you should know."

Janet watched the gold band twist and wobble at the end of

its chain until it settled.

She wasn't sure how she felt at this—both worse and better. How would things have gone had he called her? Her mind ran through her encounters with Jon; he'd never shown any signs of distress—although he *had* started calling her after their little get-togethers.

"Are you *sure* you want this, Janet? Because all that said, that DVD thrilled me to my core. We can be a bunch of cruel motherfuckers, as you once so astutely said."

Janet lowered her face again.

"Are you sure you don't want to think about it a while?"

Janet took a deep breath and looked up at Amanda. "No, Ma'am. I've been thinking about this my entire life."

It was *still* everything she had ever wanted, since before puberty, before she even knew what sex was—pictures of captured and bound maidens in fairy tale books; Andromeda chained naked to the rocks in an illustrated book of Greek mythology Janet's father had, awaiting her own sacrifice.

True, she had always thought it would be a *man* that she might find to submit to, but at least there'd be a man around, and a pretty good one, despite his flaws.

And Amanda: she did fit the life-long fantasy so well—her quiet authority, her propriety, her strictness.

God, Janet loved strictness.

Twenty lashes?

"Take me," she said. "I know what I want, I don't need to think about it. Please. Accept me as your slave. Please."

Amanda smiled her cool smile and leaned back. She was still sitting with her legs crossed, and lifted the foot hovering in front of Janet higher.

"Kiss it," she said.

Janet took the foot in her hand and held it like it was the hand of the Pope, and bent down to kiss the top of it.

"Now the other."

Amanda did not switch legs. Janet lowered her face to the floor, on all fours, and kissed the bare foot.

She kissed it three times, and felt the other foot on the back of her head. Pressing down, harder, and harder still. Janet did not fight it, resist it. She laid her head on the floor, sideways, and submitted fully, let Amanda press her down into the tiles. She whimpered when it started to hurt, but she stayed in place.

"I claim you, Janet. You are mine. You are my property, to do with as I wish, and you will obey every command, accept whatever is done to you. You will submit to my will, you will devote your body and mind to my happiness, my pleasure. In return, I promise only that no harm will come to you."

She released Janet's head, and Janet kissed her foot again, on her elbows and knees, naked ass up in the air.

She hugged Amanda's ankle, caressed her calf.

"Thank you," she whispered. "Mistress."

Good God, what have I done?

"Now. Get up. We have work to do. We're having a dinner party tonight, you know. We have a playground in the park to fund, remember?"

❖

Janet, still naked, helped Jon move furniture as Amanda directed, then set up two rows of tables and chairs in their living room. She helped Amanda set the tables, the spacing of each piece of silverware measured by Amanda with a ruler. She brought up bottles of wine, and discovered a new room down there, the wine cellar. She had still never seen their dungeon/playroom. Did they even have one?

As five o'clock neared, Janet was worried that she would have to serve their guests—the Neighborhood Association!—naked as well. But after cleaning the entire house, Janet dusting while Jon vacuumed, Amanda summoned her to the bedroom.

"Let's get dressed," she said.

Janet had never set foot in their large bedroom, and it was… surprisingly bland. Earth tones, not even a king-size bed, just a queen-size four-poster, enough to tie someone down spread-eagled, she thought. Too low for a cage underneath—did Jon sleep here with her? Every night? Where would she sleep?

Amanda opened the door to the walk-in. She already had her outfit chosen, but held up dress after dress against Janet's torso.

"You're taller than me, slightly smaller in the chest but wider shoulders," she said. "Similar waists, I think?"

She held up a little black number with spaghetti straps, and nodded approvingly.

"Here. This will do. Slip it on."

Janet modeled for her after dropping it over her shoulders.

"It's a little short on you, but that's all right. You look great."

It was short, quite high up Janet's thighs. But it fit, looked sexy. A little too sexy for a Neighborhood Association meeting, elegant dinner or not.

Amanda rummaged for shoes. She brought out a box with shiny black stilettos and set them on the floor.

"Too small?"

Janet forced a foot into one.

"Yea. At least a size."

"Put them on. You're going to have to get used to some discomfort."

"Okay." She pried on the other shoe, took a step.

"No underwear."

Janet stopped mid-stride.

"Problem?" Amanda was unbuttoning her uniform with one hand while applying lipstick in the mirror of her vanity with the other.

Janet couldn't very well start protesting *now*.

"No, Ma'am. …Mistress!"

Amanda reached up and ran the lipstick over Janet's lips. "I'll be a minute. Open six bottles of wine, start them decanting."

"Yes, Mistress."

"Don't acknowledge every order. Just carry them out."

Janet left the room in silence and painful shoes.

❖

Janet's first job was to greet people at the door, hold it open for them, welcome them as Amanda mingled. Shades of her dinner party, of Kylie's dinner party: "Hi! I'm Janet. You must be…?"

Some people she knew, some she didn't. Amanda's house and hers were at opposite ends of the neighborhood, both almost belonged to other neighborhoods.

"Carlotta! Hello! How are you? Hello, Melvin!" Carlotta's husband.

"I'm so glad you persuaded Amanda to do all this, Janet," Carlotta said. "It wouldn't have been nearly as successful without you. She's refused us before, you know."

"She was glad to help," Janet said. *Persuaded her?* "I'm so glad all her pies sold. They're wonderful, aren't they?"

"They are indeed. We bought two."

Carlotta smiled and handed Janet an envelope, the same one that everyone had given her so far. She wasn't sure what they were, as she'd never received one, but then again she wasn't exactly going to the meetings. She still hadn't even opened the letter Carlotta had sent this summer. She put the envelope on the table by the front door with the rest of them.

"Mr. Burman! I haven't seen you in forever. How are you?"

Amanda had four of her staff come in through the back door, two working in the kitchen heating and plating the food made at her shop while two others served. The aroma in the house was mouth-watering, and Janet was ravenous. It had been quite a day, and the dinner wasn't even going yet. Poor Amanda, she'd already delivered a van full of pies after supervising their baking the night before. She probably *was* going to take it out of Janet's hide.

Janet accepted another envelope from a couple she did not recognize. "Thank you so much," she said.

Dinner was as delectable as it had smelled—Beef Bourguignon, which was something between gourmet and comfort food (as any "neighborhood" gathering should impart); asparagus tips with a buerre blanc sauce; garlic mashed potatoes with a hint of horseradish. Amanda's taste in wines was superlative—guests had a choice of hearty reds, plus a Riesling she kept on hand. And for dessert, of course, a sampling of the kinds of pies many of the guests had earlier purchased and taken home for themselves.

This could only be good for her business. Janet had done her a favor, really. Janet was happy for her and hoped it would ease Amanda's annoyance at being shanghaied into this.

Janet was seated in the dining room, open to the living room through a big double doorway, and she was given responsibilities beyond those of the two servers. Make sure everyone's glass is full. Try to keep the people seated in the dining room from feeling isolated from the bigger crowd in the living room. Facilitate conversations, no politics, no religion. She ate, but frequently got up to run to the kitchen for wine or to round up a waitress or chat up a guest.

She had to be careful not to bend over. She would stoop down next to people to speak with them, thighs pressed together; she tried to keep her braless jiggling to a minimum. She couldn't shake the feeling that she was being checked out, watched, but why wouldn't she be, in this sexy short dress—this *was* the boring old Oakdale N.A. What else did these people have to do?

While crossing the room, Amanda asked her to take the envelopes into the kitchen, and tally up the totals. Contributions? She told her which drawer the calculator was in, and she was to write the total—double-checked and triple checked—on a piece of paper, and, importantly, to file the forms in order of their amounts, highest first.

Such a simple job, but Janet's mind was swimming as she sat in the breakfast nook. She began tearing open envelopes. Each was a pledge form, coupon-sized. Name, address, and email; contribution amount. There was a picture of a swing, slide and climbing bars on each one, comic sans font.

$600, wow. $400. Lots of $100's, $150's.

$1,000! From the Janskis, no less. This was amazing. Amanda was really going to clean up, in fame and karma at least, since all the money was going to the park's playground. There was easily ten thousand dollars pledged, as long as everyone followed through. Plus the bake sale? This was such a generous neighborhood! She happily tapped out the numbers on the calculator, twice, yet again.

The staff was cleaning up, though wine was still being poured. Two tables were removed from the living room to make a space under the chandelier, the outdated chandelier. The chairs were lined up against the wall and people sat awkwardly in them, their legs now exposed.

Amanda stood and clinked her glass with a fork, and the guests fell silent.

"Thank you so much for coming, everyone, it's been my absolute pleasure to host this important event." The room applauded; people from the dining room were filing in and standing against the back wall. The staff packed up and left through the garage.

"Thank *you*," someone—Mrs. Janski?—said, "for this opportunity!"

"Thank you, Carlotta," Amanda said. "And let's remember,

this *is* all for the children."

There was laughter, which Janet didn't quite understand.

"Janet?" Amanda held out her hand for the bundle of forms, and the piece of paper she'd attached to them.

"Stay here."

Janet stood next to her and beamed. Maybe she'd be thanked, it wouldn't hurt her image, either.

"Well, it *is* for the children, isn't it?" Amanda said to the room. "And as far as the rest of the Neighborhood Association goes, that's all they need to know."

The rest…?

"But some of us like a little more adult entertainment, don't we?"

Cheers, hoots from the crowd.

"And, as I promised you all,"—poignant pause—"here is our entertainment. You've all met Janet?"

Amanda stepped back, held an arm out toward Janet.

Wait, what? No.

"Yes, here she is. And I keep my promises."

She smiled at the applause as Janet stood perfectly still.

"Do *you*, Janet?" What was happening?

"Please, Amand—Mis—"

But Amanda cocked her head expectantly and Janet was silenced.

The very same day that she'd begged, pledged herself? Been claimed? This couldn't be a coincidence. Amanda *knew* she'd ask her—today. Janet had been getting up the nerve for weeks; it had been obvious to everyone.

Then it hit her: Amanda had told Jon to schedule their shoot for today, just so she would already be here and naked and primed when Amanda got back from the bake sale. She'd even prompted the discussion: *I'm not going to ask you, you have to ask me.*

"Take off your dress, Janet."

Janet stared at the crowd, faced with the same choice she'd had to make since she first agreed to Jon's idea, after she'd left that book out on her coffee table: do as she's told, or leave.

This time for good.

Do it or don't.

She closed her eyes as she pulled the thin straps off her shoulders and peeled Amanda's dress down her body. There was applause. Janet opened her eyes but looked down, too mortified to face her audience.

"Ten thousand, six hundred, fifty dollars," Amanda said as she read the total. "A promise is a promise; I said the minimum was ten. Let's get to the winning bids, shall we?"

Bids?

"Ah, very nice," Amanda said, shuffling through the cards. "Lots of five hundreds, but the top five are well above that." She looked up.

"Fifth place: the right to bind her wrists in suspension, goes to Bill Hollingsworth. Bill?"

A man Janet didn't know stood up near the back and made his way up, and Jon handed him a pair of leather cuffs, the same two he'd used on her for the photo shoot.

Janet stood, still in disbelief, as Bill fastened them on and then together, her hands in front of her. He was remarkably dexterous at it, and he clearly relished his prize.

A looped steel cable was lowered in front of Janet's face. She looked up—the chandelier? The cable came right out of it.

Jon was flipping a light switch near the door. Jesus—this house wasn't at all what Janet thought it was. No wonder they had no playroom—their whole *house* was a playroom? What other devices were hidden in its walls, its appliances?

Bill Hollingsworth hooked her cuffs to the cable, and Jon flipped the next switch on the wall. Janet's arms were pulled up, above her head. And then some—he stopped only when she was nearly lifted off the floor, struggling on her toes in her tight shoes. Right under the bright, sparkling light.

"Fourth prize—the right to blindfold her…Jack Miller?"

A little old man in the front row, who Janet only knew from saying "Hi" as they crossed paths on their daily walks, raised his hand to speak.

"If it's all the same to you, Amanda, I'd prefer that she see our faces watching her. Can I trade that for a set of ankle cuffs?"

Amanda frowned, and pointed her finger at Mr. Miller.

"Deal," she said.

He came up and Jon handed him the cuffs. He crouched behind her, old-man breath on the backs of her knees, and put one on and then the other, locked them together. She was now tottering even more precariously in her painful heels. He squeezed a buttock as he rose and returned to his chair. This couldn't be happening.

"Third prize: gag!" their hostess said. "Sally McDaniel."

"I'll pass," a voice said, a large, buxom woman. "I want to hear her scream."

Oh Jesus.

"Fine then, okay. That's your option." Amanda flipped to the next form.

"Nipple clamps! Second prize. Our girl *loves* them, don't you Janet. Janet?"

Janet shook her head between her upraised arms. How was she supposed to answer this? How was she supposed to ever face any of these people again?

"Yes, Mistress," nearly in tears.

"Jane Richards, Doctor Jane Richards—come on down!"

Jane? Her dentist? *No!* Jane lived just down the street. Janet had baked cookies and took them to her house when her beloved dog had died, even though it was sixteen years old. That was this last spring. And now—

Janet whimpered as Jane pulled her nipple harder than necessary, and clamped the little steel clip to it. These were smaller and harsher than Dmitri's sapphires, very painful. She was equally rough applying the other.

"Sorry, sweetie," Jane said, and walked away applauding herself and fist-pumping the air to cheers from the crowd. Someone high-fived her.

Who *were* these people? Her neighbors, her friends…well, maybe not close friends, but they were always friendly. Now, they were—

"First prize," Amanda said.

No. Please—Amanda held a coiled, braided whip. A single-tail, a bullwhip, whatever. The kind that she'd passed out from, in the film. The kind that felt like a steel blade. The kind she'd fantasized about her whole life.

"Melvin Janski!"

Carlotta's husband? This could not get any worse. She saw the Janskis sitting near the front, she hadn't noticed them there until now. *Oh, please, no no no.*

Her lifelong fantasy—to be whipped before a room full of people—and it's the Janskis?

Melvin, slightly chubby and wearing a very bright and unfashionable sweater, took the whip and stepped to the side of the room.

"Thank you so much for this, Amanda."

"Oh, it's my pleasure, Melvin. And thank *you*. Enjoy!"

He extended his arm back and unfurled the whip behind him and the people along the wall cleared out, some taking their chairs with them, others just their drinks.

He swung. It slashed across Janet's shoulders and she screamed, out of embarrassment as much as pain. It *hurt*. And she knew she looked foolish. She *knew* these people. This was supposed to be on a private island somewhere, a kingdom, a pirate ship. An exorbitant mansion, at least. Not in a living room six blocks from home, surrounded by her realtor, her dentist, her accountant.

Her Mistress. Janet's head was reeling with this insane day, with too much happening. She needed to *think*, to process.

The whip hit her again, across her ass, and the tip wrapped around her hip and struck into her flank. She flinched and screamed again; the little crystals in the chandelier rattled above her head and she tried to hold still.

Melvin switched grips, struck her across her upper breasts, and she cried out in agony. Mr. Janski was not new to this. He was skilled. Carlotta's eyes were gleaming with pride.

"Will we be bidding on her…other services, later?" Melvin asked.

"Of course," Amanda said. "After the whipping. We'd all want her whipped first, right?" She patted Melvin on the shoulder, reassuring him before stepping back as he wound up.

Amanda gazed at Janet, trussed up and almost hanging.

"I told you I'd take it out of your hide, remember?" she asked, remarkably collected. That was her way, collected. And she kept her promises.

"Yes, Mistress," Janet said.

Janet also remembered: *…on the auction block, nothing you can do about it. Who will buy you? Could be a real creep.* Amanda's words; Kylie's fantasy. But this was real. What would she have to do? And to whom?

But then she remembered Amanda's next sentence: *I was as wet as the ocean.* Janet looked at her new Mistress, and knew that however calm and cool she appeared, Amanda was burning inside, soaking wet. For her. And there was no question of how Jon felt about her.

Janet braced herself, grasped the cable that was supporting her weight. She would see this through, all thirteen months, even if it killed her.

She'd promised.

"Fifty dollars a stroke, and Mr. Janski has raised us one thousand dollars, ladies and gentlemen," Amanda said.

Twenty lashes? The same number Jon had taken—as punishment—for not calling her. And that Amanda had demanded be given to her.

And only three down.

The crowd looked lustful, eager—but not surprised. All these people. This had all been going on a long time, right under Janet's nose.

Melvin wound up for another stroke. Janet shook her head in disbelief but said nothing; bit her lip to keep from screaming.

She didn't want the neighbors to hear.

She laughed at the irony before the tears started for real.

Welcome to the neighborhood.

Chapter Twenty-Five

Janet's hand was not trembling in the least as she pressed the doorbell button. Not in the least.

"I still don't think this is a very good idea," she said.

"Two things, Janet," Amanda said, behind her. "One: That is dangerously close to backtalk, questioning my decision. Your opinion was not asked. You will be punished, tonight, for that.

"Two, you were told early on that you will sometimes have to do things that might not please you, because they please *me*. And while I'm at it, three, I see we still have a problem with you speaking out of turn. We'll have to make sure your mouth is kept *very* occupied, this evening."

More punishments. Janet bowed her head but didn't turn around to face her.

"I am sorry, Mistress."

It had already been quite a day. She had been awakened by Amanda early, naked in her cage (she'd finally learned what was in that relaxing-green room downstairs, where Jon had spent two weeks—a neat row of four low steel-mesh cages, only hers occupied), and allowed to pee. She was led to their bedroom, where Jon was still sleeping.

She was told to wake him up with a birthday blowjob, and then, as per his birthday request, she was whipped by Amanda, old-school dominatrix-style, ten lashes with the single-tail while she stood still for it in their big bedroom, arms held high.

She hadn't even been told his birthday was coming up.

She was then spanked by her Mistress with the crop, a stroke for every one of Jon's thirty-five years, as she stood spread-legged and counted them off while Jon, seated on the edge of the bed, vigorously fondled her wet clitoris. It threw her into an absolute begging, pleading, knee-buckling sexual frenzy, as Jon watched her face and stopped whenever she got close—and then she was abruptly told that she had better hurry and get dressed if she didn't want to be late for work. She heard the sounds of their lovemaking as she headed out the front door.

She spent most of her workday in the basement, volunteering to find lost files rather than sitting at her desk. *Thirty-five strokes.* Plus the ten whip-marks across her torso. Ron now understood, for better or worse.

"I wish I could join you," he said, grimacing as he squirmed in his seat.

One of these days, when the weather warmed up, she was going to ask Amanda for permission to go fishing with him. They had a lot to talk about.

At 11:45 she was informed by phone that she would report to the parking lot during her lunch hour, where, after telling the girls she had other plans, she had to strip naked in the cavernous backseat of Jon's Buick and suck him off again, heater running and windows mercifully fogging up. Amanda filmed the occasion on her phone from the front seat. Janet could taste Amanda on his stiff cock.

Then, at 4:45, she was phoned again and told to drive straight to their house after work, even though it was a Monday.

She couldn't help touching herself during the commute, her hand down her pants whenever traffic halted, though she knew better than to make herself come—Amanda would know. She sucked her juices off her fingers when she hit the side streets, cleaning off the scent.

After stripping and collaring, she was at least allowed to partake in Amanda's staggeringly delicious duck breast with mango compote and a wonderful tiramisu, Jon's favorites, although her place was set on the floor, not the table. Her meal was pre-cut into delicate morsels by Amanda so she could eat kneeling down with her hands behind her back; Amanda wiped off her face with a wet cloth afterward.

She had to sing "Happy Birthday to You" for Jon, solo, standing naked in the dining room. Somehow, that was the most embarrassing part of the day.

Until now. After Jon opened his birthday present from Amanda, some expensive camera lens, Janet was told to get dressed but to stay collared; they were all going out.

To here.

"You'll be fine, doll," Jon said, also standing behind her. He placed his hand on her shoulder.

"Janet, you're shaking."

"I'm shivering, Sir," she said, and hunched her shoulders inside her coat. She was to address Jon as "Sir," tonight.

"Relax," Jon said. "She's different, now. Or at least more like she used to be. Which I guess is still not exactly a walk in the park."

Janet's stomach tightened as she looked up at the door. There was a beautifully crafted wreath hanging there, something Janet would not have expected. She thought there should be Halloween bats and cobwebs and especially witches on brooms here, year round.

"Jon wanted to spend his birthday with an old friend," Amanda said.

Janet checked herself before she got caught shaking her head. Just her luck to be co-slave with a Sagittarius.

"Is this a problem for you, or is it not?"

"No, Mistress."

"When is your birthday, Janet?" Amanda said. "I can't believe I've never asked."

"April twenty-fifth, Mistress."

"Well. If you're a good enough girl, perhaps you'll get to choose where we spend your special day, too. When Jon was Carolyn's slave, she had certain male friends over who would abuse him terribly—penetrate his every orifice, harshly and repeatedly. Didn't you say one of them in particular bothered you Jon? You said he would always have this obnoxious smirk on his face."

"Yes, My Love," was all he said. Jon was to address Amanda as "My Love"—a territorial thing?

"Perhaps we can find out who this man is, tonight, Janet. Perhaps you'd like us all to spend your birthday at this smirking man's house."

"Yes, Mistress," Janet said, absentmindedly, hearing the click of footsteps approaching on hardwood floor. But then Janet raised her head at the revelation, like a burst of sunlight through a stained-glass window in a cathedral, as she realized what had just happened. Amanda had offered her revenge against Jon for this, and Janet hadn't even asked for it.

And it occurred to her, as the footsteps behind the door got louder, that there might be all kinds of ways to get what you want as a slave—to maneuver, to manipulate, even while within the strict borders of obedience. A look, a hint, a subtle gesture. Amanda could no doubt see through anything obvious—she'd seen it all—but there were subtleties and complexities possible that Janet had never even foreseen. Things could get very complicated, back at the House of Amanda Martin.

This was all too much to think about right now, with the

footsteps approaching. She would have to pack it away for later. Carolyn opened the heavy wooden door. She was dressed more casually than Janet had ever seen her, except for that mess of a day at Kylie's: heels, of course, and a skirt, but not a stiff gray pencil skirt, more of a sexy black thing slit up the side, with an eggplant-colored 3/4-sleeved top that was cut wide and down to her modest cleavage rather than a starched blouse buttoned to the collar. A black bra strap was visible. Even her hair was down; shiny, beautiful. Of course. She looked like...a normal person. A normal, sexy person. But Janet was skeptical.

"Come in," Carolyn said, and stepped aside. She hugged her arms. Her cast and sling were gone, replaced by a snug black brace. "It's cold out."

The house was warm. Janet had a feeling it would need to be. Carolyn shut the door.

"You let her lead?" Carolyn asked Amanda.

"She asked to ring the doorbell." This was a complete lie.

They followed Carolyn down the narrow hall: bamboo flooring, relaxing green. Asian textures, dim warm lighting; tranquil. *Ha.*

"And who is this?" Jon asked, stopping in front of a beautiful Asian girl standing naked in a recessed, arched alcove about a foot off the floor. Her eyes were lowered, and she wore a wide, polished steel collar with a thick rope leading down her back to a massive coil of more rope beside her. She kept her hands behind her back and stood perfectly still, one knee slightly bent. There was a recessed light above her in the alcove, and her erect nipples cast sharp shadows down her small, pert breasts.

"This exquisite creature is named Mai," Carolyn said, turning around to look at her. "Isn't she luscious?"

"Yes, she is," Jon said.

"Who is she?" Amanda asked.

"I call her Mai Responsibility," Carolyn said, grinning. "Your...?"

"No; Mai. M-a-i. She is my housekeeper. And my art, as you can see."

"She's beautiful. She looks awfully young."

"She is a nineteen-year-old virgin, isn't that right Mai?"

The girl, eyes already downcast, lowered her gaze even further.

"Yes, Miss Carolyn." Her voice was soft, shy. Vulnerable.

What, no "Mistress"? Janet thought.

Amanda must have read her mind—"Janet, why are you still dressed? And why am I still wearing my coat?"

"I'm so sorry, Mistress," Janet said. Another apology. These things were tallied every night; they kept getting away from her. She undressed in seconds, leaving only her collar. She pulled Amanda's coat off her shoulders, and then Jon's.

Despite being Amanda's slave as well, Jon's status was infinitely higher than hers. Amanda wore his ring after all, even if around her neck, not on her finger. They were Serious. Which was why Amanda's hint at getting back at Jon was so intriguing.

"There's the closet," Carolyn said, and pointed to a narrow door by the wide front one.

"Anyway?" Amanda said.

"Mai is in my charge, my…responsibility," Carolyn said, gesturing at the joke. "Her father works at my old company."

Janet returned empty-handed and stood naked behind Jon and Amanda.

"Young Mai here was brought up in a very strict, very traditional household. She was home-schooled, for chrissakes. Once she was almost old enough to leave home for school, her father was terrified of all the temptations out there in our hedonistic American universities. But he didn't want to deny her an education, now did he?" she asked no one, admiring the supple young woman.

"Her father had always admired the strictness with which I ran my department. The discipline I maintained there."

Janet tried not to recoil.

"And I respected him. So he asked me for advice. He wanted suggestions for ways to keep a young attractive girl out of trouble while still letting her go to school, and going out into the working world. She had always done chores at home, but she needed to start learning how to hold down a job. He said she was very hard-working, very responsible. Hints, yes? So he ended up asking me a *huge* favor—he would be deeply in my debt if I would be interested in taking her in. He would pay me room and board to ensure her safety, her...virtue, while taking classes and working for me. He saw me as a role model!

"The poor bastard—sorry, dear," Carolyn gently touched Mai's shoulder, "The poor gentleman had no idea what goes on around here, what my hobbies are. But Mai had been around the office, while growing up. Everyone likes her. And somebody, who later paid dearly for it, told her a little about my home life. Either as a warning, or to tease her.

"And you know what? The little harlot begged her father to convince me to take her in!"

Carolyn laughed, and Mai's face turned a deep, crimson red.

"She told him she would work *so* hard. She had never so much as held hands with a boy, and she was dying to come here. Kinkiness and all. Ready to bust out, weren't you dear?"

Mai nodded, not looking up.

"Yes, Miss Carolyn."

"Well, this was all just too delicious. So I told her father, of course I would take her in. And I would maintain her virtue. I wouldn't take a dime from him—as long as Mai worked hard, I would be glad to pay her a wage. Let her build up some savings and learn responsibility.

"I promised her father that she will graduate with her virtue fully intact. And I keep my promises. So she's been taking online classes, in addition to her housekeeping duties. And her duties…here." Carolyn waved at the arch of the alcove that Mai was displayed in.

"Absolutely no one touches her. Understand?" She looked at Jon. "I usually don't allow anyone to gaze upon her, I want to keep her humble. But you're special guests."

She stroked a strand of Mai's black hair off her face.

"Wow," Jon said.

"Isn't it too wonderful? Her father's wishes are fully honored: school, job, strict supervision. If he only knew how strict. She wears a steel chastity belt when I'm out and to sleep in. And we do a virginity check, every single night. A little examination. And she's as wet…as…the ocean."

Another deep blush. *Very* deep. Janet nearly blushed for her.

"*She* chose this life. But she will not participate, ever, while still in school. And it drives her insane. That's why I place her here on display. I get this beautiful art, and she has to watch it all happen, every night. Even though she's not 'allowed'"—finger-quotes—"to watch."

Janet had to admit, Carolyn had an ironic if cruel sense of humor. Which did not portend well for this evening.

"How long has it been since you've worn clothes, Mai?"

"Since I moved in, Miss Carolyn."

"My getting fired almost cost us the whole arrangement. Her father was *not* pleased, to say the least. Who could blame him? So Mai stepped in—she told him that under my supervision, she was doubling her classwork, taking twice as many classes, and still getting straight A's. And he relented; he had to admit he was impressed."

Jon stood wide-eyed, enthralled.

"But of course, she's really just a clever little minx—she took advantage of the wording of my promise: that she will remain a virgin until she graduates. So she asked for more time to study, if she can get her housework done. She is now going to finish school in two years, with summers, not four."

Carolyn paused to admire her handiwork, this little sex-starved creature she had created.

"Because while she remains a virgin until the day she graduates, the *night* she graduates, she is *aaaaalll* mine. Good God, is she in for it. You're all welcome to attend; we'll have quite a crowd. I've told her every single thing that will be done to her, over and over and over. And she is doing everything she can to bring that day sooner."

Everyone watched poor Mai try to maintain her composure.

"Isn't that right, sweetheart?"

"Yes, Miss Carolyn."

Carolyn looked prideful, happy; a balance to Mai's shame.

"Once she's gone, I'll be down to one," she said, and Janet expected a harsh look, or anger, but Carolyn was smiling, something new in her eyes. Janet thought she had an entire stable of slaves, out here.

"She'll be needing a place to live after that, if you're interested," Carolyn said. "If she finds a job here in the City. She's never made a single decision on her own, so it'll be entertaining to see what she does."

"That *is* interesting," Jon said, his mind clearly in overdrive.

As Janet watched Mai struggle to retain her serenity as her dignity crumbled, something occurred to her: Mai was Carolyn's art, requiring daily, almost constant supervision, but Mai was also *Mai's* art. Whatever her reasons, Mai chose to stay here and strive to fulfill her duty, to be this beautiful sculpture, a mere object for her Mistress's appreciation. It had to be difficult work, attaining this level of exactitude for hours at a time, that heavy weight around her neck.

Jon and Dmitri had their art as well, and while Janet was model and even muse, their projects were not hers.

So what *was* her art? When Jon had once told her that she

should be an artist, so long ago now, she'd assumed her house was her art—she'd certainly transformed it.

But looking at Mai standing there so still, so ashamed yet thrilled, so *flawless*, it hit Janet: she could be her own art, too, just like Mai—but even more so.

She had agreed—hell, begged—to be Amanda's slave. She had imagined an ideal world of total obedience, but over the last few weeks she'd learned that real life didn't quite match the books—she had expected this perfection to just *happen*.

She did talk out of turn. She *was* intrigued at the possibility of intrigue, of using her charms to get her way. She was always wishing for more attention, just as Amanda had predicted.

Janet saw now that she could still be the clay in Amanda's hands, pliable in body and mind—but she could also be the sculptor. She could be both art *and* artist, transforming herself like she had her house.

Janet straightened her posture. She brought her shoulders back, but not so stiff as to look like a soldier at attention. She pushed her chest out to accentuate her breasts, to offer them. She placed her arms not straight at her sides but tucked her elbows in at the waist, so that her forearms and wrists conformed to her hips, emphasizing her figure.

There would be no more whining. There would be no more losing track of her duties, even if she was distracted by a hot Asian chick in an alcove. There would be no more talking out of turn.

…Well, maybe. But she would *try*, and accept the punishment with grace if not silence.

And what about that clue Amanda had given her, that there were gains to be had by playing the game well? Did being a perfect slave—to the level of Art, even—mean giving up on all such manipulations?

Oh hell, no. Jon still needed to pay for bringing her *here*, of all places.

"Amanda," Carolyn said, "May I get Janet started?"

"Of course. Janet, f—"

Amanda stopped short as she noted Janet's new stance. She raised her eyebrows, pleased and perhaps a bit confused, as she scanned down Janet's body, suddenly so properly presented.

"Follow her, Janet," Amanda said softly, and turned back to Jon and Mai.

Carolyn beckoned Janet with two fingers.

"We should consider taking Mai in, My Love," Jon said, appraising the girl. "Janet should be in the guest room, by then. They could share."

"That would likely require restraints for both of them," Amanda said. "And you seem awfully confident that Janet will sign on for another year."

"You mean, you're not? Besides, we've always got the cages."

"I'm *not* taking in a harem, Jon," Janet heard Amanda say. "What would the neighbors think?"

Janet walked behind Carolyn the few steps into the living room. The woman did have excellent taste in décor—a mix of low-ceilinged Modernist cool and traditional Asian materials that somehow all fit together. Restrained, coordinated—and yes, disciplined. A small, sedate Christmas tree graced the far corner.

"Oh," Janet said, surprised.

Across the room, in front of the polished concrete fire-place, was a young man standing naked but for his padlocked collar, his hands locked behind his head, elbows back and his legs spread wide. Light-skinned, dark red hair. The leashed boy from the film premier, not the one from Jon's—or rather Amanda's—driveway, who did look so much like this one. (And why were there two?) There was a fire in the minimalist fireplace; his backside was likely getting pretty warm.

"Beautiful, isn't he?" Carolyn said.

Janet had always preferred her men darker—dark hair,

dark eyes, possibly dark soul, which this boy looked entirely too sweet to have. But he was fit, handsome, muscular. And that cock—thick, straight, fully erect over tight shaved balls…

"Yes, Ma'am," she said.

Carolyn crossed her arms and looked at Janet a long time—not at her body, at today's new bruises, but in the face, her blue eyes.

Janet demurred, looked away.

"I'm not going to touch you, tonight," Carolyn said. "I will give you no orders." She paused.

"This is not out of respect for Amanda, although I certainly respect her. It's…"

She stopped.

The young man in front of the fireplace cleared his throat.

"Yes, *thank* you. I know," Carolyn said over her shoulder at him, annoyed.

"It's out of respect for you."

Another long pause.

"I was wrong, about you. That's all I'm going to say."

Janet wasn't sure what all that meant. Whatever speech she'd intended to make, that was apparently the end of it. What was a promise from Carolyn worth?

"Jon wanted to spend his birthday with me, God knows why," Carolyn said. "And Amanda consented."

She closed her eyes and shook her head. Remembering her own behavior?

"I proposed we play Puppets. Amanda will have you, and I will have him," gesturing at the redhead. "We'll see how Jon fits in, tonight. He may only get to watch. Wouldn't that be funny?"

Janet nodded, faint smile on her lips. That oughta teach him.

"Yes, Ma'am," she said. "It would."

She *still* didn't trust Carolyn—how could she?—but at least she had her Household with her, her backup. She was Owned, claimed by someone she did trust, despite them both sometimes being cruel motherfuckers, and she felt safe. No harm would come to her. Amanda had promised.

Carolyn turned and walked across the center of the living room, covered with a rug so complex in its evolving patterns that Janet chose to not let herself be distracted by it.

Janet saw that the coffee table, made of polished steel and heavy glass, had been moved to the edge of the room to make a large space in the center of the furniture. Very familiar. She thought it very unlikely that there would be any blue bubble gum stuck to the bottom of this table. There were two floggers on its glass surface but no quirts or long whips; she saw eight cuffs laid out, eight coils of rope in two neat rows.

... *"Puppets"*?

"Janet, this is Ken. You two will be...interacting, tonight. You will get to know each other very well, and yet you will not know him at all."

Janet looked at the naked and splayed young man, ramrod straight and disciplined, perfectly still—but beaming, his chest out, wearing an expression of...pride, of all things.

"Hello, Ken."

"Ken," Carolyn said, her hand on his shoulder, same look on her face—"Meet Janet."

Acknowledgements

You have no idea how awful the first version of this novel was. Or the second. Any indications of quality writing must be credited to the most talented, perceptive, supportive and generally amazing crew of readers and friends a writer could hope to have: Siri Ousdahl, Blue Toggle, Barbara J. Webb, Jessica Taylor, and my Beloved, who insists on remaining anonymous. Any faults in the writing and storytelling belong to me alone.

I would also like to thank Rachel Kramer Bussel for teaching me a thing or two in my early days, and for always answering my annoying requests for advice with kindness and support.

www.ingramcontent.com/pod-product-compliance
Lightning Source LLC
Chambersburg PA
CBHW071634260626
47170CB00001B/101